The Dragon's Descent

The Dragon's Descent

AN ETHER NOVEL

BOOK THREE

LAURICE E. MOLINARI

WITH CHRISTOPHER MOLINARI

ZONDER**kidz**

Also by Laurice Elehwany Molinari:

BOOKS

The Ether: Vero Rising (Book One)

Pillars of Fire (Book Two)

Screenplays

My Girl (Columbia Pictures)

The Brady Bunch Movie (Paramount Pictures)

The Amazing Panda Adventure (Warner Bros.)

Anastasia (Uncredited) (Fox Animation Studio)

Bewitched (Uncredited) (Columbia Pictures)

ZONDERKIDZ

The Dragon's Descent
Copyright © 2016 by Laurice E. Molinari

This title is also available as a Zondervan ebook.

Requests for information should be addressed to:
Zonderkidz, 3900 Sparks Drive SE, Grand Rapids, MI 49546

ISBN 978-0-310-73557-1 (hardcover)

ISBN 978-0-310-73563-2 (softcover)

Library of Congress Cataloging-in-Publication Data

Names: Molinari, Laurice E., author | Molinari, Christopher, author.

Title: The dragon's descent / Laurice E. Molinari with Christopher Molinari.

Description: Grand Rapids, MI : Zonderkidz, [2016] | Series: An Ether novel;
    book 3 | Summary: The young guardian angel Vero faces his greatest
    challenge when he must locate the lost Book of Raziel before the forces of
    darkness can use it for their own purposes.

Identifiers: LCCN 2016004836 | ISBN 9780310735571 (hardcover)

Subjects: | CYAC: Guardian angels—Fiction. | Angel—Fiction. |
    Demonology—Fiction. | Good and evil—Fiction.

Classification: LCC PZ7.M7337 Dr 2016 | DDC [Fic]—dc23 LC record available
    at http://lccn.loc.gov/2016004836

Illustrations: Randy Gallegos
Interior design: David Conn and Ben Fetterley

Printed in the United States of America

16 17 18 19 20 21 22 23 24 25 / DHV / 15 14 13 12 11 10 9 8 7 6 5 4 3 2 1

For Grace and Luke: may the angels
always keep watch over you

CONTENTS

1

❖

TRAIL OF LIGHTS

A panther's piercing gold eyes gazed through shimmering leaves as it relaxed on the well-worn curve of an ancient tree branch. As the large, black cat looked upon the green, conical mountain in the distance, it yawned, losing the fight to an afternoon nap. Above, a chattering family of langurs carelessly stuffed their gray-black faces to their heart's content, allowing shreds of leaves to fall onto their white beards. Below, in the marshy lowland, a small herd of shaggy-coated Sambar deer stood shoulder deep in the water, eating water lilies and refreshing themselves in the cool water. A petite white egret hitched a ride on the back of one of the deer, pecking insects from its fur while green and brown frogs made their presence known with boisterous croaks.

Silently, heavy clouds rolled into the jungle, burying the tranquil afternoon in mist. The vibrant ecosystem was transformed into a blur of fog in a moment's time. And then, just as quickly, the mist dissipated, revealing the now quiet darkness of night. On the face of the distant mountain, an illuminated trail wound its way up the mountainside. The zigzagging path seemed endless, lit up by thousands of flickering lights that stretched into the stars.

Clover woke with a start. After sweeping her long blonde hair from her face, she grabbed a small journal and a pencil off her nightstand and began to cover the blank pages with detailed images from her dream. Moments later, she glanced at her old princess alarm clock: 5:22 in the morning. She would need to be up for school in an hour, but something screamed to her that she had to record what she had seen before the images faded from memory.

Clover had kept a dream journal ever since she was a little girl. She felt her dreams were special, and as she grew older she found it harder and harder to shake them—in fact, her dreams had always been so vivid, so real to her, that she often needed to stay in bed for a few moments to reorient herself after waking. Clover knew the images she dreamt were trying to tell her something, and had discovered that many did hold messages. These visual messages used to terrify her, but finally, at the ripe old age of fifteen, she had learned to embrace them—and not only her dreams, but also her visions. She had once thought she was seeing hallucinations, that she was crazy. But in time, she had come to realize she saw real things other people could not see. And she saw them because of Vero, her guardian angel brother. Her prophetic gifts were meant to somehow support Vero in his mission. Of this, she was one hundred percent sure. And that's the reason she took such painstaking efforts to sketch the mountain, the animals, and jungle as accurately as possible.

Clover walked past Vero and playfully boxed his ear while he sat in the kitchen eating an egg-in-the-hole. It was his favorite breakfast—an egg fried inside a hole cut in the middle of a slice of bread.

"What was that for?" Vero scowled, tugging on his left ear.

Clover opened the refrigerator door and pulled out a peach-flavored Greek yogurt. "Making sure you were awake." Clover smirked then picked up a spoon from inside a drawer before slamming it shut with her hip. "Where are Mom and Dad?"

"Dad went in to work early," Vero said, shaking the salt-shaker over his egg. "And Mom's out jogging."

"Good. Hold on . . ." Clover said, dashing out of the kitchen.

"For what?" Vero asked, but Clover was already gone.

When she rushed back with her dream journal, he had stuck his fork into his egg, and yolk spilled out onto the fried bread. Before he could take a bite, however, Clover slammed the book down on the table with a thud. It was open to a sketch of the landscape from her dream.

"Does this mean anything to you?" she questioned urgently and curiously.

Vero's gray eyes narrowed as he studied the drawing. He looked thoughtfully at it, as if trying to trigger some sort of recognition. He focused on the winding trail of lights up the side of a steep mountain that rose high above hills, and the exotic animals below.

"Anything?"

Vero shook his head.

"Are you sure?" Clover tapped her index finger on the drawing. "Because I have a really strong feeling about this."

"Nothing," Vero mumbled in between bites of egg. "Maybe in time, it'll make sense."

The front door opened and quickly shut. Clover snatched the journal from Vero and snapped it shut just as their mother, Nora, walked into the kitchen. Nora's face was bright red. Sweat had formed on her forehead.

"The bus is almost here! What are you doing still eating? Go! Get ready!" Nora yelled, out of breath.

"Shoot! I gotta brush my teeth," Vero exclaimed, jumping up from the table and sprinting out of the room.

"I'm ready," Clover said to Nora. "But I totally miss when Molly would pick me up."

"Well, you better make friends with the bus, because Molly graduated, and I'm sure not driving you." Nora studied Clover's face. "Why do you look so tired? Were you on your phone last night? Because you know, no electronics in your room."

"No, Mom." Clover rolled her eyes. "I just woke up super early."

"You probably heard Dad. He went to work while it was still dark," Nora said as she pulled a bottle of flavored water from the fridge. "He's worried about his project."

"He worries about every project," Clover said.

"Why don't you want me to see that?" Nora asked, motioning to the journal tucked under Clover's arm.

Clover froze.

"You don't have to show me. I'll just sneak a peek like I normally do once you're on the bus." Nora smiled.

"You do?!" Clover asked with a look of outrage.

Nora laughed. "Oh yeah! And I also throw out all your old toys too!"

Clover eyed her, not sure if she was joking.

"But you have no problem showing Vero," Nora said, a bit hurt.

Clover considered for a moment. "Fine," she said as she handed her mother the well-worn journal. "It's on the next-to-last page."

Nora flipped to the sketch of the mountain. Clover watched her mother's eyes soften as she studied the drawing. At forty-two, Clover thought her mother looked great. Sure, she had to highlight her hair to remain a blonde, but she could still fit into most of her college clothing, and last week when Nora bought a bottle of champagne for a housewarming gift, she was carded! Clover hoped she had inherited her mom's genes.

"You're really good."

"Thanks, Mom." Clover blushed.

"Was this in one of your dreams?"

Clover nodded. Down the block, the school bus horn blared.

"Gotta go!" Clover snatched her journal from Nora's hands and zipped it inside the front pocket of her purple backpack. "I'll take it with me. That way you won't be tempted to snoop around for it." Clover smiled.

As Clover left, Vero ran down the stairs with frothy toothpaste around his mouth. Nora chuckled to herself.

❖

Clover got off the bus before Vero. The high school was the first stop, followed by the middle school then elementary. Vero always felt a tinge of sadness when he watched Clover step off the bus without him. Even though he would join her at the high school next year, it was of little consolation because he knew that someday the separation would become permanent. He hoped and prayed they'd both be given the strength to survive once that time came.

"Hey, move over," a boy's voice cracked.

Vero looked up and saw Tack standing over him. Sometimes he thought his eyes were playing tricks on him when he looked at his best friend of twelve years, because Tack no longer resembled the pudgy little kid Vero had grown up with. Tack was now nearly six feet tall, and all the places that once had been prone to baby fat had transformed into well-defined muscles. As Tack sat down next to him, his hairy, long legs bumped up against Vero's, who had also grown considerably. And Vero had even started wearing deodorant a few months ago, after Clover complained that he stunk up the whole room with BO, as well as mentioning the pungent aroma whenever he took off his socks.

But it wasn't only Tack's physical appearance that had changed—he had become more serious. He no longer held the title of class clown and had even made honor roll for the first time in his life. Most people attributed the change in Tack to the natural transition to maturity. But as Vero glanced at the stack of books on Tack's lap, he wondered— was Tack being prepared for whatever part he was to play in helping Vero find the Book of Raziel? The archangels had told Vero that it was his mission to retrieve the all-knowing book. It blew Vero's mind when he thought about all the knowledge contained within its pages: the laws of the universe and of creation, the names of every human ever born and those yet to be born, and the names and duties of each angel. It was mind-boggling. The book had originally been given to Adam to console him after he was expelled from the garden, then passed down for generations until it eventually became lost. And though it was up to Vero to find it, the archangel Uriel had told Vero that Tack would play some part. Maybe Tack could somehow sense he had a higher purpose . . . he was a proven dowser, after all, and could sense things ordinary people could not. Perhaps that was why childish things were falling so quickly by the wayside?

"Did you figure out what you're going to do for service hours?" Tack asked Vero as the bus drove away from the curb.

"I'm not sure yet," Vero said. "How many do we need to do?"

"Fifteen hours or else they won't pass you to ninth grade."

"My mom wants me to volunteer at the hospital. She says lots of kids do. Plus, I can drive in with her to work," Vero said.

"I'll do it with you," Tack said. "My sister volunteered there and said she was delivering flowers and reading books to little kids, stuff like that."

"I can handle that," Vero said.

"Then ask your mom to sign us up."

"Okay."

"Oh, but I can't do Saturday mornings," Tack said. "That's when my dad takes me out on dowser jobs with him."

Vero nodded. He knew how important being a dowser was to Tack. Up until last year, his friend had shown no aptitude in the ancestral talent; then Tack's abilities sprung forth with a vengeance when he sensed that a busted pipe had caused water to pool in the gym's ceiling. He'd led everyone outside moments before disaster hit.

"Hi guys."

Vero and Tack looked up and saw Davina Acker quickly move to the seat next to them as the bus rounded a corner. Davina always made Vero smile. She was stunning, with sparkling blue eyes and soft brownish hair, but it was her warm smile that Vero found most endearing.

"Hey, Davina." Tack nodded.

"I thought I heard someone say service hours," she said. "I worked this weekend at the nursing home."

"How was it?" Vero asked.

"Sort of sad at first, but then you start to notice how grateful all the residents are that you're there, and then you're glad you went," Davina said.

"I hear you. My grandma lives in one in Virginia," Tack said. "When you first get there, the place kind of smells like mothballs . . . sort of like Vero's feet."

"Hey!" Vero looked offended.

"But then my grandma and her friends are so happy to see me, it kind of becomes fun."

"Then you guys should volunteer with me," Davina said.

"We're gonna do the hospital," Tack said as the bus came to a stop in front of Attleboro Middle School.

"My mom works there," Vero added.

"Oh, there's Danny." Davina smiled dreamily, glancing out the cracked, finger-smudged window.

Vero followed her gaze. Danny Konrad stepped off his black skateboard and kicked the tail with his right foot, flipping it into his hands. Danny looked like the all-American boy—blond, dimpled, and confident.

Tack nudged Vero. "And this is where we become invisible."

"That's not true!" Davina exclaimed indignantly.

"Really?" Tack smirked.

"Well, maybe a little, but only because I need to talk to Danny," Davina said as she walked up the aisle.

Tack rolled his eyes as he and Vero followed her off the bus. Danny walked toward the school's metal front doors as Davina chased after him.

"Danny! Danny!"

Danny stopped and turned around. Vero and Tack stood behind Davina.

"Hey . . . How come you didn't text me last night?" Davina asked.

"I was busy." Danny shrugged.

"Really?"

"My dad was home . . ."

"And?"

Vero watched as a flicker of anger crossed Danny's face.

"And what? I don't have to tell you stuff that's between my dad and me," Danny snapped.

Hurt instantly clouded Davina's eyes as Danny turned and walked away. Tack elbowed Vero, who was concerned.

"The universe must be off," he whispered to Vero, watching Danny make his way into the school.

Deep beneath the ground wriggled the bodies of creatures—so many that they crawled over and under one another like clumps of earthworms. These beasts lived underground because light was the enemy. Darkness sustained them.

Each monster was equally hideous. Sparse, matted bunches of fur clung to their nearly emaciated bodies—bodies that resembled decomposing corpses. They hissed with grotesque, dirt-covered fangs. Their clawed hands swiped at one another, cutting into scaly, sallow skin. The lone eye that penetrated their heads could not see beneath the dark earth, yet somehow they knew the master had come into their presence. Their anger intensified, their attacks becoming more furious. The violent frenzy pleased the master. The creatures were tired of waiting for the master to release them so they could do the thing for which they were created—spread hatred. But it was not the right time. So their master kept them hidden beneath the surface, seething with chaos and hunger. When the time came, their festering hatred would erupt with a vengeance.

2

◆

HOSPITAL ROUNDS

Tack pushed the hospital's hospitality cart down the hallway as Vero walked in front guiding it. A balding male aide hurried past, offering the boys a slight smile.

"Ouch!" Vero yelled, spinning around to Tack, who had run over Vero's right foot and hit his ankle with the heavy cart.

"Sorry," Tack said with a guilty look.

"Watch where you're going!" Vero complained, as he hopped on his left foot, waiting for the pain to subside.

"This thing is so tall, I have a hard time seeing around it," Tack said, craning his neck.

It was true; the top of the cart reached Tack's eye-level. While the lower half of the cart had small drawers for candy, decks of cards, magazines, coloring books, and crayons, the upper part held a large coffee and hot water dispenser along with cups, tea and sugar packets, creamers, and freshly baked cookies.

"Look where you're going," Vero said as he resumed walking.

Tack placed his hands on the cart and pushed it while Vero held one hand on its front, guiding it.

"Leland! Kozlowski!" a harsh voice rang out.

Startled, Tack accidentally gave the cart a shove right into Vero's other ankle, tripping him.

"Tack, you big dummy!" Vero yelled, falling to the floor.

Rubbing his new injury, Vero looked up to see the hulking figure of Nurse Kunkel standing over him. Vero had always thought that Nurse Kunkel was as wide as she was tall, and from his current vantage point, it seemed to be true.

"What are you two doing here?" she barked.

Nurse Kunkel held out a hand to Vero, who grabbed it. She pulled him to his feet with such a force that his head nearly hit the wall.

"Our service hours," Tack said.

"Very good," she said as she grabbed a warm chocolate chip cookie from the cart.

Tack nodded to the sign hanging over the cookies. It read, "Patients Only."

"Are you a patient?" Tack sheepishly asked.

"No," she said as she shoved the cookie into her mouth. "I pick up a couple of extra shifts a month to pay for my synchronized swimming classes. They're not cheap, what with budget cuts and all." Cookie crumbs shot out of the side of her mouth.

Vero and Tack exchanged looks. *Synchronized swimming?*

"Well, carry on, men," Nurse Kunkel said, snatching another cookie before walking down the hall.

"Come on," Vero told Tack. "We've got to finish our rounds."

Tack resumed pushing the cart. As they continued down the hospital corridor, Vero heard the faint whisper of a voice.

"Vero, Vero," it softly called.

Vero stopped abruptly. The cart slammed into both his heels. He winced.

"Not my fault that time!" Tack yelled.

Vero didn't answer Tack. He was looking around for the source of the voice.

"What are you stopping for?" Tack asked.

"Vero, please . . . Room 217," the voice said.

Vero's eyes scanned the sterile corridor. His eyes then landed on door 217, and he headed for it.

"Hey, that's not on our route!"

Vero ignored Tack and opened the door and walked inside. Tack stayed behind, nervously. Once Vero stepped in the room, he saw an angel hovering over a young woman who slept with a newborn in her arms. The angel's wings were translucent like crystal and continuously changed colors. The angel looked to Vero.

"The mother won't listen to me. She's just too exhausted," the angel said with a sigh of frustration.

"You're her guardian?" Vero asked, surprised.

"Yes," the angel replied. "Why so surprised?"

"I've never seen guardians here before . . . only in the Ether."

"Oh. Well, I need your help, which is why I'm allowing you to see me."

"What's wrong?"

"The baby was born tongue-tied. Right now it will affect her ability to feed. But later down the road, if not detected, she'll grow up with a speech impediment, which could impact her self-esteem as a child and carry through into her adult years. I want to spare her all that and have a doctor look at it now."

"What do you want me to do?" Vero asked.

"Wake the mother up and tell her."

"Wake her up?" Vero repeated, a bit unsure. "I don't think I'm supposed to . . ."

"Have your friend come in here with the cart. That will do it."

Vero looked to the angel as he thought for a moment, then turned and walked to the door. He opened it and called to Tack, who was still waiting in the hall.

"Get in here." Vero waved to Tack.

"What are you doing in there?"

"Just bring the cart."

Tack sighed. "Okay, but if we get fired on our first day, it's your fault."

Vero held the door open. Tack struggled to push the cart through the door, running it smack into the side of the wall. *Crunch!* The baby cried, waking up her mother.

"Oh, sorry," Tack said, his face turning red.

"See?" The angel smiled to Vero.

Vero chuckled.

"It's not funny," Tack said.

Vero then realized that Tack had no clue the angel was in the room with them. Vero stood next to the bed and turned to the mother.

"Hi ma'am, would you like a snack?"

"Cookies or coffee?" Tack added. "Tea?"

"No, thank you," the woman answered.

The angel motioned to Vero, who began to sweat. Vero snatched a cookie and held it to the woman.

"Would the baby like a cookie?"

The angel rolled his eyes.

"You idiot!" Tack slammed his hand to his forehead. "Everyone knows babies don't eat cookies!"

"Oh, yeah, I forgot." Vero's face flushed red.

"Everyone knows they eat soft stuff," Tack said as he reached for a bag of candy. "Like gummy worms." He held up the bag.

It was the angel's turn to slap his hand to his forehead.

"Thanks, guys, but we really need to get some rest," the woman said over her newborn's cries.

Vero bent down to the baby. He smiled at her.

"She's really cute."

"Thank you. This is Claire. She's about three hours old."

As Claire cried, Vero moved closer to her. A concerned look clouded Vero's face. The mother noticed.

"What? What's wrong?"

"It sounds like Claire might be tongue-tied. I can hear it when she cries."

Tack gave Vero a look. The angel breathed a sigh of relief.

"What do you mean?" the new mother asked, suddenly worried.

"Yeah . . . she 'wahs' a little funny when she cries. It's not a big deal. It's easy to fix."

"How do you know?" the woman asked.

"Oh, because I 'wahhhed' really funny when I was a kid," Vero said, thinking quickly. "I would just ask the doctor to look at it."

The mother looked strangely at Vero as if trying to figure out something. She hesitated for a moment before she answered.

"Okay, I will," she said, somewhat puzzled.

Vero turned to leave.

"Thank you, Vero," the angel said.

Vero nodded to him and placed his hands on the cart. He turned to Tack. "Get the door, will you?"

Tack scrambled to open the door, and Vero wheeled the cart out. Once alone in the hallway, Tack turned to Vero.

"I never heard you were born tongue-tied," Tack said, narrowing his eyes suspiciously at Vero. "Whatever that is."

"I never said I was . . . I said I 'wahhed' really funny. Tongue-tie is a real thing, and I think her daughter may have it. So she should have her checked."

"I think you've been watching too many medical shows."

Vero saw his mother standing in front of them, hands on her hips. "Boys, what are you doing?" Nora asked.

"Nothing." Tack shrugged.

"I'm on break, you are not," Nora scolded them. "Now get to your rounds."

"We're on it," Vero said, pushing the cart.

Vero and Tack walked from room to room, offering snacks and magazines. Everyone was grateful to see them. The little kids especially loved Tack. He taught them how to burp the alphabet, the proper way to shoot a spitball, and his favorite game—"The Nurse Kunkel Shuffle." A kid would press the call button, and when Nurse Kunkel walked in, he'd yell, "Psych!" After three rounds of the game, Nurse Kunkel had had enough and told Nora. Nora walked into the children's ward ready to fire Tack and Vero, but forgave them when she saw how it made the sick kids laugh—something they rarely did.

"You guys are done for today," Nora told the boys as they walked down the hallway pushing the cart. "Return the cart, then get a snack in the cafeteria—I still have another forty-five minutes on my shift."

"Okay, Mom," Vero answered.

Nora walked away. "And stay out of trouble."

"Come on," Vero said as he pulled the cart while Tack pushed it.

"Vero, quick!" another voice said. "Hurry!"

Vero's eyes scanned the hallway.

"You just passed my room! Come back!"

Vero abruptly stopped. The cart smashed into him.

"What is your deal?" Tack yelled. "You can't pin that on me!"

"Go ahead without me. I need to use the bathroom!" Vero said. "I'll meet you in the cafeteria."

"Whatever," Tack said, and continued down the hallway.

Once Tack turned the corner and was out of sight, Vero slipped into the room. He saw an angel lying next to an elderly man in bed, cradling him with his wings. When Vero stepped closer, he saw that the man was unconscious and struggling to breathe.

"It's almost time. I need you to get his son. He went to the cafeteria for a bite. He'll be very upset if his father passes when he's gone!" the angel told Vero, urgently.

It was then that Vero noticed another angel sitting patiently in the corner of the room. He was brighter than most angels he'd seen. A kindness and gentleness emanated from the angel.

"Vero, now!"

"How will I know him?"

"Mr. Berger's son, Frank. He's wearing a red shirt, and has messy brown hair and glasses! Go!"

Vero tore out of the room. He ran down the hall, dodging a gurney pushed by an aide in full scrubs. A nurse walked toward him carrying a tray of food, and Vero nearly knocked it out of her hands.

"Hey!" the nurse shouted.

"Sorry!" Vero yelled as he burst through the cafeteria doors and scanned the room. It wasn't crowded. He saw a red shirt, but it belonged to a woman who stood at the salad bar scooping croutons onto her plate. Vero saw a middle-aged man who looked like he hadn't slept in days, sitting at a table drinking a hot coffee, rubbing his eyes. His shirt was a muted red, but he wasn't wearing glasses. Vero decided to approach him anyway.

"Excuse me."

As Vero got closer, the man pulled something out of his shirt pocket—a pair of glasses! He put them on to see Vero.

"Are you Frank Berger?" Vero asked hurriedly.

"Yes."

"It's your dad! You have to come now!"

The man sprung from his chair. With Vero on his heels, they dashed out of the cafeteria. The double doors flew open and nearly hit Tack, who was strolling in. He quickly jumped aside.

"Vero? Where you going?"

Vero didn't answer as he ran after Frank. They finally reached the room and ran inside, where Mr. Berger lay in the bed. His breathing was even more labored. Frank ran to his bedside and took his father's hand in his, then began to cry. The angel's wings wrapped tighter around the dying man. Vero turned to leave.

"Stay," the angel told Vero.

Vero nodded. As Frank continued to hold his father's hand, the angel who sat in the corner arose. He gently flapped his wings and floated over to the bed. A bright pink light emanated from this angel, as well as a peaceful feeling that overtook the room. Vero looked into the angel's face and saw only compassion and love as he looked upon Mr. Berger. The angel reached over Frank's head and placed the palm of his hand on Mr. Berger's slowly rising and falling chest. Something Vero recognized as a soul began to rise out of his body. Mr. Berger's guardian angel rose with the soul, enclosing it within his wings, never letting go of it. Vero noticed the silver cord that tethered the soul to the body. When the soul was floating about two feet over the body, the glowing angel, with his other hand, tenderly squeezed the silver cord, severing it. Vero then realized who the angel was—the Angel of Death.

In the arms and wings of his guardian angel, Mr. Berger's soul grew more radiant. A nearly blinding light surrounded both the guardian angel and the soul, and enveloped them. Vero felt pure joy and elation from the soul and guardian. There was no fear. No anxiety. Vero never realized death could be so peaceful, so wonderful. The ball of light that was the guardian and soul shone even more brightly as it floated toward the ceiling and then vanished. The Angel of Death looked to Vero, solemnly nodded, then also vanished.

Vero looked over to the bed. Mr. Berger lay lifeless. Tears ran down Frank's cheek. He looked up to Vero.

"Did you feel it?" Frank asked. "That feeling of peace when Dad passed?"

Vero smiled sadly. "I did."

3

FAITH MAZE

Vero walked down the basement stairs in his house, feeling tired. His first day in the hospital had been exhausting and all he wanted to do was eat dinner and go to bed. He saw his dad, Dennis, sitting at the worktable in the middle of the room, surrounded by red and green plastic storage boxes and an artificial Christmas tree with probably five seasons' worth of tinsel still stuck to it. Dennis was hunched over the table, building some sort of small model village.

"What's that?" Vero asked.

Dennis looked up. "Come to help?"

"No, Mom needs milk." He crossed over to the old refrigerator that sat in the corner.

"Come here."

Vero opened the refrigerator door, pulled out a gallon of milk, then shut it. He walked over to his dad and sat on the stool next to him, while placing the milk on the floor at his feet. Glancing down at the model, Vero saw what looked like a town with several canals alongside of it.

"It's the project I've recommended for a village in Sri Lanka. During the monsoon season they can get torrential rains that completely flood the place. The people often lose their homes, their crops, even their lives."

"So the World Bank is giving them money to build these canals?" Vero said as he ran his finger along the blue strip of painter's tape representing water.

"Yes, they've already begun digging, but for the canals to be really effective, I need to build another three, and the budget won't allow for it." Dennis sighed weakly. "So the project's engineer and I have been trying to reconfigure what already has been started so it will work with the given budget."

"What if you can't?" Vero looked at his father, unsure.

"I won't go down without a fight," Dennis said as a determined look came over him.

Vero nodded, knowing it was true.

"Vero, where's that milk?!" Nora's voice rang down to the basement, muffled through the closed door.

Vero picked up the milk and ran up the stairs. But as his foot landed on the top step, it slipped off the edge of the tread, and he tripped and fell forward. His head smashed into the basement door as the gallon of milk flew out his hand, hit the stairs hard, and sprayed open. Vero then tumbled down the stairs to the basement floor.

As a massive stone door opened, Vero staggered inside. He face-planted into something solid. As soon as Vero righted himself, he saw the angry face of the archangel Raziel glaring down at him. His features were harsh, severe—making him seem even more intimidating. Raziel never gave Vero a warm and fuzzy feeling. Vero always felt that the archangel didn't like him.

"Oh . . . sorry," Vero stammered, rubbing his forehead. "Do we have to keep doing this? Can't you just text me when you want me?"

"Let's go," Raziel sternly said as he snapped around.

As Vero followed Raziel, he slowly began to realize he was walking through C.A.N.D.L.E., the Cathedral of Angels for Novice Development, Learning and Edification, otherwise known as the guardian angel school. He recognized the impressive front hall of the massive Greco-Roman temple. It was jaw-dropping due to its walls of gold mixed with spectacularly shinning diamonds. The domed ceiling was so tall that Vero had to crane his head back to see all the way to the top. Yet, despite the distance, somehow his eyes could make out every intricate and colorful tile pattern on the dome and in the rows of columns that lined the walls and held up balconies. C.A.N.D.L.E. looked the same, but yet something was different.

"Where is everybody?" Vero panicked, noticing that the place was empty.

"There is no one else," Raziel said, picking up the pace.

"But the others are coming? Right? Greer, Pax, Kane—"

"No one is coming," Raziel said harshly, cutting him off.

"I'm not here for training?"

Raziel did not answer. He led Vero underneath a balcony then down a dark, narrow staircase. With each step, Vero grew more and more uneasy. Where was Raziel taking him? Raziel had never warmed up to Vero. The other arch-angels had always seemed to like him, but not Raziel. Vero could never make any inroads with him no matter what he tried. As they walked down deeper into C.A.N.D.L.E., Vero's heart began to race, but he dutifully followed.

They entered a room—an empty space not much bigger than the inside of an elevator. Perspiration formed on Vero's forehead as he noticed that the entrance they had just used seconds ago was now a wall. As a matter of fact, as his eyes scanned the room he realized four white walls surrounded them, and none had any doors.

"Why isn't Uriel here?" Vero nervously asked, his eyes looking for an escape route.

Vero desperately wished the archangel Uriel would show up. Vero looked to Uriel as his mentor and protector. Uriel had watched over him ever since he was a baby, and it was Uriel who took Vero to the Ether for the first time.

"This is something between you and me," Raziel harshly said.

Vero gulped, knowing anything between him and Raziel was bound to end badly.

"No one will be joining you. No other fledglings have been called back. This one is all you."

Vero's eyes filled with confusion.

"Time runs short, and we need to know for whom you fight. Darkness or the light."

"Of course, the light," Vero blurted out, hurt that it was even a question.

"Prove it." Raziel looked hard into Vero's eyes. "Find your way out of the maze."

"A maze?" Vero asked while scanning the solid walls. There was no way out. Panic came over him. "How?"

"If you truly believe faith can move mountains, then four walls should be no big deal." Raziel smirked, then simply walked through a wall and disappeared.

Vero stood there, considering what Raziel had said. "Time runs short? What is that supposed to mean?" Vero ran his hands over the walls, hoping there was some secret door, a way out. He'd even settle for a doggie door. But the walls were solid stone.

"Ahh!" he screamed in frustration and banged his fists on a wall. "How the heck did he just walk through the wall?!"

Vero slid to the floor. He put his head in his hands.

"There's got to be a way out of this," he mumbled to himself.

But then he had another thought. *What if there isn't?* Raziel had never liked him. What if Raziel had called him back to the Ether without the others knowing? What if Raziel was trying to do him in?

Vero lifted his head out of his hands. Were his eyes playing tricks on him or did the wall across from him suddenly seem closer? He jumped up, and the top of his head scraped the ceiling. Then it dawned on him—the room was closing in! He began to shake with fear. He was going to be squished to death, and end up in the choir of angels—if that was even still a possibility for him! He was completely distraught. But then Vero remembered his Vox Dei—the voice of God. He could always rely upon it no matter what the situation.

As the walls grew closer, Vero closed his eyes, placed his hand over his heart, and began to pray with such intensity that beads of sweat dripped down his face. With all his heart, he beseeched God to guide him. After a few moments, a confident smile formed on Vero's lips. He stretched out his arms. His fingers spread apart on the dense walls and then he simply pushed.

They fell away easily. The sidewalls crumbled upon the ground, yet the ceiling held above him. It had stopped moving. Vero had no idea what was holding it up, but he was grateful. He climbed over the rubble for a few feet then stood and looked around. Before him was a narrow space, wide enough that maybe only three people standing shoulder to shoulder could pass through. Dark, curved stone walls—easily fifteen feet tall—stood on either side of him. Somehow, this place felt very surreal to Vero. As if he were inside someone else's dream . . . a feeling he was familiar with. During the angel trials, Vero and his fellow fledglings—Greer, Pax, Kane, X, and Ada—had all been inside one of Greer's dreams. Vero remembered how quickly things could change in that sleep-induced world; how frightening it could be, and how not everything made perfect sense.

A short distance ahead, he saw that the walls formed multiple pathways—here was the maze that Raziel spoke of. When Vero looked up, he saw that terrifying gargoyles lined the tops of the walls, appearing to leer down at him. The pathways were so narrow that the stone creatures nearly touched one another overhead. He could see slivers of sky sneaking through, enough to provide light below. Only a few inches separated the frightening statues, which meant Vero could not fly out. His only way out was to find his way through.

As Vero walked ahead, he stared at the gargoyles. It appeared to him that no two were alike. Some were winged.

Some were half human, half animal. Others resembled human ghosts. One appeared to be a dragon while another looked like an oversized bat. All were grotesque, with distorted human or animal forms. Each was scary, especially the monkey with sharp, webbed wings that held a dagger in its paw while baring its teeth. Vero shuddered.

After just a few yards inside the maze, he came upon a fork in the path. Vero had no idea which way to turn, as both options looked the same. Vero looked left, then right, and left again, totally perplexed. Then he saw something out of the corner of his eye. As he turned his head toward it, a shadowed blur quickly disappeared. Were his eyes playing tricks on him?

Vero then heard what sounded like the slow inhale and exhale of a person. A blast of hot air hit the back of his exposed neck, sending chills down his spine. He spun around, looking for the source, only to see a shadow that flickered out of his peripheral vision. Vero was suddenly overcome with the unsettling feeling of impending doom. He needed to get out of there! Again, he considered left, then right, but when he looked back to the left, fear seized him. A strange, human-shaped silhouette with glowing green eyes stood staring at him from only a few feet away.

The decision resolved, Vero sprinted down the path on his right. As he ran, he continuously glanced over his shoulder, catching glimpses of darker-than-night shadows pursuing him in earnest. He couldn't outrun them, but after several minutes the shadows disappeared. Vero's legs burned, and he needed to stop for air. He turned his back to the wall for protection and put his hands on his knees, catching his breath.

Moments later, Vero lifted his head. His eyes drifted up to the eerie gargoyles above him, then suddenly he felt ice-cold hands closing around his neck. They felt bony, yet Vero could only see dark shadows tightening around his throat. The hands squeezed harder and harder until Vero thought he'd pass out. Losing air, he jerked away from the wall and landed in a heap on the ground. His eyes caught a black mist disappearing back into the wall, and a different shadow drifted down the path above him. Its green eyes illuminated the horrific faces of the gargoyles as it passed. Nowhere was safe. Vero leaped to his feet and ran deeper down the path.

The faster he ran, the more shadows appeared and pursued him. Soon, the path behind Vero became a sea of burning green eyes and dark apparitions. Vero was already badly outnumbered, and he realized that running only made it worse. He came to an abrupt stop, taking the shadows by surprise. They too stopped, malevolent eyes watching for his next move. Vero closed his eyes, and instantly his sword sprung forth from the palm of his hand. He grabbed it by the hilt and swung the blade at the dark entities, slicing one from head to bottom. Vero's eyes widened when he realized that his blade had passed right through it, the entity unharmed. A sinister laugh echoed through the hallway. His sword was useless against these things. His weapon disappeared back into his palm as he momentarily considered his options. There weren't any, so he turned and ran again.

His level of fear rose as the number of shadows continued to grow. The swarming mass of black chased him, pushing him deeper into the maze. Vero's heart skipped when he saw the original lone shadow standing a few feet ahead of him, blocking his way forward. He was trapped, in front and behind. Sweat ran down his flushed face as he turned to the tangled mass of black clouds and green eyes. He was sick of these creepy shadows. He realized he was powerless and could run no farther. The thought made him angry, and that anger spurred a moment of courage. Vero stood tall before the charging mass and bravely faced them. As an angry pair of glowing green orbs darted at his face, Vero refused to blink. The shadow stopped and inched away, staring deep into Vero's unwavering eyes.

"What?" Vero screamed. "C'mon . . . let's see what you got! Do it . . . I'm not afraid!" For a split second, the brooding green eyes gave a look of surprise, and then, *poof!*—the dark entities all disintegrated and disappeared.

Vero turned. The lone creature was also gone. Vero let out a sigh of relief and looked up at the gargoyles. No black shadows clouded their faces. As he headed down the path encased by walls and towering gargoyles, Vero wondered what had caused all the shadows to vanish. The thought of the solitary black figure sent a shudder through his body. As he looked down the path, he once again saw a pair of the green eyes staring menacingly at him. "Oh, man! Not again!" Vero yelled.

Vero turned and ran back the way he had come. He glanced over his shoulder. The figure slowly and methodically followed him, as if it knew Vero could not escape and so there was no need to rush. Vero's fear spiked. Suddenly, scores of the black shadow creatures streamed from the mouths of the gargoyles. He ran even faster. *What had made them vanish before?* Vero wondered. *Had they just been messing with me?*

But then a thought occurred to him. They had disappeared the moment he stood his ground—when he stood tall, and his fear had vanished. And they had reappeared when his fright had returned. Was it his own panic and lack of confidence that drew the black shadows to him?

Vero looked every which way for an out—every single inch of the narrow path was dark with the entities and their glowing eyes. And then one grabbed Vero around his neck with both hands and lifted him off the ground. Vero gagged as he struggled for air. An angry mob began to swarm beneath him, clawing at him, each one trying to take a piece of him away. As the hands around his neck tightened, Vero eyed the shadow creature. Once again, his fear gave way to anger. His defiant resolve returned, and Vero spat at the creature. "Get off of me . . . now," he said calmly and firmly. His fear abated, Vero again produced his sword. Looking the creature in the eyes, he fearlessly cut the shadow hands from around his neck. This time, his sword had power.

The creature's eyes went wide as it vaporized into thin air. Vero fell back against the wall and watched as the swirling horde of shadows vanished. Moments later, he stood. There was no sign of the entities anywhere. He retracted his sword. His theory had been correct—his fear of the shadows was what drew them to him. And it was his own lack of confidence that had initially rendered his sword powerless. Vero straightened his back and raised his head high, determined to no longer fear the shadows, or his ability to vanquish them.

As Vero continued down the path, he glanced up once more at the rows of gargoyles. He had read about them last year in his seventh-grade World History class. Placed on top of cathedrals and castles, they served as waterspouts that directed rain off the roofs through the gargoyles' mouths, but no one really knew the exact reason why the statues were so unappealing and frightening to look upon. Some historians felt they were placed to ward off evil spirits. Others claimed the gargoyles were evil themselves and were meant to frighten people so they would run into the church for protection. Staring up at a particularly scary statue with a distorted, angry, ape-like face with horns protruding from its head, Vero hoped the former was the correct explanation.

As he walked, Vero noticed that sparse clusters of grass broke through the stone ground like weeds clinging to life between cracks in the sidewalk. He started to hear the song of crickets and he crinkled his nose. The musty-smelling air gave way to the smell of a barnyard. Vero was suddenly reminded of the small petting zoo that had taken over their backyard for Clover's ninth birthday. As he rounded a corner, Vero was faced with another split in the path. Taking a step toward the right side, he heard the faintest sound of a running river. Thinking of the three beautiful waterfalls in the far more forgiving region of the Ether, where souls cleansed themselves before meeting God, he decided to follow the sound. Vero's excitement increased as the sound grew clearer and louder with every step he took. As he rounded a corner, he stepped out into a wider, taller corridor.

Vero hadn't realized how claustrophobic he had been in the smaller corridors of the maze until he stepped into this new, bigger space. To accommodate the added width, the gargoyles had also gotten bigger, maintaining a canopy top that prevented any escape by flight. There was flowing water here, though the trickle of the stream that cut right across the path in front of him could not be the source of the sound he had been following. As he stepped over it and walked ahead, the noise of rapidly flowing water became almost deafening. Vero's head whipped around. A feeling of dread came over him. The tiny stream had somehow magically swelled into a raging river.

"Weird," Vero said aloud. "Guess I won't be going back that way."

Ahead on the wall to his left, Vero saw a large cave-like entrance, illuminated by flickering torches. Vero rested against the stone wall for a moment, trying to gather his thoughts. Moments later, he walked into the cave. The deeper he went into the cave, the fainter the sound of the river became. He started to hear a new sound. "Is that the clucking of chickens?" Vero wondered. This maze was so weird.

Confused, Vero wearily approached the source of the sound. Before him, the cave seemed to open into a much larger chamber. He distinctly heard a great multitude of chickens, echoing against every crevice of the cave. Scattered around the chamber were what appeared to be life-size statues of angels, made of some sort of whitish plaster. Some had their wings fully open, while others did not. Vero noticed looks of either shock or terror on every face. He was reminded of Medusa's garden from the mythology stories his dad had read to him as a little kid. One glance at Medusa's hideous face instantly turned the viewer to stone trophies she kept in her garden. Mindful of this, Vero decided to keep his eyes on the floor, as a precaution.

He darted through a multitude of statues, making sure to stick to the wall of the ever-expanding chamber.

Wondering what could have transformed these angels, he bumped into a statue of a young girl of about nine or ten, who had her mouth open in terror, her head turned away from the wall. She was holding on to a pencil, which was still touching the wall, as if she had been trying to write something. Vero saw faint letters, faded with time. All he was able to read on the wall was "c katr ce."

Pondering what letters were missing, Vero pushed on. On the other side of the large chamber, a smaller passage-way led into a smaller chamber. He continued into the inner cave. Suddenly, a rush of feathers hit his face. He coughed as he spit a plume out of his mouth. He wiped his mouth with his sleeve, still careful to keep his eyes down. On the ground, surrounding him, were hundreds of drab-colored hens pecking the dusty floor of the cave. Peeking through his half-closed eyes, Vero saw that these hens were maybe two or three times the size of the ones on earth, standing well above his knee height. Vero wondered what this place was. What had the terrified statue girl been trying to write? Was it a warning? He recalled the letters, "c katr ce."

"Who are you, and why have you come to my den?" a smooth, deep voice called out to him, startling Vero, who opened his eyes wide and took in his environment. He saw a cave about the length of a basketball court, full of hens and statues, before quickly returning his glance to the floor.

"Who are you?" Vero shouted.

"I am called the cockatrice," the voice replied, sounding only a few feet away.

Cockatrice! That's what the girl had written. Vero now knew exactly what the creature was. The books of Isaiah and Jeremiah had both mentioned the cockatrice—the half rooster, half serpent creature that, like Medusa, possessed a gaze that turned living things to stone. If Vero looked it in the eyes, he'd be added to the cockatrice's collection of statues. Vero tightly shut his eyes.

"I'm not here to harm you," Vero shouted over the clucking hens. "Just passing through. I need to make my way through the maze. Any chance you could tell me the way out?"

"Forget the maze! You should be asking how to leave my den," the cockatrice said.

"Great! Tell me which way, and I'm gone," Vero said.

"To leave here, there is but one way. You must outwit me . . . or remain my 'guest' forever."

Vero gulped.

"It's not so bad. I've never heard even a single complaint from anyone here." The cockatrice smirked.

"On second thought, never mind. I'll just go back the way I came."

"No, fledgling. You must succeed where all the others have failed. You must outwit me. How hard could that be? After all, I'm nothing but an overgrown rooster." The cockatrice laughed nastily.

"You're also half serpent, with a killer gaze," Vero added.

"Ah, but I am so beautiful to behold, one look at me is worth ten thousand deaths."

"I don't think so. I already got a peek at some of your hens," Vero said. "And they didn't exactly do it for me."

"They are not as beautiful as I am. I am one of a kind," the cockatrice said in a soothing voice. "Open your eyes and stare at me. I'm right in front of you."

Vero instinctively stepped back. His sword sprung forth from his hand, and he held it out defensively.

"There's no need for violence," the cockatrice scolded.

"If I slay every chicken in here, eventually I'll get to you," Vero said as he swung his sword, keeping his head down.

"You'd senselessly slaughter all these innocents?" the cockatrice sneered. "That would be a huge sin, angel."

"As opposed to using those innocents to hide behind?"

The cockatrice snickered. "I'm no angel."

Vero knew it was true. But he had learned his lesson from the shadows—he would show no fear. Fear gave his opponent an instant advantage. How was he going to outwit the cockatrice . . . especially since he couldn't even look at it? And if he could—did he look like all the other birds? *Except,* Vero thought, *he has a serpent's tail, and the others would not.*

"Look at me," the cockatrice said in a soothing voice. "You can't keep your eyes closed forever."

Vero closed his eyes even tighter.

"Eventually curiosity will get the better of you. It always does," the cockatrice chuckled.

Vero was working on a plan. If he could keep the cockatrice talking, he might be able to zero in on it.

"Don't you have better things to do than prey upon fledgling angels?" Vero asked.

"Not anymore. There was a time long ago, when I preyed upon humans."

"I doubt that," Vero said as he stepped forward, following the voice.

"I once dwelt in the cities of Sodom and Gomorrah," the cockatrice boasted. "I was there when the angels destroyed the cities."

Vero inched a few feet to his right, toward the voice.

"I overheard the angels tell Lot to flee before fire rained down from heaven onto the cities, and I followed them out."

Vero knew the story of the two cities. They were so corrupt that God destroyed them, sparing only Lot and his family.

"The angel warned them not to look back at the burning cities, but Lot's wife couldn't help herself."

"It was you? You were there when she turned around, turning her to a pillar of salt!" Vero said.

"Yes. I was there. But I had no idea she was going to turn around, so I can't really take the credit for that one. After the destruction, those two angels put a sack over me and brought me here, where you, too, will become a pillar of salt."

Vero wielded his sword. The immediate group of birds around him flew a few feet away, avoiding the blade.

"Missed," the cockatrice teased.

Vero noted that its voice seemed to come from behind him.

"Open your eyes, and let's get this over with," the cockatrice sneered.

Vero thought for a moment. It would be near impossible to slay the creature without being able to see it. How would he do it? The demigod Perseus used his shield as a mirror to see Medusa. He'd been able to approach her by watching her reflection. If only he had a mirror. But he did—his sword! Vero raised his sword to eye level. He looked into the blade, hoping to catch an image of the cockatrice. But he only saw the reflected faces of the hens.

"Nice try," the cockatrice smugly said. "But aren't you familiar with the cockatrice? Everyone knows I'm far too beautiful to have a reflection."

Vero sighed. *How am I going to get out of this?*

But then Vero again remembered the cockatrice's tail. His tracks would be the only ones with a serpent's tail mark between the feet. He lowered his head and slightly cracked open his eyes, keeping them intent on the ground so the cockatrice could not see that they were slightly ajar. Vero saw the tracks of giant rooster feet on the sandy floor every which way he turned. Which ones belonged to the cockatrice?

"Come on, angel. Just take a little peek at me . . ." the cockatrice enticed.

The low, velvety voice was hypnotic, tormenting Vero. He tried to ignore it while he continued to search the ground.

"I am more beautiful than the most glorious sunset, more stunning than the vibrant wild poppies swaying in the wind . . ." Its voice was soothing, tempting.

Vero saw an imprint in the dirt between two footprints. It was a solid line that seemed to follow between the tracks. If he followed it, the trail would lead him to the creature. With his eyes glued to the ground right in front of his feet, Vero stepped forward, following the tail's path along the ground.

"Come closer," Vero called to the cockatrice. "When I do look, I don't want to miss out on any of your beauty."

The cockatrice did not answer. Vero saw that the trail he followed took an abrupt circular turn. He looked between his legs and saw what appeared to be a large lizard's tail in the dirt right behind him. Vero could feel breath on his neck as the cockatrice hissed an unearthly sound, now trying to both scare and surprise Vero into looking at him. But

Vero did not turn to face the beast. With his eyes tightly shut, Vero swung around in one fluid motion and sliced the head off the cockatrice! He opened his eyes slowly and watched as the body ran around headless, wings flapping. He had to admit, the cockatrice was stunningly beautiful. Its body was covered in royal blue feathers with red, yellow, and green feathers peppered in.

The cockatrice's head lay face down in the dirt, away from Vero. He was afraid to approach it, recalling that Medusa's head could still turn people to stone even after it had been severed from her body. Vero then heard what sounded like falling rocks. He looked back to the larger chamber, where the once-angel pillars of salt had stood. They were all crumbling as they came back to life. Vero walked over to the girl writing on the wall, and the flock of hens followed. The girl's rock eyes began to crack, and soon Vero could see her sparkling blue-green eyes peering out at him. The rest of her body cracked, and chunks of salt fell to the ground. A young fledgling stood before Vero. She nodded gratefully to Vero.

"Thank you," she said before vanishing into thin air.

The rest of the pillars also crumbled, freeing the remaining angels and fledglings. Some smiled to Vero while others nodded before they all disappeared from sight. Vero walked straight ahead, out of the empty cave and back into the maze, happy to have outwitted the cockatrice.

4

❖

DRY BONES

Vero rounded the corner and picked up his pace. His right hand was over his heart as he waited and listened for his Vox Dei to guide him. He felt as if he was going in the right direction, though he couldn't be completely sure. But one thing he was sure of was that he was lonely. He missed the other fledglings. He wished Greer were here to hurl some kind of insult at him. He chuckled just imagining the expression on Ada's face had she seen the headless cockatrice running around. Yet his thoughts always came back to Kane. Vero was increasingly worried about him. When they had last parted ways, Kane had been in a bad place due to the Angel Trials, where the fledglings had competed against angels from other spheres. Kane felt the trials had been unfair to him—that he should have won—and when he didn't get the recognition, he had become bitter and angry. The hardest moment had been when Vero sent a fort-i-fire Kane's way to help him restore hope, but

Kane had blocked it in anger and despair. Vero hoped that over the past few months, his friend had made peace with the outcome of the Trials and was back to his old self.

The outcome of the Angel Trials didn't really change too much, anyway. Though Vero himself had been a winner, here he was, alone in this maze, trying to prove himself yet again. The Archangel Michael had promised Vero that he'd never be alone, yet here he was—all by himself. In fact, he had always felt alone. On earth, Vero never really felt he fit in with the other kids, except maybe Tack. It wasn't until he'd discovered he was a guardian angel that he realized how correct he'd been in thinking so. And even among his fellow guardian angels, Vero was different: somewhat isolated. There were constant whispers behind his back of rumors that he wasn't like the others, that he was special. But Pax was more gifted at reading minds than he was. Ada knew much more about religious scriptures, folklore, and traditions than he did. X was physically stronger than all of them. Greer was so tough and fearless, and Kane . . . he'd shown Vero up on several occasions, and even earned the unicorn's blessing during the trials. Truth was, at the time, it hurt Vero that he wasn't selected to receive the special blessing from God. He had felt that he had needed it more than Kane. However, Michael had told Vero that because he was given much, more was expected of him. But that didn't make it any easier to be alone now. *Please don't let me be alone . . .* Vero prayed.

He heard the rustling of feathers. His face lit up. Were the other fledglings here? He turned in the direction of the noise, though his face dropped when he saw what was behind him—it was just the flock of hens. They had followed him out of the cockatrice's den.

"Why are you guys following me?"

"'Cause we think you're cute," a voice said.

Vero's heart skipped a beat. His head whipped around, and a befuddled look came over him when he saw Pax standing behind him, laughing. With his big ears and bad haircut, he was unmistakable.

"Pax?"

"Don't look so surprised," Pax said. "You called me."

"I willed you to the Ether?" Vero asked, astonished.

Pax nodded. "I was in the middle of surgery. The doctor was putting a stint in my heart . . ."

"You're sick?"

"Yeah, I have a congenital heart defect."

Vero looked at him, perplexed. "On top of the autism?"

Pax shrugged. "So anyway, I heard you calling, and next thing I knew, I saw you talking to a bunch of chickens." Pax chuckled.

"It's really cool that you're here. I wonder if the others are coming."

"Vero . . . where is here?" he said, looking around, his eyes taking in the canopy of gargoyles. "And I guess we can't fly out."

"We're in a maze somewhere underneath C.A.N.D.L.E."

"Why?"

"They're testing me. Raziel said they need to know which side I fight for . . . like it's still a question," Vero said, hurt and frustrated. "Why do they still doubt me?"

"I don't know. But I do know that at some point they'll stop doubting you. But until then, I guess you've got to get through this maze."

Vero nodded. He was so grateful Pax was with him. The boys walked ahead while the hens trailed closely behind.

"I saw the Angel of Death the other day," Vero said.

Pax stopped and looked at Vero, very curious.

"I watched him take an old man's soul from his body. It was actually really beautiful, so peaceful. You know what? If people could see that, I don't think they'd be so afraid to die."

"But I'm still afraid," Pax sheepishly said.

"I promise you, when the time comes, you won't be." Vero patted Pax's back, comforting him. He turned, and the boys continued walking with the hens following.

While still on the path, a glimmer of light up ahead caught Vero's eye. Had they reached the way out?

"Pax, come on!" Vero yelled.

Vero ran down the path toward the light until his foot hit something, causing him to trip and land on his face. The flock bunched around him. Pax picked up what had caused the fall—a decaying bone.

"Looks like a leg bone," Pax said, quickly dropping it.

Vero's exuberance instantly turned to dread. Looking ahead, he saw several more bones scattered on the path. With a deep breath he stood and dusted himself off.

"Come on, there's no going back," Vero said as he slowly walked ahead.

The light in front of them continued to offer guidance, and soon they reached a large white, open arena so bright they had to shield their eyes. After a few moments, their eyes adjusted. They were standing in a rounded field of bones—a boneyard. A sickening feeling formed in the pit of Vero's stomach. Thousands of skeleton pieces lay on the ground—skulls, shinbones, collarbones, as well as pieces of arms and legs were scattered in piles.

Worst of all, there was only one path through the massive, circular arena. The gargoyles lining the walls stood on top of one another, forming a dome-shaped ceiling above. It reminded Vero of the Capital Dome, which he and Tack had visited on a fourth-grade field trip to Washington, D.C.—except this ceiling was constructed out of many frightening-looking gargoyles. The hens flocked around him. They, too, were weary of this forsaken place.

"Where are we?" Pax asked.

"Wherever we are, it sure is creepy," Vero said.

"Look at those." Pax pointed to rusted pieces of metal scattered among the bones. "They look like swords and shields."

Vero looked closer. "They are swords and shields. These guys must have died in battle."

"Let's hurry and get out of here," Pax said, nervously looking to the lone exit on the other side of the arena.

Heading toward the escape, they carefully sidestepped around the bone piles, trying not to touch any of the remains and accidentally desecrate them. Little by little, Vero began to feel uneasy, like he was being watched. He quickly spun around. Only Pax was following with the hens.

"What?" Pax asked.

"Nothing, guess I'm just feeling paranoid."

"How could you not in here?"

As they continued forward, Vero could feel his heart racing and the blood pounding through his veins. Then he heard what sounded like a pebble hitting the ground. He stopped. The hens hop-flew behind him.

"You hear that?"

Pax also stopped. "Yeah."

Stone gargoyles peered down on them. The sound of crunching bones filled the chamber. Chunks of stone were raining down from the dome's ceiling, smashing the bones below. Then, to their horror, they realized where the stones had been falling from—the gargoyles! They were shedding their stone shells much the same way the statue angels had shed their salt shells, revealing real flesh and bones and muscles.

"They're alive!" Vero yelled, horrified, as one by one living gargoyles broke free.

The gargoyles had black, slimy hides. Some had wings, while others did not. But all of them smelled foul, like stagnated sewage water. Vero and Pax scrambled over rocks and bones to get out. Just as they reached the exit, a huge gargoyle with sharp black wings and a face that resembled a troll's flew at the boys, picked both up in his claws, and threw them back into the center of the bone pile.

"That hurt!" Vero yelled as he sat up, holding his injured backside.

"I can't find my glasses!" Pax shouted, his hands blindly searching through bones. "I'm practically blind without them!"

Vero quickly glanced around. They were badly outnumbered—about fifty gargoyles were advancing. Some of the living statues flew above him, while others crawled closer.

"Well, you may not want to see this!" Vero yelled.

Vero's sword shot out from his hand. He wielded it at the creatures while he scrambled to stand. Once on his feet,

Vero backed up. He grabbed Pax by the collar, trying to escape the way they had entered.

"Stay away and I won't have to kill you all!" Vero shouted to the approaching creatures, knowing it was an idle threat the moment it escaped his lips.

Unfazed, the gargoyles hissed at him. Vero felt a tinge of regret for not having taken the slain cockatrice's head. Perhaps he could have turned the gargoyles to salt. Vero backed up farther with Pax, crunching bones as he went.

"Your glasses!" Vero shouted, eyeing the pair under a stack of bones.

Vero released the back of Pax's collar and picked up the glasses. He stepped, and was handing them to Pax when his foot became stuck in a ribcage.

"My foot's stuck!"

Vero tried to kick it free, but the ribcage would not budge. Pax shoved his glasses back onto his face and tugged at Vero's foot. The terrified hens also joined in, pecking at the bone, trying to free Vero.

"Take my sword!" Vero yelled to Pax.

Pax grabbed the sword and waved it threateningly at the approaching gargoyles. With both hands, Vero pulled on his ankle. He was surprised when the bones shattered to pieces as his foot came loose.

"Good thing these bones are so dry. They break easily!" Vero shouted.

"Dry?" Pax said, scrunching his brow in thought. "The bones are all dry . . . They're all 'dry bones'!"

"That's what I said," Vero shouted, grabbing his sword from Pax. "You know, you really should grow your sword . . . I could use a little help!" Vero yelled as the gargoyles inched closer.

"One sword won't help, but I can get you a whole army!" Pax yelled.

"What?"

"We're in the valley of dry bones from Ezekiel! God told Ezekiel to speak to the bones and let them know that He would breathe life into them. Ezekiel did, and the bones fused together, flesh and muscle formed on them, breath entered into them, and they stood up in a vast army!"

"Really?"

"Yes. Ezekiel had faith that God would restore the bones. So maybe if you do too, God will raise you an army!"

A gargoyle resembling a wolf with an elongated face snarled at Vero and Pax. Several more gargoyles circled them. As the ring tightened in, Vero shouted to the bones, "Arise, and God will breathe life into you!"

Nothing happened. The wolf gargoyle swiped his paw at Vero, catching his shirt and ripping it. Vero lost his balance and fell back into a mound of skeletons, which crashed down on top of him. Using his snout, the wolf gargoyle began to throw bones off Vero in an attempt to reach him. As he came face to face with the gargoyle, Vero closed his eyes, prayed with all his heart, and yelled, "Arise!"

A loud rattling sound shook the chamber. Vero felt the bones around him stir. The gargoyles backed off, concerned by the ruckus, allowing a short reprieve. Vero stood and backed up. Pax and the hens also moved away. The boys watched as thousands of bones fused themselves together and formed into human skeletons. Each picked up a rusted sword and shield off the ground, then at the same moment they all stood up, forming a protective circle around Vero and Pax, who watched in amazement. Vero noted there had to be at least a hundred skeleton soldiers to the fifty gargoyles. But that didn't stop the gargoyles. The wolf gargoyle pounced on a skeleton, biting its fibula and dislodging it. The skeleton stumbled a bit on one leg, but then its fibula fused back into position. The skeleton once again stood tall. Seeing this, Vero realized there was no way to defeat these old guys—they were already dead.

The gargoyles advanced. Vero backed up. He needed to think fast.

"Fall in, soldiers!" Vero yelled in a commanding voice. "I want two straight lines protecting me to the exit!"

The skeleton army formed into two lines of soldiers standing shoulder-to-shoulder all the way to the exit. The skeletons held the gargoyles at bay, brandishing their shields and swords. As Vero and Pax walked in between the flanks of skeleton soldiers, the frustrated gargoyles shrieked in angry rage.

The wolf gargoyle attacked the skeletal soldiers. A skeleton swung its sword, hitting the gargoyle across its midsection and wounding it. The once fierce gargoyle yelped and whimpered away.

The other gargoyles launched an attack on the army of the dead. But the fearless skeletons held their ground courageously. The horrific sounds of battle enveloped Vero and Pax, but the line of fighting skeletons held firm, allowing the boys to walk unscathed toward the exit—even the hens kept pace with them.

Vero and Pax exited the tumultuous arena, and saw a yellow, glistening staircase. As quickly as they could, they ran up.

5

❖

VERO'S MISSION

With great relief, Vero found himself back in the main hall of C.A.N.D.L.E. as he stepped off the last stair.

"Vero," a fatherly voice called out.

Vero turned to the voice and saw Uriel standing in the hall. Vero smiled to the silver-haired archangel, happy to see him.

"Congratulations," Uriel said, his violet eyes twinkling. "You made it through, and I see you made some friends." Uriel chuckled, looking at the multitude of dazed hens gathered around Vero. Suddenly, Uriel's smile turned to surprise. "Pax?"

Pax walked into the main hall. "Vero called me to the Ether."

"But he was to go through the maze alone," Uriel said, thinking aloud, putting it all together. "You willed him here?"

"It was a surprise to me too," Vero said. "Wait . . . does this mean I have to go back and go through it again?" Vero looked terrified at the thought.

"No, but Pax, you must go back."

"Into the maze?" Pax yelled, scared.

"Back to earth."

Pax let out a sigh of relief. Vero turned to Pax.

"Thanks. I wouldn't have been able to outsmart those gargoyles without you."

Pax smiled and nodded. He closed his eyes and vanished.

"Come on, take a walk." Uriel motioned with his head.

With the hens following at Vero's heels, Vero and Uriel walked through the main hall of the school. It was still completely empty; Vero could not spot a single angel anywhere.

"Why is it so quiet?" Vero asked.

"Only you were called back for training," Uriel answered as they walked out the massive main stone doors and into the outside light. "Pax being here was not supposed to happen."

"Why, Uriel? Why am I always singled out?" Vero asked, desperation in his eyes. "Why do I keep having to prove myself? I wish I could be like everyone else."

Uriel stopped. He scratched his closely cropped beard. "You are like everyone else."

"No, I'm not!" Vero yelled. "If I was like everybody else, I wouldn't be here right now!"

Compassion filled Uriel's eyes. "Sit," Uriel said, motioning to a glossy marble step.

Vero hesitated, then sat. Uriel joined him. A hen fluttered into Vero's lap.

"Vero, God asks certain things of all of us. And that request is different for every person, every angel, so in that regard you are like the others."

Vero looked at him, confused. He petted the hen.

"Everyone plays a part in God's plan, and He gives them exactly what they need to accomplish whatever it is He asks of them. And for you, He is tasking you to find and return the Book of Raziel. And the time has come."

Vero's steely gray eyes went wide. Michael had told Vero previously that he was to find the book, but now that the mission was actually upon him, he was scared.

"But I'm not ready. I thought I'd have more time to . . ."

"Lucifer is closing in on it. You have no more time."

"Closing in? But how?"

"Unfortunately, the Angel Trials confirmed it. He now knows you are the one who has the ability to find it."

Vero considered for a moment. "But why do I have to find it now? What's the rush?"

"You are still a fledgling. You are still vulnerable. Unlike archangels or full-fledged guardians, you have not decided for whom you fight."

"Yes, I have!" Vero shouted. "Why doesn't anyone believe me?"

Startled by Vero's outburst, the hen flew off his lap.

"I believe you." Uriel looked into Vero's eyes. "But Lucifer wants you badly. Be on guard, Vero."

Vero looked to Uriel, trying to process the enormity of it all.

"And you are ready." Uriel nodded to Vero. "You made it through the maze. You proved that you could overcome your fear. By controlling your fear, you were able to stop the shades from overpowering you."

"That's what those black shadows were?"

"Yes, they live off your fear. And by outwitting the cockatrice, you showed great strength by resisting temptation. It's nearly impossible not to look at the cockatrice."

"What happened to the angels who'd been turned into pillars?"

"You freed them. They had been trapped there for a long time, but now you've enabled those angels to move on. Just as it's probably time for them to also move on." Uriel nodded to the hens that gathered around Vero's legs.

Vero smiled at the birds. "He's right, guys. You'll like this part of the Ether. There are lots of wide-open green fields over there."

Vero pointed ahead. The birds looked dejectedly at Vero.

"I promise you'll like it here," Vero said. "And no cockatrice . . . Now go on."

The hens looked up to Vero with blinking, sad eyes. Vero nodded his head, hoping to convince them. After a moment, the hens turned and hop-flew toward the distant green fields. Vero wistfully smiled as the birds receded from sight. He then turned to Uriel.

"So what were the bones all about?" Vero asked.

"By commanding the bones the way you did, you showed great faith in God. You had the faith that He would hear you and breathe life into the skeletons," Uriel said, then placed his hand on Vero's shoulder. "You're ready."

Vero met Uriel's eyes. He nodded solemnly. Vero suddenly realized something, and his chin dropped to his chest. A look of intense compassion came over Uriel as he had heard Vero's thoughts. With his thumb and index fingers, Uriel tipped up Vero's chin, and held his gaze.

"Yes, you will be leaving your family soon."

"But I thought I'd have more time with them . . ." Vero said, tears forming in his eyes.

"God will give them the strength to accept your death," Uriel said.

"But what about me? Will He give me the strength to leave them?" Vero asked, tears streaming down his face.

"Yes, He will."

"Was it hard for you to leave your family?"

"Archangels aren't placed on earth with a family, so I wouldn't know," Uriel said with a tinge of sadness. "I have to admit I always feel a bit of longing when I see guardians finally reunited with their earthly families . . . when their families return to God after they pass on."

Vero suddenly felt sorry for Uriel. This kind angel had never known the love of a human family. He had never known that joy.

"But I do know that once reunited, any lingering sadness is forever turned to joy," Uriel said in a consoling voice.

Vero looked down. Despite the reassurance, it was still overwhelming. So much was being asked of him. Vero looked up at Uriel. "What if their course in life does not lead them back to God before they die?" Vero asked, biting his lip.

Uriel chuckled. "You think Greer will have problems keeping Clover on the right path?"

Vero had forgotten. His fellow fledgling, Greer, was his sister's guardian angel. Greer was about as tough as anyone could be. Vero knew Clover was in good hands.

"Probably not," Vero answered.

Vero watched as Uriel closed his eyes, then quickly opened them. Suddenly two angels appeared on either side of him. Both of the male angels were very tall and robust, wearing dazzling white robes. They exuded incredible strength and purpose. Something about them felt familiar to Vero, though he couldn't recall ever having met or seen them before. Uriel turned to the angel on his right.

"Vero, this is the guardian angel Leo."

Leo bowed to Vero.

"Leo is your father's guardian," Uriel said.

A look of surprise came over Vero. Uriel turned to the angel on his left.

"This is Karael, your mother's guardian angel."

Karael bowed to Vero.

"I love your father very much," Leo said to Vero. "As Karael loves your mother."

"Nothing can deter us in our mission to bring them back to God," Karael said.

Vero nodded, appreciatively.

"And if you ever need us, we're always here for you," Leo said.

"Thanks, but I thought we never leave our humans for even a second," Vero said. "How can you be here?"

"One of the perks of being a full-fledged guardian," Karael said. "We have the gift of bilocation."

"Being in two places at once?" Vero asked.

"Actually, even tri-locating if necessary," Karael said. "Depends on what is needed."

Vero looked confused.

"Location is a human concept," Uriel explained. "But we angels are pure spirits, and a spirit is wherever he is *acting*. We can be acting in more than one place."

The two angels nodded to Vero.

"God be with you, Vero," Leo said before he and Karael vanished from sight. Uriel turned to Vero.

"Families of guardians have some of the most powerful angels because God knows the loss of their child will be devastating and can easily shake their faith. So He assigns only the strongest angels to sustain them."

Vero wiped his face with his sleeve and stood. He quickly walked down the stairs of C.A.N.D.L.E.

Uriel called out to him, "Vero!"

Vero did not stop. He continued to walk down the school stairs.

"Vero, stop!"

Vero wouldn't listen. He stormed past a cluster of plump fruit trees, trying not to notice that Uriel chased after him. When the archangel reached Vero, he placed his hand on his shoulder and spun Vero around.

"What if I fail?" Vero shouted. "What if I can't find the book?" Vero looked hard into Uriel's eyes.

Uriel sighed. "You wouldn't be the first one."

Vero looked surprised.

"Another angel before you tried and failed."

"What happened to him?"

Sadness flooded Uriel's eyes. "He is in the Lake of Fire. Abaddon claimed him."

Vero gasped. His breathing intensified as panic overtook him.

"But how? I thought if I failed, I'd just go to the choir of angels!"

Uriel shook his head. "Because the book means so much to Lucifer, he will do anything, including turning your heart to the darkness in order to get it. The other angel, named Sora, fell prey to him and wound up in the lake."

"For all eternity . . ." Vero interrupted.

Vero's eyes closed for a moment as he lowered his head, feeling his legs might buckle out from underneath him. Uriel placed his hand on his shoulder to steady him.

"The news just keeps getting better and better!" Vero shouted. "Is this book really even worth it?"

"The Book of Raziel lists the names of every person to be born. A baby is to be born in the coming years who will do much good in the world. This child will grow up to be a great spiritual leader, and many will hear his message and come back to God . . . thousands and thousands of people." Uriel looked squarely at Vero. "Now do you think it's worth it?"

Vero hesitated for a moment, then slowly nodded his head.

"But what if I mess up?"

"Should the Book of Raziel fall into Lucifer's hands, and he were to learn the name of the child, he'd do everything in his power to stop the baby from ever growing up in the light. He will stop at nothing to keep that from happening."

"How?"

"He'll go after the parents, corrupting them or leading them to despair. Even convincing other humans to kill them. Nothing is off limits for him if it will prevent the child from his or her mission."

"But what if no one can find the book? Then it will just continue being hidden and everything will be okay."

Uriel shook his head. "Lucifer has always been in fanatical pursuit of the book. Events are unfolding that we cannot stop. I wish I could."

Vero looked to Uriel with eyes full of uncertainty. "I'm scared, Uriel."

"That's okay. God knows you are ready for the task. Everything you've done up to this point has prepared and proven you." Uriel paused. "You are not alone. Others will be of great help to you."

"Okay," Vero said, accepting his fate.

Uriel placed his hand on Vero's shoulder. "Most importantly, God does not want to lose you."

Vero looked into Uriel's eyes. At that moment, he felt his Vox Dei so strongly, and it made him feel loved by God. And he knew it was true—God did not want to lose him, ever.

"Go and enjoy your family and friends, Vero," Uriel said. "We'll call you back when it is time."

"All right."

Vero closed his eyes.

"Vero."

Vero opened his eyes. Uriel still stood before him.

"It's not only God who would hate to lose you," Uriel said with heartfelt emotion.

"Thank you," Vero said before he disappeared.

6

TACK THE MAGNIFICENT

"Vero! Vero! Are you all right?" Dennis yelled, distraught. Vero heard his father's familiar voice. He opened his eyes and looked around, realizing he was lying on the basement floor at the bottom of the stairs. A trail of milk dripped all the way down the steps and puddled at the bottom around him. As Dennis ran over to him, Nora opened the basement door.

"Vero!" Nora yelled, racing down the stairs while careful not to fall herself.

Dennis helped Vero sit up on a step.

"I'm fine," Vero said, resting his forehead in his hands. "I just tripped."

"You hit your head," Dennis said. "Hard."

Nora knelt down in front of Vero. She moved her index finger left to right in front of his eyes.

"Can you see my finger okay?" Nora asked.

"Yes."

"How about over here?" Nora asked as she moved her finger to the left of his face.

"Yes."

"Any blurriness?"

"No, Mom," Vero answered. "I'm fine."

"Sure?" Dennis asked as he ran his hand over a newly formed bump on the back of Vero's head.

Vero nodded. He got all choked up when he looked into his parents' worried faces. If they got this upset over a trip and a little lump, how would they ever handle his for-real death? Tears streamed from his eyes at the thought.

"I'm sorry," Vero cried.

His parents pulled him into them and hugged him tightly. All three sat on the steps in a tangled ball of arms.

"I'm sorry," Vero said between sobs. "I'm so sorry."

"It's just a gallon of milk," Nora said. "It's no big deal. I'll send Clover next door to the Atwoods to get a cup."

Dennis placed his hands around Vero's ears, and looked him head on. "Vero, listen to me. I've told you a hundred times before . . . there's no point in crying over spilled milk." He chuckled, worry lines creasing his forehead.

Vero couldn't help but to laugh through his tears. One day, he would miss even his dad's bad jokes.

Tack and Vero sat in the school cafeteria eating lunch with Nate Hollingsworth. Each had a tray of food on the table in front of them. Tack stuck his beefy index finger into Nate's mashed potatoes.

"Are you gonna eat those?" Tack asked while poking his finger around.

"Not after your disgusting finger's been in 'em . . . I saw you pick your nose earlier." Nate's prominent Adam's apple bounced up and down in annoyance.

Nate had always had huge feet, and it was only now that he had grown into them. He was even taller than Tack, and at times Vero had mistaken Nate for a teacher from behind.

"Great, I'll take 'em." Tack pulled out his finger and licked it.

As Tack grabbed his spoon and scooped the buttery potatoes from Nate's tray onto his own, Davina walked over with Missy Baker, whose white-blonde hair was unmistakable.

"Can we sit with you guys?" Missy asked the boys. "Danny's being a real jerk to Davina."

Vero looked across the cafeteria and watched as Danny angrily sulked to a table and sat with a group of jocks.

"Yeah, sure," Vero said.

"Davina went to sit with him, like she does every day, but get this . . . He said he was sitting with those other jerks." Missy nodded to the group of jocks.

"He was being rude to you the other day when we got off the bus," Tack said through a mouthful of Nate's mashed potatoes.

"Did you two have a fight?" Vero asked Davina as she scooted in with Missy.

Davina shook her head.

"Please . . . Davina doesn't fight with anyone," Missy said admiringly. "It's like she's a saint."

It was true. Vero had never seen Davina have any cross words with anyone. For that matter, she never had a bone to pick with anyone. She was a nice person to the core.

"You gonna eat that?" Tack asked Missy as he stuck his finger into her dinner roll.

"You jerk! Actually, I *was* going to ask if anyone wanted it," she yelled, slapping his hand away. Missy picked up her roll, dropped it to the floor, smashed it with her shoe, then handed it to Tack. "Here you go. You can have it." Her hazel eyes narrowed.

Tack eyed the flattened roll, then looked at the floor, and back to the roll; Vero couldn't believe he was actually considering it. Davina handed Tack her dinner roll.

"Just take mine," Davina said.

"Thanks," Tack replied as he shoved the whole thing into his mouth.

Nate flashed him a disgusted look.

"What do you think is up with Danny?" Vero asked Davina.

After all, Vero was Danny's guardian angel, so he had to be interested in what was going on with his future charge.

"Don't know." Davina shrugged. "I asked him and he won't tell me."

It didn't make any sense to Vero. He knew that Danny was crazy about Davina. She had such a positive influence on him. It would be a shame if Danny cut her out of his life.

"I could ask him," Vero said to Davina.

"Dude, if he won't tell Davina, he's definitely not about to tell you," Tack said, chunks of bread stuck between his teeth.

Tack was probably right. Danny had hated Vero since way back in the sixth grade, when Davina had been new to the school. Back then, Vero had the biggest crush on her. Problem was, so had Danny. But last year, Vero felt that he had made some inroads. A rumor had been going around that Danny was the one who'd destroyed the gym. Vero had refused to believe the rumors. Even though he was confused by it, Danny had really appreciated Vero's support, so maybe he would now confide in Vero.

"Thanks, but just let it go for now," Davina told Vero. Vero nodded.

"How's your volunteering going?" Missy asked the boys.

"Great," Nate said. "It's a lot of fun."

"You are not volunteering!" Tack said.

"Of course I am!" Nate yelled.

"You're working at a place called Puppy Love," Tack said. "Your job is to play with puppies all day!"

"I also have to pick up their poop! And puppies eat a lot, so they poop a lot."

"Get real. You're not dealing with life-and-death situations like Vero and me down at the hospital."

"What life and death? You hand out magazines and coloring books." Nate rolled his eyes.

"Oh, really? You think that's all we do?" Tack asked.

"No, they probably let you wash the dirty bedpans." Nate now full-out laugh-snorted.

"Yeah." Missy laughed along.

"Very funny. For your information, Vero here properly diagnosed some baby as being tongue-tied, and he knew when a man was about to flatline even before the doctors did," Tack said proudly, puffing out his chest. "He ran and got the man's son, and he was right there when it happened."

"Is that true?" Davina turned to Vero.

"Well, sort of . . ." Vero stammered.

"That's pretty awesome," Missy said.

"I think Vero's on his way to becoming the most famous doctor since Dr. J." Tack slapped Vero's back.

"Dr. J was a basketball player in the seventies, you idiot," Nate said, shaking his head.

❖

Tack held up a card to a curly redheaded little boy wearing Spiderman pajamas. He and Vero were playing with several kids in the children's playroom at the hospital. The room was decorated with bright, colorful wallpaper of circus scenes. The boys and kids sat on a red rug with a yellow circle pattern on its edges.

"Is this your card?" Tack asked the boy.

The boy shook his head.

Tack pulled out another one and held it up.

"Is this one your card?"

"No," the boy said with a laugh.

"How about this one?" Tack flashed another card.

The boy shook his head. Tack flashed card after card.

"This?"

"No."

"This?"

"No."

"It's gotta be this one, right?" Tack asked, holding up the Jack of Hearts.

The boy's baby-blue eyes lit up. "Yeah!"

"Yes! Tack the Magnificent strikes again!" Tack said to his audience.

"But you went through half of the deck," a seven-year-old girl in a pink bathrobe protested.

"That's called 'creating suspense.'" Tack smirked.

"You're crazy," the girl said through a chortle.

"I'm crazy? You think I'm the crazy one?" Tack asked as he leaned over her.

"Yeah." She giggled.

"You're the crazy one, storing quarters in your ear . . ." Tack proceeded to pull a quarter from the back of her ear. Then a second, then a third.

The girl, along with the rest of the kids, smiled, astonished.

"Tack the Magnificent." Vero chuckled under his breath.

"Can you do any tricks?" a girl hooked up to an oxygen tank asked Vero, her breathing labored.

"Not really."

"Me either." She sighed. "But if I could, I wish I could fly."

"Really?" Vero asked, his curiosity piqued. *Was she a fledgling?*

"I always felt like I could," the girl said. "If it weren't for this oxygen tank . . ."

"Then you could sail through the endless blue skies, breathing in the pure white clouds that billow past your face," Vero said dreamily. "Over rivers so crystal clear, that from half a mile up you can make out every single stone in the riverbed, and over fields of wildflowers so brightly colored, you'd need to squint your eyes. Feeling weightless . . ."

Vero then realized that he'd gotten carried away. He abruptly stopped speaking. Tack gave him a curious look and said, "Wow, guys . . . looks like we found who the real crazy one is in here!"

Vero blushed. Nora walked in the room, interrupting them.

"Boys, back to your rounds," she told Vero and Tack.

"Okay, Mom," Vero replied as he stood.

"No, stay," the kids protested.

The girl approached Nora, dragging her oxygen tank. "You're Vero's mom?"

"Yes."

"Vero was telling us about flying. Did he ever fly?"

Nora began to shift uncomfortably. "Of course not."

"He tried once." Tack chuckled. "He jumped off the roof of his house . . ."

"Tack, get to work!" Nora's eyes insistently darted toward the door.

"Really?" the girl asked, wide-eyed.

"He fell, and nearly broke both his legs," Nora adamantly stated. "He did not *fly*."

Nora locked eyes with Vero. He knew his mother was upset. Anything that reminded her that he was different troubled her greatly. She did not know that he was a guardian angel, but she had always known there was something otherworldly about her son, and Vero knew it scared her. So he quickly crossed over to Tack and pulled him by the arm and led him out, waving good-bye to the kids.

"Now it's time for Tack the Magnificent to make himself disappear!"

The hospitality cart was waiting up against the wall in the hallway. Tack stepped behind it and began to push it while Vero walked alongside it. As they wheeled forward they came past a petite woman standing next to a stretcher. Vero recognized his next-door neighbor.

"Mrs. Atwood," he said, with a curious tone.

He looked down at the stretcher. He saw Mr. Atwood asleep.

"Hello, Vero," Mrs. Atwood said, then glanced over to Tack. "Hello, Thaddeus."

"Hi."

"Is Mr. Atwood okay?" Vero asked, as worry lines formed across his forehead.

"He's fine. He's just coming out of surgery. We're waiting for a room."

Mrs. Atwood saw the look of concern on Vero's face. She leaned into the boys.

"Hemorrhoids. He'll be fine," she whispered.

Tack chuckled. Vero elbowed him.

"We're going home later today."

"Would you like some coffee or tea while you wait?" Vero asked.

"No, thanks, but that chocolate bar looks good."

Tack handed Mrs. Atwood the candy bar. Mr. Atwood groaned.

"He's in and out of it," she said.

Mr. Atwood's eyes fluttered. Vero stepped over to him.

"He's waking up!" Vero said.

Mr. Atwood's eyes opened. As his head turned to Vero, his eyes went wide and his heart monitor began to spike.

"Hi, Mr. Atwood." Vero smiled.

Tack also leaned over his head and smiled at him.

The heart monitor spiked even higher. Mrs. Atwood rushed over to his side. She turned to Vero.

"Vero, Mr. Atwood really needs to rest right now," she said, in a way that was clear she was trying not to hurt Vero's feelings. "Why don't you come visit Albert later when he's home."

"Oh, okay," Vero said. "Bye, Mr. Atwood. Feel better. I'll come visit you later."

As Vero and Tack walked away, Mr. Atwood's blood pressure alarm went off.

Over the next hour, the boys visited several rooms and gave out candy, magazines, freshly baked cookies, and coffee to patients and their visitors.

"My feet are killing me," Tack told Vero. "When's our shift over?"

Vero glanced at his watch. "Five more minutes."

A short, older woman wearing a hospital gown wandered over to them. Her hair was a mess, and she looked a bit out of it.

"Can I help you?" Vero asked her.

"Um, yes, I'm lost," she said, confused. "I can't find my room."

"Do you know the number?" Vero asked her.

"231."

"That's up a floor," Tack said.

"We'll take you there," Vero said as he took her arm and walked her over to the elevator.

Tack left the cart and followed. He pushed the elevator button, and the doors instantly slid apart.

"You must have the magic touch," she wheezed to Tack.

"As a matter-of-fact, I do." Tack puffed out his chest.

They stepped inside the elevator. The doors began to close. Vero reached for the second-floor button when the woman immediately snatched his wrist and squeezed hard. Her face contorted into one of complete anger. Tack's eyes shot wide.

"We know it's you, Vero," she growled.

Her hand pressed even tighter around Vero's wrist.

"Hey, get off of him!" Tack yelled as he tried to pull Vero's arm from her grasp.

"Where is it?" she shrieked.

"We left the cart in the hallway!" Tack screamed, yanking on Vero. "But we could go back and get you some cookies or something!"

The old woman would not release her grip. Her fingers began to smolder on Vero's skin. Tack looked as if he couldn't believe what his eyes were seeing. Vero gazed into the woman's eyes, and he saw red—the red flecks of a malture.

"She's burning you, dude!" Tack screamed. The woman's arm was as hot as fire. Tack instantly let go of it, and shook his hand in pain.

Vero's eyes narrowed at the woman. A determination came over him and then one by one he pried her fingers off his wrist. Tack watched in horror and disbelief as Vero bent each of her fingers back, systematically breaking them. In a total panic, Tack hit random buttons on the elevator panel.

"We gotta get out of here!"

The woman hissed at Tack, displaying a mouth full of rotted teeth. He recoiled. She was about to pounce on Tack when Vero ran straightforward. He took two big steps right up the elevator wall before him, got airborne, and back flipped, landing behind the woman. He put her in a choke-hold, while Tack gripped the handrail. The elevator finally stopped on a floor.

"Run, get out!" Vero shouted to Tack.

Tack held on to the rail, frozen with fear.

"Tack, go! Get out of here!"

"I can't leave you!"

"Do it!" Vero shouted as the woman tried to break free from his grasp.

"I'll get help!" Tack shouted as he let go of the railing and ran toward the open elevator door. A massive, slimy, one-eyed creature stood blocking his way. Tack stopped dead in his tracks and stumbled back into the elevator. He tripped and fell on the floor. The creature stood over him.

"Tack!" Vero shouted as he released the old woman and threw himself between the new malture and Tack.

The malture stepped forward. As it reached out to Vero and Tack, a black iron chain shot out of its clawed hand. The cuff at the end of the chain flew over their heads and wrapped around the woman's neck and clasped. She shrieked. Then in one forceful tug, the malture pulled her toward him. He grabbed her, and they vanished instantly before the scared boys' eyes.

Tack's eyes went back into his head. He passed out. Vero kneeled over him, desperately hoping that when he woke, Tack would think it had all been a dream.

7

❖

WORLDS COLLIDE

Vero stood over Tack, who lay on a gurney in the emergency room. They were alone behind a curtain that hung all the way around the bed. Vero lightly slapped his friend's face, hoping to wake him.

"Tack, Tack, wake up . . ."

Vero was nervous. Had Tack really been able to see that malture? Would he remember the attack? If he did, how would Vero explain it? He had other questions as well—like why did the second malture rescue them from the malture posing as an old lady? What was that all about? Before Vero could think about it further, Tack's eyes started blinking—he was coming to.

"Tack, you all right?" Vero asked.

Vero watched as Tack's eyes slowly began to focus.

"How do you feel? You okay?" Vero asked, leaning over the gurney. "You passed out in the elevator."

Tack's eyes instantly shot open. Vero saw terror in them.

"Get away from me!" Tack told Vero, as he bolted up and pushed himself away.

"Tack . . . what?" Vero said, hurt.

"Who are you?" Tack yelled.

"It's me, Vero."

"No, they knew you. Those freakin' monsters in the elevator knew who you were!" Tack shouted as he raised the bedsheet instinctively up to his neck, shielding himself.

Vero was at a loss for words. Tack had seen both maltures. Worse, he remembered it all. Could Vero reveal his true identity to him, even though Uriel had always warned him not to? The thought left Vero feeling like a deer caught in the headlights. At the same time, his heart was breaking. How could his best friend now be afraid of him?

"Tack!" a woman's soft voice cried out.

The curtain pulled open, and Tack's parents, Marty and Mary, rushed over to him. In this case, it wasn't true that opposites attract, because Marty and Mary looked more like brother and sister than husband and wife. Both had husky, robust physiques. Each had a wide forehead with a narrow chin that made their faces look heart-shaped. Their eyes were a similar lively blue. And on top of their heads, the famous Kozlowski strawberry blond hair, which they had passed down to Tack and his sisters.

"Are you okay?" Mary asked, caressing her son's cheek.

Tack nodded.

"What happened?" Marty turned to Vero.

"He fainted in the elevator," Vero said, hoping there'd be no more questions.

Nora walked over to them while holding a blood pressure monitor.

"He's awake." Nora smiled, relieved.

"Nora, is he okay?" Mary asked, her brow furrowed.

"Doctor said he's fine," Nora told them as she strapped the blood pressure cuff around Tack's bicep. "I just need to take his pressure."

"Do you know what caused you to pass out?" Marty asked Tack.

Tack looked to Vero. Vero wondered what Tack would say and nervously shifted. But then Tack shook his head, in a small sign of loyalty to Vero.

"It's good—110 over 70," Nora said as she ripped off the Velcro cuff. "Did you get enough sleep last night?"

Tack nodded. He then locked eyes with Vero. "But I won't tonight," he muttered under his breath.

"What was that?" Marty asked.

"Nothing."

"Did you eat today?" Nora asked automatically.

"Nora, this is Tack we're talking about." Mary smiled.

"Oh, right," Nora said. "They did an EKG, and his heart's fine, so I think it was just a sudden drop in his blood pressure. Standing up too quickly or standing too long on your feet can trigger it. Or sometimes you can faint from anxiety or fear."

Tack's eyes darted back to Vero.

"Can we go home?" Mary asked Nora.

"Sure," Nora said. "But Tack should rest."

Mary turned to Vero. "You want to come with us while your mother finishes her shift?"

"No," Tack said a little too quickly.

"Tack!" Marty said.

"I just mean, I really need to go home and sleep," Tack covered.

"Well, Vero can still come and watch TV . . ." Mary said suspiciously, staring into her son's eyes.

"No thanks, Mrs. Kozlowski," Vero interrupted. "I have a lot of homework. I'm gonna go to the cafeteria and study."

Vero turned and walked away, and Tack made no attempt to stop him.

"I've requested to go to Sri Lanka for a few days," Dennis said as he stuck his fork into a piece of chicken. "The trip could help me push my project through."

Clover sat across the kitchen table from Vero and her mother. Using her fork, she surreptitiously pushed some peas from her plate into a waiting napkin she held under the table.

Vero sat with his head down, quietly eating. He was clearly deep in thought, and had been since coming home from the hospital earlier.

"When would you leave?" Nora asked Dennis as she got up from the table and walked to the stove.

"Few weeks if it all gets approved."

"I've always wanted to see that part of the world," Nora said, grabbing a saucepan off a burner. "You better take a lot of pictures."

"So, Vero, how was the hospital today?" Dennis asked.

Vero looked up from his food. "Fine," he said a little too quickly, then went back to eating. Clover eyed him suspiciously.

"Poor Tack passed out," Nora said.

"Really?" Dennis said. "Is he feeling okay?"

"Yes, but remind me to call Mary after dinner to check on him."

"What happened?" Clover asked.

"He fainted in an elevator," Nora answered. She turned to Vero. "Was he acting differently just before?"

"No."

"Did he complain of dizziness or did he look clammy?" Nora asked, holding the saucepan.

"I don't know. I'm not a medical person," Vero said with a definite annoyance in his voice. "Everybody says he's fine, so what's the big deal?"

"You don't have to bite my head off," Nora said.

"Sorry," Vero said, getting up from the table. "Can I be excused? I have a ton of homework."

"Okay." Nora sighed.

As Vero placed his dirty dish into the sink, Nora scooped a spoonful of peas onto Clover's plate.

"Hey! I didn't ask for more!" Clover protested.

"Well, I just assumed you wanted more, because you seem to be saving those in your napkin for later," Nora said, her voice dripping in sarcasm.

Clover rolled her eyes. She was busted. Vero chuckled as he walked out of the room.

Minutes later, Clover made her way to her brother's bedroom. The door was open, and Vero was lying on his bed playing a video game on his old PSP.

"Studying real hard, I see," Clover said, narrowing her eyes.

"Maybe I was and now I'm taking a break."

"Liar." Once inside, Clover shut the door and walked over to his bed. "What went on in that elevator?" She yanked the digital game from his hands. "And don't lie to me, because I'll know!"

She placed the game on his desk. Vero looked up at her, hesitant.

"I can handle it," Clover said as she sat on his bed.

"I was attacked by an old lady pretending to be a patient. Tack saw it all."

"What do you mean?"

"A malture disguised like an old lady."

"An undercover one like Blake and Duff?"

"Yeah."

Blake and Duff were maltures who had disguised themselves as two teenage thugs, who then hung out with Danny Konrad at school. They had tried to lead Danny down the path to ruin, but Vero had fought and defeated them.

"Did Tack see her? Is that why he passed out?"

"I was hoping he'd forget or think it was all a dream, but yeah, he definitely saw them and remembered."

"Them?" Clover asked, feeling her heart skip a little.

"Two of 'em."

Clover tried to process that.

"It doesn't make sense, though," Vero said. "The old lady patient attacked me, but then another malture, one not in disguise, showed up. And instead of going after me or Tack, it went after the old lady and then they both disappeared." Vero got more upset as he talked. "Tack saw me fighting with the old lady. I had to break her fingers to get her off of me."

Clover was terrified by the nonchalant manner in which Vero was describing his fight with a malture.

"Wait . . . You broke an old lady's fingers while you were volunteering at the hospital?" Clover exclaimed.

"Well, yeah. I mean, she was a malture, and she was grabbing me. What would you have done? Anyway, now Tack's all freaked out by me. You're still the only one who knows what I really am."

Clover took a moment to get over the horror. Apparently, she was a little freaked out by Vero too. But eventually, after several deep breaths, she was able to process it.

"Then you have to tell him the truth."

"I don't know if the archangels will let me. Before, whenever I tried to tell someone something I wasn't supposed to, they always sent a fire truck past with its siren blaring or something loud to drown it out."

"But they didn't when you told me," Clover said.

Vero nodded.

"Did you ever think that maybe the archangels want Tack to know? I mean, why else was he even able to see the maltures? And though the truth is definitely shocking at first, when I started to think about it, it all made sense. Like when you kept trying to fly or jumped two hurdles at a time. Maybe when Tack puts it all together, it will make sense for him too."

Vero shrugged.

"But why were you attacked? They just don't randomly attack people, right?"

Vero looked down. He clearly didn't want to answer. Clover punched him in the shoulder to get his attention. "Tell me."

"It's almost time for me to fulfill my mission. And I think it's making the maltures nervous."

Clover looked down and closed her eyes tight, trying to hold back tears. When she peeked up, Vero looked at her, his expression full of compassion and longing—longing to stay on earth with her. After a few moments, Clover composed herself and looked straight at him.

"You told me I was going to help you with whatever this mission is, so let me know when it's time," she said before getting up and walking out of his room.

Clover sat two seats behind Vero on the bus ride to school the following morning, next to her best friend, Vicki, who was trying to apply mascara to her close-set, brown eyes while Clover held up a small mirror. The bus hit a pothole, causing Vicki's hand to hit her forehead, smearing it with mascara. The black mascara was about the same color as Vicki's hair, so it almost looked like she simply had a few hairs out of place . . . almost.

"Does he have to hit every single bump?" Vicki asked, outraged. "It's like he does it on purpose! And this is waterproof!"

Clover didn't answer. She couldn't care less. All her thoughts were of Vero. The thought of losing her brother was unbearable, yet she had faith that she could survive Vero's death. She was convinced beyond a shadow of a doubt that one day she would be reunited with her brother forever.

"Mr. Harmon, I think there are a few potholes you missed!" Vicki shouted, glaring at the back of the bus driver's head.

When Mr. Harmon had first gotten the job, he had been a baby-faced nineteen-year-old, straight out of high school. The kids had treated him with little respect. But even though he was a few years older and looked the part, his passengers still treated him with little respect, so he made sure to hit the brakes . . . hard. Vicki's mascara wand poked her forehead once again.

"Ah!" Vicki screamed. "I *know* he's doing it on purpose."

Clover actually managed to giggle at the sight of her friend's forehead, black with mascara. Once the bus stopped, a group of kids walked on. Clover looked up and saw Tack walking down the aisle. When he got to Vero, her brother pushed toward the window to make room for him. Tack looked at Vero for a moment then continued down the aisle. Clover watched as a hurt look came over Vero's face when Tack took a seat farther back. Clover wanted to yell at Tack and cuss him out for being so mean, but she remembered she had once treated Vero the same exact way. When strange things were happening around Vero, she too had been afraid of things she didn't understand.

The bus came to a stop in the circular driveway of the high school. As Clover stood, she felt Tack's eyes on her. As she walked down the aisle alongside Vicki, Clover leaned over Vero and whispered in his ear, knowing that Tack was secretly watching.

"Tell him," she said in a low voice.

Vero looked hesitant, but then nodded.

Before the bus came to a complete stop at the Attleboro Middle School, Tack raced up the aisle to the front. He was the first person off the bus. Vero looked out the window and watched as Tack hurried into the school, avoiding him.

It didn't get any better during the remainder of the school day. Wherever Vero went, Tack gave him the cold shoulder. Every time Vero approached him, Tack either turned his back or simply walked away.

After lunch, a rowdy group of boys ran down the school hallway. One shoved a stack of books out of Nate's hands, laughing as Nate bent down to pick them up. As Vero leaned over to drink from the hallway water fountain, another boy smacked the back of Vero's head into the stream of water. Vero turned around, water dripping down his nose.

"Hey, Leland, looks like your nose runs and your feet smell . . . you must be built upside down!" the boy yelled as he ran past with his friends.

While the boys laughed at Vero, he spotted Tack standing in the hallway. They made eye contact, but Tack shook his head at him. Even though he wasn't hanging out with the obnoxious group of boys, Tack had not come to Vero's rescue. The boys continued down the hall, slamming any open locker doors shut in kids' faces. And Tack just turned and walked the opposite way.

Davina approached Vero. "Did you and Tack have a fight?" she asked innocently.

"Not really, but he's mad at me."

"Sounds like we're in the same boat," she said sadly. "I still have no clue why Danny won't talk to me."

"I'm sorry," Vero said.

"I'd like to know what I did wrong to make him hate me," Davina said. "Do you know why Tack's mad at you?"

Vero nodded. "But it's something I can't do anything about."

"You guys have been friends forever. I'm sure it'll just blow over."

Recalling Tack's terrified face in the hospital, Vero didn't share her confidence.

"How'd it go?" Clover asked as she looked up at Vero, who was standing on a metal ladder while cleaning out the gutters in the front of their house. Her backpack was still slung over her shoulder, and she was wearing a school T-shirt and shorts. "I've been dying to know all day. I almost skipped volleyball practice so I could come home early."

Vero dropped a soggy handful of decomposing leaves to the ground with a loud splat. He started making his way back down, and Clover supported the ladder until he reached the ground.

"So? How did he take it?"

"I didn't tell him. He avoided me the whole day." Vero sighed as he leaned against the bottom rung.

"Seriously?"

"Yeah, I think he really hates me, and I can't blame him. I put his life in danger. But worse, I've been hiding who I am from my best friend."

"It's not your fault—those are the cards you've been dealt," Clover told him.

Vero shrugged.

"Take this," Clover said, shoving her backpack into his chest. "I'm taking your bike."

She walked over to the open garage, grabbed a helmet, got on Vero's mountain bike, and pedaled down the street.

Tack was shooting hoops in his driveway when he heard Pork Chop, his English bulldog, barking excitedly. He held the basketball to his chest and turned around to see Clover dropping Vero's bike to the ground on his front lawn. His heart sank at the sight of her unfastening her helmet. He didn't want to hear what she had to say, and fought the urge to bolt.

"I know how you feel," Clover said, kneeling down to pet Pork Chop.

Tack stood, looking at her, waiting to hear what she had to say next.

"He didn't know what he was until two years ago. He was as clueless as the rest of us."

Tack looked at her, unsure what she was talking about, and afraid to ask. But the part of him that needed to know said, "What is he?"

"He's one of the good guys." Clover locked eyes with Tack. "He's a guardian angel, or will be one day."

The basketball dropped from Tack's hands. His mouth dropped open as he staggered back. He sat on a small retaining wall, stunned. Clover stopped petting Pork Chop and joined him.

"It all makes sense. Doesn't it?" Clover said. "Always trying to fly. Jumping the hurdles in track. And remember when he was kicked off the bus?"

Tack remembered. Two winters ago, Vero yanked the wheel of the school bus during a blizzard. He had claimed a car was heading straight for the bus, but nobody else saw it happen.

"One of those creatures that attacked you in the elevator had been in that oncoming car. Vero saved us all."

Tack took that in for a moment. His brain scrambled to connect the dots representing all the strange events surrounding Vero through the years—flying, pulling the snake off Davina, the amazing feats in track and field, and the bus freak out. All the incidents he had tried to brush off, unable to understand them until now.

"I was terrible to him for so long because I didn't understand . . . I thought if I was mean to him, it'll all go away, that it would stop," Clover said, shaking her head. "I'm embarrassed to say, but I was afraid of him."

Tack looked at her. "I still am."

Clover grabbed his face and turned it toward hers. "Don't be. He's the same Vero, the one who's been your best friend since preschool. That hasn't changed."

"Are you one too?"

"No."

"Your mom or dad?"

"No, and they don't know."

"But how can he be an angel? He's a kid! I can't believe it." Tack put his head in his hands.

"Don't you believe in angels?" Clover asked.

"Yes, but . . ."

"But what?"

"I just never thought I would share a toothbrush with one," Tack said.

Clover chuckled. "That's really gross."

"But he doesn't look like an angel. And I thought angels were in heaven, not here on earth."

Clover's eyes welled up with tears.

"What?"

"He won't be on earth for much longer," Clover told Tack.

"What do you mean?"

"He's on earth to learn and train and understand what it means to be human, and once that's completed, once he becomes an angel, he'll die."

Tack's eyes went wide with fear. "Vero's gonna die? How? When?"

"I don't know. But one day soon he'll become a full-fledged guardian angel and leave us . . . It's not too far away."

Pork Chop slobbered over to Tack, who picked him up and buried his face in the dog's neck. Though he tried to muffle his sobs, he was aware Clover could hear them.

"How could your parents not know?" Tack sniffled, looking up at her.

Clover shrugged, wiping a tear from her face. "They can't know. You and I are the only two." She cleared her throat and composed herself. "But we need to get a grip here, because Vero needs us."

"What do you mean?"

"He has a special mission to complete and somehow we're supposed to help him. He said that God has given us gifts and talents that he will need."

Tack felt even more surprised. "Me?"

"Trust me, Vero and I were just as shocked." She laughed. "We're hoping it's your dowsing ability, not your talent to burp the alphabet."

Tack managed a slight smile. Clover reached down and picked up her bike helmet.

"It's going to take a while for all this to sink in, but just know that whether human or angel, Vero has been and will always be your best friend, and he would do anything for you."

Clover walked over to Vero's bike, picked it up, and started to ride down the street. Tack watched her go, knowing his life would never be the same again.

8

※

READY OR NOT

Vero went the whole weekend without hearing from Tack. The only other time he could recall that happening was years ago when Tack had gotten his tonsils removed, and that had only been because he was unable to speak for several days after. With each hour that passed without word from his best friend, Vero became more depressed. Clover assured him that Tack would come around, but Vero wasn't as confident. Asking Tack to accept him as a guardian angel was just too much to ask. But Clover would not waiver.

"Give him a little more time," Clover said. "Do you really think the archangels would allow you to reveal your identity otherwise? Dude, you're an angel. Have a little more faith."

Late Sunday afternoon, Vero once again stood on the ladder against the backside of the house in order to finish cleaning the gutters. As he dropped a slimy, moldy clump of leaves below, he heard someone yell. He looked down and saw Tack standing at the base of the ladder, brushing the rotten leaves off the top of his head.

"Thanks. I come over here to talk to you, and this is how you treat me?" Tack quipped.

"Sorry," Vero said as he climbed down.

"Why can't you fly down instead?" Tack asked, eyeing the ladder.

"It doesn't work that way," Vero said as he stepped onto the ground.

The friends stood face to face. Even though Vero had shared everything with Tack—food, measles, toothbrush, even underwear—he felt uncomfortable. Neither seemed to know what to say. Then Tack's bottom lip began to quiver.

"I promise I'll visit your mom all the time, you know, to make sure she's all right," Tack said.

"What do you mean?" Vero asked, confused.

"Clover said you're gonna . . . that your time on earth is ending soon." Tack sniffled.

Now Vero's eyes began to tear up, touched by Tack's offer. He nodded.

"Clover too, and your dad," Tack said. "You won't have to worry about them . . . I promise."

Vero looked down, overcome with emotion.

"Thanks," he muttered. "I'm sorry I didn't think I could even tell you."

"It's okay. If I hadn't seen that creature, I probably wouldn't have believed you anyway. Those creatures, do they come after you all the time?" Tack asked.

Vero nodded. "And worse."

Tack looked scared for his friend.

"But they mostly come after me in the Ether."

"Where's that?"

"All around us."

Tack glanced around him as if looking for anything unusual—but around him was only the Lelands' house, the yard, the sky.

"You can't see it. But trust me, it's there. The Ether is the spiritual realm that surrounds the earth. It's where angels and demons battle over human souls."

"So you mean to tell me that right now there's this whole war going on that people aren't even aware of?"

"Not everyone is unaware, but yeah, basically."

"And in this Ether, you have wings and fly?"

"Yep."

"And fight demons with swords and stuff?"

Vero nodded.

"Hard to believe you're the same guy who got shoved into a locker not too long ago." Tack chuckled.

Vero cracked a smile.

"Clover said I'm somehow supposed to help you with some mission?"

Vero nodded. "I need to find something and return it. I'm not sure I can tell you what it is yet."

"Okay," Tack replied. "Whatever it is, you can count on me. I won't leave you hanging."

Vero look at Tack, gratitude seeping into his eyes. "I know."

Tack shot what seemed like a million questions at Vero. He wanted to know everything about Vero's secret life. How did he get to the Ether? What was the food like there? Were there any cute angel girls? Vero answered all his questions, and Tack seemed satisfied.

There was only one question Tack didn't ask—how would he feel when it was his time to leave earth? Vero was grateful Tack didn't ask, because he did not want to sob in front of his friend.

Once Tack turned and walked down the sidewalk, Vero climbed back up the ladder. A powerful gust of wind came out of nowhere and blew the ladder over, taking Vero with it. He fell hard on his back, hitting the ground as the ladder smashed on top of him.

Vero felt pressure on his chest. He opened his eyes and saw a combat boot pressing into his upper body. He looked up and saw the boot belonged to a tall teenage girl with short brown hair spiked with blonde highlights. In both her ears were three small hoop earrings. Vero instantly recognized her.

"Hi, Greer."

"Just a friendly little wake-up call," she said as she harshly nudged her foot into his chest.

Vero sat up, and Greer pulled her foot away. She held out her hand to Vero, who grabbed it. As Greer pulled him to his feet, she stumbled under his weight.

"Somebody gained a little extra since last time I saw him. I won't be helping you up again."

"It's called filling out," Vero told her.

"More like pigging out." She smirked.

Vero smiled to her. He loved Greer. It had been several months since they last saw one another, and he had missed her. She had a tough exterior, but Vero knew underneath Greer had a heart of gold. She was a faithful friend, and had definitely proved it last time they were together in the Ether. Greer had been the only fledgling who had ventured down into the demoness Lilith's castle to save Clover. Greer had risked everything to help him.

"It's great to be back . . . Can't believe we haven't been here since the trials last year!" Greer said as she eyed C.A.N.D.L.E. in the distance.

"Not for me," Vero said as they walked past a group of trees toward the angel school. "I was just here."

"Without us?" Greer asked, outraged.

"Yeah," Vero said. "Uriel and Raziel said it was sort of a personal training session only for me, although somehow I summoned Pax near the end."

"You can do that?" Greer asked, wide-eyed.

"Apparently."

"I'm a little hurt you summoned Pax over me," Greer said as her eyes narrowed.

"I think it was because he's best at speaking mind-to-mind."

"Oh, guess I should work on that. So why did they call you back for training? Maybe because you need more help than the rest of us," Greer quipped.

"No," Vero said firmly. "Because the time has come to find the Book of Raziel."

Greer froze. "Already?"

Vero nodded.

"But we're not ready. We need more time. More training."

"They say otherwise."

"But what do you think? Are you ready?" Greer asked him, incredulously.

Vero held her gaze for a long moment, then turned and walked toward the school without answering. Greer chased after him, and once she caught up grabbed his shirt from his shoulder and spun him around to face her.

"I didn't hear an answer . . . Are you ready?" she asked while still clenching his shirt.

"Hardly," Vero shouted while jerking free of her hold. "But it doesn't matter. I have to do it anyway!" He walked ahead.

"Then tell them you don't feel ready."

"I did."

"And . . .?"

"It can't be changed."

Greer took that in for a moment. She sighed, following after him.

"Were you ready to take on the Leviathan or the golems?" Greer asked.

"No."

"Or how about Lilith? Would you say you were ready to take her on when you did?"

"No, I guess not."

"And you whipped her good."

"We whipped her good," Vero corrected.

"Maybe the archangels have more confidence in you than you do yourself," Greer said. "They haven't been wrong yet."

Vero mulled that over for a moment, then nodded.

"You're right. Maybe I am ready," he said, puffing out his chest. "I can do this. And I won't let anything get in my way."

Just then, Vero tripped over a rock jutting up from the ground and fell facedown, ruining his moment.

"Then again, maybe the archangels are just flat out wrong this time," Greer said with a smile as she eyed Vero's dirty, beet-red face.

As Greer and Vero headed up the massive steps into C.A.N.D.L.E., both looked around. There were no other angels to be seen.

"It's like the place is deserted," Greer said, her eyes scanning the area.

"It was like this the last time I came. Must be Angel Spring Break at C.A.N.D.L.E."

"There is no such thing. Everyone just shows up when needed," Greer said.

The front doors were wide open. Vero and Clover walked inside. In the main entrance, they saw Ada and Pax walking toward them; Ada, with her curly auburn hair, and Pax, with his ears sticking out far from his head, were a welcome sight to Vero. Ada ran and hugged Vero. Greer high-fived Pax.

"Have you guys seen anyone else here?" Vero asked, his voice echoing in the empty hall.

"Not yet," Pax said. "You're the first."

"Did we miss some memo about where we're supposed to meet?" Greer asked as she took in the stillness of the hall.

Suddenly, a wind rushed into the hall, and the heavy stone doors slammed shut. The fledglings jumped back. When the wind stopped, Uriel, Raziel, and Raphael stood before Vero and the others. Vero smiled when he saw Raphael. With his jolly, round, wide face and friendly smile, Raphael always made Vero feel at ease.

"We're missing two," Raziel said dryly.

As if on cue, there was a knock on the front door. Raziel rolled his eyes. The doors swung open, revealing X and Kane standing on the threshold, unsure whether or not to enter.

"Come on, come on," Raphael motioned. "Get in here."

X and Kane walked inside. Vero thought X looked even bigger than the last time he saw him, if that was possible. X was powerfully built, especially his upper body. Kane was also very muscular, though he was much shorter than X. But it was Kane's expression that Vero was trying to gauge. Last time they had been together, Kane had been in such a bad place. As Kane got closer, Vero smiled to him. Kane returned the gesture. Vero took that as a good sign.

"Let's do this in the courtyard," Uriel told them.

As the group headed outside, Vero shimmied over to Kane.

"Hey," Vero said to him in a low voice. "How are you?"

"Doing good," Kane said.

"I mean, are you okay?" Vero hesitantly asked.

"You mean because of the whole Angel Trial thing?" Kane said.

Vero nodded.

"Yeah, I'm over it. It took a few months, but now I realize it didn't really matter."

Vero smiled ear to ear. He was thrilled to have the old Kane back. The group stepped outside into a lush courtyard, something Monet would have loved to capture on canvas.

"Sit," Uriel instructed, pointing to several benches.

The fledglings sat down on stone benches surrounded by immaculately manicured bushes and flowerbeds.

"Ada," Uriel said, "what do you know about the Book of Raziel?"

Vero looked, trying to make eye contact with the other fledglings. Did they also think it was strange that there were no pleasantries? That Uriel was jumping right into it?

"Well, not too much. There's really nothing about the Book of Raziel in the Torah or other sacred scriptures, but according to Jewish mythology, the Book of Raziel was given to Adam after he was kicked out of the garden. Adam and Eve were so repentant for their sins, and so unprepared to deal with life outside the garden, that God sent a great book to Adam that contained many great secrets of nature that would help him adapt to life on earth," Ada said while twirling her curly hair through her finger. "Supposedly it listed secrets of the universe . . ."

"Such as?" Raphael interrupted.

"The laws of creation and of the planets and stars. It listed the names of all the angels and how to summon them," Ada said. "It contained the names of every human yet to be born. The book had information that even the angels don't know . . ."

Vero looked over to Raziel, wondering if it were true. Vero knew that Raziel was the angel who had stood next to God's throne and had written down everything he had heard—hence the name of the book. So how could he not know certain things that were written in the book he'd compiled? Raziel caught Vero looking at him and glared back. Vero quickly returned his attention to Ada.

"Some of the angels grew jealous and took the book from Adam, throwing it into the sea, but per God's instructions, the angel Rahab retrieved it and returned the book to Adam. From there it was passed down through Adam's generations and eventually given to Noah. Its secrets taught Noah how to build the ark. It was also passed down to Abraham and to Joseph. Joseph used the book to discover the true meanings of dreams. Moses had it at one point and took the book with him as he fled Egypt. Eventually the book taught King Solomon great wisdom, and he used the secrets to help build his temple, where he kept the book with the Ark of the Covenant," Ada said. "The temple burned to the ground, and the book was lost."

There was a moment of silence as everyone digested the information. Then Greer responded, rolling her eyes. "I thought you said you didn't know much about this book!"

"Oh, I don't. Like I said, there is no direct reference to the Book of Raziel in the Torah, or scriptures. Though Genesis 5 does mention Adam's Book of Generations, and some say that is a reference to it."

"So what happened to the book after King Solomon?" Pax asked.

"No one knows. It disappeared. Thousands of years later, in medieval times, there was an actual published book that went by the same name, and was full of Jewish mysticism and magic, but no one knows what happened to the original book," Ada said.

"It just vanished," Raziel said, matter of fact. "Never to be seen again."

"What does the book have to do with us?" X asked.

Uriel spoke next. "The book was and is very real. Abraham, and mankind itself, could never have adapted outside the garden without this precious gift from God. Vero must find the book—and soon. Lucifer and his demons are searching for it, desperate to possess all of its knowledge. We need to find it and return it to its proper place before he can seize it. If he gets his hands on it first, his ability to sway and influence humanity will be unimaginably multiplied."

"But Raziel"—X turned to Raziel—"don't you know everything in your book? Couldn't you just rewrite it?"

"No. I have no recollection of what is written in the book. The memory of its contents was taken from me," he humbly admitted.

Uriel looked to Raziel, his eyes full of empathy.

"Is there anything in particular that Lucifer wants from the book?" Pax asked, pushing up the bridge of his glasses.

"Yes. It's the list of humans yet to be born that most interests him. I explained this to Vero earlier, but there is a child to be born. A child who will do much good in the world and lead many souls back to God," Uriel said. "This child is very important to God's plan for mankind. If Lucifer learns the name of this child, he will stop at nothing to prevent him from reaching maturity."

"Who is the child?" Kane asked.

"We don't know," Raphael answered. "We have told you everything we learned."

"But his name is written in the book. And Lucifer knows that," Raziel said, and Vero had never seen the archangel look so dejected.

"But why is Vero the one who must find the book?" Kane asked. "He's only a fledgling. Why wouldn't God want full-fledged angels or you guys?" Kane looked at the three archangels.

"Kane, we don't question God's will," Uriel said. "Vero has been given the gifts needed to find the book."

"Of course. Vero," Kane said with a slight tinge of envy in his voice.

"Yes, Vero," Uriel repeated, "and all of you must do whatever is necessary to help him succeed." As Uriel said this, he studied Kane with some concern.

Vero looked down, almost embarrassed. Raphael placed his hand on Vero's shoulder. "Don't ever be ashamed of what God has given you. Everybody gets exactly what they need."

Vero nodded.

"What does the book look like?" Pax asked. "How will we recognize it?"

"There are many rumors, but we don't know for sure," Raphael said.

"But Raziel, you have to at least know what the book looks like." Pax looked eagerly at him.

Raziel sadly shook his head.

"We will help you in every way we can," Raphael said. "Don't be afraid to ask us. We want you to succeed."

Raziel stepped dangerously closer to the fledglings. "We *need* you to succeed."

9

SEVERE BEASTS

Vero, X, Pax, Kane, and Greer tried to keep pace with Ada, who beelined toward the library with arms swinging by her side.

"Slow down," Greer yelled to Ada. "The book's been out there for thousands of years. What are a few more minutes?"

Ada didn't answer. She instead walked up the steps to the library two at a time and went inside. Standing in the great library, Vero wished he had sunglasses—not that he had any choice in what he wore to the Ether. Bright light shone through the windows, creating a blinding glare off the stark-white walls, ceiling, floor, tables, and benches. Shading his eyes, Vero saw thousands and thousands of scrolls stacked from floor to ceiling. After walking past several stacks, he and his friends found seats on benches around a stone table.

"You remember how this works? Right?" Ada asked the group.

"Yeah," X said.

Vero recalled the first time he had been in the library. They had been looking to do research on unicorns, but none of the fledglings had known how to locate the scroll they needed. And suddenly, just at the mere thought of the mystical creatures, an ancient scroll had separated from all the others on the shelves, flown into the air, and landed on a table before them. When they unrolled the parchment, a teeny tiny unicorn had materialized and flown into Pax's ear and out the other! The information they had needed soared directly into his head, and the knowledge of unicorns had remained in his brain.

"So start thinking 'Book of Raziel,'" Ada told everyone.

Greer closed her eyes and concentrated, as did Pax. Kane tilted his head back and looked up at the many scrolls.

"Book of Raziel," Ada whispered to herself.

Vero was lost in thought as he pressed two fingers on either side of his temples. After a few seconds, he lowered his hands, looking discouraged.

"Nothing's happening," he said.

Greer opened her eyes. "Yep. I'm striking out too."

"It always worked before," Ada said, worried and nervous.

"Try again," Kane said. "But this time, concentrate on *any* information about the Book of Raziel."

Everyone closed their eyes and focused, but yet no scroll flew to them and presented itself. Vero sighed, opening his eyes.

"I'm not feeling it," he said. "Maybe the Book of Raziel is so secretive there is no scroll on it."

"Then we need to go to Solomon's temple, if that was the last place it was seen," X said.

"Great idea!" Greer said.

X proudly smiled.

"Except for the fact that it burnt to the ground!" Greer narrowed her eyes at X.

X's smile dropped. "Oh, yeah . . ."

"At least you're thinking along the right lines," Pax said to X.

Greer leaned back, her eyes scanning the library.

"I'd really hate to be the guy who has to keep this place so pristine. There isn't a smudge of dirt anywhere," Greer said.

"Greer! Who cares?" Ada shouted. "You're supposed to be concentrating on the book!"

"None of the archangels can tell us anything on the book, even Raziel," Greer yelled. "So what chance do we have? It's a lost cause!"

"Don't ever become a motivational speaker," X smirked to Greer.

"She is right though," Kane said.

"Thank you." Greer flashed the others a smug look.

"But if Uriel, Raphael, and Raziel have no clue . . ." Kane said.

"Rahab!" Pax suddenly shouted. "He might know something!"

"He's the angel of the seas, right?" X asked.

"Yes. When the jealous angels threw the book into the sea, Rahab retrieved it," Ada explained.

"Exactly," Pax said. "Maybe he'd be easier to find than Solomon's temple."

"You're right. He might know something. If not where it is, maybe at least what it looks like," X said.

"Or he may know bupkis!" Greer added. "We could waste all this time tracking him down only to find out that the memory of the book was taken from him too!"

"I think you can also scratch life coach off your career list," X told Greer.

"I'm just the voice of reason," Greer shot back.

"We have no other leads." Pax looked to the rest. They nodded in agreement.

Greer threw up her hands. "Okay, so where do we find Rahab?" She sighed.

Vero looked over at Ada. Her eyes were closed in deep concentration. A scroll shot down, barely grazing Greer's head and causing her to duck. At the soft rustle of ancient paper landing on the stone table, Ada opened her eyes and unrolled the ancient-looking scroll. The parchment crinkled with her touch. A tiny angel with wings about an inch tall materialized from the parchment. It flapped its wings then shot into Ada's right ear, disappearing. Ada's eyes rolled around in their sockets for a few moments, then the tiny angel shot out of her left ear and back onto the unraveled scroll. Once the angel disappeared into the parchment, the paper rolled itself back up and flew up to the shelf from where it had come.

"Okay, so where do we find him?" Greer asked Ada.

"The sea," she answered.

"Duh." Greer rolled her eyes.

❖

The angels flew high in the clouds over the mountains of the Ether, their wings flapped against the cool mist. Greer kept pace with Ada.

"How much farther?"

"Just on the other side of the mountains," Ada said.

"I hope it's more like a real ocean, and not like that last sea we had to deal with in the Ether," Greer said.

"Oh, that was disgusting!" Pax said as he caught up to Greer. "It was like an ocean full of motor oil."

Greer and Pax were referring to the sea where they had encountered the Leviathan—the sea dragon. The water there had been thick and black, tar-like. It had also smelled like decaying flesh.

The angels continued on for a while longer before glimpses of deep blue peeked through the clouds. The group dropped below the clouds, and before them was a magnificent ocean, clear and sparkling.

"I need to take a break!" Kane said to the group as he headed for the shoreline.

Kane touched down on a white sandy beach as the others landed near him. Vero looked out to sea. It was vast, endless. He turned around and took in the tall, jagged green mountains in the distance, which peered down upon the sandy shores edging its forested base.

"Okay, we're here. Now what?" Kane said to Ada as he picked up a handful of sand and let it sift through his fingers.

"Rahab lives somewhere by the Great Sea."

"Somewhere . . . as in where?" Kane asked.

"I'm not sure. All the scroll told me was that he dwells by the sea, and that he surrounds himself with 'severe beasts.'"

"'Severe beasts.' Now you tell us that?!" Pax said.

"Kind of a big detail to leave out!" Greer shouted.

"I knew if I told you, you'd probably not want to come!" Ada cried.

"Guys, knock it off!" X said. "We're here now, so deal!"

Greer's eyes became mere slits as she looked at Ada. "If I get eaten or killed by some 'severe beast,' it's on your head."

"Don't worry. I'll protect you," Ada said.

Greer rolled her eyes. "Thanks. Now I feel perfectly safe."

"Ada, what kind of beasts are we talking about?" Vero tentatively asked.

"A beast more severe than Greer?" X chuckled.

Greer shot him a look. "And I guess you can cross comedian off *your* career list."

"I don't know." Ada shrugged. "All it said was that Rahab, the angel of the sea—or as he's sometimes called, Euroclydon—dwells at the Great Sea, and that he keeps 'severe beasts' for company," Ada said, motioning. "And this is the Great Sea."

Greer gave her a look of contempt. Ada picked up on it.

"At least I got us to the right place."

"Then he dwells here somewhere," Pax said, staring out over the water.

"Let's look around the shoreline to start," Kane said. "If he has beasts, they probably would live near the forest, right?"

Vero stared at the towering reeds atop of the dunes behind them. The green shoots were just taller than X, who was nearly six foot, and they grew between the sandy beach and the wooded area. The fledglings would have to make their way over the dunes and through the wall of reeds in order to get as far inland as the forest.

"Wait! Look out there," Pax said as he pointed over the water. "See?"

The others followed his gaze. Out on the distant horizon, a large outcropping of rocks protruded high above water. The boulders were stacked in a way that resembled a teepee made out of stones. In the center appeared to be a V-shaped opening.

"It could be a shelter," Pax said, squinting through the lenses of his glasses.

"I say we check it out first." Vero looked to Kane. "You okay with that?"

"Yeah, I guess. Why not?" Kane said, glancing around. "As good a place as any to start."

Kane lifted off the ground, and had started out over the water when powerful gusts of wind began to churn up the sea. The winds seemed to come from nowhere, and were so strong that Kane was blown back to the shore. Instantly, the gale-force winds were whipping the fledglings on the beach. Ada grabbed onto Vero, who tried to stay on his feet.

"Quick! Behind the reeds!" Kane shouted over the howl of the wind.

With their heads held low to block the pelting sand, the fledglings raced toward the dunes. With each step Vero had to steady himself to avoid being blown over. Beside him, Pax held on to his glasses with one hand and Greer's hand with the other. Walking amongst the squalls was exhausting. Kane was the first to reach the protection of the reeds. He grabbed the others' arms, and one by one guided them into the cove of the thick, stalwart reeds. They crouched down against the wall of stalks.

"Whatever this wind is, hopefully it will pass," Vero said, surprised at how much quieter it was behind the dunes given the gale-force winds.

"Yeah, let's just hope the wind will break." Pax nervously chuckled.

"What's so fun—? Oh, I get it, breaking wind." Greer rolled her eyes.

"Until these freak winds settle down, we'll have to stay put," Ada said. "Might as well hunker down."

"Agreed," X announced, as he sat and tried to get comfortable.

As he stretched his legs out on the sand, X leaned back against his wings, using them both to support his back and cushioning him from the reeds. Vero looked over to X.

"Don't get too comfortable. We're out of here soon as it stops."

"I know," X said, reclining farther back.

Vero looked to Kane, who was keenly staring at something in the crowded stalks. Vero followed his gaze and saw what looked like weathered, once-white planks. Kane walked over and parted the reeds, revealing a rowboat. Even though it looked like it had been through quite a number of storms, it was still intact.

"Wonder why that's up here?" Vero asked.

"Probably washed up on shore," Kane said. "Maybe we can use it to look for Rahab."

Kane picked up a thick rope tied to the front and pulled the boat a few feet through the reeds. "We don't need a boat!" Greer said. "Last time I checked, we still had wings. Why would we paddle when we can fly?"

"Good point," Kane said, dropping the towrope.

X screamed.

"See? X agrees with me," Greer said.

X's screams grew frightening loud. "Help me!"

The fledglings' heads whipped around to see X being dragged deeper into the reeds. Kane and Pax ran over and grabbed X's legs and held firm with all their might.

"What is it?" Vero shouted as he grabbed X around the waist.

The reeds parted, and Vero saw what had grabbed X—a bear! It had a large head with a long snout and small, rounded ears, and a stout body matched with strong muscular legs and a distinctive shoulder hump formed by powerful back muscles. The bear had X's wing in its mouth, and was dragging him even farther into the reeds. X yelled in agony as the stocky animal shredded a hunk of flesh from the meat of his wing, then momentarily released him when Greer's sword shot from her hand.

"Pull him back!" Pax shouted.

Kane, Vero, and Pax quickly pulled X away from the bear. Greer swung her weapon at the giant bear and sliced the tip of its nose. Enraged, the bear roared and stood threateningly on its hind legs. His head easily cleared the tops of the reeds. Using her sword like a trainer's stick, Greer poked at the bear, aiming for its light-brown shaggy coat, but only caught air. The animal swatted its sharp black claws at her. Vero's sword shot out into his hand. Standing next to Greer, he swung at the animal and caught its midsection. The bear yelped in pain. It dropped down to all fours, and retreated back into the reeds.

Ada ran to X's side. She looked down on the ground and saw what looked like three ribs on the sand. She looked to X's chest—they were not his.

"How bad?" Ada asked X as Greer and Vero rushed over.

"Real bad . . ." X moaned as he stretched his hand to reach his bleeding wing.

"Retract them," Pax said. "It will stop the bleeding, and you won't feel it so much."

X rolled over onto his stomach. He winced as his wings slowly disappeared into his back. He sat up.

"Better?" Pax asked.

X nodded. "Yeah, now it just feels like I pulled a muscle."

"We need to get out of here," Vero said. "That bear will probably come back."

"We're gonna have to brave the winds," Kane said, his eyes trying to see over the reeds.

This time it was Greer who screamed. Vero looked over. She was face to face with a gigantic golden leopard. And then the head of another leopard broke through the stalks to the right of the first, joined by a third one on the left side. Vero was still doing a double take when a fourth leopard poked its head through, right alongside the other three. As the snarling creatures stalked out of the reeds in unison toward the fledglings, Vero and the others stepped back.

"We're doomed!" Pax said, his hands shaking.

Vero's eyes bugged out of his head. It wasn't four leopards approaching, but rather one massive, spotted leopard easily the size of a Clydesdale horse, with four heads and two sets of giant wings. At that moment, Vero couldn't think of anything that could be worse, until—

A ten-horned lizard, the size of a rhinoceros, emerged from the reeds. It snarled, revealing razor-sharp iron teeth.

"Oh no," Ada said, staggering back. "Brace yourself. If I'm right, we'll be seeing a lion break through . . ."

A lion with a pair of wings pounced through the thicket of reeds. The others looked to Ada, incredulous.

"Rahab's 'severe creatures' are the four beasts from Daniel, the ones that rise up out of the sea," she said. "I can't believe I didn't think of that sooner!"

Vero brandished his sword before the four-headed leopard, stopping the advancing beast. Kane did the same, holding the ten-horned beast at bay, while Greer flashed her sword to the lion. The bear rushed out of the reeds straight at X, determined to finish him off. X's breathing intensified as his sword sprung from his hand. Running on pure adrenaline, X swiped at the bear, slicing its ear to the ground. The bear whimpered as it pressed its claw over the bloody gash where its ear had been moments ago. It turned and ran back into the reeds for the second time.

"And don't come back!" X yelled. "Unless you want some more of that!" He turned to the others, proudly holding up his weapon. "Guys, my first sword!"

"Might be your last if you don't help us fight these beasts!" Kane yelled.

The leopard head on the far left side of the beast snarled and snapped at Vero. He swung his sword and managed to nick it across its forehead. Its head jerked back, but then the one next to it hissed at Vero, while at the same time the head on the right opened its mouth to bite down on Ada. She screamed in terror and rolled out of its way just in time.

"Your sword, Ada!" X yelled as he struck at the leopard. "Use your sword!"

"It's not happening!" she screamed, looking into her empty hand.

"For once, don't use your brain, just feel it!" X yelled, sweat dripping into his eyes.

A sword unexpectedly popped out of Pax's hand. A huge smile spread across his face.

"That's what I'm talkin' about!" Pax bellowed. "I've got sword!" He held his sword up to the horned beast and turned to Kane. "I've got this guy," Pax said as he bumped Kane out of the way.

A determined look on his face, Pax shoved the tip of his blade into the ten-horned beast's mouth. The beast bit down on Pax's blade with its large iron teeth, dislodging it from Pax's hand, then swallowed it in one gulp. Pax looked like he was going to cry.

"Easy come, easy go." Kane shook his head.

As the iron-toothed creature lowered its head, like a bull ready to charge a matador, it aimed for Pax. Catching the beast's angry glare, Pax began to panic. As the creature bolted toward Pax, he took cover behind Vero.

"Fight it Pax!" Vero yelled to him.

"It ate my sword!"

The lion fiercely roared, bearing down hard on Greer. As she slowly backed away behind her upheld sword, the feline pounced. She rolled underneath the beast, barely escaping its slashing claws.

"We've got to get out of here!" Vero yelled.

"Get airborne!" Kane shouted.

"I can't!" X screamed. "My wing's busted!"

Vero grabbed X by the waist and tried to lift off the ground with him, but X's weight made it hard to fly. Seeing Vero's struggle, Kane grabbed X underneath his armpits and helped Vero raise their friend into the air. Instantly, fierce winds knocked them to the ground. Ada, Pax, and Greer collided with one another in the air as the winds bashed them around as well. They dropped back to the sand.

The horned beast, the lion, and the four-headed leopard charged the fledglings. About to be trampled, Vero and the others retreated to the beach. With sand and flecks of water whipping against his face, Vero stepped out of the reeds onto the shore. The others followed. The gale-force winds nearly pushed the fledglings back into the reeds. Their heads down, they fought against the gust. Vero glanced over his shoulder. The creatures were nowhere to be seen.

"Where'd the beasts go?" Vero yelled over the howling wind.

"I don't know!" X answered.

"We can't fly out of here, and we can't go back to the reeds!" Kane shouted. "We're totally stuck!"

Ada searched the shore. Vero noticed a panicked looked come over her.

"Where's Pax?!" she shouted.

Vero looked up and down the beach. Pax was nowhere to be found.

"I'm going back for him!" Kane yelled.

"Me too!" X shouted.

Vero pointed to the stalk tops, which were moving in the opposite direction of the blowing wind.

"The beasts!" Vero exclaimed.

But then Pax broke through the wall of reeds, pulling the rowboat by the rope.

"What are you doing?" Greer screamed. "You almost gave us all heart attacks!"

"We can't fly out of here, and we can't go inland," Pax said. "So we row out."

"That boat could be smashed to pieces in this wind," X shouted.

"Maybe, but look out there . . ." Pax said, pointing to sea. "The water's calm on the other side of this storm."

Vero looked to sea. The sky was sunny only a few hundred feet away.

"I'd rather take my chances on the water instead of the air or land right now," Ada shouted.

"But those beasts have wings!" Kane said. "We could be sitting ducks in that rowboat!"

"I doubt they can fly any better in this wind than we can!" Greer responded.

"Let's do it!" X yelled.

Vero looked behind him. He saw the tops of the reeds fall to the ground as if being trampled. Knowing what was coming, Vero ran to the boat and helped Pax pull the boat. Kane and X also grabbed the towrope and scrambled to drag the boat into the water. Violent waves crashed the vessel on all sides.

"Everybody hurry!" Kane yelled as he tried to steady the bow of the boat.

One by one, the angels climbed into the small rowboat while X stood knee-deep in the water, holding the stern firm. Vero could feel the ground underneath his feet shake. With one foot in the boat, he turned and saw all four beasts charging—even the bear had rejoined the ferocious stampede. Vero spun back quickly and tumbled into the boat. Standing on the bench closest to the bow, Ada pointed at the four-headed leopard, which rose up on its hind legs. All four heads snarled down on Greer, who was oblivious to the deadly threat.

"Greer, behind you!" screamed Ada.

Greer turned in time to see the heads looming over her. She hoisted her upper body into the boat when the head on the far left side of the leopard bared its teeth, ready to sink them into her chest. Sweat mixed with the rushing seawater ran down her face as she looked into the beast's hungry eyes. A high-pitched scream, like the cry of a warrior, split the roar of the wind. In a single, fluid path, a sword sailed like a boomerang, slicing off the leopard's outermost head, and then lopping off the remaining three in a clean sweep. The wind lifted the severed heads briefly into the air before they all dropped to the ground. Their wide eyes were forever caught in shock.

The fledglings' eyes too were wide as they looked at Ada standing on the bow.

"Told you I would protect you," Ada said to Greer.

10

RAHAB

The rough seas pushed the tiny rowboat around. Water splashed over the boat's sides as X tried to row through the storm. The other fledglings clung to each other and their seats for fear of being tossed into the high seas. Greer's face had even turned a shade of green.

"Want me to take over?" Kane yelled to X. "You're injured."

"I got it!" X shouted. "It was just my wing. Rest of me is fine!"

Anguish etched across his face, X continued rowing against the wall of waves and finally broke through. Rays of sunshine and calmer skies greeted them on the other side, though the water was still choppy, and the air too windy to fly. But everyone slowly released one another and their grip on the boat.

"I still can't believe you were able to slice their heads off like that," Greer said to Ada, shaking her head in disbelief.

"And yet I did." Ada flashed a cocky grin.

"She's been holding out on us," Pax said with a chuckle.

"How did that happen?" Vero asked.

"I just wanted a sword so badly when I saw Greer in trouble that it happened, I guess."

"I get that part," Vero said. "How did you throw it like that?"

"I play a lot of Frisbee with my dog."

Vero gave her a look. "That's it?"

"It's all in the wrists." Ada smiled, proudly.

Greer shook her head. "The universe has turned upside down . . . and you . . ." Greer nodded to Pax. "You should feel bad. A girl showed better swordplay than you."

Pax became visibly upset. Greer had hit a sore spot.

"I'm only joking," Greer apologized.

"Well, I don't think it's funny!"

"Look, you've got something that goes a lot farther than sword skills . . ."

Pax looked to her, curious.

"Guts and heart. With that combo, you'll do better than all of us."

Pax smiled. "Thanks, Greer."

"Friends?"

"Always," Pax said. "But I'm bummed that thing ate my sword. How am I gonna get it back?"

Ada frowned dejectedly. "I didn't think of that."

"Well, we can't go back for them," Greer said to Ada. "Sorry, you might just be a one-hit wonder. Well, actually a four-hit wonder."

"I don't think so," Vero said. "I think swords are like lizards' tails. You might be able to grow another."

"I hope," Ada said, looking into the palm of her outstretched hand.

Kane stood. "X, I can row for a while," he said as he climbed over the seat, inadvertently rocking the boat.

"Stop doing that!" Greer chided.

"Sorry," Kane said. "It's hard to balance."

"Yeah, well, I get seasick," Greer said. "So knock it off!"

Vero stood up in the boat. "What, Greer?" Vero teased. "This makes you sick?" Vero shifted his weight from leg to leg, rocking the boat from side to side.

"Sit down!" Greer roared.

Vero laughed and then sat next to her.

"If I throw up, I'll be sure to aim for you," Greer told Vero as her right hand white knuckled the side of the boat.

Vero inched away from her.

X looked to Kane. "I'm all right for now."

Kane nodded and sat back down.

"Turned out to be a nice day after all," Ada said, her face turned toward the warm light above.

"We're not here so you can get a tan," Greer quipped.

"Yeah, I get that, but why not enjoy it while we have the chance," Ada said.

Vero looked upon his fellow angels with affection. Greer noticed his stare.

"What's your problem?"

"I just want to say thank you . . . for helping me," Vero said. "You guys are all great."

Pax and Ada smiled to him.

"Hey, it's what angels do," X said, purposely skidding the oar against the water, drenching Vero.

"Thanks a lot," Vero said with a smile, wiping water from his face.

"We'll find that book," Kane told Vero. "We won't let you fail."

"But if on the off chance we don't," Greer said to Vero, "you're taking the blame one hundred percent."

Vero chuckled. "Okay. But I really am grateful."

"He's getting too sappy," Greer said. "Feed him to the sharks."

X continued to row, and soon they were nearly upon the rock formation. Waves lapped up on the submerged boulders. Vero noted that, up close, the teepee-shaped outcropping was much larger than what he had expected.

"Anybody else feeling nervous?" Pax asked as his eyes focused on the opening in the rocks.

"Rahab's an angel. He once found the book and returned it. He's gotta be good," Vero said.

"Oh yeah, sure," Greer said. "We'll just go tell that to Lucifer, and maybe he'll stop looking for the book." She turned to Kane. "You believe this kid?" she scoffed.

"Yeah, Vero," Kane said, shifting uncomfortably. "Duh."

Vero held Kane's gaze for a moment. Kane appeared to be nervous. It wasn't like him to be on edge.

Crash!

The front of the boat smashed into the boulders.

"X! Stop rowing!" Ada shouted.

"Sorry, guess I don't know my own strength," X commented, slightly embarrassed.

After grabbing the towrope, Vero climbed out the boat and onto the large rocks, which were covered in slimy algae. He slipped and did an embarrassingly bizarre dance to keep from falling into the water. A few seconds later, he regained his balance.

"Nice moves," Greer teased.

Vero blushed. Then carefully, keeping the rope securely in his hand, he pulled the rowboat closer to the rocks.

"Come on," Vero said, holding out his hand.

Kane stepped out and helped him secure the boat. Then one by one, the others climbed onto the mossy rocks. As Greer grabbed on to Vero's arm and stood, her boot became lodged between two rocks, causing her to stumble and face-plant straight into Vero's chest. They both fell off the boulders and into the sea. Greer spit a mouthful of salt-water into Vero's face.

"Thanks for the help."

"You pushed me in!" Vero shot back.

"Guys, are we going to find Rahab or not?" X asked, holding out his hand to Greer.

X pulled Greer up onto the rocks, while Vero climbed up himself. With small, deliberate steps, the fledglings made their way over the slick rocks. In front of the opening, the boulders flattened out into a level ledge of solid rock. They gathered around the large gap and looked inside. Vero felt his hopes plummet. It was just a small, dark cavern. The ocean waves hit the ledge where they stood and lapped into the cavern, forming a pool before the water seeped out through gaps in the rocks. Vero scanned the area. Neither Rahab nor anyone else was anywhere to be found. The cavern was uninhabited.

"Okay, that was a phenomenal waste of time," Kane said, irritated.

"He has to be here somewhere," Ada said. "Maybe he lives underwater."

"Then we'll never find him," Pax said.

"Ada, the scroll must have given some other info," Vero said. "Something you're not remembering."

Ada shook her head. "I told you everything."

The sky began to darken. The wind began to blow in the distance. Greer looked up to the clouds.

"Another storm," she said, her eyes full of dread.

Vero turned to Ada. "You said he's also called Euroclydon. What does that mean?"

Ada shrugged. "I don't know everything!"

The winds began to whip up harder. Claps of thunder rang out. The air turned cold, and the sky grew nearly dark. The faint shape of a funnel formed in the distance, and appeared to be the front edge of a big hurricane. Greer pointed to it.

"We either need to fly out of here or take shelter in this cavern!" Greer called. "Because that looks like we're in for a hurricane!"

"Or we fly right into it," Kane said.

"Are you crazy?" Greer shouted. "Did that bear hit you in the head and we missed it?"

"*Euroclydon* means *tempestuous wind.*"

"How would you know that?" Pax asked.

"Vocab word," Kane said while pointing to the oncoming storm. "That is Rahab."

Vero looked to Kane as he processed the information.

"He's a storm?" Greer asked, staring at Kane as if he was the dumbest thing she had ever seen.

"No, but he's causing the storm. He must be in the middle of it," Kane answered. "That's why we have to fly into it."

"Because it's always calm in the eye of the hurricane," Vero finished.

"Yes." Kane nodded.

"But we can't fly in those winds," Ada said. "They're too strong."

"Airplanes can," Kane said, looking up. "If we get high enough, we can fly above it, then drop down into the eye. Where I come from, we have to deal with monsoons all the time."

"That's just nuts," X said, as the winds picked up speed. "But if we're going to do it, we have to go now or we won't be able to get airborne."

"Go for it!" Kane yelled in a rallying cry.

The angels' wings shot out in unison.

"We'll fly in a V formation," Vero said. "Everyone hold hands and don't lose anyone!"

X tried to lift off. His injured wing dangled from his back.

"I can't fly!" X yelled, frustrated. "Go without me. I'll wait out the storm in this cavern."

"Pax, stay with him!" Vero shouted over the winds.

"No, I'll be okay!" X yelled as sprays of water hit his face.

"If there's any trouble, Pax can communicate with me mentally!" Vero said.

X didn't argue further. The storm was nearly upon them, leaving no time for debate. Vero, Ada, Kane, and Greer shot like missiles straight into the dark, heavy clouds. They rose higher and higher, but were still not able to get above the storm due to the pelting wind and freezing rain.

"Keep going!" Vero shouted as they tossed around inside the tempest.

They flew even higher. Finally, patches of light broke up the dark, stormy clouds. The rains and winds gradually subsided. Upward they flew, and moments later each broke out above the billowing thunderclouds. They were now safely above the storm, where it was surprisingly sunny, dry, and calm.

"Hey, this is nice," Greer said, raising her head toward the warm light shining on her.

"Stop going up," Kane said. "We need to fly straight ahead and find the eye."

The angels glided across the calm skies. Vero was amazed how peaceful their flight was in contrast to the turbulent storm directly below. After flying for a few miles, Vero saw a circular, well-defined eye up ahead. He estimated it to be about a mile in diameter. It looked exactly like the images he had seen of hurricanes taken from space stations—a donut hole surrounded by clouds swirling counterclockwise. It was dangerous, surreal, and beautiful all at the same time.

"We have to be sure to drop down exactly in the eye," Kane said, pointing to their target. "The eye is surrounded by the eye wall. That's the most dangerous part of the hurricane. It's a dense wall of thunderstorms. You don't want to go there."

"Let's go single file. Everybody grab someone's ankles!" Vero said. "I'll lead!"

Greer grabbed on to Vero's ankles. Ada held on to Greer's, and Kane completed the chain. Vero narrowed his eyes, carefully zeroing in on the hole that was the eye.

"Aim dead center!" Kane shouted.

Vero gave him the thumbs-up sign, lowered his head, and nosedived toward the opening. With the others holding on to him, Vero landed smack in the center of the eye.

It was mostly calm weather inside—a light wind and clear skies. But surrounding Vero and the others were the towering, symmetric eye walls. It reminded Vero of the tornado booth he and Clover had once stepped into at the science museum—a cylinder-shaped glass booth that simulated a mild version of a real tornado.

"Can we let go?" Ada shouted.

"Yes," Vero said.

Ada took her hands off Greer's legs and Kane and Greer also let go. The group hovered in the center of the eye, careful not to fly close to the edges.

"We're here, so where is he?" Greer asked, looking around. "Rahab, come out, come out, wherever you are!"

Vero scanned the swirling eye walls. Stormy weather was all around him. Looking up through the cylinder eye, he saw blue sky. Looking down, he saw blue water.

A deep, gravelly voice cut through the howling winds. "You killed my pet."

The fledglings' heads darted around. The huge, weathered face of a middle-aged man broke through the eye wall so smoothly, it was like he was made of the thunderclouds. His skin was leathery, as if he had spent his entire existence in the blazing sun. The man was completely bald, and a scar ran across his forehead. But his brown beard was so long and bushy, Vero thought a family of birds could build their nest in there, and this guy would never even notice.

But what was most shocking was the empty eye socket. And in the remaining eye, there was no twinkle—it was as cold as the water in the deepest depths of the ocean. Vero then realized that they had found Rahab.

"By pet, you mean the leopard?" Vero asked.

"Yes," Rahab answered, exposing teeth coated with algae.

"Ada did it!" Greer said, pushing Ada forward toward Rahab. Ada quickly retreated.

"Sorry about that," Ada said. "But it was trying to kill us."

"Who are you?" Rahab yelled as he moved farther out of the storm, exposing more of his body, as well as a long, greenish robe covered in barnacles, which covered his feet.

Vero noticed Rahab had a barrel-like chest, and gigantic wings that were not white but blue. As Rahab hovered, it became clear those wings were whipping up the winds around them.

"Why are you bothering me?" he shouted.

"We want to talk to you." Vero wrinkled his nose. Rahab reeked of fish. "We're guardians in training."

"You can have all the training you want, but it won't save you," Rahab snarled.

Vero and Ada exchanged puzzled glances.

"Why should I talk to you?" Rahab said.

"Because we just braved your hurricane and were almost eaten by your *pets*!" Greer snapped. "You owe us a little courtesy!"

"I owe you nothing!" Rahab spat.

"Please," Vero said. "We need to know about the Book of Raziel."

Rahab's face twisted with anger at the mention of the book. He began to thrash and kick. His feet came into view, and Vero saw that both ankles were shackled to a long, thick iron chain that stretched down into the water below. The angel tried to grab Vero, but the chains kept

Vero just out of his grasp. Rahab swiped and clawed at Vero with vicious fervor, and then calmed, putting his head in his hands.

"I'm sorry," Rahab said through his fingers.

Vero looked at him with empathy. "What happened to you?" he asked. "Why are you here?"

"I rebelled."

Ada's eyes went wide.

"During the Great War, I decided to leave God, but at the last moment I changed my mind," Rahab said. "This is my punishment."

Rahab spread his arms toward the winds surrounding him. Vero noticed Kane watched Rahab with keen interest.

"You didn't become a demon?" Kane asked.

Rahab shook his head. "I'm stuck here making weather . . ." He lifted his foot, exposing the heavy chains. "I do whatever He asks of me, in the hopes that one day He'll free me."

Rahab's contrite face suddenly turned irate once more, and he screamed, "I found the book for Him. I returned it. Did as I was told, but He didn't free me!"

"How were you able to find the book at the bottom of the ocean?" Vero asked.

"Beginner's luck." Rahab laughed.

"No, there's more," Vero said. "Please. It's my mission to find it . . ."

"We'll tell them you helped us," Ada said. "We'll tell Michael."

Rahab's head whipped around to face Ada. "You'll tell Michael?"

"Yes, and Uriel and Raziel, all of them." Ada nodded.

"We swear," Kane said.

Rahab looked Kane in the eyes. "You, I don't trust."

"I'm telling the truth," Kane said, a pleading tone in his voice.

"I may only have one eye, but it sees more than a hundred eyes together."

Kane looked uncomfortable.

"He's telling the truth." Vero nodded to Kane.

"You need to trust us," Greer said.

"Why? Go away, all of you!" Rahab yelled.

"You're right. You don't know if we're telling the truth or not," Vero said. "But you have nothing to lose. If we don't tell Michael, nothing here will change for you. But if we do tell Michael, you just might have everything to gain."

Once again, anger rose like a geyser in Rahab. His face turned furious.

"Why you?" he screamed at Vero. Seaweed flew into Vero's eyes. "Why not me? I found the book once for Him. I returned it as I was told! Why not me?!"

"This guy is totally nuts," Greer said in a low voice to Ada.

"I don't know why it's me anymore than you know why it's not you!" Vero roared, unable to hold back his own geyser of emotion. "But like you, I do as I am told!"

Rahab's face seemed to soften. "Like I said, this one eye sees more than most. Despite all the coral reefs, rocks, as well as caves and plants and endless miles, I was able to find the book on the ocean's floor because He gave me the vision to see things that no one else can."

Vero looked at him, feeling a connection forming.

"You have it too, don't you?" Rahab said softly.

Vero nodded, recalling how, near the beginning of his training, he was the only one able to read the mysterious writing on the golems' parchments. No one else could even see a single letter.

"It's not a book like you think. There are no pages or a bound cover."

Kane looked to him, more curious than ever.

"It's the most beautiful gem you've ever seen."

"A gem? Not a . . ." Vero couldn't finish his sentence. High-pitched, ear-splitting shrieks caused him to shudder. A shadow overhead clouded his vision, blotting out the clear blue sky above. Rahab began to beat his wings faster in an attempt to sustain the storm.

"Dreadful bird!" Rahab shouted, his wings beating furiously.

Ada linked hands with Greer to steady them both as the winds intensified around them. Everything went dark.

"What's going on?" Kane yelled, his words echoing in the winds.

And then the winds died down as light broke through from above and the rains turned to sprinkles. Rahab looked defeated.

"They send that bird just to vex me," Rahab said bitterly.

"Who sends it?" Vero asked.

"The Virtues," Rahab said. "They can command the weather."

Vero knew all about the Virtues. He had competed against them in the Angel Trials. They were invisible angels who were extremely smart and could see the future. He just hadn't known that they also had power over the weather.

"Was that bird the Ziz?" Ada asked.

"Yes! The foul creature," Rahab said.

"What's the Ziz?" Kane asked, stuttering with fear.

"A bird as large as the Leviathan," Ada said. "Its wing-span can block out entire storms."

"Obviously," Greer said, looking up at the now clear skies.

Vero turned to Rahab. "You said the book was a gem. What kind of gem? What does it look like? Do you have any idea where it could be?"

Rahab began shaking and his eyes darted around wildly. "I have to leave!"

Vero looked at the shackles around the angel's ankles. *Where is he going?* Vero wondered. Rahab grabbed Vero by the front of his shirt and shook him. "It's so dark down there! Tell Michael to release me! Tell him!"

"I will," Vero yelled. "But you have to tell me everything about the book first!"

Rahab let go of Vero. The storm had mostly dissipated.

"It is blue . . . the most beautiful ocean-blue sapphire. About the size of a sand crab," Rahab said, pinching his fingers as if imagining he was holding the precious stone.

"When I found it, I returned it to Adam. But it didn't even belong to him. It needs to go back to where it came from. Others have tried. Others have gotten close, but no one has succeeded."

"Solomon had it last," Ada said.

"Is that what you think?" Rahab scoffed.

"Didn't he?" Ada asked, twirling her hair nervously.

"Wise old Solomon was even wiser than you know . . ."

Vero moved closer, anxious to hear Rahab's every word.

"Haven't you ever heard of Solomon's ring? Also known as the 'Seal of Solomon' . . . ?"

Vero shook his head.

"Of course," Ada said. "It was also called the Seal of Solomon. What about it?"

"Why am I wasting my time with such ignorant creatures?" Rahab spat.

"Because we have access to Michael," Vero said forcefully.

Rahab's face twitched with anger, but then he took a deep breath. "Everyone knows that Solomon was wise, and God did give him the gift of wisdom, which served him better than you know in the end," Rahab said. "But in addition to wisdom, Solomon had great knowledge that came from the book, which he wore on his finger. Solomon's ring held the Book of Raziel."

"Did Solomon know?" Kane asked.

"Of course," Rahab said. "In addition to God's great gift of wisdom, the book would have provided him with immense worldly knowledge."

"Besides being able to design and build his temple, it was said that Solomon was able to control demons and speak with animals," Ada added.

"Correct, fledgling," Rahab said, scowling at Ada. "This fledgling is not as stupid as the rest of you . . ." His gaze extended to the others. "I might have even liked her, if she were not such a cold-blooded killer!"

"I said I was sorry. He was going to kill Greer . . . It was self-defense. Now please, tell us about the ring if you want us to speak for you," Ada said.

Rahab considered her words, and composed himself again. "Over time, Solomon began to feel superior to all those he ruled . . . He felt he was practically a god himself, and he fell into sin. There has always been a saying about the ring he wore—that it could make a sad man happy and a happy man sad. But it was through the wisdom God gave him that Solomon finally understood the saying. For when he looked into the book upon his finger, he read the words, 'This too shall pass.'"

"I've heard that before," Vero said.

"At that moment, King Solomon knew that all his riches, his temple, and his kingdom would not last forever—that Israel would be divided into two. That only God was everlasting. So Solomon repented. And in his wisdom, he realized that the book was too powerful for men and it had to be returned. He sent his oldest and most trusted captain, Benaiah, to return the book."

"So it didn't perish in the temple fire . . ." Vero said, thinking out loud.

"He understood that the book's power was too much for any man to handle. Once man had settled in the world outside the garden, it needed to be returned to its origin."

"Where, Rahab?" Vero asked. "Where does it need to be returned to?"

"To the Tree of Knowledge of Good and Evil, of course," Rahab said. "In the middle."

"In the garden of Eden?" Kane asked.

"Yes, and Solomon would have known the location of the garden, and directed Benaiah where to voyage in order to find it. Of course, Solomon—with his wisdom and knowledge—helped Benaiah plan the trip, and take every precaution to ensure the secrecy of the mission. Benaiah traveled by land and by boat. Even back then, there were trade routes from the Middle East to the Orient."

"The entrance to the garden is in the Orient?" Vero asked, feeling his pulse quicken. "You mean somewhere in Asia?"

"Well, that is where Benaiah traveled, yes. But even though old Benaiah followed Solomon's directions to the letter, ultimately he was not able to find the entrance to the garden. Instead, he hid it as best he could . . . and to his credit, he must have done a very good job. My guess is that Solomon may have told Benaiah of another place to hide it, were he unable to find the garden. Somewhere very close to the entrance of Eden."

"Where?" Vero asked, his breathing becoming faster.

"The answer to that died with Benaiah. Not even the angels know where, not even Michael." He grimaced.

"But how do you know all this?" Greer asked Rahab.

"Remember, I found the book once myself . . . My fish tell me all sorts of things." He snorted. "And crabs are the best sorts of gossips. That was my 'gift.'"

Suddenly, right before their eyes, the chain yanked Rahab straight down. As his body hit the water's surface, Vero and the others watched as his wings morphed into scaly fins. The chain tugged him under the surface and he disappeared from sight.

"What a complicated guy," Ada said.

"No kidding. I'd hate to be his therapist," Greer said.

11

SRI PADA

With the storm gone, Vero, Ada, Greer, and Kane flew back to the rock cave, where Pax and X waited for their return.

"Thank God you're all okay! So tell us what happened!" Pax called.

"Did you find Rahab?" X asked anxiously.

"Yeah, we found him. And he's stinkin' crazy!" Greer volunteered.

"What do you mean?" said Pax.

"We'll tell you all about it on the flight back," Vero said, eager to leave the cave. "X, we're going to have to take turns carrying you."

As the fledglings flew back to C.A.N.D.L.E., they regularly shuffled X between them while filling X and Pax in on what Rahab had said. As they landed on the steps of the school, Greer and Kane let go of X.

"Thanks for the lift," X said to them as he stumbled onto the stairs.

"What's next?" Greer asked Vero.

"I don't know." Vero stared into the wall.

Pax chimed in. "I think it's obvious. The entrance to the garden and the location of the book are near one another, so we search for both and see which one turns up first."

The fledglings heard the sound of a massive door closing shut. They turned and saw Uriel walking down the stairs with Raziel.

"What's the latest?" Uriel asked them.

"We found Rahab," Kane said.

"Charming, isn't he?" Uriel said.

"Yeah, and his pets," X groaned, putting a hand to his shoulder.

"It will heal when you return to earth," Uriel told X.

"What did he tell you?" Raziel asked eagerly. "What did Rahab say?"

"That the book isn't a book. It's a blue gemstone, a sapphire." Vero said. "Is that true?"

Raziel looked at Vero, as if trying to recall. After a few moments, he shook his head. "I don't remember," he said with sadness in his voice.

"Anything else?" Uriel asked.

"That it is somewhat near the entrance to the garden of Eden, which is where it needs to be returned," Vero said.

"The garden?" Uriel mused.

"Raziel said Solomon's trusted captain, Benaiah, tried to return it, but fell short. He hid it somewhere near the entrance," Ada said. "Uriel, you were in the garden—do you have any idea where it is?"

Uriel shook his head. "Like Raziel, the memory of it was taken from me when I failed and gave the serpent access to the garden."

"Oh, sorry," Ada said.

"But I do know there is an entrance, a portal to the garden, from the earth," Uriel told the group. "When Adam and Eve were expelled, they traveled through it."

"So the garden isn't on earth?" Greer asked.

"The garden is partitioned off in the Ether."

"But the only way to get access is from earth?" Vero asked, wanting to be sure he understood.

Uriel nodded. "Yes. There is an entrance somewhere, that much I know."

Vero and the others mulled that over for a moment.

"This is just like in the Trials, when we had to find the portal to Jacob's Ladder!" X suggested.

"Yes," Uriel said, smiling at the connection.

"Might the library have a scroll on the garden?" Ada asked.

Uriel shook his head.

"No scrolls at all?" Vero asked.

"Not on the garden."

"I'm starting to get real discouraged here. In the whole entire world, I'm supposed to find a small gemstone—oh, and a portal to the garden of Eden?" Vero said, his voice dripping with sarcasm. "Oh yeah, while fighting off maltures at the same time."

"You were attacked again?" Uriel asked with keen interest.

"In a hospital elevator with my friend, Tack."

Uriel looked to Raziel with concern.

"And Tack saw them too."

"Them?" Uriel asked, seemingly more surprised that there had been two than the fact that Tack had seen them.

"It was weird. One rushed us in the elevator, and while I was fighting with her another one showed up," Vero said. "I thought they would both be going after me, but instead the second one actually took out the first malture. It basically saved me."

Uriel looked to Raziel. They were communicating mind to mind.

"The first one must have acted too soon. That's why the second one was sent," Raziel said.

"I don't get it," Vero said.

"At this point, they don't want to harm you. They've figured out that you are the key to finding the book," Uriel said. "So they need you, but Vero, you're not safe."

"Because the moment you discover the book's location, they will come after you. They are watching you more closely than ever," Raziel said in an almost threatening tone. "Trust no one . . ."

Vero locked eyes with his fellow fledglings. Only Kane dropped his gaze.

"Even yourself," Raziel said with utmost seriousness.

"What do you mean?" Vero looked panicked.

"I remember nothing about the book except for the feeling it gave me. With access to that much knowledge, you become in danger of feeling like God."

Vero lay on the ground of his front yard. He felt something heavy pressing on his chest. He opened his eyes—the ladder pinned him to the ground. As his senses returned to him, he looked around. No one had seen him fall. He lifted the ladder and squirmed out from underneath it, then lay on the ground next to it. He stared up into the sky, taking a moment to readjust. Everything was going too fast. The pressure was on, and he had no clue where the garden could be. Because the entrance to the garden lay on earth, Uriel had suggested he must return, as the answers would have to be found on earth rather than in the Ether. But Vero wasn't so sure.

"Taking a break?"

Vero heard his father's voice. He looked over and saw his dad standing over him. Dennis got down on the ground.

"Not a bad idea," Dennis said.

He lay on his back next to Vero, looking up to the sky.

"I miss being up there in the clouds," Dennis said.

"What?" Vero said, alarmed.

"When I flew for the Navy."

"Oh." Vero sighed, relieved his dad wasn't about to reveal that he, too, was an angel.

"When you're up there, everything else down below no longer seems so important. You know, we get so caught up in our little lives down here that sometimes we can't see beyond that. Up there, everything just sort of feels right, quiet."

"Yeah, the best feeling is when you're just about to break through the clouds and you can almost feel the wind blowing right through your body . . ."

Vero realized his dad was staring at him.

"Oh, well, you know, I can imagine," Vero backpedaled.

"I never told anyone, but on one of my flights, I saw a 'pilot's halo.' Do you know what that is?"

"No."

"When you fly over a cloud deck, and you see a rainbow halo around the shadow of the plane. Some people also call it a 'glory.' There's an old story that says when you see it, it means an angel is flying with you."

"Really?" Vero asked, intrigued.

"Yeah," Dennis said. "Of course scientists will tell you the halos are formed by water vapors in the air refracting the light that bounces off the clouds. But no one has ever been able to replicate the phenomena in a lab."

"What do you think?" Vero turned his head to his father.

"All I know is that whenever I flew . . . I never felt alone."

Vero smiled.

"Back in the mid-1980s, several cosmonauts on a Soviet space station were doing their routine assignments when a strange orange gas suddenly surrounded the station followed by an intense bright light."

"A bright light?" Vero thought aloud.

"Yes," Dennis said. "Right after their eyes adjusted, all the cosmonauts reported seeing seven tall figures with large wings and halos over their heads surrounding the station."

"Angels?"

"I think so. They reported it to the ground control team, who dismissed their sightings by saying it was a mass delusion brought on by the stress and fatigue of prolonged space flight. But eleven days later, a fresh crew of another three cosmonauts joined the first crew, and right after they arrived, they, too, saw the bright light and the seven beings with wings. They were reported as saying that the beings' wingspan were the size of a 747. And because the second crew had just gotten there, they could no longer blame the sightings on fatigue."

"So what happened?"

"Weeks later when they all got safely back to earth, they put the cosmonauts through a battery of physical and psychological tests. They all passed with flying colors."

"So do you believe them . . . that they saw angels?"

"Vero, before you can even think about becoming an astronaut, they make sure you're of sound mind. So, yes, I think they saw angels. Maybe it's not a scientific explanation, but isn't it comforting to think about?"

Vero sat in front of a computer in the school library. It was lunch break, and despite his growling stomach, Vero was determined to learn everything he could about the garden of Eden; but in everything he read, nothing new jumped out. There were many theories on the location of the garden, which ranged from places in the Middle East to the Far East. And some said the garden was destroyed during the Great Flood. Vero was left even more confused than before. Uriel had told him the garden was partitioned off in the Ether, but there was an entrance somewhere on earth. All Vero could come up with was that the entrance might be near where the garden had originally been. But where was that? Vero's thoughts were interrupted by a familiar voice.

"Danny, what is it?" Davina cried.

Vero looked up and saw Davina standing with Danny in front of the checkout desk. As Danny slipped a book into the return slot, Davina grabbed his arm.

"Can you at least tell me what I did?" she asked, her face troubled.

Danny didn't answer. He yanked his arm away from her, letting another book slip into the slot. Without a word, he turned and walked out of the library. Davina watched him leave. Vero got up and walked over to her.

"Davina . . ."

Davina turned to Vero.

"Are you all right?"

Davina shook her head. "He hates me for some reason, but he won't tell me why. I don't know what happened. He won't even talk to me!"

Seeing Davina near tears sparked Vero's anger. His eyes became slits as he watched Danny walk down the hallway. He charged off after him.

"Danny!" Vero yelled.

Danny continued walking. Vero chased up to him and grabbed his arm, spinning Danny to face him.

"Get off me, Leland!"

"Why are you so mad at Davina?" Vero shouted. "You act like such a jerk to her!"

"What do you care? Isn't this the moment you've been waiting for? It's your big chance to swoop in and make her your girl," Danny said.

"It's not about that," Vero said. "She's really upset, and she's like one of the nicest people in the world."

Danny's face softened. "I found out I'm moving. When school ends, my whole family is going to Colorado."

"Why?"

"My dad's sick of always being on the road."

Vero recalled that Danny's father drove a tractor-trailer.

"His route's from here to Colorado, and the trucking company offered him a desk job out there so he can stay in one place."

"That's not all bad. You'll get to see him all the time."

"But Davina and I will be over," Danny said with emotion.

Panic came into Vero's eyes as he put two and two together, and remembered he was Danny's guardian. Which meant when he became a full-fledged angel, he would be with Danny all the time—in Colorado! Vero had thought that when the time came to leave his family, he would at least be in the same town with them. That he would still be able to see them going about their lives.

"You're right! You can't go!" Vero blurted out.

"What?" Danny asked, confused.

"You have to stay here!"

"But you just said it was good—"

"Forget what I said!" Vero said. "Tell your dad you're not going! You belong here with Davina and your friends."

Danny looked at Vero, uncomfortable with his outburst. Did Vero just say he was his friend? The bell rang. Lunch was over.

"You're a weird dude," Danny said, shaking his head as he walked off to class.

A blast of hot steam hit Vero smack in the face as he opened the dishwasher. As he jerked his head back, Nora walked past him.

"Clover is supposed to unload those," she told Vero.

"I'll do it," Vero said.

"No, it's her job," Nora said. "Tell her to come down."

Vero walked out of the kitchen to Clover's bedroom. He opened the door without warning her first. Clover spun around in her chair. She was sitting at her desk studying.

"You should knock first!" she yelled at him. "What if I was getting changed?"

"Then you would have locked it," Vero said. "Mom said you need to empty the dishwasher."

"Tell her I'm studying."

"She doesn't care. I tried to do it for you, but she said no."

"Yeah, I bet you tried real hard."

Vero didn't answer. Something had caught his attention. Clover followed his gaze. Vero was staring at her drawing of the mountain with the forest below—the one from her dream that she had shown him a few weeks ago. Only now, the image was much more detailed and vivid.

"What?" Clover asked.

"You're still working on this drawing."

"Yeah, I can't shake it," Clover said. "I keep seeing it. It has to mean something."

"What's this triangle?" Vero asked, pointing to a triangular shadow that cast over the valley.

"It's the mountain's shadow," Clover said.

"Except the mountain is shaped more like a cone. It shouldn't cast a perfectly triangular shadow like that."

Clover shrugged. "It's what I see."

"Well, I've learned some things about the Book of Raziel," Vero said with a pause. "This book isn't like any book you've ever read . . . It's an actual gem. And it's somewhere near the entrance to the garden of Eden," Vero told her.

"This"—Clover held up the drawing—"has to be it. I'm telling you, I feel real strongly about it."

"Maybe, but where *is* this?" Vero said, feeling his frustration grow the more closely he studied her drawing. "There are tons of places on earth that have jungles and mountains. We'll never figure it out from this. It's impossible," Vero said, totally exasperated.

"Clover," Dennis said, walking into the room. "Mom said now for the dishes."

Dennis glanced down at the drawing.

"Beautiful drawing of Sri Pada," he said, then turned and walked out.

Clover and Vero looked to one another, astonished.

12

FLYING COACH

It makes perfect sense," Vero told Clover as they sat in front of the big computer screen in the downstairs study.

"It seems like too much of a coincidence," Clover said as she clicked the mouse.

"It is!" Vero said. "That's why it can't be a coincidence. There are forces at work here."

Vero looked at the image of the majestic mountain of Sri Pada on the screen.

"A holy site for many different religions . . ." Vero read. "In the country of Sri Lanka."

"You're right," Clover said. "Dad's been working on the Sri Lanka project for over a year. It's no coincidence."

"The mountain is located in the Central Highlands of the island nation. It's surrounded by forested hills below, and is home to a wildlife preserve of many species including panthers, Sambar deer, and elephants," Vero read.

Clover pointed to the black panther and Sambar deer in her drawing. Vero nodded then turned his eyes back to the bright computer screen.

"The mountain soars upwards to almost 7,360 feet. Half of the year, it's shrouded in cloud cover. At certain times of the year, torrential rain runs down the sides, which over time has eroded away the hillside and exposed some of the richest gem mining in the world."

"The book is a gem!" Clover said with awe.

Vero nodded.

"But why is it a religious site?" Clover asked.

"I don't know," Vero said, his eyes scanning the screen.

"It says more than three million pilgrims travel yearly to the mountain," Clover said. "Including Hindus, Buddhists, Muslims, and Christians . . ."

As he read, Vero's eyes went wide. "Sri Pada. It means 'sacred footprint.' There's a rock formation near the summit, which bears a huge imprint in the shape of a foot. Many Buddhists say it belongs to Buddha. Some Hindus say it's Lord Shiva's, and many Muslims and Christians believe it's Adam's first footprint on earth after he was exiled from the garden of Eden."

"Sri Pada is so beautiful that Adam stepped there to make his transition from the garden of Eden less painful," Clover read. She turned to Vero. "Everything points to Sri Pada. It's where you need to go! I'm sure of it!"

Vero nodded. "I think so too."

"So now what will you do?" Clover asked.

"I have to get there," Vero said with determination.

"Can you just fly there?"

"I wish," Vero said, shaking his head. "The book is on earth, not in the Ether, so I have to figure out a way to get to Sri Lanka."

"Maybe if Dad goes, you can go with him. You'll just have to convince him."

"Is he going for sure?"

"He was talking about it," Clover answered. "You've got to get him to take you."

Vero was thinking. How could he get his dad to bring him along? The trip would be expensive, plus he doubted his dad would allow him to miss school just because Vero wanted to travel out of the country for no reason.

"Dad! Come here!" Clover yelled. "Dad!"

"What are you doing?" Vero panicked.

"Just ask. What if he says yes?"

"What?" Dennis yelled from down the hall.

"Can you come here? Vero wants to ask you something!" Clover yelled.

"Tell him to come here! I'm busy! And the dishes are *still* waiting for you!" Dennis shouted.

"Go," Clover said to Vero. "I'll help."

Clover stood and grabbed Vero's arm, pulling him up out of the chair. They walked down the hall to the family room. Dennis was reading a book while Nora was watching television. Vero glanced at the television. It was a cooking show. His mom was always looking for new recipes to try.

"What is it?" Dennis asked, looking up from his book.

"Um, it's well . . ." Vero stammered.

"Vero wants you to take him with you to Sri Lanka," Clover blurted out.

"You do?" Dennis looked surprised.

"Um, yeah. I've always wanted to go there."

"Well, he's certainly not going to go before I do," Nora said, hitting the mute button on the remote.

"Since when did you become interested?" Dennis asked Vero.

"Last year, when I had to do a report on it for Social Studies."

"I remember that report," Dennis said with suspicion in his voice. "It was the one you wanted me to write for you because you were bored with it."

"No, that's all Vero talks to me about. How fascinating he found that country," Clover said a little too quickly.

"I think someone just wants to skip a week of school." Dennis smiled to Vero.

"Oh, so you're going?" Nora asked Dennis.

"Not a hundred percent confirmed, but it looks like the week after next."

"That's perfect!" Vero shouted. "That's winter break, so I won't miss any school!"

"Vero, you're not going," Dennis said. "If I could take anyone, it would be your mom."

"Then we'll all have to go," Clover said. "We'll make it a family vacation."

"Yeah!" Vero said excitedly.

"Guys," Dennis said. "Calm down—you're getting yourselves all worked up here. Tickets to Sri Lanka cost an arm and a leg . . ."

"I'll chip in," Vero said.

"Me too," Clover said. "I have a couple hundred bucks saved."

"Look, I love the idea of all of us getting away to some faraway, exotic land, but sorry, it's just not going to happen," Dennis said.

"Oh, I just remembered," Nora said. "Mary called me yesterday and asked if we could take Tack for that week. They have to go to visit Marty's mom. They're moving her to an assisted living facility and selling her house."

"Well, that ends it. Sorry, guys, it's a no," Dennis said. "But I'll be sure to send you a postcard, and take lots of videos on my phone."

Clover exchanged a look with Vero. This hadn't gone exactly as they had planned. Vero walked back to the study and Clover followed. Once inside, she shut the door behind them.

"What are you doing?" Clover asked as Vero sat in front of the desktop.

Vero typed on the keyboard, an idea growing in his mind. Clover sat next to him. She stared at the screen.

"You're searching for flights to Sri Lanka?"

"Yeah."

"They're nine hundred and fourteen dollars!" Clover said. "Dad's never gonna pay that for all of us."

"No, he won't." Vero sighed.

"We have college savings accounts," Clover said. "Maybe we could take the money from there?"

"They won't do it," Vero said with frustration.

"I'll keep working on Dad," Clover said. "It's meant to be. I've got a feeling on this one. I'll convince him."

Vero didn't answer. His mind was elsewhere.

That night, Vero tiptoed down the hall to his parents' bedroom. He poked his head into the room. His mom lay fast asleep with her eye mask around her head—she always needed the room to be completely dark to fall asleep each night. His dad was on his back, snoring loudly. Vero often wondered why his mother chose an eye mask rather than earplugs. Some nights he could hear his dad snoring all the way to his room.

Vero gingerly walked back, careful not to wake anyone. He stood at the base of his bed. Last year, when he was terrified for Clover's safety, he got himself so worked up that he produced a heart attack, which caused him to transition to the Ether. Raphael had told Vero that he had actually willed himself to the Ether. So if he could do it once, Vero reasoned he could do it again. He closed his eyes and had one single thought—to get to the Ether. He desperately wanted to go there. He needed to find two angels in particular. The thought consumed him. He felt pain in his chest and grabbed over that area, then collapsed on his bed, his head hanging over the side.

Vero removed his hand from his chest and he looked around him—green stalks met his eyes in every direction. He was lying in a field of sunflowers. He stood up and screamed— the angels Leo and Karael, his parents' guardian angels, stood before him.

"Well, you called us," Leo said defensively.

"Oh, yeah, I did," Vero said, slapping his hand to his head in an attempt to recover from the jarring transition.

"When you're a full-fledged guardian, you'll no longer feel the transition," Karael told Vero. "It gets much easier."

"What do you need, Vero?" Leo asked.

"I have a pretty good idea where the entrance to the garden of Eden is," Vero said.

"You do?" Leo asked, surprised.

"Sri Lanka," Vero said.

Karael looked to Leo. Vero could tell they were speaking mind to mind. He picked up on snippets of their conversation.

"Yes, my dad's going there," Vero said.

"You can read minds?" Leo asked Vero.

Vero nodded. "A bit. Look, I'm here because I need you to convince him to take me with him to Sri Lanka." Vero looked to Karael. "And convince my mom too. If she puts pressure on him, he'll take me."

"We can't just do that," Leo said. "It has to be approved."

"What do you mean?" Vero said, the panic rising in his voice.

"Well, of course we need to confirm that it's God's will," Leo said.

"But I need to go there! It's what I must do! You promised to help me!" Vero pleaded.

"And we will, Vero," Karael said. "If God allows us."

"How do we find out if He will?"

"Ask Him." Leo smiled. "It's not only human prayers He hears."

Karael flapped his wings. "If He grants your prayer, we can get on it much quicker if we're already at the prayer grid."

Vero nodded and sprouted his wings. Off the three angels flew. Vero soared over the vast green hills below. He saw animals of every type peacefully grazing. Soon they reached the crystal coliseum that was the prayer grid. As Vero, Leo, and Karael hovered above, they saw the thousands and thousands of angels who were seated in the stands. Brightly colored rays of light shot up from the grid in the middle of the coliseum, which angels caught into their hands. Soon each flew off and other angels arrived to catch new shards of light. Vero was in awe of the spectacle.

"Go ask," Leo said to Vero. "We'll wait here."

Vero nodded and flew off to a peaceful cluster of trees just outside the prayer grid coliseum. He landed on the thick branch of one and pulled in his wings, then sat and closed his eyes. The atmosphere around the prayer grid was so tranquil that Vero had no problem concentrating. He asked God with all his heart to hear his prayer. After a few moments, he opened his eyes, grew his wings, and flew back to the prayer grid.

"Vero, over here!" Karael waved to him.

Vero looked over and saw Leo and Karael sitting on the top bleacher. He flew to them and sat down.

"Any word?" Vero asked.

"Not yet," Leo answered. "Patience."

"We need to hurry. Because I willed myself here, time hasn't stopped on earth for me," Vero said. "Can you see if my dad is still asleep?"

"Sawing wood." Leo chuckled.

Without warning, two vivid purple rays of light shot straight toward Leo and Karael. Their hands instantly went up, and they caught them.

"All good?" Vero asked them.

Karael smiled and nodded. "But remember, all we can do is plant the seed in his mind."

"I know," Vero said.

"And don't expect me to push for first class." Leo smiled.

"No worries. Business class will be fine with me," Vero said, meaning it.

Vero woke the next morning with a crick in his neck. When he returned from the Ether, he was so exhausted that he'd slept with his head hanging off the bed, the exact position from when he had transitioned to the Ether. He threw on a pair of jeans and a T-shirt, then went to find his father.

"That one could work," Vero overheard his mother say.

He walked into the kitchen and saw his parents sitting at the table, hovering over his dad's laptop.

"What are you doing?" Vero asked.

"After sleeping on it, I sort of had a change of heart," Dennis said, looking up from the screen.

"Dad's taking the whole family to Sri Lanka with him!" Nora said excitedly.

"Really?" Vero asked.

Clover walked into the kitchen in her pajamas.

"What's going on?" Clover asked.

"We're going to Sri Lanka!" Vero said.

"All of us?"

"Even Tack," Dennis said. "We called his parents and they're okay with it. He already has a passport. I guess he was supposed to go on some dowsing trip to Central America with his dad last summer, but then the trip never happened."

"And our passports are still good from when we went to Cancun. Dad just needs to get the visas," Nora said.

"This is crazy," Clover said. "What changed your mind?"

"When I woke up, for some reason I felt like we really needed to spend more time together as a family," Dennis said. "And then everything just seemed to magically fall into place. You guys won't miss any school. And some-how I had a ton more frequent flyer miles than what I had remembered . . ."

Clover shot Vero a suspicious look. He shrugged.

"So we're only actually paying for one ticket."

"Come on, you two." Nora turned to Clover and Vero. "Hurry up and eat so we can get your pictures taken."

"Dad," Vero said. "This is all so amazing. But is there any chance you have enough miles for business class?"

"As a matter of fact, yes."

"Really?"

"Yep," Dennis said. "Mom and I will be in business. You, Tack, and Clover can sit in coach." Dennis smiled. "Unfortunately, the only seats available for you kids were the ones right across from the bathroom."

Somehow, Vero knew that Leo was also smiling.

13

TRACKING SAPPHIRES

Sri Lanka?" Tack said to Vero as they pushed the hospitality cart down the sterile hospital hallway.

"Yeah."

"Why can't the book be somewhere like Hawaii or Alaska," Tack said. "I always wanted to see Alaska."

"Sri Lanka's supposed to be beautiful," Vero said. "After we're done here, can you come over to my house?"

"Yeah, why?"

"I need you to practice looking for the book," Vero said. "I now know what it is, so we can fine-tune your dowsing skills. Okay?"

"What is it?"

"A gem."

Vero saw a worried look come over Tack. "What?"

"I've only ever detected water. I'm not so sure I can find a gem."

"I thought dowsers can find a whole bunch of stuff like oil, metals . . ."

"Some can. I just hope I don't let you down," Tack said.

Tack's face then turned white. Vero saw fear in his eyes. Then he realized they were standing in front of the same elevator where they were attacked, and that Tack had stopped pushing the cart.

"It's all right," Vero said. "They're not gonna come back . . . at least for now."

"How do you know?"

"Because they need me right now. They need me to lead them to the book."

Tack shook his head.

"What?"

"It's still hard for me to make sense of all this," Tack said. "How did you deal with it? You know, when you first found out."

"Part of me was relieved because it explained all the weird stuff that was happening. I really thought I was going crazy. But then I worried that my family would hate me if they knew the truth . . . You too."

"I'll admit it freaked me out, but I could never hate you," Tack said. "You know my family. We go to Mass every Sunday, but I guess I focused more on video games than religion. I kind of thought all those old Bible stories were just stories about how not to behave."

Vero nodded. He understood.

"But here you are, an angel," Tack said. "I don't know if I would have believed if you weren't here, and if I hadn't seen those monsters."

The elevator bell dinged, signaling its arrival. Vero looked to Tack.

"I'll get in," Tack said, eyeing the elevator. "I'm not scared anymore."

The elevator door opened, and Tack screamed at the sight before him. Not a malture, but Nurse Kunkel walking off the elevator. She gave him a look.

"Get a grip, Kozlowski," Nurse Kunkel told Tack as she walked past.

Vero searched through his mother's jewelry box, which sat on top of Nora's dresser in her bedroom. Tack stood in the doorway keeping watch.

"I feel weird about this," Tack said.

"We're not stealing, just borrowing them," Vero said as he pushed a pearl necklace to the side of the box.

"Hurry up."

"I can't find them," Vero said, frustrated.

"Can't we just use something else?"

"Wait! Here we go!" Vero said, excitement in his voice.

He held up two blue stone earrings. Tack looked closely at the earrings in Vero's hand.

"So that's a blue sapphire?"

"Yep," Vero said.

"You sure?" Tack asked.

"Yeah, let's go."

Minutes later, Tack stepped out of the Leland's back door into the backyard. Vero stood under a tree.

"You ready?" Vero asked Tack.

"Did you hide them together or separately?" Tack asked.

"You tell me." Vero grinned mischievously.

Tack narrowed his eyes at Vero. "Okay, I will."

Tack spread his fingers and held both hands out over the ground. A serious, focused look came over his face. He walked toward the picnic table then stopped. He stood still for a moment, concentrating. Vero watched, with bated breath. He was hopeful Tack would find the sapphire. But then a look of disappointment came over Vero as Tack turned and headed toward the house next door.

Vero shook his head as Tack walked into the Atwood's yard. Tack made his way around Mrs. Atwood's vegetable garden and walked up their back porch. Panic flooded Vero's eyes. He raced over to Tack.

"Come back, I didn't hide it in their yard!" Vero called to Tack.

It seemed as if Tack was in some sort of trance. He stood staring into the Atwood's family room. Vero arrived just in time to see Mr. Atwood's eyes shoot wide as he lay on the sofa watching a basketball game on TV.

"What in the world?!" Mr. Atwood shouted through the French doors.

"It's not here. Let's go," Vero grabbed Tack's arm.

Tack didn't budge.

"Wendy! We have unwanted visitors at the back door!" Mr. Atwood shouted. "Get rid of them!"

"Great, now look what you did!" Vero tugged on Tack's arm.

The door opened. Mrs. Atwood stood there, her hair done, wearing a long overcoat.

"Hi, boys," she said. "Can I help you with something? Or are you looking for Angus? Because he's not home right now."

"Um . . ." Vero faltered. "We were checking up on Mr. Atwood."

"Oh, aren't you sweet," Mrs. Atwood said. "He's doing much better."

The loud, unmistakable sound of someone passing gas reached their ears. Mrs. Atwood cringed. Vero smirked. Tack remained serious.

"You'll have to excuse Albert," Mrs. Atwood said. "The doctor has got him on all kinds of medications . . . including laxatives. I'd invite you in, but it's really awful in here right now. Mr. Atwood can't entertain guests for the time being."

"Are they gone?" Mr. Atwood shouted.

"Quiet, Albert!" Mrs. Atwood yelled.

"We'll just be going," Vero said as he stepped toward the stairs.

"You look nice," Tack said to Mrs. Atwood.

Vero abruptly stopped and gave Tack a look.

"Thank you. I'm on my way to a dinner at my women's club."

"Okay, we have to go now," Tack said.

Vero arched his eyebrows. *What was Tack doing?*

"Oh, Mrs. Atwood, before we go, do you happen to have the time?" Tack asked.

Mrs. Atwood pushed her right sleeve up, revealing her watch.

"Five forty-seven."

"Thanks, and what a stunning watch," Tack said, smiling the biggest smile.

Vero glanced over at the watch. A jolt of surprise shot through him.

"I know it's hard to believe," Mrs. Atwood said. "But Albert got me this for my fortieth birthday. I was born in September. The sapphire is my birthstone."

She pointed to the twelve tiny blue sapphires on the face of the watch. Vero smiled to Tack, who gave him a sly look.

"That was pretty impressive, if I do say so myself," Tack said to Vero as they sat on the picnic table.

"Yeah, since I thought you had totally lost it," Vero said. "But you still need to find my mom's."

"Fine."

Tack stood. He took a deep breath and tried to focus. He held his hands out over the yard, but after a few moments, he shook his head.

"I got nothing at all."

"It doesn't make any sense," Vero said. "How were you able to find Mrs. Atwood's? Especially since these were right under your nose."

Vero pulled both earrings out from the bottom of the picnic table. He had used a piece of duct tape to tape them to the underside.

"Really? That is bad," Tack said, sadly.

"It doesn't make any sense."

"Hide them again. We've got to keep practicing," Tack said.

"Okay."

"Boys!" Nora called from the kitchen window.

Vero quickly stuffed the earrings into his back jean pocket.

"Mary called. She wants Tack home for dinner."

"Right now?" Vero asked.

"Yes. He was supposed to be home a half hour ago." Nora shut the window.

"We'll practice tomorrow," Vero told Tack.

Tack nodded.

As Vero lay on his bed in sweatpants, studying from his science textbook, Clover barged into the room.

"You want to explain why I found these in your pocket when I was doing the laundry?" Clover asked, opening her hand to reveal the sapphire earrings.

"Oh, I forgot to put them back," Vero answered, sitting up.

"Answer the question. You going to pierce your ears?"

"No," Vero answered, shocked by the question.

"Nose?"

"No."

"Belly button?"

"NO!" Vero shook his head. "I was using them to train Tack."

"Okay, now I'm even more confused," Clover said.

"They're blue sapphires. The Book of Raziel is a blue sapphire. I hid them in the backyard to see if Tack could find them. We're practicing for when the time comes."

"It can't be going well."

"Not with those," Vero said. "But how did you know?"

"Because these are fakes." Clover sighed. "Mom bought these because she needed them to match a dress."

"That would explain it!" Vero excitedly said. "So it wasn't Tack!"

"Use this."

Clover lifted a necklace out from under her shirt and unclasped it. She put it in Vero's hand. It was a small blue stone.

"This is the real deal."

"Where did you get it?"

"When I graduated eighth grade, Mom and Dad gave it to me. It's my birthstone. So don't lose it!" Clover said. "Give me the chain back."

Vero took the stone off the chain.

"Thanks, I won't lose it."

"Not to change the subject, but what's this I hear about you losing it with Danny Konrad the other day?" Clover asked.

"It's true," Vero said as he placed the sapphire on his nightstand. "He's moving to Colorado. His dad's not gonna drive a truck anymore."

"So? Now he won't be able to pick on you," Clover said as she sat down on his bed. "You should be happy."

"I'm Danny's guardian angel."

Clover looked straight at Vero.

"Serious?"

Vero nodded.

Clover laughed.

"What?"

"Well, it's kind of funny," Clover said. "You can't stand him, but you're stuck with him."

"He's not so bad anymore." Vero shrugged.

"So why are you upset if he moves?" Clover asked.

"Because he'll be in Colorado, far from you guys . . ."

"And your point is?" Clover asked.

"I'll have to go with him. I thought I could at least be around you guys, you know, when the time comes."

Sadness came into Clover's eyes.

"Vero, you're Danny's guardian, which means you have to support what's best for him. Going to Colorado and being settled with his dad will be good for Danny."

Vero looked down. "I know."

"I've only ever thought about how hard it will be for us to live without you, but I never really thought how hard it will be for you to live without us," Clover apologized, her eyes swelling.

Vero wrapped his arm around his sister's neck. Clover rested her head on his shoulder.

14

THE OTHER SIDE OF THE WORLD

Mrs. Luckett squinted through her cat-eye-style glasses at Tack and Vero, who stood before her. She was about seventy, and while her eyesight wasn't what it once was, her hearing was still fantastic. And right now, she probably wished it wasn't—for Tack was singing in music class. While Vero stood next to him, the rest of the class was sitting on plastic blue chairs that had tennis balls attached to the base of their metal legs.

"Thaddeus, try that note again," Mrs. Luckett said, pointing her conductor's stick at him. "'Hallelujah' in B flat."

"Okay."

"Now I've heard there was a . . ." As Tack sang, a look of pain came over Mrs. Luckett. She looked as if an elephant just stomped on her toes . . . all ten . . . twice.

"That is enough!" Mrs. Luckett shouted to Tack, then turned to Vero. "You try."

Vero started. *"Now I've heard there was a secret . . ."* Once again, Mrs. Luckett's face squished up in pain—this time as if someone had slammed the car door on all ten of her fingers, then opened the door and slammed it shut again. She repeatedly tapped her wand on her music stand. "Thank you! Stop! Enough!" Vero closed his mouth.

"It's all art," Mrs. Luckett told the entire class. "Whether you sing, dance, act, write, or draw, all art should be respected and held in high regard. And another wonderful form of artistic expression is pantomime . . ." She turned to Tack and Vero. "So from now on in my music class, you two will be performing pantomime whenever we sing. You will mouth the words while the rest of the class uses their full voices."

Davina giggled along with Nate and Missy. Vero and Tack looked confused.

"You may sit down," Mrs. Luckett told the boys.

Vero and Tack took their seats. Davina leaned over to Vero.

"I thought you sounded okay," she whispered to Vero.

"Thanks," Vero half-heartedly said, knowing she was only being nice.

"Danny Konrad, could you please stand and sing the few bars of the song?"

Danny stood. Tack elbowed Nate.

"This ought to be good," Tack said in a low voice to Nate, who snickered.

Vero thought Danny looked uncomfortable as he put his hands into his pockets and fidgeted. He hesitated. Mrs. Luckett raised her conductor's stick.

"On the count of three . . ."

She tapped her stick in the air three times, signaling Danny. He looked down at his feet, and began to sing, faintly, *"Now I've heard there was a secret chord that David played . . ."*

All murmurs in the class instantly dissipated as Danny sang Leonard Cohen's lyrics. His voice was stellar. Vero exchanged surprised looks with Tack. Nate's eyes practically popped out of his head. Davina gazed wistfully upon Danny.

". . . And it pleased the Lord . . ."

As Danny sang, Mrs. Luckett placed the tip of her wand under his chin and raised his head. She smiled encouragingly to him. The bright-red coloring of his cheeks gradually disappeared the louder his voice grew. The class didn't dare make any moves, afraid they would ruin the moment.

". . . But you don't really care . . ."

As Danny sang, Vero watched Davina as she looked upon Danny. His beautiful voice captivated her, yet there was a melancholic look in her eyes.

". . . for music, do you?"

Once Danny stopped singing, there was an awkward silence. Then the class clapped and broke out into shouts and cheers. Danny's face flushed red once again, and he cracked a smile. Vero turned to Davina.

"Did you know he could sing like that?"

Davina shook her head. "He doesn't share anything with me anymore," she sadly said.

Mrs. Luckett smiled to Danny. "You, my dear, will never be one of those annoying, ridiculous mimes."

Tack and Vero exchanged offended looks. After music class let out, Vero caught up with Danny in the hallway.

"Dude, that was pretty amazing," Vero said.

"Thanks," Danny said.

"Davina thought it was great too," Vero said, pulling Davina over by her arm.

"Oh, yeah, it was beautiful," Davina said, awkwardly.

Danny held her gaze. He looked into her sparkling blue eyes. "I'm sorry. I know I've been a jerk to you lately . . ."

Davina's face softened.

"I'm moving to Colorado."

"Colorado?" Davina said, a mix of sadness and surprise on her face.

"In the summer," Danny said. "I thought that if I was mean to you, somehow it would make leaving easier."

"That's dumb," Davina said.

"I'm sorry," Danny said, looking down.

"We'll FaceTime each other every day, and my aunt and uncle live out there. We go every year for a visit. If your town isn't too far away, I can come see you."

"Really?" Danny's face lit up.

Davina nodded. She turned to Vero. "You knew he was moving?"

"He did," Danny answered. "Kind of freaked when I told him."

"Yeah, well, it was unfair of me to make you feel bad for moving," Vero said. "It's just hard to lose a friend."

Danny looked to Vero with a faint smile. "Thanks, Vero."

The following Saturday afternoon, Tack's parents drove everyone to the airport. Marty pulled the dented red minivan to the curb and turned off the engine.

"Okay, this is your terminal," he said.

"I'll get the bags," Dennis said, getting out of the car.

Dennis walked behind the car and opened the back door. As he began pulling suitcases from the trunk, everyone else stepped out of the car and onto the curb. Marty walked over to Dennis and helped grab suitcases. Mary looked at Tack with tears forming in her eyes.

"Don't worry, Mary," Nora said as she hugged Tack's mom. "We'll take good care of him."

"I know. It's just so far . . ." Mary sniffled as they broke apart.

"It's only a plane ride away, Mom," Tack said.

"Actually, it's four plane rides away," Vero said. "New York, Zurich, Mumbai, then Sri Lanka."

Mary burst into sobs. Tack flashed Vero a look over his mother's shoulder as he hugged her. Vero felt guilty, and was glad Dennis finally had all the bags on the curb.

Dennis shook Marty's hand. "My cell phone will work once we get over there."

"I've got the number and the contact info for the hotel," Marty answered.

A *ding* came from Clover's jacket pocket. Dennis's head whipped around.

"Did you bring your cell phone?" Dennis asked.

Clover pulled her cell phone from her pocket.

"Clover, I said to leave that home," Dennis said, annoyed. "Do you have any idea how expensive it is to make international calls or to surf the net abroad?"

"You're bringing yours," Clover protested.

"That is a World Bank phone, not mine!"

"I'll hold on to it till you get back," Marty said, holding out his hand to Clover.

Clover huffed then handed over her phone.

"And remember only drink bottled water," Mary told Tack, fixing his collar. "And that includes even when brushing your teeth."

"Okay, Mom," Tack said.

"Oh, don't go anywhere without sunscreen on. Sri Lanka is very close to the equator," Mary said. "And no eating salads that haven't been washed with purified water, and eat only thoroughly cooked meat, and no shellfish . . ."

"All right, Mary," Marty said, nudging her toward the car. "Dennis and Nora know what to do."

"And I read you're not allowed to take photos in any of the Buddhist shrines," Mary told Tack, ignoring her husband. "And no exporting any wild animals or antiques older than fifty years . . ."

"Really, Mom?" Tack said, rolling his eyes.

"And one more thing," Clover said. "No annoying Clover."

"Yes." Mary smiled, though it was wobbly. "No annoying Clover."

Mary grabbed Tack again and hugged him tightly. She then let go and grabbed Vero and Clover and hugged them too. As Marty hugged Tack, an airport policeman walked over to him.

"You've got to move your car," the policeman told Marty.

"Yes, Officer," Marty said, releasing Tack.

"And you're allowed ten kilograms of tea duty-free," Mary said to Tack as her husband opened the passenger's door and guided her inside. "Bring me back some."

"I don't even know what a kilogram is." Tack shook his head.

Marty shut Mary's car door. He got in, and the Lelands and Tack waved good-bye as the car drove off.

The flight to New York took just under an hour. On the flight to Zurich, Vero sat by the window with Clover in the middle and Tack on the aisle. This was the flight Vero had been half dreading—they were in the row across from the bathroom.

"At least it's convenient," Tack said to Clover, who pulled the front of her shirt over her nose.

Nora and Dennis, as they'd said they would, sat up in business class.

Tack elbowed Clover. "Go ask your parents to get us more of those chocolate chip cookies."

"The stewardess has already kicked us out twice," Clover said through her shirt. "I'm not going back up there." Clover rearranged her pillow in an attempt to get comfortable. "Now be quiet so I can sleep."

"Vero?" Tack asked.

"No," Vero quickly answered.

"Okay, yeah, fine. Here I am, traveling halfway around the world to help you save the universe or something, and you can't even ask for a few cookies for me?"

"My mom said they were trying to sleep," Vero said. "I'll go up there later."

"Fine," Tack huffed.

"But I do appreciate you coming along to help me." Vero smiled.

"Apparently not enough," Tack shot back. "And besides, have you figured out how we're going to convince your parents to take us to Sri Pada? I read it's a few hours' drive from Colombo."

"No, not yet. I'm confident it will all come together when we get there. Even if I have to sneak away to get to the mountain, I will."

"I hope it doesn't come to that."

Vero nodded. But the truth was, he was nervous. How *would* they get away? How could he convince his parents they needed to go to Sri Pada? It was a problem Vero needed to solve. But for now, he decided to rest his head against the window and sleep.

After a grueling eight-hour flight followed by a two-and-a-half-hour flight, the plane finally touched down on the outskirts of Colombo, Sri Lanka. Tack, Vero, and Clover walked through the airport like zombies, dragging their luggage behind them. As Vero nearly tripped over his own feet, he noticed his parents had a spring in their step. They also looked completely refreshed. Apparently, they'd slept well in business class.

"If you're up to it, we could go sightseeing later today after we check into the hotel," Dennis said.

"That sounds like fun," Nora answered, almost giddy.

"Sounds like agony," Clover said. "I need a bed. You didn't have Tack sleeping on your shoulder halfway around the world!"

Vero had woken up several times during the flights to discover that Tack's head had slipped onto Clover's shoulder. He found the sight to be touching. He secretly hoped that one day Tack and Clover could be a couple. It would be nice if, after he was gone, they had one another. Then Vero would feel a lot better about leaving them.

"Sorry, I didn't know," Tack told Clover. "But hey, at least I didn't drool on you."

"Wrong. My shirt was soaked." Clover shot him a look.

Tack winced. Vero smiled. He thought they sounded like an old married couple already.

"We'll let you kids sleep when we get to the hotel," Dennis said. "Colombo is only about a half hour ride from here."

A little while later, Vero stared out the window of the cab as it made its way through the streets of Colombo, Sri Lanka's capital. The city was busy, vibrant. People of a deep-brown complexion navigated their way through the wide, tree-lined streets. Vendors stood at small stalls selling their goods and foods—different seafood and fruits Vero had never seen before. As they rode, Dennis talked about the architecture of the buildings, which ranged from modern to colonial, as well as some of Buddhist and Hindu influence. The cab crossed over many canals, keeping speed with buses and tuk-tuks—three-wheeled, covered motorcycle-taxis. Despite the exhaustion, the foreign sights were riveting to him.

The car pulled up to the hotel. On the horizon, Vero saw nothing but blue—the Indian Ocean. As he stepped out of the cab, he noticed the air felt tropical and humid. The hotel was about eight stories tall. It was a colonial style, yet it appeared to be fairly new. Leafy trees and green grass adorned the grounds. Guests played tennis on a clay court. Beyond that, other guests sunned and swam in an elegant pool.

"This is the life," Tack said, taking in the sights.

"Let's get settled, take a nap, then we can explore," Dennis said as he gave the cab driver his fare.

In the two-bedroom suite, Tack, Vero, and Dennis shared a room, while Clover bunked with Nora. Their nap lasted longer than expected—in fact, it extended into the night, and Vero, Tack, and Clover didn't wake up until late the next morning. After a breakfast of egg hoppers—a crisp, edible bowl made from rice flour and coconut milk with a cooked egg in the middle—Tack was ready to hit the pool and beach.

"I say we stay by the pool all day, and order room service," Tack said to everyone.

Vero kicked him under the table. Tack looked over, not sure why he was kicked.

"I'd rather sightsee," Nora said, turning to Dennis. "Are you working today?"

"Yes, but that shouldn't stop you from hitting some of the sights."

"I want to go to Sri Pada," Vero said.

"Of course you do," Dennis answered. "But that's a few hours from here."

"But we all really want to go there," Vero pressed.

"Yeah, we do," Clover said. "Right, Tack?"

"Um, yeah."

"What exactly is Sri Prada?" Nora said.

"Sri *Pada*. It's also called Adam's Peak. The mountaintop is sacred to four of the world's major religions," Dennis explained, and told Nora about the footprint at the top and what it meant to Hindus, Buddhists, Muslims, and Christians. "It is supposed to be beautiful. In fact, that's the mountain Clover drew in her journal. The picture was stunning, by the way."

Clover blushed.

"There are stairs to the top of the mountain. They say the best time to climb is in the early morning so that when you get up there, you can catch the sunrise," Vero said.

"Sounds dangerous," Nora said, narrowing her eyes in maternal worry. "Wouldn't it be completely dark in the early morning?"

"No," Vero said. "The path is lit all the way up. They say it looks like lights that reach the sky."

"You wouldn't have to do your morning run," Clover added. "Just walking up those steps would be enough exercise for a few days."

"We'll see," Dennis said.

"'We'll see' means 'no,'" Clover said, shooting her parents a look.

"Not always," Dennis said.

"Yes, it does," Clover said. "Every kid knows that."

"And there's a wildlife preserve at the base of the mountain," Vero said. "With elephants."

"I do love elephants." Nora smiled.

"But there's so much to see around here," Dennis said. "And I don't think I could go. I am here to work, after all."

"Mom could take us," Vero said.

"I don't know, guys," Nora said. "It sounds a bit too adventurous. Plus, I don't have a guide or speak the language . . ."

"Vero?" a young male voice said, cutting off Nora.

Vero looked up. A complete look of shock came over him as he saw Kane standing before him.

15

LOCAL TOUR GUIDE

What are you doing here?" Vero asked Kane.

"I live here."

Then Vero remembered. When they had first met, Kane had said he was from an island in the Indian Ocean.

"You two know each other?" Dennis asked with a confused look.

"Um, yeah . . ." Vero stammered, shooting Kane a nervous look.

"We went to school together," Kane said, cool as a cucumber. "I was a student in a special student-exchange program."

Not exactly a lie, Vero thought. Although the exchange was from earth to the Ether. Vero noted that Kane spoke English with a different accent from the one he had in the Ether.

"That is so unbelievable! We're on the other side of the world and Vero runs into a classmate . . . What are the chances? But you look a little older than Vero," Nora said.

"I am, Ma'am. I wasn't in Vero's grade."

"I don't remember you from school," Tack said, with a furled brow.

Once again, Vero kicked Tack under the table. Tack looked to Vero, realizing he just said something he probably shouldn't have.

"That's because we didn't meet at school," Kane said. "But I remember you . . . We actually met at an arcade at the mall, but I don't think Vero introduced us."

Vero then remembered. When they were competing in the Angel Trials' final challenge, Vero and his fellow fledglings all wound up in an arcade at the mall by Vero's house. They had stumbled upon Tack there.

Tack squinted his eyes, thinking hard. "Oh, yeah, I do remember you now."

"This is Tack," Vero said to Kane.

"Hi," Kane said, shaking Tack's hand.

"And my mom, dad, and sister, Clover," Vero said as Kane shook hands with Dennis and Nora.

"So nice to meet you all!" Kane said with a winning smile.

"I still can't get over this . . . It's such a coincidence! Dennis, can you believe it?" Nora said.

Dennis looked a bit stunned himself, and Vero could tell he was considering how unlikely it would be to find someone you know so far from home. "It's almost unbelievable."

"Here in Sri Lanka, we say all things happen for a reason," Kane said to Dennis with a confident smile. "There is a quote written on the back of my tuk-tuk that reads 'Coincidence is God's way of remaining anonymous.'"

Dennis looked surprised to hear the quote. "Albert Einstein said that, and ironically, I was just thinking about that quote a few weeks ago as I was booking our tickets."

Clover gazed squarely at Kane. She looked as if she had recognized him. Kane nodded and smiled to her.

"So what are you doing in Sri Lanka?" Kane asked Vero.

"My dad's here on business for the World Bank, and we tagged along. We're all on Spring Break."

"Awesome," Kane said. "If you like, I could show you some of the sights, or at least point you in the right directions."

"Are you staying in this hotel?" Vero asked.

"No," Kane said. "I live in Colombo, but we're also off school for two weeks so I'm driving a tuk-tuk around to make some extra money. I just dropped someone off here."

Vero and Kane shared a glance. Vero was thinking about that quote and how appropriate it was . . . It was no coincidence Kane was at the hotel. Vero knew that his fledging friend was there to help him in his search for the Book of Raziel.

"What are you planning to do while you're here?" Kane asked.

"We want to go to Sri Pada," Clover said.

Kane shot Vero a suspicious look. Vero nodded.

"I can help make that happen!" Kane said. "My aunt does tours to Sri Pada."

"She does?" Vero practically shouted.

"Yeah. She'll take us," Kane said. "It's about a three-hour bus ride from here. She speaks English pretty well. I'm sure she'll let me go too."

"So can we, Dad?" Vero turned to Dennis.

"But it's like I said. I'm here on business, I really can't get away for an overnight excursion."

"I could go with them," Nora said.

Dennis looked at Nora, considering.

"We need to meet and talk with Kane's aunt first, of course. But if Kane and his aunt are willing to be our guides, it sounds like it could be a great—and safe—adventure," Nora said.

"You sure you want to do this?" Dennis asked Nora.

"The kids want to go on a religious pilgrimage—who am I to say no?" Nora threw up her hands.

"Okay," Dennis said.

"Thanks." Vero smiled.

Vero quickly spun around to Kane. "Can we go this afternoon?"

"Hey, relax a bit," Dennis said to Vero. "You just can't go tonight. I'd like to meet his aunt first. Got it?"

"Yeah." Vero nodded.

Dennis glanced at his watch and stood. "I need to leave. I have a meeting in a half hour." Dennis extended his hand to Kane. "Kane, just let us know how we can reach your aunt. Make sure Vero has your phone number."

"Will do."

Dennis grabbed his briefcase, kissed the top of Clover's head, then kissed Nora's cheek before walking out of the restaurant.

"I should move my tuk-tuk before it's stolen," Kane said. Then he turned to Vero. "If you walk out with me, I can give you one of my cards with all my info."

"Okay," Vero said, rising from his chair.

"It was nice meeting you, Kane," Nora said.

"Me too, Ma'am," Kane said. "I'll call my aunt later today and be in touch."

Kane nodded to Tack and Clover, then walked toward the lobby. Vero kept pace with him.

"So how did you know I was here?" Vero asked Kane when they were out of Nora's earshot.

"I didn't. I just had a really strong feeling that I needed to come here," Kane replied. "Had to be my Vox Dei."

"So you didn't know I would be here?"

"No clue."

Vero thought about that for a moment.

"You must be here because of the book?" Kane said. "Is it in Sri Pada?"

"I think so."

"Where?" Kane's eyes went wide.

"That I don't know."

"It's a pretty big place. You must have some idea?"

Vero shook his head. "But I got this far, so I have to just keep going," Vero said. "I'm sure something will lead me to it."

"Of course I'll go with you," Kane said.

"Do you really have an aunt who does tours, or were you just trying to help me out?" Vero asked.

"Yes, and I'll bring her by tomorrow to set everything up with your father," Kane said. "He'll love my aunt. She's great."

"Are you sure she can take us?" Vero was worried.

"She will."

Vero turned to Kane. "Do you ever feel helpless here on earth? I wish we could just fly there right now."

"I'm sure I'm the only one in this whole hotel who understands how you feel." Kane chuckled.

As they reached the tuk-tuk, Vero thought it looked like it would be fun to drive; the driver seat had motorcycle-style handle bars that steered the front tire, and there was a covered three-seat section behind the driver. The car was painted a fire-engine red, with lots of decals all over it—some in English and some in what Vero assumed was Sinhala. Written on the back of the tuk-tuk, just under the window, was the quote about coincidence. Kane reached into the glove compartment and pulled out a crumpled business card. He handed it to Vero.

"Here's my card. Call that number to reach me. I finally got a cell phone."

Vero nodded.

Waves gently broke upon the shore. The glistening, clear ocean water looked turquoise in color. Vero and Clover sat on lounge chairs on the fifth-story hotel balcony, hovered around a laptop. Tack stood leaning over the railing, looking down with longing at the sunbathers stretched out on the golden sands.

"Sure you don't want to go for a quick dip?" Tack asked, turning around.

"Later," Vero said without glancing up.

Tack sighed. "Have you figured anything out?"

"Not yet," Clover said. "Maybe we would, if you tried to help us."

"I say we go there and just wing it," Tack said.

"We're going to be there less than forty-eight hours," Clover said. "We can't just *wing* it."

"Does Kane have any ideas?" Tack asked. "He's a guardian too. He should know something."

"He doesn't know any more than what I do," Vero said.

Tack sat down with a huff, his chin in his hands.

"If you want something to do, I hid the sapphire somewhere in the two rooms. Go find it . . . Gotta keep practicing."

Tack jogged back inside the room, whistling cheerily. He was actually learning to like this game . . . He was so surprised and impressed every time he got it right, and with all the practice he'd been doing, he was getting noticeably better.

He walked over to the coffee table and picked up the TV remote. He ran his hand over it, then popped open the battery compartment and smiled.

A moment later, Tack emerged onto the balcony, with both hands extended in fists toward Clover. "Which hand?" Clover picked one, and Tack turned it over to reveal her small sapphire stone.

"Where was it?" Clover asked.

"Inside the TV remote's battery compartment," Vero answered, impressed.

Tack extended his other hand as if to introduce himself to Clover. "Hi, name's Tack the Magnificent, expert dowser."

Clover shook his hand, and playfully rolled her eyes at him. "You know, if the whole dowsing thing doesn't work out, you could make a serious living finding women's lost jewelry," she said, as if seeing Tack in a new light.

"That wouldn't be the first time for a Kozlowski," Tack said, handing the stone back to Vero.

"What do you mean?" Clover asked.

"Back in Poland, there was some rich couple who were getting divorced, so the husband hid his wife's jewelry. He buried it in the ground somewhere so she couldn't find it, thinking he could go dig it up for himself once they were divorced. But the wife hired my great-great-grandfather to locate her jewelry. She suspected her husband hid it somewhere on their property. Even though their land was about one hundred and twenty acres, my great-great-grandfather went right to it. He found the burial spot under a maple tree."

"That's impressive," Vero said.

"Yes, but it turned out the husband was a Polish crime boss. When he found out what happened, he tried to have my great-great-grandfather eliminated. And that, folks, is how the Kozlowskis came to America."

"Really?" Clover asked.

Vero shot him a perplexed look.

"Yeah, he had to flee from Poland."

"Oh," Vero said, finally understanding.

"Coming up with anything on the book or the garden of Eden?" Clover nodded to the computer.

"Nothing."

Clover pulled her journal from her backpack and opened it to her drawing of Sri Pada. "There's got to be something here that we're not seeing," Clover said, studying the image.

Tack looked over her shoulder.

"Your perspective is off. You've got a river running right through the side of a mountain," he said, pointing to it.

"I just draw what I see. I don't care about perspective," Clover huffed, annoyed. "How about you? Can you feel anything from the drawing?" Clover looked to Tack.

"No. But I still don't get why you drew the shadow of the mountain as a triangle," Tack said. "You really need to take an art class in perspective."

"No, that's real. Even though the mountain is shaped like a cone, it casts a perfect triangular shadow," Clover said. "And nobody knows why."

"Yeah, there are tons of images of it on the Internet. Tourists posting their photos," Vero said.

"Doesn't make sense," Tack said.

A mini-twister disturbed the still air. It instantly stopped spinning, and Uriel, Raziel, Raphael, and Gabriel—an impossibly beautiful female angel with shoulder-length, copper-colored hair—emerged from its center. They turned to Michael, who always looked intimidating. Well muscled and around ten feet tall, Michael also towered over the others. The angels stood on the edge of a desolate mountain in the part of the Ether that belonged to Lucifer. Rocks were all around them, as nothing green grew here. It resembled a desert after a nuclear bomb had exploded— dead beyond dead. Michael turned to the other archangels.

"I wanted all of you to see this. There is great commotion down below," Michael told the others, speaking mind to mind.

He nodded to the flat, barren wasteland below. The others followed his gaze and saw the land move as if there were waves beneath the surface. Though muffled, the shrieks and cries coming out of the dirt were almost deafening. An intermittent glow of red covered the rolling land, making it appear to be made of volcanic hot spots.

"How many do you think he will release?" Uriel asked Michael with concern.

Michael caught Uriel's eyes. "All of them."

Uriel's chin slumped to his chest.

"But Vero's only a fledgling," Raphael said.

"He's becoming more and more powerful," Uriel said. "He can summon now."

"Impressive," Gabriel said.

Raziel shook his head. Michael read his thoughts.

"No, Raziel, do not blame yourself," Michael said. "This is meant to be."

Raziel slowly nodded.

"We are to trust."

"I do trust," Raziel said.

"Then what is it?"

"I've resented the boy," Raziel said, his eyes down in apparent shame.

"Vero?" Gabriel asked.

"Yes. I lost the book. I should be the one who is in danger. What I did a long time ago has put Vero in harm's way . . . I allowed myself to be fooled by Solomon when he switched the gem in his ring and sent the book away. I should be the one to correct my mistake."

"As I would like to correct mine," Uriel said, recalling his lack of judgment that allowed the serpent into the garden. "But He has forgiven us."

"This is a chance to make things right," Raphael said.

"Which is why we must do everything we can to ensure Vero does not fail," Michael said. "Because there will not be another chance."

A pit formed in Raziel's gut as his eyes drifted out to the land below. The red, glowing ground was seething—it was only a matter of time before it would burst open.

16

CHIKO

Vero shoved several bottles of purified water into his backpack and zipped it shut. Tack was busy with his backpack as well.

"That reminds me," Tack said as he grabbed a box of Ding Dongs from his suitcase on top of the bed.

"How many of those did you bring?" Vero asked.

"Just one box for each day."

Tack shoved the entire box into his backpack and zipped it just as Clover stuck her head into the bedroom.

"The bus is out front," she announced. "You guys ready?" Clover looked over and saw the other box in Tack's suitcase. "Really?"

"Yes, Clover, Ding Dongs," Tack said, very dramatically. "For your information, the heavenly chocolate cake and exterior glaze shell both contain cocoa, which scientists have proven greatly enhances concentration and mental abilities, and the divinely creamy center contains vanilla bean extract—a fragrant spice used by Zen masters for thousands of years for its nerve calming effects and promotion of an overall feeling of relaxation. It's no exaggeration at all to say that Ding Dongs are the greatest performance-enhancing snack ever known to mankind," Tack picked up his backpack in a lofty manner for effect. "Don't mock that which you do not understand." He then purposefully walked past her into the main room.

Vero rolled his eyes at Tack's performance, as Clover laughed at the speech. "I guess that explains why I don't need them . . . I'm cool as a cucumber," she said.

"Let's go," Vero said, slinging his backpack over his shoulder as he walked out of the small bedroom. "And Clover, don't forget to bring your drawing."

"Don't need it," Clover said. "I've committed every detail to memory."

"Really?"

"Yeah."

"Okay," Vero said as he held the door open to the hallway. Tack walked out. Clover hesitated.

"Go ahead, I'll be down in a minute," she said to Vero. "I forgot something."

"I'll wait, get it."

"No, you go. Mom and Dad will get worried wondering where we are," Clover said.

Vero walked out and closed the door after him. Once he was gone, Clover walked over to Tack's open suitcase and pulled out a plastic-wrapped Ding Dong. Her hand shook as she unwrapped it and shoved the whole chocolate cake into her mouth. When she was done, she grabbed another and then walked into the main room, unwrapping it. The door opened. Clover panicked, but it was too late. She was busted.

Tack stood in front of her, grinning ear to ear. "I think this could be the start of something beautiful."

The bus was about half the size of a regular school bus. It was green and pretty old, with lots of rusted metal spots. Vero saw his mother looking at their transportation with a look of disappointment and doubt as they stood under the hotel porte cochere.

"I'm not so sure it's even going to make it out of the driveway," Nora said while staring at the bus.

"Yes, it will be good," a woman said with a strong Sri Lankan accent. "It ees only fort-ee years old," she said playfully. "For Sri Lanka, it just broken in."

Nora turned and focused on Kane and his aunt, who'd introduced herself as Adrik. She was a tall woman with tanned skin, and short, dark, spiky hair. If Vero had to guess, he'd say she looked about sixty.

"Oh, Adrik, hello," Nora said.

Nora and Dennis had met Adrik the day before, when Kane had brought his aunt to the hotel to introduce her and to work out all the arrangements for the journey. They were taking a bus to Dalhousie, the access town to Sri Pada. According to Adrik, it would be about a four-and-a-half-hour drive. They were scheduled to arrive around two in the afternoon, check into the hotel there, and begin the climb late that night along with the other pilgrims. That way, they'd be able to observe the breathtaking sunrise as well as watch the shadow of the mountain form on the distant horizon and then recede back across the plains below.

"Now that you all are going, I'm a bit jealous," Dennis said.

"It's only one night," Nora said as she hugged her husband. "We'll be back before you know it."

Dennis hugged his children, then Tack. After saying their good-byes, the bus driver—a short, stubby man with a thick, full beard—opened the door, and they stepped onto the vehicle.

About an hour into the ride, Tack and Clover had fallen asleep. Apparently the travel and time change had taken a toll. Both were sprawled out across a bus seat. Vero wondered how they could get comfortable enough to nap, because springs were pushing up through his seat, and the antiquated bus seemed to hit every pothole along the way. Kane was listening to music on his earphones, and Nora and Adrik were sitting two rows up, talking.

"Kane loved lee-ving in Washington . . ." Adrik was saying.

This snippet of conversation caught Vero's attention. He leaned forward to listen.

"I wanted to vee-sit him," Adrik said. "But he was there so short a time."

Vero knit his brow in confusion. Kane was never an exchange student in Washington, D.C. Why was his aunt lying for him? *It's bad enough when a kid lies, but an adult?* But then Vero wondered if Adrik was like Clover. Had Kane confided his real identity to her? Maybe Adrik knew Kane was a guardian, and she was helping him out. It was unclear to Vero, but he decided all that really mattered was that he would be in Sri Pada in a few short hours, as unbelievable as that seemed. He rested his head against the window and tried to get some rest as well. He watched the green landscape pass by—palm trees, banana plantations, and rice paddies. And despite the cushion springs pushing against his bottom, he soon fell asleep.

"We're here," Tack said while shaking Vero's shoulder. "Ew, gross, man! Hey, guys, look! Vero drooled all over the window!"

Vero opened his eyes. Spit dribbled down his chin. He quickly wiped it with his sleeve.

"I must be jetlagged too," Vero said.

"We here!" Adrik yelled. "Don't forget your bags!"

Vero reached down below the seat and pulled out his backpack. He stood and walked down the aisle, stopping to let his mother out first.

"You have a good nap?" Nora asked Vero.

"Somehow, I guess." Vero rubbed his backside.

"Good. You needed it. You have dark circles under your eyes."

Vero stepped off the bus. The first thing that hit him was the mist. He felt as if he was smacked in the face with a blast of cold, wet air. He looked around. The bus had stopped in the central square of the town. Before him were rows of shoddy wooden booths with people hanging their goods for sale. Peddlers were busy selling snacks, flashlights, warm clothing, hiking boots, and bottles of water and soda to pilgrims. He also noticed the main street was paved with asphalt, but side streets were dusty, hard-packed earth. A river ran alongside the town and beyond that, dense forest stretched forward.

As Vero's eyes drifted high above the town, he saw the mountain's summit—Adam's Peak. From a distance, it looked as if a walled castle sat on top of a sheer mountain, with nothing but jungle directly below. But Vero knew it wasn't a castle—it was a Buddhist temple. He was where he needed to be to find the Book of Raziel, yet, as he looked at the vast landscape, his heart sunk. He had no idea where to even begin the search. Just as he was about to groan in desolation, Vero felt a hand on his shoulder, jarring him from his thoughts.

"My aunt says we need to check into the hotel," Kane said.

Vero nodded. He followed the others as they walked through the town. It was crowded with locals and pilgrims. Vero saw the travelers were from many different backgrounds—from obvious Westerners in jeans and shorts to Buddhist monks with shaved heads in orange robes.

The hotel was about a half a mile walk off the main street, and appeared to be made up of charming cottages surrounded by eucalyptus trees on the edge of endless tea plantations. The soothing sound of rambling water only enhanced the tranquil setting.

"You'll be in one cottage, and my aunt and I will be in the one next door," Kane said as he held open the cottage door for Nora.

"Where is Adrik?" Nora asked, stepping into the cottage.

"She went to check on dinner for tonight."

Tack, Clover, Vero, and Kane followed Nora into the cottage. It was a quaint room with bamboo floors and a terrace that overlooked a green lush courtyard. Two beds sat in the middle of the room, enclosed with mosquito nets.

"They must have some killer bugs here," Tack noted as he touched the fine white mesh over one bed.

"Yeah, but I'll deal with the mosquitoes any day over the leeches." Kane chuckled.

"Leeches?" Clover said, her face white.

"Be sure to wear long sleeves and long pants when we hike up the path," Kane said. "You can get leeches just by brushing up against leaves."

"Noted," Clover said, and swallowed hard.

"Here's what we're going to do," Nora said, placing her backpack on the bed. "We'll take a nap—"

"But we just did on the bus," Tack interrupted.

"You could use another." Nora eyed Tack. "Then we will have a late dinner and begin our ascent around eleven o' clock."

"I agree with Tack," Clover said. "I'm not tired."

"Guys, it's a four-hour hike up 5,200 stairs to the summit. I don't want you pooping out halfway up," Nora said.

A worried look came over Tack. "That reminds me. Are there bathrooms on the climb?"

"Yes," Kane answered. "But I can't promise toilet paper."

"I'll bring a roll in my backpack," Clover said.

"And hand sanitizer," Nora added.

Vero drew the curtains, shrouding the room in darkness.

"I guess that means we're taking a nap," Tack said.

"I'm tired," Vero said.

"Then I'll see you in a few," Kane said as he stepped out, shutting the door behind him.

As Vero lay in the bed, the fine mosquito net swaying in the wind reminded him of graceful angel wings, and his mind was racing. He couldn't sleep. How was he going to do this? He had come so far, all the way to the other side of the world, yet he still had no idea how to find the book. What if it wasn't in Sri Pada at all?

Vero sat up. He saw Tack zonked out next to him. In the other bed, his mother slept soundly with Clover. He was jealous of their peaceful minds. He longed to be able to turn off his brain and relax, but it wasn't happening.

Vero swung the mosquito netting aside and stood. He put on his sneakers and walked out the door. The sun wasn't nearly as bright as it had been when they had arrived in the village—he realized it would soon be dusk. Vero strolled to a meandering river. The region was so fertile—clotted, dewy plants and shrubs clung to the gently sloping hills. It was so verdant and picturesque that, for a moment, he thought he was back in the Ether.

As Vero made his way through the greenery, he saw a cluster of large boulders nestled at the edge of the river and headed toward them. As he got closer, he saw someone sitting on one of the largest boulders, facing the water. It was a boy who, based on size, looked to be about eight or nine years old. When the kid turned his face in Vero's direction, Vero saw that his head was completely shaved, and that he wore a saffron robe with a yellow sash tied across his waist. The boy was sitting in the lotus position with his legs crossed and his palms turned upward.

"Oh, sorry . . ." Vero said as he backed away.

"It's okay," the boy said.

"Hey, you speak English," Vero said.

The boy nodded. "My grandmother went to English schools in India and taught it to me."

"You were meditating?" Vero asked.

"Yes, I'm getting much better at it."

"Are you really a monk? I mean, how old are you?"

"I'm only nine. I'm not yet a monk."

"So how does that work?" Vero asked, sitting down on the adjacent boulder. "Aren't you kind of young to make a decision like that?"

"Are you too young to be an angel?"

Vero's eyes went wide, suddenly alarmed. "What are you talking about? Who told you that?"

"No one told me. I saw it when I was meditating. I'm Chiko. It means 'light of wisdom.'" Chiko bowed his head to Vero.

"I'm Vero . . . um . . ." Vero stammered.

"Truth. Latin for truth." Chiko smiled.

"Really?"

"Yes."

"You're pretty smart for a little kid," Vero said.

"I'm on the road to enlightenment, but I'm not there yet. I have many years of life at the monastery before that moment happens."

"You live in a monastery, away from your parents?" Vero felt troubled at the thought.

"Since I was seven. I haven't seen them since."

"Don't you miss them?"

"Every day it gets easier, but this is who I am now. I cannot change that any more than you can change who you are."

Vero took in those words for a moment then nodded, while his eyes drifted to the monastery at the top of the mountain. "Is that where you live?"

"No, my monastery is far away. We are here on a pilgrimage."

"Have you been to the top?" Vero excitedly asked.

"Yesterday, and I am going back again tonight."

"It's so beautiful here. Some people think that the garden of Eden was near Sri Prada," Vero said. "Have you ever heard that before?"

Chiko's head bobbed once.

"Then is it true?"

Chiko shrugged. "I don't know."

"Thought I'd give it a shot." Vero sighed. "Because I really have nothing to go on. I'm hoping to find it."

"But you do have the information you need," Chiko said.

Vero looked to him.

"Meditation brings wisdom," Chiko said. "The masters tell us that."

A lightbulb went off for Vero. His face lit up as he thought about his Vox Dei. The archangels had taught Vero that whenever he reached a crossroad, he should train his mind to listen for his Vox Dei—God's voice. And it was true. In times of uncertainty, his Vox Dei would always be there for him. It was just tricky to clear his mind of other thoughts so he could hear what God wanted to say. Vero thought that if he learned to meditate, he might hear his Vox Dei more clearly.

"Can you teach me to meditate the way you do?" Vero asked. "Sometimes I can concentrate, but not always. I need to get better at it."

"For starters, it helps to be in a comfortable position," Chiko said.

Vero crossed his legs like Chiko.

"This position is comfortable for me, but if it's not for you, find a different one," Chiko said. "Some people like to kneel, or I've seen some monks do it while standing or walking."

"I'll try your position for now," Vero said, straightening his back and laying his forearms onto his thighs with his palms facing up.

"Close your eyes," Chiko said. "When you exhale, count your breaths. Concentrate on it entering and leaving you. Breath is the absolute essence of life."

Vero closed his eyes.

"You will become distracted by the sounds that surround you, and the thoughts within. Acknowledge them, but do not attach yourself to them. Let them roll off you. There are many obstacles to concentration—hatred, anger, laziness, worry—but the worst is . . . doubt."

Vero opened his eyes and looked at Chiko. The boy was right. Doubt was something he had always struggled with. Even though he had many moments of unwavering faith in God, eventually doubt always seemed to creep back into his mind. But Vero was determined that he would erase doubt forever from his mind.

"But, Chiko, how do the masters tell you to clear your mind?"

Chiko did not respond. He was staring straight ahead as if he was in some sort of trance. Vero then realized that he was meditating with his eyes open. This little kid didn't even need to shut his eyes for concentration! A pang of jealousy shot through Vero. He closed his eyes and tried to concentrate. But he heard the splish-splash of the water as it rushed over rocks and twigs. The distant sounds of car engines distracted him. The chatter of a flock of wild parrots rang in his ear. Every little sound seemed amplified. But when something landed on his nose, he had had enough! Vero's eyes shot open as he swatted a bee from his face.

He looked over at Chiko, who was still meditating with his eyes wide open. Vero watched as the bee landed on Chiko's arm. Vero raised his hand to swat it away, but then lowered his arm. He watched, fascinated, as Chiko did not stir even with a bee on his arm. *What amazing concentration*, Vero thought. After a few moments, Chiko turned to Vero.

"Why did you give up?"

"I had a bee about to sting me!" Vero yelled. "So did you, on your arm."

Chiko turned his arm—there was a throbbing, red welt.

"I guess it stung me," Chiko said.

"How can a bee sting you, and you don't even flinch?" Vero shouted with frustration.

"It wasn't always like this," Chiko said, smiling. "When I first started to meditate, I once got so distracted by a butterfly that I ran off to chase it."

"So how did you overcome the distraction?"

"One day, when the masters were ready to give up on me, I watched a monk walk barefoot across hot, burning coals. Afterward, his feet were not even burned."

"Yeah, I've heard of fire walking."

"I talked to the monk later and asked him how he was able to do that," Chiko said. "And you know what he told me?"

Vero shook his head.

"He said, 'Before I start my way across the hot embers, I do not think that I can get burned. Rather, I think that I have already successfully made it across . . . Where the mind leads, the body follows."

Vero took that in for a moment.

"Maybe you should think about that the next time you try," Chiko said, standing up. "Good-bye, Vero."

Chiko extended his hand to Vero, who shook it. "I will send many good thoughts your way as you continue on your quest."

17

❖

ASCENT INTO
THE NIGHT

After Vero said good-bye to Chiko, he walked back to the bungalow and fell asleep. His encounter with the boy gave him a renewed sense of peace, enabling him to finally relax and get a few hours of shut-eye. The next thing Vero remembered was Tack standing over him, shaking him awake for the second time that day.

"Dude, it's time to get up," Tack said. "Your mom and Clover went with Kane and Adrik to get food."

Vero looked out the window. It was dark outside.

"What time is it?" Vero asked, rubbing his eyes.

"Nine at night," Tack answered. "After we eat, we start the climb."

Vero looked closely at Tack. "Are you ready?"

"Yeah, I packed my backpack."

Vero shook his head. He gazed at Tack, refusing to look away. "I mean, are you really ready?" Vero asked with the utmost seriousness.

Tack held Vero's intense stare then nodded a moment later. "I am."

Clover and Nora walked into the bungalow carrying several Styrofoam boxes of food.

"Dinner's here!" Clover announced as she placed the food on the bamboo desk in the corner.

"Lots of rice to keep us full," Nora said, opening a box. "We also bought protein bars and bottled waters."

Vero sat up. "Thanks. Where are Kane and Adrik?"

"We're to meet them outside as soon as we're finished," Nora said. "I still can't believe the coincidence. What are the odds that you run into a kid you know in Sri Lanka?"

Tack, Vero, and Clover all exchanged secret glances.

"Yeah, what are the odds?" Vero said with a forced smile.

Despite the darkness and the late hour, the town center of Sri Pada was bustling with activity. Storefronts lit up the streets as people ranging from old men in traditional flowing sarongs and sandals to teenagers in jeans and T-shirts hustled to and fro, making last-minute preparations before their ascent up the seemingly endless mountain. Vero stood on a dusty street looking up at the mountaintop. The five thousand stone steps were illuminated by electric lights, creating a glowing line that spiraled around the mountain until it reached to the summit. The lights seemed to reach heaven itself. Kane put his hand on Vero's shoulder as he too looked upward.

"It's beautiful, isn't it?" Kane asked Vero.

"Yeah, it's hard to believe from down here that I'll ever make it all the way to the top."

"It does seem a long way away," Kane said. "But look . . ." Kane nodded in the direction of an elderly man wearing a sarong. "If he can do it, then so can we."

Vero nodded, noting that the man wasn't even wearing shoes or sandals. He was going to climb the mountain barefoot!

Adrik walked over flanked by Nora, Clover, and Tack.

"It is time to begin," Adrik told the group.

"Does everyone have their backpack?" Nora asked.

"I do," Tack answered, slinging his backpack onto his shoulder. "Although it feels kind of heavy."

"It's the bottled waters," Nora answered. "As you drink them, your load will get lighter." Nora turned to Clover and Vero. "You two have yours?"

Each nodded.

"Okay, follow me," Adrik said as she turned and wove her way through the village center.

Adrik walked briskly, and the others had to quicken their pace to keep up with her. They dodged cars, buses, and other pilgrims on their way. Vero nearly lost sight of Adrik in the crowd.

"Can you tell your aunt to slow down?" Vero said to Kane.

"She wants to beat the crowds—that's why we're starting so early," Kane said. "She prefers to climb when the stairs aren't packed with pilgrims."

Vero's eyes stayed on Adrik, who stepped over a muddy puddle. Then she disappeared from sight after turning the corner of a hotel building. Vero looked over at his mother, who had a panicked look on her face as she scanned the area for Adrik. Vero's eyes went wide with horror—an ox-drawn cart was careening toward his mother, who was oblivious.

"Mom! Stop!" Vero yelled at the top of his lungs.

The ox cart did not slow down, and soon plowed through the intersection. Nora was on the other side of it, and Vero lost sight of her. He held his breath, silently praying she was okay. As the ox cart moved past, it revealed Nora stood unharmed in the intersection. Vero felt his chest loosen as he began to breathe again. He ran over to his mother.

"I was so focused on Adrik that I wasn't watching where I was going," Nora said, dazed.

Vero took her arm and walked her to the side of the street, right in front of a wooden stand selling trinkets. Kane, Clover, and Tack were already waiting there. Pale and shaken, Clover hugged her mother.

"I'm fine," Nora said. "Thank God Vero yelled at the last second."

Adrik walked over to them. She had a look of concern on her face.

"Is everything okay?" she asked. "Why you no follow?"

"Because you're walking too fast and we can't keep up!" Kane yelled at her.

"Why no tell me?" Adrik said.

"You were too far ahead to hear us," Vero said with a razor edge to his tone.

"Boys, stop, everything's fine," Nora said. "Besides, this is no way to start a pilgrimage."

"I am most sorry." Adrik smiled, bowing her head. "I will slow down."

Nora bowed in return. Vero noticed that Adrik's smile quickly faded, leaving him with the feeling that he needed to keep his mother close.

They made their way across a narrow bridge with a slow-moving river below. On the other side Vero saw a forty-foot-long statue of a Buddhist woman in a maroon robe, lying on her side. On second glance, maybe it was a man? He shone his flashlight at the face for closer inspection, but he still couldn't decide one way or the other. About twenty feet away from the statue, a stone arch marked the base of the stairs—the entrance gate. Vero looked closer at the arch. It was made completely of stone, yet the top was highly ornamental. Carved into it was an image of a man in prayer flanked by two elephants on either side. Their trunks formed a heart-like image over the man. On top of that was a carved face of a creature that Vero did not recognize. It had large, round bug eyes and a row of long top teeth that appeared to be smiling. Vero thought it was some kind of mythological animal.

Vero heard a British accent, and discovered it belonged to a couple in their early thirties. They were taking a selfie while standing under the arch. Only a handful of other pilgrims began the climb.

"Where is everybody?" Tack asked. "I thought the climb was supposed to be crowded."

"Most begin at two in the morning," Adrik said. "I like to climb now before too crowded."

"So what was the rush?" Vero said in a low voice to Tack, who shrugged.

Nora looked up the trail of stairs. Dim lights lit the path in a shroud of mystery. Nora looked disappointed.

"I was hoping for more light," Nora told Adrik.

"More light the higher the climb," she answered. "You weel see."

"Good thing we brought plenty of flashlights and batteries," Nora said as she stepped upon the first wide step. She turned back to the others and smiled. "Let's do it!"

Readjusting their backpacks, the group climbed upon the concrete stairs. A two-foot stone wall edged the stairs on both sides. The path was sheathed in a white mist as if the night fog was claiming its hold on the mountain.

"One," Clover said as she stepped on the first step. "Two," she said with her foot on the next one. "Three," she continued. "Four . . ."

"Are you going to do that the whole way up?" Vero asked, already irritated.

"Thought it might make the climb more interesting if we kept track of our steps," she answered.

"Well, count them in your head," Vero said.

Adrik took the lead with Nora keeping pace directly behind her. Vero walked slightly behind his mother.

"Is anybody else ready for a break?" Tack asked, out of breath.

"We just started!" Clover shouted at him.

"I should have brought my iPod." Tack sighed.

"Guys, you've got to keep it down. Walking up these stairs is supposed to be a religious experience," Kane scolded.

The stairs grew steeper and narrower as the path twisted around a dense clump of trees. The small retaining wall that flanked the path had crumbled on one side, which Kane explained was from years of encroaching tree roots.

"Careful through this stretch," Adrik told the group.

The overhead lights flickered. Vero looked around nervously when, suddenly, the trail was plunged into darkness. An earsplitting shriek split the night air. Vero instantly knew the voice.

"Mom!" he yelled.

Vero shone his flashlight in the direction of the scream, but Nora was gone. The crackling sounds of splintering bramble filled Vero with dread. He raced to the edge and peered over, searching with the flashlight. The others raced over to Vero, crowding around him, their eyes following the beam.

"There she is!" Tack pointed.

The shaft of light illuminated Nora, who was lying on her side about thirty feet below them. Her eyes squinted from the bright glare.

"Mom, are you all right?" Vero shouted.

Before Nora could answer, Adrik jumped down off the stairs. Swatting tree branches out of her face, she beelined straight for Nora. Vero followed, climbing over rocks and fallen tree trunks to reach his mother.

"Mom!" Vero yelled. "Are you okay?"

"My ankle! I really hurt my ankle," Nora answered, grimacing in pain.

Adrik reached Nora and placed her hands on her ankle, examining it. Nora winced at the touch. Vero knelt beside his mother. He saw her face was scratched and dirtied.

"Maybe broken," Adrik said.

"Is it only your ankle?" Vero asked.

"Yes," Nora said, sitting up while holding her leg.

"Can you walk out of here?"

"We help," Adrik said. "Grab under arm," she told Vero.

Vero and Adrik hoisted Nora to her feet. Vero's mom tried to put a little pressure on her left foot, but wasn't able to.

"I can't do it," Nora said.

"Lean on us," Vero told her.

Adrik and Vero walked Nora back up the hillside. With one hand, he clasped his mother, while the other held the flashlight and lit the way. When they reached the steps, Kane and Tack jumped down and lifted Nora onto the stairs. Vero noticed the trail's lights had turned back on.

Nora sat on a step, her leg straight out in front of her. "I'm sorry, guys, but I can't go on."

Clover bit her lip while anxiously glancing at Vero.

"We have to take her back to the room," Vero said. "And find a doctor."

"Agree," Adrik said.

"How did you fall?" Clover asked.

"When the lights failed, I must have misstepped and lost my balance," Nora said.

"You don't sound so sure," Clover said.

Nora had a puzzled look on her face, as if she was lost in thought.

"What?" Vero asked.

"It's crazy, but it almost felt as if I was pushed."

Vero's eyes narrowed at Adrik.

18

BRIDGE IN THE SKY

"But I . . . *we* . . . have to go," Vero pleaded to his mother as she lay in bed inside their bungalow, her foot propped up on pillows. "We've come so far, and it's the chance of a lifetime."

"Sorry, but I'm not comfortable sending all of you . . ." Nora said as she looked to Clover and Tack, who sat on the bottom of the bed. "Without me."

"But we'll be okay," Clover said. "It really wasn't that tough a climb. We're just walking up a really big set of stairs."

"Yeah," Tack said. "I saw old people doing it barefoot."

"Just because you fell doesn't mean we will," Vero said. "And besides, the doctor said it's only a sprain. You can sleep and we'll be back by the time you wake up."

Nora shook her head. There was a knock on the door, then Kane walked in with Adrik. She was carrying a bag of ice.

"How you feel?" Adrik asked as she placed the ice on Nora's foot.

"Better, thank you," Nora answered as she sat up and repositioned the ice bag.

Adrik turned to the kids. "Ready to go?"

"Mom won't let us," Vero said.

"Ah, no," Adrik said. "We must go to top."

"Me lying here changes things," Nora said.

"I take good care of them," Adrik said to Nora.

Vero looked to Adrik, doubting her sincerity. He didn't trust something about her, but she was his ticket to the mountain. There was no way his mother would allow him to climb it without Adrik.

"It's a shame to come all this way and not climb it," Kane said.

"I know, but . . ." Nora said.

"Mom, I have to climb that mountain," Vero said forcefully, looking into his mother's eyes with conviction.

Nora looked taken aback. She held Vero's gaze for a few moments, then slowly nodded.

"We'll be all right," Vero said to her.

"Now I really wish we had let you bring your cell phones," Nora said, sadly.

"They no work here anyway. But not to worr-ee. I take good care of the children." Adrik smiled to Vero.

⬩❖⬩

The path was more crowded than it had been when they had first started climbing with Nora. They had lost a few hours while taking Nora back down the mountain, and then waiting for the doctor; it was now nearly two in the morning, and most pilgrims had begun their ascent. Despite the path being well lit, Vero and Tack had put on headband flashlights. They would be ready should the lights unexpectedly go out again.

Kane, Adrik, and Clover climbed a few steps ahead of Vero and Tack. Vero's legs burned as he climbed. Oh, how he wished he could fly to the top! Vero looked over to Tack, who seemed exhausted. Sweat dripped down Tack's forehead over his headband. A Sri Lankan man giving his young son a piggyback easily climbed past them.

"Really?" Tack said as he watched the father and son begin to fade from view. "Why doesn't he just climb two at a time?"

Then Tack watched as the man climbed two steps at once.

"Show off . . ." Tack groaned.

"Are you feeling anything?" Vero said in a low voice to Tack.

"Yes. Pain."

"I mean which way to go."

Tack nodded. "Higher."

After climbing another twenty minutes, they reached a tea stall. The group took off their backpacks and sat on a bench while Adrik brought them cups of hot tea to help defend themselves against the frigid night air. The black tea tasted harsh without sugar, but Vero was grateful for its warmth. They relaxed for a few minutes. Clover moved to sit down next to Vero.

"Anything?" she asked in a low voice.

"Not yet."

Tack suddenly stood. Vero watched as he walked from the bench onto a dirt path. Vero could tell that his friend had picked up on something. Tack turned on his headlamp as he walked farther into the brush. Vero got up and followed him.

"Where they go?" Adrik asked.

"I think nature calls," Clover quickly answered.

Vero followed Tack for a few minutes, until Tack abruptly stopped and spun around.

"It's this way."

"Are you sure?"

"Yes. I think so."

"How far away?"

"I don't know," Tack said, his eyes fixed in the distance. "But it's far enough away that Adrik will never let us go there."

"We have to ditch her," Vero said.

"Ditch who?"

Vero and Tack turned and saw Kane walking up to them, his flashlight beaming.

"We need to go this way," Vero told Kane. "We're sure of it."

"So we need to ditch my aunt?" Kane asked.

"Yeah, though we're worried she'll never let us leave the pathway," Vero said.

"So let's just go now," Kane said.

"We need Clover," Vero said.

"Then let's climb a little higher, let my aunt take the lead, and we'll duck out when we can," Kane said.

"Okay," Vero said, nodding. "I'll clue Clover in."

The group climbed for a few minutes longer with Adrik ahead of them all. The path was now teeming with pilgrims, as the sun would rise in less than three hours. The large crowd seemed like another divine coincidence, as it made sneaking away much easier than if they'd followed Adrik's original departure schedule.

Vero eyed Kane; he could not wait any longer. Kane dipped his head in agreement. It was time. Vero threw his arm out in front of Clover and Tack, stopping them. He waved his head to the right. Tack and Clover nodded back in understanding. All four let a group of pilgrims pass and then slipped behind a wooden food stand. Vero peered out from the stand; Adrik was lost in the sea of travelers. He did not see her anywhere.

"Let's go," Vero whispered. "Tack, lead."

Tack turned on his headlamp. "Stay close behind."

Tack took them through a forest so dense that even the moon's silvery rays could not penetrate the canopy above. Although they all had either flashlights or headlamps, it was of little comfort in the utter blackness. Every crunch of a twig or dead leaves underfoot echoed forebodingly into the thick night air. Clover suddenly stopped.

"I just remembered something," she said with fear etched across her face.

"What?" Kane asked.

"Leeches," Clover said to Kane. "You said they're all over these woods."

"Yeah, but you're wearing long pants and a long shirt. If you get any, they'll only stick to your clothes."

"And that's supposed to make me feel better?" Clover said.

Kane shrugged.

"Tack, how much longer?" Clover asked.

"It's a ways still."

"Are you still convinced it's a blue sapphire?" Kane asked Vero.

"Yeah, that's what Rahab said." Vero noted the discouraged look on Kane's face. "What?"

"This mountain is supposedly loaded with sapphires. Sri Pada and some of the surrounding peaks are considered one of the richest gem-mining areas in the world—and not just for sapphires, but rubies, emeralds, and topaz too." A puzzled look came over Kane as he just put two and two together. "Now that I think of it, they say that the footprint is actually a blue sapphire."

"What do you mean?" Vero asked.

"The rock footprint at the top, the one you can see, isn't the real one."

"What?" Clover looked outraged.

"The real footprint, the sacred one, is actually protected underneath it. And supposedly, the sacred footprint is imprinted on a large sapphire."

"You don't think that's the Book of Raziel, do you?" Clover asked.

"I hope not," Kane said. "The visible footprint is always under the careful guard of the monks."

Vero's heart sunk. He'd never be able to get to it.

"That may be," Tack said. "But I'm feeling that it's this way," he said, pointing straight ahead.

"Doesn't sound right." Kane's voice was hesitant.

"I know what I'm doing," Tack said, unwavering.

Vero looked from Kane to Tack as he tried to decide.

"We follow Tack," Vero said.

Kane nodded.

As they made their way through the woods, Clover yelled. She thrashed around, entangled in something. The others shined their lights on her. Clover had walked right into a tree heavy with moss.

"Clover, chillax, it's only moss," Tack said.

"Sure? 'Cause it felt like a giant spiderweb," she said as she pulled a chunk of green moss from her hair and flung it to the ground.

"You gotta toughen up, because we're not there yet," Tack scolded Clover.

As if on cue, Tack began to scream at the top of *his* lungs. A face appeared before him in the trees. It was ugly, with deep-set eyes, a pink, wrinkled snout, and a whorl of hair on its head.

Kane put his hand on Tack's shoulder. "Dude, it's a monkey."

Tack stopped screaming.

"They're all over Sri Lanka."

Clover grabbed Tack's arm and dug her nails into him. "Where there's one, there are more," she said.

The monkey ran back up high into the tree.

"They won't bother us if we stay out of their way," Kane said. "Just keep your knapsacks on your backs or else they'll steal 'em!"

As Tack continued walking, Clover held on to the back of Tack's shirt. They walked a few feet ahead, until Clover pulled Tack toward her. "Look where you're going, bozo!" she yelled, reminding Vero of Greer. How he wished Greer could be here right now to toughen everyone up, himself included.

Tack looked below. They were standing on the edge of a steep cliff.

"Thanks for the heads up." Tack nervously smiled to Clover.

"Be careful," Clover chided him.

"Now which way?" Vero asked.

"Same direction—straight ahead," Tack said.

Vero shined his light out in front of them. On the other side of the deep ravine below stood another steep cliff, about a hundred yards away.

"We need to get over there." Tack pointed.

"It'll take forever to climb all the way down and up the other side," Kane said.

"Not to mention dangerous," Clover added.

"Looks like it's our lucky day," Vero said as he illuminated a rope suspension bridge to their left that stretched high above the ravine below.

Kane walked over to the bridge. Wooden planks lined the floor of the bridge while rope railings on either side supported it. Kane tapped his foot on the first wooden plank, testing it.

"Is it sturdy?" Vero asked.

"Could probably hold us," Kane said.

"I'll go across first," Vero said. "If I make it, then you guys follow me."

"Sure you can't fly us across?" Tack asked.

"Do you think I would have walked up all those stairs if I could fly?" Vero answered, feeling aggravated.

Vero stepped onto the bridge, holding tightly to the rope. The raging river sounded below, and his headlamp caught a glint of the water. Vero realized he was already more than halfway across.

Clover turned to Tack. "Somehow, I don't think this is what my mom had in mind when she agreed to let us come here."

Tack sighed, nodding.

Suddenly, there was a loud crack. Vero's foot had broken through a wooden plank.

"Vero!" Clover screamed.

Never letting go of the ropes, Vero managed to regain his balance.

"I got it!" Vero shouted.

"Come back!" Clover shouted. "It's not safe!"

Vero didn't answer. He walked ahead, his foot testing each plank before he placed his weight upon it. Finally, he made it across to the other side. He waved to the others.

"It's okay, you just have to be careful where you step! There are a few planks missing," Vero shouted across the ravine. "Better go one at a time. Don't want to put too much weight on it!"

"I'll take your backpacks across for you," Kane said. "It'll make it easier."

"You have your own to deal with," Clover said.

"I can handle them," Kane said, his hand outstretched.

"Thanks," Tack said as he took his backpack off and tossed it to Kane.

Clover also handed Kane her pack. Kane held one and strapped the other to his chest. He grabbed the rope rails and stepped onto the bridge. Vero watched from the other cliff as Kane easily traversed the bridge.

"Ladies first," Tack said to Clover.

Clover placed her hands on the rope, but hesitated. Her breathing became quite rapid and her hands shook.

"I can't do it," she said, her face completely pale. "I mean, even in daylight I'd have a problem with it, but when it's pitch dark . . ."

"I'll go right behind you," Tack said.

"But Vero said it may not support the weight of two people . . ."

"Kane plus those backpacks, with the way your mom packed 'em, was easily the weight of three people."

Clover managed a brave smile. "Okay."

From behind, Tack gently put both his hands on top of Clover's. He then placed her hands a bit farther ahead on the ropes, and she took her first step onto the bridge.

"I'm right behind you," Tack said.

Clover tentatively took a few more steps. Tack stayed with her.

"You know, it might be better to do this in the dark," Clover said. "It's probably a good thing that I can't see down."

"You're doing great," Tack said. "We're halfway across."

Clover took a few more steps before a freak gust of wind shook the rickety bridge. She screamed, white-knuckling the rope. The winds intensified, jostling the bridge.

"Clover!" Vero shouted as he ran toward the bridge.

Tack grasped Clover's arm to steady her. He looked her square in the face with a serious yet stern gaze. "You can do this."

Clover swallowed hard then took a step forward. Tack kept a tight grip on her arm. Vero and Kane walked out onto the bridge.

"We're almost there," Tack said in a comforting voice as Clover walked. "A few more feet . . ."

The bridge swayed in the wind. Clover's face turned completely pale as she made her way across. When she neared the other side, Vero clasped his hand around hers and pulled his terrified sister off the bridge and onto solid ground. Kane grabbed Tack's arm and also pulled him to safety.

"I am never doing that again," Clover shouted, catching her breath.

"Me either," Tack said, completely ashen faced.

"You seemed okay out there," Kane said to Tack.

"Are you kiddin'? Tack's totally afraid of heights," Vero said.

"He was just being brave for me," Clover said, smiling gratefully to Tack.

Tack actually blushed.

19

✦

PATH OF THE PANTHER

Vero surveyed the terrain around them. It seemed even darker on this side of the rickety bridge. Even his bright headlamp struggled to penetrate the utter blackness.

Kane shook Vero's shoulder. "What's he doing?" Kane gestured to Tack, who stood with both arms spread wide above the ground.

"Dowsing."

"Yeah, but he's been standing like that for a few minutes now, and we really need to get going," Kane said.

Vero nodded. He walked over to Tack and tapped him on the shoulder.

"I lost it," Tack said.

Kane and Clover walked over as Vero asked, "What do you mean, you lost it?"

"I really felt that we needed to cross that bridge, but now I've got absolutely nothing," Tack said as he hung his head. "Sorry."

"Great," Kane said, looking like he was about to punch something.

"Can't you even feel the general direction we should head in?" Vero asked.

Tack shook his head. As Kane looked off in the distance, Vero noticed his eyes suddenly went wide.

"What? What is it?" Vero asked.

"Panther!" Kane screamed.

Vero and Tack looked at one another, panicked. Kane ran into the dense forest.

"Run!" Clover screamed as she sprinted past them.

Vero and Tack took off, running blindly into the forest. Vero could hear the guttural roar of a panther, and it felt so close that Vero imagined he could feel its hot breath down his neck and its drool down his back. In reality, it was the sweltering heat of the forest, together with his own sweat. As they ran, everyone became separated; time seemed to melt away as they imagined the panther in close pursuit.

Suddenly, Vero screamed, "The trees! Quick! Get in the trees!"

They each clambered up the closest mossy tree they could locate.

"Vero, where are you?" Clover yelled, her voice sounding isolated and scared.

"Over here!" Vero answered. Their headlamps found each other and allowed them to make eye contact.

"What do we do?" Tack howled from a tall tree to Vero's right.

"Hopefully wait until he leaves!" Clover shouted.

"Except panthers are amazing climbers," Kane shouted, the only one Vero couldn't locate. "We're not that safe in these trees!"

"Then why did we climb them?" Clover shouted, her voice shaky.

"Could be worse. It could have four heads," Kane said.

Vero knew exactly what Kane meant.

"Okay, that's really dumb," Clover called out.

"No, last time we were in the Ether, we had to deal with a four-headed leopard," Kane said.

"Well, we're on earth. As far as I'm concerned, what happens in the Ether, stays in the Ether," Clover quipped. "Right now we need to deal with a *one*-headed panther! It is one-headed, isn't it? Did anyone actually see it?"

"Yes, a big cat with a sleek black coat," Kane answered, annoyed. "I think I know what a panther looks like."

"It's too quiet. Maybe it's gone?" Tack asked, with a tinge of hope.

"Who knows?" Clover answered.

"Does anybody see it?" Vero asked.

"No," the others answered simultaneously.

The crunch of twigs and dead leaves silenced everyone. The panther was on the ground, approaching Tack's tree. Tack screamed then scrambled, grabbing a branch and climbing higher as the panther drew closer to his hiding place.

"What did you guys do to escape the four-headed leopard?!" Tack howled.

"We cut its heads off!" Kane yelled.

"We had swords there!" Vero shouted.

The large cat leapt onto a low-hanging branch on Tack's tree.

Vero could hear Tack pleading and crying, "Please, God, if I make it out of this alive, I swear I'll do all my homework on time and wash the dishes and—"

Thwack! A stick hit the big cat in the side, stunning it. The panther turned its head. Kane stood on the ground underneath the cat, holding the stick. Kane's bravery quickly faded as his eyes then went wide, and he ran for the closest tree.

The panther bounded down out of Tack's tree, seeming almost wounded. As it pranced over toward Vero, he threw down his backpack, hitting the cat squarely in the head. The panther blinked and turned, appearing to decide Vero wasn't a meal worth the effort.

The lithe animal found its way to Clover's tree, where it circled, sniffing the air for the girl who hid in crevices of the tree above, camouflaged by the dark night.

The big carnivore made up his mind and bounded up into the tree. He wasted no time weaving his way upward. Clover held her breath, afraid any movement would get her killed. As silent tears rolled down her face, all was noiseless and immobile.

The hot breath of the panther sent chills down Clover's back. She peered up momentarily to see the menace right before her face.

Saliva dripped onto Clover's pant leg. She wanted to scream, but willed herself to stay smart. She knew that wild animals liked to kill their prey themselves, and not eat anything that was already dead. So she remained unmoving and held her breath.

And held her breath.

And held her breath.

And held her breath.

Her vision was starting to blur as she turned purple and refused to blink.

I'm going to die. Right here. Right now. In a tree. In the middle of Sri Lanka.

Her body rebelled against her will.

She sucked in air. A deep breath. And blinked rapidly.

The panther continued to stare at her. The fiend was stoic and frozen.

Why hasn't it tried to kill me yet? I'm clearly alive and an easy target. Why aren't I dead?

She looked up into the creature's eyes and felt the wind knocked out of her once she recognized the golden-green eyes. It was the panther from her dream! And then the large cat leaned into Clover and nuzzled her face with the top of its head.

The panther then backed away and climbed down the branch. It turned back to Clover, beckoning her to follow.

Clover took a moment to start moving. The panther was waiting for her at the bottom of the tree. Clover climbed down as a beam of light hit her.

"Clover, watch out!" Tack yelled, pointing his flashlight at her. "The panther's there!"

"It's all right, everyone," Clover calmly said. "Come down. I know this guy. He's okay. He's here to help us . . . he's here to guide us."

Clover followed the panther. Vero, Tack, and Kane raced down their trees, then watched, almost in reverence, as Clover trailed the cat through the trees. Then they too began to follow.

As they stealthily made their way through the forest, no one spoke a word, as if they were afraid any sound would break the panther's enchantment. They followed the fluid movement of the feral cat as it led them to a glade in the forest where the moon shone brightly.

The panther guided them through a tract of low-lying, soggy soil. Vero could feel his sneakers sinking into the mud with each step. They trudged through a cluster of bamboo stalks taller than any of them. It reminded Vero of walking through a cornfield during Halloween. Clover was the first to emerge from the bamboo forest. When Vero arrived next, he found Clover alone, staring at a large rock outcropping atop a high and craggy hill. Her eyes scanned the area, searching for the panther. It was nowhere to be seen. Kane and Tack emerged from the bamboo as Vero made his way to stand alongside Clover.

"Where's the panther?" he asked.

"He's gone," Clover answered. "He just vanished."

"It led us to here?" Kane said, staring at the rock wall. "A dead end?"

"No, it's not," Tack said, his hands splayed on the rock. "This is exactly where we need to be."

20

DISAPPEARING ACT

I got my mojo back," Tack said proudly as he ran his hands over the sheet of rock jutting out of the mountainside.

"Good, so where do we need to go?" Vero asked, his headlamp shining on the rock wall.

"Through this rock," Tack said.

Vero and Clover exchanged confused looks.

"How can we go through solid rock?" Kane asked, annoyance in his tone.

"Hey, my job is only to tell you where to go, not how to get there!" Tack shot back.

"Thanks—you led us to a dead end!" Kane replied.

"You know, for an angel, you're kind of a jerk!" Tack shouted.

"What's that supposed to mean?" Kane yelled in Tack's face.

"Exactly what it sounds like!" Tack shot back.

"This isn't going to get us anywhere," Vero told them. "Just cool it!"

Kane and Tack eyeballed one another. After a few tense moments, Tack lowered his eyes and backed away. Clover stepped over to them.

"If Tack says we need to get inside that mountain, then we have to find a way," she said. "Don't forget, the panther led us here. I'm sure it was for a reason."

Kane nodded. "Okay, fine. Vero and I will look over here . . ." Kane pointed to his left. "And you and Tack can search that way." Kane pointed to his right.

Tack, Clover, and Kane turned on their headband flashlights. Beams of light lit up the area as Vero walked off with Kane. Tack paced around the rock formation, then climbed over boulders and stepped over fallen, rotted tree trunks, all while scouring the ground for any sort of opening. But he seemed to be growing more and more discouraged by the moment. Clover stepped up behind him.

"Any luck?" she asked.

"No," Tack sighed as he sat down on a large rock with a fairly flat top.

Clover sat next to him.

"I still believe in you," she said, patting his knee reassuringly.

Tack's eyes went wide when he looked at Clover. He quickly put his arm around her neck and drew her in toward him. He then kissed her on the lips! A look of shock came over Clover. With his lips still pressed against hers, Tack pulled something off Clover's neck. She abruptly stood.

"How dare you!" Clover shouted. "I can't believe you . . ."

"Wait, no!" Tack yelled. "It's not what you think!"

"Are you gonna say it was an accident? That your lips just *accidentally* pressed up against mine?!"

"No, I kissed you on purpose, and I'd do it again!"

"What?"

"I did it to distract you."

"Distract me from what?" Clover shouted.

"This."

Tack opened his hand, revealing a big, fat leech. Clover looked at it. She thought her legs might buckle out from underneath her.

"The kiss was the only way I could pull it off without you knowing, 'cause I knew you'd freak otherwise," Tack said, flinging the leech to the ground.

"Are there more on me?" Clover panicked. "Quick, look!"

Tack removed his headlight and shone it up and down her body. Clover turned around so he could check her backside. Tack put the headlight back on his head.

"You're good," he said.

"Sure?"

"Yeah, but what about me?"

Clover then shone her headlight over the front of his body.

"Turn."

Tack turned his backside to her. She ran the light from his neck down to his shoes.

"I don't see anything," Clover said, strapping her headlight back on.

"Thanks," Tack said.

"Ahh!" Clover shouted with frustration. "That was my first kiss ever . . . and with my little brother's best friend!"

"Your first? Really?"

"You sound surprised."

"As pretty as you are, I just thought for sure someone would have kissed you by now." Tack shyly smiled.

"Thanks, but no," Clover said. She began to chuckle.

"What?"

"It's kind of funny. I never thought my first kiss would involve a guy pulling a blood-sucking leech off my neck."

Tack smiled and let out a little laugh.

"But thank you," Clover said, blushing. "Thanks for kissing me."

Kane and Vero arrived just in time to overhear Clover. Vero looked at Tack, dumbfounded.

Tack smiled and shrugged to him. "Tack the Magnificent strikes again!"

"You still think it's through there?" Kane asked, pointing to the rock wall.

"Yeah," Tack answered. "And the feeling just keeps growing stronger."

"The sun will be coming up soon," Kane said, looking into the night sky.

"Mom's gonna really panic when we're not there," Clover said with sadness in her voice.

Tack stood. "Look, maybe I'm wrong, but I really don't think so. But if you don't trust my dowsing ability and want to go on without me, I'll totally get it."

"No, we stay together," Vero said. "Just try again. There's got to be something we're not seeing. C'mon, Tack, try to concentrate as hard as you can."

Tack nodded. He turned off his headlight.

"Why are you doing that?" Clover asked.

"I want to rely totally on my feelings," Tack answered. "Turn yours off too so I won't get distracted by anything."

Kane looked to Vero. "Really?"

Vero nodded. He turned off his headlight, as did Clover. Bowing to peer pressure, Kane huffed then also turned his off. Tack held his palms over the terrain and began to walk. No longer having any light to see with, the others followed closely behind him. Clover held on to the back of Tack's shirt, and Vero and Kane held on to Clover so as not to become separated. Vero watched as Tack closed his eyes, allowing himself to be guided solely by his hands. He walked a few feet to his left then stepped over an old tree stump that housed growing fungi. Vero, Kane, and Clover stayed right on his tail, holding on. Vero could feel his thighs working hard; he knew they were walking up a steep slope. Tack walked up even higher, when Vero felt hard rock underneath his feet. They had reached some sort of plateau. They walked a few feet ahead on the flat surface, and Vero heard Clover scream.

Soon everyone began to scream. They had walked straight off the plateau . . . sinking into . . . something really mushy and thick. Vero began to flap his arms around, but only felt himself getting stuck further. A light shone on him. He looked over. Kane had managed to turn on his headlight.

"What is this?" Clover yelled.

Vero's heart sunk. Looking out over the terrain, he knew exactly what it was.

"It's dry quicksand," he said, with dread in his voice.

As Kane turned his head around, Vero saw Clover and Tack up to their waists in the quicksand.

"Thanks, Tack, now we're really stuck," Kane said.

Panicked, Clover began to thrash around in the dry, loose sand. "I have to get out of here!"

"Clover, you're making it worse!" Vero shouted. "You'll only sink faster that way!"

Clover stopped moving, but she was now covered up to her chest. She took labored breaths of air.

"Guys, I'm having a hard time breathing," she said.

"Take slow breaths," Vero said. "Stay calm."

Clover closed her eyes and began to breathe more normally.

"How are we going to get out of this?" Kane asked. "There's no one to pull us out!"

"Guys, this is the way in," Tack said, looking down at the fluffy sand below him.

And then Vero remembered. He had once slid through a similar sinkhole with the fledglings when they had been looking for Kane during an early training exercise in the Ether.

"Forget what I said! Fight! Fight as hard as you can," Vero shouted. "It will speed up the inevitable."

Kane's head whipped around toward Vero. "Are you crazy?"

"Tack's right. We're supposed to be here. This is the way through the rock," Vero said, feeling the sand tighten around his chest. "When you were in the pit of acid, and we were looking for you, we had to jump through a sinkhole just like this sand. We slid right through it and landed safely in a tunnel beneath."

"But that was the Ether! This is earth. Big difference!" Kane shouted nastily.

"Dude, you can argue all you want, but it's not gonna change a thing," Tack said. "You're going down whether you like it or not."

"You're nothing but a fake!" Kane shouted at Tack. "We put our trust in you!"

"And I'm right." Tack glared at Kane.

"Tack, are you sure?" Clover asked, her eyes trusting.

"One hundred percent."

"Tack's right," Vero said to Clover, the sand up to his neck. "You said it yourself—why else would your panther have led us here?"

Clover nodded.

"Just hold your breath when the moment arrives," Tack said, as he sunk farther down into the fluffy, porous sand. He was disappearing like a little kid in a bounce house filled with plastic balls.

"This is insane," Kane shouted. "Vero, you can't be serious!"

Kane looked over to Vero, but he could only see a sliver of his friend as Vero allowed the sand to cover his eyes, and soon his hairline. Seconds later, he was gone.

21

BENAIAH'S CAVE

Vero landed in a frigid pool of water, accompanied by some of the dry quicksand, which rained down all around him from above. His headlamp revealed he was in a subterranean pond in an ovoid cavern. Tack was the next to fall through the ceiling, and landed belly-first into the pool, spraying Vero with an icy wave. Clover then fell through the dry quicksand and into the water. Her head quickly broke through the surface, and she sucked a huge breath of air into her lungs.

"Told you." Tack smiled. "Looks like Tack the Magnificent is on a roll today!"

"We're never going to hear the end of this." Clover rolled her eyes.

"Any sign of Kane?" Tack asked.

"Not yet," Vero answered. "He's probably still trying to resist."

"This water is freezing," Clover said. "Can we get out of here?"

She swam with her backpack still strapped around her shoulders over to a ledge of rock jutting out into the lake. Tack and Vero followed. When Clover reached the ledge, she placed her palms onto the rock's surface and pushed the rest of her body out of the water. Tack and Vero climbed up next to her. The three sat for a moment, taking in the sight.

"Thank goodness Mom bought waterproof flashlights," Clover said. "Or else we'd miss this." Her voice was full of wonder.

The water was a beautiful emerald-green color. Ornate stalactites and stalagmites grew out of the sheer rock, decorating the cavern. They looked magical, but Clover knew from her science classes they were the result of thousands of years of dripping water. Yet it was the deep silence of the cavern that Clover found most intriguing. It felt almost sacred.

"It is beautiful in here," Clover said, looking around. "Nature's art."

"Yeah," Vero added.

"Where is Kane?" Tack asked.

"Give him a few minutes," Vero said. "It's not like he's going anywhere else."

"I don't know what you see in that guy," Tack said.

"He can be kind of intense," Vero said. "But overall he's a good guy. And trust me, it's not an accident that I happened to run into him here in Sri Lanka—remember, he is the one who got us to Sri Pada. There are bigger forces at play here."

"Guys, I'm still freezing," Clover said, her teeth chattering.

"Did you bring any extra clothes in your backpack?" Vero asked.

"No—but if I did, they'd be soaking wet as well!"

Vero reached around and touched his backpack.

"Mine's wet too," he said.

"Good thing Ding Dongs are waterproof," Tack announced as he opened his pack and pulled out a Ding Dong. He tore open the plastic wrapper and shoved the cake into his mouth. "Want one? They're still good."

Both Clover and Vero shook their heads. Clover unzipped her backpack and pulled out two power bars and handed one to Vero. As they ate their bars, Kane fell into the water without warning, splashing them. He swam to the surface then toward the rock ledge. Vero stood, extending his hand to Kane and pulling him up on the ledge.

"That's okay," Tack said as Kane looked in his direction. "I don't need an apology. I'm not the type of guy who says I told you so."

"Sorry," Kane said. "I just lost it. But you've got to cut me some slack. It's not every day I get trapped in quicksand."

Tack considered for a moment. "We're cool," Tack said.

"Cool? Freezing is more like it," Clover said as she stood. "Can we go find somewhere warm?"

"Any idea?" Kane asked Tack.

"We need to follow the ledge that way . . ." Tack pointed directly ahead of him.

"Be careful," Vero said. "The rock is slippery."

Tack stood, staring at the jewel-toned water beside them. "This isn't a lake. There is a current running through it—watch." With that, Tack took the plastic wrapper from his Ding Dong and turned the bottom edge inside out so the packaging stood upright in his hand. He placed it on the water's surface, and it started to move with the small current.

"That's weird," Vero said with a curious grin. "I didn't feel any current when I was swimming."

"Well, it's there. This isn't a stagnant pond," Tack said. "It's a pool that's fed by an underground river. I think we should follow the current and see where it takes us."

They set off in the direction Tack's makeshift boat had set sail. It was a vast cavern, and after only a few minutes Vero counted at least five separate pools. He knew Tack was doing his best, but he was growing impatient. Where would they wind up? And how could they find a single stone in the massive, complex cavern? What if—

"Hold up." Tack raised his hand.

Vero looked out over the ledge. They stood before another pool in the subterranean river. It was the same sparkling green color as the others.

"This pool," Tack said. "I'm feeling it in this pool."

"Don't even think about it. I was just starting to feel dry again," Clover said.

"You think it's in the water?" Vero asked.

"Yeah." One side of Tack's mouth edged up in pride.

"Not in the walls or ceiling?" Vero said, eyeballing the stalactites hanging down from the ceiling.

"Nope."

"Okay," Vero said, taking off his sneakers and socks.

"I'll go look for it," Kane said, also taking off his shoes. "I was being kind of a jerk, so I guess I have it coming to me."

"No," Vero said. "I need to do it."

"I'll go with you," Kane insisted. "I don't want you down there alone."

Vero considered his fellow fledgling. "Okay, but let's see how deep it is." Vero picked up a rock and dropped it into the water. He leaned over the ledge to see if he could see or hear it hit bottom. The rock never made a sound.

"Guess it's pretty deep," Vero said.

Kane nodded. "Let's do it," he said, removing his backpack.

Kane sat down on the ledge, about to slide in, when Vero grabbed his arm, stopping him.

"You're gonna need this . . ."

Vero handed Kane a waterproof flashlight as Clover grabbed his backpack. Vero then adjusted his headband flashlight.

"Thanks," Kane said before pushing off the ledge into the pool.

Vero followed Kane into the water. After they'd swum down a few feet, Vero opened his eyes. He was surprised how well he could see. The water was completely clear. Swimming away from Kane, Vero began to explore. He noted that there wasn't a single plant growing in the lake. When he couldn't hold his breath any longer, Vero headed to the surface and broke through. Seconds later, Kane's head surfaced as well.

"See anything?" Tack yelled.

"No," Vero answered, then nodded to Kane. "You?"

"Nothing," Kane said.

"I think we need to go down deeper," Vero said. "I wish I could hold my breath longer."

"Push yourself," Kane said.

Kane ducked back into the water and swam straight down. Vero sucked in a deep breath then kicked his feet up and shot down like a missile, deeper into the water. He swam down much farther than last time and was rewarded with a beautiful sight for his efforts.

Underwater stalagmites grew up from the floor and provided a breathtaking display. Each column was different from the other and all were stunning. Vero felt as if he was in a forest of tall rocks—so many that they seemed to form a maze. He twisted his body around them for closer inspection. Their beauty enchanted him to the point that he forgot that he couldn't hold his breath any longer. Silence began to fill his ears. He felt as if he would drift off into sleep.

Whack! Vero felt a punch to his arm. He whipped his head around to see Kane motioning with his thumb to swim up to the surface. He suddenly became very aware that his body was running out of oxygen. Panic set in, and Vero kicked his legs so hard and fast that he lost sight of Kane. He needed air and quick! *Just . . . a . . . little . . . higher . . .*

He felt life pour back into his lungs. He spotted Tack and Clover on the ledge, and knew he had made it back. He panted, taking in big gulps of air; stale air, but it would do. Kane popped up beside him.

"You all right?" Kane asked.

"Yeah," Vero said. "Thanks."

"What happened down there?" Clover asked.

"There is the most amazing group of stalagmites growing up from the floor," Vero said, treading water.

"And Vero got a little too distracted by them," Kane chimed in.

"Really?" Tack asked.

"Dude, couldn't you tell you were drowning?" Kane asked.

Vero shook his head, but then his face lit up as he put two and two together. "Maybe I was close to the book!" Vero said. "Maybe that's why I lost track of time, and didn't notice I needed to breathe?"

"You think the stalagmites are there to stop people from finding the book?" Clover asked.

"Maybe," Vero said. "Or maybe proximity to the book causes an overwhelming sense of peace. Whatever, but nearly falling asleep on the bed of a freezing subterranean river isn't normal, so I think we're close."

"You think it could be hidden in one of the pillars?" Kane asked, also treading water.

"Could be, but which one? There are dozens of them down there," Vero said. "Tack, you need to get in the water with us. Maybe you'll feel something."

Tack nodded and began to take off his shoes and socks. He handed his backpack to Clover.

"Don't eat all of my Ding Dongs," he warned.

"Don't you want a flashlight?" Clover asked.

"Not for this," Tack answered as he jumped feetfirst into the pool and swam over to Vero.

"Does it feel any different being in the water this time?" Vero asked.

"No, it's just as freezing!" Tack shouted, teeth chattering.

"You get used to it," Kane said.

"Just let me concentrate," Tack said.

Tack closed his eyes and spread his hands out over the surface of the water. Vero watched as Tack began to swim toward the middle of the pool. When he appeared to be dead center, Tack stopped swimming and opened his eyes.

"It's right under this spot," Tack said.

"Let's go diving," Kane said as he swam to the center then dove down under the surface.

Tack turned to kick down into the water, but Vero grabbed his shoulder before he could descend.

"You should go back by Clover," Vero said.

Tack nodded. He looked grateful to be getting out of the frigid water. As Tack swam back to Clover, Vero kicked his feet and dove below. Within several feet, the stalagmites came into view. Vero willed his mind to ignore their bewitching beauty and focused solely on finding the Book of Raziel. He swam to a pillar, which he imagined to be the exact center. Examining it up close, he saw nothing blue on the pillar—no sign of any sapphire. He began to feel out of breath, so he kicked his feet from off the bottom of the water's floor and bulleted up to the surface.

As Vero bobbed up out of the water, he saw Kane, who had also come up for air.

"You see anything?" Kane asked Vero.

"Not yet," Vero said. "But keep looking. We gotta be close."

Vero and Kane kept searching the bottom for any sign of a sapphire or other gemstones. It seemed like finding a needle in a haystack, but neither knew what else they could do. During one attempt, Vero touched the base of a pillar. His hand accidentally scraped the lake's floor. It felt warm, and when he looked at his hand, he could feel the current in the water—it was stronger down here at the bed. He got an idea. He swam back up to the surface, took a huge breath of air, and swam back below. But this time, instead of heading to the center of the pool, Vero dove down to the bottom and swam his way across it. His hands swept against the floor as he let the current take him, allowing him to crawl across the bottom. He did this for about ten yards, until water suddenly shot up his nose. Vero's head unexpectedly tucked into his chest as he was pulled forward off what he had thought was the bottom. As he somersaulted off a ledge, Vero realized he was caught in a powerful current that was drawing him toward an opening in the sidewall of the cavern.

Vero struggled to fight the current, trying to go back to the ledge he had fallen off of. It wasn't easy, but he was making headway and putting some distance between himself and the hole in the wall. As he swam back toward the ledge, he noticed there was an underside to it, and it seemed as if there might be an air pocket there! Vero kicked with everything he had and made it to the underside of the ledge.

Suddenly, air came back into his lungs. Vero realized his head was no longer under the water; he had indeed found an air pocket under the ledge. He looked up and saw light above him, and it wasn't from his flashlight. He was under a dome-shaped ceiling. After he caught his breath, he understood that what he and Kane had thought was the floor of the cavern was actually a massive, curved dome of rock beneath the surface.

As Vero surveyed the inside of the air pocket, he noticed a flat outcrop of rock in the middle. Vero climbed up out of the water underneath the dome of rock. When he stood, his head nearly grazed the ceiling. But when he tilted his head back and looked up, he saw nothing but blue, and it wasn't sky.

22

BOOK OF THE ANGEL RAZIEL

Kane's head broke through the water. A panicked Clover and Tack leaned over the rock ledge.

"Did you see him?" Clover shouted, her eyes full of fear.

"No," Kane said. "I don't know where he is. I looked everywhere down by the stalagmites, but he wasn't there!"

Clover dove into the water, shoes and all.

"Clover!" Tack yelled, then jumped in after her.

Tack raced over to her and turned her around by her arm.

"Let me go, Tack!"

"Okay, but we'll search together," Tack said. "You're not going there alone!"

"Fine," Clover yelled. "But we have to go!"

They dove headfirst under the surface.

Vero stared at the dome's roof with his mouth agape. Inlaid throughout the craggy knots of the stone ceiling above him were ridge upon ridge of deep-blue sapphires as far as his eyes could see. The entire ceiling sparkled blueness as if one giant gemstone.

"The Book of Raziel . . ." Vero said aloud, smiling.

His smile turned to a frown when he realized that there must be thousands of sapphires embedded in the ceiling. How would he know which one was the book? He examined a few of them by running his finger over their surface. Nothing distinguished them apart from one another. His heart sunk. He had come so far . . .

But then one particular sapphire began to twinkle like a tiny star. Vero walked to it and stood directly underneath. As he stared up at the stone, no bigger than a small rock, he wondered how he would get it out of the rock ceiling. Why hadn't he thought to bring a pick?

He looked around the small cavern. There had to be something he could use to chip the sapphire from the rock. When he saw there was nothing, he took off his headband flashlight. Turning the light upside down, he carefully smashed at the rock around the sapphire, hoping to chisel it free. With the first thrust, the sapphire loosened and dropped to the floor of the cavern even easier than he would have hoped. Vero scrambled to grab it.

That was way too easy, he thought as he looked upon the beautiful sapphire. Was this the Book of Raziel? Vero looked intensely into the stone, hoping somehow it would tell him. But all he saw was a pretty blue gem. He was furious with himself. How could he not know if this was the right stone?

Vero sunk to the floor. His mind changed to thoughts of Tack and Clover and Kane. They must be worried about him, but he didn't dare leave the cavern—what if he couldn't find his way back to this location? Uriel had told him that he possessed the gifts to find the book. But how? Then a thought came to Vero: *Vox Dei*.

He recalled Chiko's story of the monk walking across hot coals. The monk had already visualized himself safely across the embers—the power of the mind. Vero tilted his head back and stared at the blue-speckled ceiling. He took deep breaths to relax himself, becoming very conscious of the air coming in and out of his body. Time and space gradually began to disappear. He became of one thought— *God, please show me the Book of Raziel.* As he continued to pray, Vero visualized himself holding the blue sapphire safely in his clutch.

The blue stones above began to twinkle so brightly that Vero felt he should have been blinded from their brilliance. But somehow he was able to stare straight at the stones, not even blinking. And then, directly over his head, flames rose and fell inside one of the blue sapphires . . . one about the size and shape of peach pit. The tiny flames began to form into shapes inside the stone. Ancient symbols appeared before Vero's eyes, archaic symbols that he had never seen before but he could somehow read.

"Book of the angel Raziel."

His palm reached for the blue stone. It willingly released from the imbedded rock and into Vero's hand. He turned his palm upward and looked down at the stone. This wonderful, magical stone held the secrets of the universe. The stone's power was infectious—Vero felt mighty. With what he held in his hand, he could accomplish so much! He started to have thoughts of grandeur, and felt all-knowing, invincible. The emotions began to frighten Vero. He forced himself to think about what his mission was—to return the stone safely to its rightful place. And then he remembered what the angel Rahab had said about the power of the book . . . Even wise King Solomon had begun to feel almost like he was a god himself. And Raziel, too, had warned him of its allure. Vero squashed all thoughts of greatness, and the rock's flames began to diminish as the symbols completely disappeared. The blue twinkling lights overhead dimmed. And moments later, they looked like ordinary sapphires. Vero quickly shoved the stone into his pocket.

Clover sat on the rock ledge, tears streaming down her face. Kane's head popped up from the water, along with Tack's. She momentarily stopped crying and looked up at Kane, who shook his head. Tack also motioned in the negative.

"If he had drowned, I would have found his body," Kane told her.

That wasn't exactly reassuring. Clover closed her eyes, trying to hold back the sobs. They came anyway.

"I wish I never led us here," Tack said, sadness in his eyes. "But I swear it's where I felt the stone."

"Do you still feel it?" Kane asked.

Tack paused to consider. "I do . . . I DO! And it feels like it's getting closer!"

Clover's eyes shot wide with hope. "Vero? Do you think he . . .?"

With that, Vero's head broke through the surface. A massive wave of relief swept over Clover at the sight of her brother safe and sound. She broke out into a smile.

"Thank God you're not dead, Vero! But I'm gonna kill you! Where have you been?" Clover yelled.

Vero swam over to them and lifted himself out of the water. Kane and Tack headed to the rock ledge and also climbed up onto it.

"I was actually under the bottom," Vero said.

"What do you mean?" Clover said.

Vero turned to Kane. "What we were thinking was the bottom of the pool, well, isn't. It's the topside of the ceiling for an underwater dome beneath it. I found the edge accidentally. There's a hole in the wall over on the other side that almost sucked me in. When I swam away from it, I got under the dome. There's a big air pocket where I could breathe."

"What did you find?" Kane eagerly asked.

They all stared at Vero in anxious anticipation.

"Well?" Tack practically shouted.

Vero paused for dramatic effect. "The whole ceiling is full of blue sapphires," he said. "It was amazing."

Tack and Clover shouted for joy, unable to control their excitement.

"Really? You found it?" Kane asked impatiently.

Vero beamed, then reached into his pocket and pulled something out, which he held tightly in his fist. The others crowded around. Vero opened his hand, and a blue sapphire—what Clover sensed was the Book of Raziel—lay there. Kane's eyes nearly bugged out of his head. Tack smiled, proud he had led them to it. But Clover was puzzled.

"That's it?" she asked. "It's a nice gemstone, but it doesn't exactly look like a book."

"Don't you see the writing in it?" Vero asked. "The dancing flames?"

"No," Clover said.

"Me either," Tack said, eyeing Kane curiously. "Maybe it's just an angel thing?"

Kane put his head closer to the stone. He squinted as he examined it closely. After a few seconds, he shook his head.

"I can't see it either," Kane said. He looked to Vero. "It must be like with the golems. You were the only one who could see the writing on the parchments."

"Golems?" Tack said. "What are those?"

"Long story," Vero said.

"Now that you have it, what are you supposed to do with it?" Clover asked Vero.

"Return it to the garden of Eden."

"I don't know if I can help you with finding that," Tack said.

"Is it in the book?" Kane asked. "Can the book tell you?"

"No!" Vero snapped. He then caught himself after looking at everyone's surprised faces. "Maybe . . . I don't know . . ."

"What's wrong?" Clover asked.

"I'm afraid to read it. It's got some sort of power that scares me. My mission is to return it, not read it."

"Okay," Clover said softly, wishing her brother didn't have to face this internal struggle. "First, let's figure out how to get out of here," she said, eyeballing the cavern. "I'm ready for some fresh air."

"Me too," Vero said as he closed his fist around the sapphire.

A soaking-wet Kane stepped toward Vero and took his arm. "Look, I hate to tell you this, but like Uriel said, now that you actually have the book, they're really going to come after you."

"Who's coming after him?" Tack asked, panicked.

"Lucifer and all his minions," Kane said, his eyes locked with Vero's.

Tack gulped.

"Let me carry it," Kane said, holding an open hand to Vero. "They won't expect me to have it."

Vero held Kane's gaze as he considered. Tack looked to Vero then to Kane, waiting.

"Thanks, man. I appreciate it," Vero said. "But I couldn't put you in danger like that."

Vero put the sapphire back into his pant pocket. A flicker of disappointment shot across Kane's face.

"Clover's right. We need to figure out how to get out of here," Vero said.

"I hope you have a plan," Clover said. "Because we can't get out the way we came in. And we've pretty much walked the whole way around the cavern—I haven't seen a way out."

"I'm not sure yet," Vero replied. Kane shook his head as well.

"I'm starting to get claustrophobic in here," Clover said, her heart beat intensifying as her eyes darted around the dark chamber.

"Tell me about the hole in the cavern wall. The one that almost sucked you in," Tack said to Vero with interest.

"It's over on the far wall over there, about eight feet below the surface," Vero replied, with intrigue in his tone. "It's about five feet around. Why?"

"Because like I said before, these pools actually have flowing water through them. I'm thinking that hole might be where the underground river empties out of the mountain . . . Maybe it's the source of a river or stream. I need to look at it."

"I'm going with you guys," Kane announced with conviction.

"No. Stay with Clover. We're just going to swim over and check it out," Vero said.

"You already said there are strong currents, which means you may need my help if you get sucked in," Kane said forcefully.

"Forget that! I'm not staying here alone," Clover said. "And I'm too cold to sit here like a big dope doing nothing."

"Okay," Vero said. "But we all swim to the air pocket together, and then Tack and I will examine the hole." Vero looked directly at Clover. "But you stay away from it. Got it? Those currents are strong . . . and Mom would kill me if anything ever happened to you."

Clover nodded then picked up the backpacks and handed them out.

"All right, let's go," Vero said.

With their headlamps on, everyone jumped into the water. Vero swam with Tack, Clover, and Kane following. As he tread water, he looked down at the bottom. A few feet out, he announced, "Here . . . The edge of the dome is right below me. Follow me straight down and under!" And with that, Vero swam down with the others following close behind.

❖

Vero's head popped up inside the sapphire cavern. Moments later, the others also surfaced.

"This is it." Vero nodded to the sheet of flat rock.

He climbed up onto the surface then helped everyone up as well. Their headlights lit up the sapphire ceiling. Clover tilted her head back, staring with her mouth agape at the sparkling gems. Equally fascinated with the sapphires, Tack ran his hand over a few of them.

"This is what we call the mother lode in dowsing."

"You guys did it, Tack and Clover," Vero said. "You got me here."

"Yeah, we did, didn't we?" Tack said, proudly, and Clover smiled.

"That's a ton of money sitting up there," Tack said. "Your mom packed our backpacks well, but she should have packed a pickaxe."

"That thought occurred to me too," Vero said, smiling.

"Guys, we need to get out of here," Kane said with a sense of urgency.

"He's right. Tack, come on. Hold on to the edge of the dome," Vero said as he sat back down on the edge of the rock platform.

"Okay. Let's go see that hole in the wall," Tack said as he jumped into the cold water feetfirst. Vero held his breath and slipped into the water after him.

Vero grabbed Tack's shirt by the shoulder and swam him over to the edge of the domed ceiling. He then placed Tack's hands on the edge and held him there, as the current was already pretty strong. A few yards in front of them lay the opening in the side of the wall. Vero watched Tack as he studied the opening and the currents around them. Vero was impressed by how long Tack could hold his breath.

Eventually, Tack looked over to Vero and gave him the thumbs up, letting him know it was time to go back to the air pocket. Tack and Vero emerged from the water simultaneously, both gasping for air. They swam to Clover and Kane, who were waiting.

"We can do this," Tack said. "That hole definitely leads to the outside, and I don't think it's very far to the other side."

"Sounds good," Vero said at the news.

"But . . ." Tack added with some insecurity in his voice.

"But what?" asked Vero.

"Well, I'm ninety-nine percent sure we can swim through the tunnel and get outside. But I have no idea where we'll wind up. It could be a river, another pool, or even a waterfall."

It was silent for a moment, as they all considered the possibilities.

"It's not a waterfall!" Clover shouted with excitement, shattering the silence. "I saw it in my dream! It's a stream. Vero, remember in the picture I drew? There was a stream that started right in the middle of the mountain. That's it . . . it has to be!"

Vero did remember the stream in her picture, but still wasn't so sure they should risk it.

"I say we go for it," Clover said, exuding confidence. "I mean, did we know what was on the other side of the dry quicksand? And what other choice do we have? Die in here?"

The boys all looked at each other and nodded. There was no other way.

"Okay, guys," Tack said. "Everyone breathe in and out a few times to get the biggest breath of air . . ."

They all started inhaling and exhaling, deeply and audibly. "Okay. Follow me, and everyone grab the feet of the guy in front of you," Tack said as he jumped back in.

Vero, Kane, and Clover entered right behind him. They formed a chain, holding on to each other's ankles as Tack swam confidently toward the hole in the wall with Clover right behind him, Vero grabbing on behind her, and Kane bringing up the rear. They didn't have to swim for long, as the current quickly caught their body mass and pulled them straight to the wall. Vero was grateful Tack had his headlight on, so he could gage his speed as they were drawn inside the water tunnel.

The four of them zoomed through a water maze inside the mountain rock. Vero was thinking if they weren't in a life-threatening situation, this would be an awesome water-park ride. And just when he felt he couldn't hold his breath a moment longer, they shot out of the side of the mountain and into the fresh night air. A second later, they all splashed down into a large pool of water below.

"That was awesome! We're free!" Clover screamed as she stood up in the waist-deep water.

"Tack the Magnificent, at your service," Tack said. Standing up, he struck a pose like a character in a Bernini fountain, and spit water out of his mouth.

Vero and Kane also stood. It was still night; the sun had not yet risen as they waded over to the edge of the pool. As they looked behind them, they saw the water shooting out of the side of the mountain from where they had just come. They all watched in silence.

A low, guttural growl shattered the quiet. Clover dug her nails into Vero's arm.

"What was that?" she asked, her eyes wide as saucers.

Kane gave Vero a foreboding look. "Not a dog."

Vero held Kane's gaze. He knew the growl wasn't an earthly one.

"Give Kane the stone, Vero," Clover urged. "He's right. They won't suspect him. You and the book will be safer that way."

"I don't know if that's true . . ." Tack shook his head at Vero.

Vero considered for a moment then pulled the blue sapphire from his pocket and held it out to Kane. "Maybe you *should* take it."

Kane's eyes lit up. "Really?"

"Yeah." Vero nodded.

Kane took the gem. Vero watched as he stared at the jewel, captivated by it. Tack also noticed Kane's fascination. He shot Vero a look that said, "Are you crazy?"

"Put it in your pocket," Vero told Kane. "And protect it with your life."

Kane hastily shoved the stone into his pants' pocket.

"We need to get back on the path," Vero said, looking up to the light path winding around the mountain in the distance.

"Not if that involves going over that bridge again," Clover said. "No way."

"I'm not sure where we've landed. But we need to follow the lights back to the trail."

"You think the entrance has something to do with the trail?" Clover asked.

"Not sure. But you and Tack should be safe there."

"You're ditching us?" Clover huffed, outraged.

"We have the book. I don't want to put you guys in more danger."

"But maybe we're supposed to help you find the entrance too, not only the book," Clover said.

"Except I'm not feeling anything, and have no idea what I'd be looking for," Tack said.

"You're just chicken. You want to go back!"

"Kind of," Tack said. "Call me crazy, but I don't think I'm really equipped to come up against Lucifer! I passed out when I saw a couple of his maltures, and they're bad enough."

Vero looked hard at his sister. "Clover, you're going back."

Clover held his gaze as she considered Tack's point. "Fine," she said, gritting her teeth.

The four walked through the forest. Their headlights and flashlights pierced the darkness as they worked their way toward the trail. Kane and Clover walked ahead of Tack and Vero.

"Are you sure it was a good idea to give him the sapphire?" Tack whispered to Vero once they were out of earshot. "I don't trust him."

"He's kind of a hothead," Vero said in a low voice. "But I trust him."

"I hope you're right."

As they forged ahead, the forest became increasingly overgrown. The more they fought their way in and out of trees, the more disoriented they became, and soon no one could see the trail's lights.

"Anybody else feel like we've been walking in circles?" Tack asked, out of breath.

"And it feels like we've been going uphill," Clover said.

The not-too-distant sound of crunching leaves stopped everyone in their tracks. Vero's eyes darted around, searching for the source.

"What was that?" Clover said, her voice strained.

"I don't see anything," Vero said.

"Well, we definitely all heard something," Clover said.

"We've got to keep going," Kane said, quickly stepping ahead.

"This forest is so overgrown!" Clover shouted as a branch flicked her in the face.

"I know the way," Kane said, not slowing down.

Clover, Tack, and Vero trailed Kane—stumbling over low-growing shrubs, fallen tree trunks, and mossy rocks. Tack's foot slipped off a log covered in slimy fungi. He fell, hitting his head on the ground.

"Tack!" Vero yelled.

Kane turned. Clover and Vero kneeled down to Tack.

"Are you okay?" Clover asked, worry lines on her forehead.

Tack sat up, a bit dazed. He rubbed his head. "Yeah . . ."

Vero pulled Tack to his feet.

"We need to slow down." Tack gave Kane the hairy eyeball. "Remember what happened when your aunt wouldn't slow down."

Kane nodded. The group walked farther ahead in silence. Gradually, slivers of moon began to break up the blackness of the forest, and they finally broke through the dense woodland. But then their faces dropped.

"No way!" Clover shouted.

They were back at the gorge. They stood on the cliff before the suspension rope bridge. Clover turned to Vero.

"Don't even think about it," she said in a threatening tone.

"I thought you knew where you were going?" Tack yelled at Kane.

"Aren't we going back to the trail?" Kane shot back.

"Yeah . . ."

"Well, this is the way!"

"We'll walk down the side and across the ravine," Vero said. "But we'll need to do this fast and make up some time."

As Vero turned back to climb down the side of the mountain, Kane stepped in front.

"This could take hours," Kane said, looking at the ravine below. "We need to go back over the bridge."

Clover threw Vero a furious look.

"We don't have a lot of time," Vero said to Clover, his eyes full of apology.

"It's no more than thirty feet across," Kane said.

"Yeah, except if you and Vero fall, you go to the Ether," Clover said. "Tack and I fall, we're dead. There's no way I'm going across that bridge!"

Suddenly, the air was filled with the sound of dozens of birds screeching in unison. Startled, everyone looked around. A massive flock of sparrows flew out of the trees. Branches snapped. The earth began to tremble under their feet. Clover grabbed on to Vero as a herd of Sambar deer crashed through the blackness. Wild boars let out high-pitched squeals as they kept pace with the deer. Terrifying cries of langurs shrieked above them as the monkeys swung from branch to branch overhead, desperately trying to flee the forest.

"What's going on?" Tack asked.

Vero had the unnerving feeling that someone unseen was watching them. He'd barely processed that thought when a pair of red eyes shone through the blackness—red eyes were never a good thing.

"We need to get out of here!" Vero shouted.

A demonic growl split the air. Fear spread across Clover's face. She looked to the suspension bridge. Vero watched as she sped toward it. Without a second thought, she grabbed on to the support rope railings and ran across the bridge. Tack followed Clover. Vero looked behind—the red eyes were nearly upon him.

Kane shouted at Vero. "Hurry! Go! Go! Go!"

Vero latched on to the rope and looked back at Kane.

"Go!" Kane yelled. "I'm right behind you."

There was no time to debate. Vero ran onto the bridge as a heart-stopping screech filled his ears from behind him. And then Vero felt as if he was flying. Only he wasn't.

The support rope had broken! Planks broke off the bridge and fell to the ground below. Vero, Tack, and Clover were swinging through the air like Tarzan on a vine. Clover screamed as they plunged toward the other gorge wall.

"Aahh!" Tack yelled, clinging for dear life to the rope as he tucked his head to his chest, bracing for impact.

Smash! Their bodies crashed up against the side of the other cliff. The impact nearly caused Clover to let go of the rope, but she managed to hold on, if barely. She cried and screamed hysterically. The rope now hung vertically, swinging from its anchor above. Vero's headlight shone up to the top.

"I'm getting vertigo!" Tack shouted, becoming clammy. "I feel dizzy!"

"Then don't look down!" Vero shouted. "We can do this! Clover, climb up the rope!"

But Clover continued to cry hysterically.

"Clover, please," Vero said, trying to maintain a calm voice. "It's only a few feet to the top. Pretend you're climbing the rope in PE. That rope's way higher."

Clover took in deep breaths, trying to calm down.

"Vero's right," Tack said. "I've seen you climb it a bunch of times."

Clover's hysteria settled to a hiccupping cry. She kicked her right leg out onto one of the support ropes that held the slats to the anchored hand ropes. Her left foot went onto the next rope above her right, giving her some traction, and she began to pull herself up like she was climbing a rope ladder.

"You're doing it! Keep going!" Vero yelled as both he and Tack followed her example and placed their feet onto the support ropes.

She struggled upward, clutching to the rope. Clover finally reached the top, and crawled along the ground to safety. Tack climbed up the rope, but stopped.

"Vero," Tack said, his face etched in worry. "My arms and legs are killing."

"Drop the backpack!" Vero yelled to him. "It'll make you lighter!"

Tack hesitated for a moment. Vero knew what was going through his friend's head: dropping the pack meant that, for a few seconds, he'd have to hold on to the rope with only one hand. Clover lay on her stomach out over the ravine, her arms outstretched.

"I'll help you!" she shouted to Tack.

Tack quickly took his left hand off the rope and put it under his backpack's strap to release it. His arm became entangled in the strap, and within seconds he lost his grip and slid downward, scrambling to grab back onto the rope. Clover screamed. Tack's arm slipped out of the backpack strap and he managed to grab the rope with both hands, stopping his downward slide. But his foot was using Vero's head as a support. Vero winced.

Tack released his other hand and let the heavy backpack fall into the gorge below. The sound of it landing was drowned out by Vero's screams.

"Get off my head!"

Suddenly lighter, Tack started to climb again. As he approached the top, Clover tried to reach out and grab him.

"No!" Tack yelled at Clover. "I'm too heavy! I'll pull you over!"

Clover moved back, out of his way, as Tack grabbed the bridge's moorings and finally pulled himself onto solid ground. He sprang to his feet and turned around to the dangling rope. Vero was already climbing up. Tack and Clover reached for him. Once he was safely onto the cliff, all three promptly collapsed in exhaustion. No one spoke for a few moments, then Tack got to his knees then kissed the muddy ground underneath him.

"I am *never* doing that again!" Tack huffed, giving the ground one last kiss.

Vero stood and looked out over the gorge. Clover and Tack flanked him on either side.

"Kane!" Vero shouted into the darkness.

"Kane!" Tack yelled.

"Kane!" Vero tried again.

The only sound returning their cries was an echo.

"He's gone," Clover said sadly. "Do you think he fell when the bridge collapsed?"

"He said he was right behind me, but the bridge collapsed almost the second I stepped on it. So I don't think so, no. I don't think he was on the bridge. But he does seem to be gone somewhere," Vero said, with grave concern.

"And so is the Book of Raziel," Tack's eyes narrowed.

23

✦

ADRIK

Kane stood in the middle of a thicket of trees, out of breath. "You didn't have to cut the bridge," he spoke to a form lurking in the shadows.

"You still have a conscience, fledgling?" a woman's voice said. "Maybe you're not quite one of us?"

"I am," Kane said, his eyes steely.

"You have the book—why should you care? Let me see it," the voice hissed, keen with anticipation.

He reached into his pocket and pulled out the blue sapphire. Before he knew it, it was snatched from his hand as "Aunt" Adrik walked out of the shadows. His eyes locked with hers, which had changed from red to a black, dead hue that made him shiver. Her long, spindly fingers wrapped around the gem.

"You did well," she told Kane.

"I told you I would get it," Kane said. "But it's mine to give, not yours."

Kane instantly regretted his remark. Adrik's eyes turned red again with hate, and she hissed, exposing yellow, rancid fangs.

"Who do you think you are, fledgling?" Adrik screamed. "You will stay in this spot and wait."

"No," Kane said. "I'm coming." As he moved to follow her, a flame shot from Adrik's fingers and landed on the cuff of his pants, catching the material on fire. Kane screamed and rolled on the ground, extinguishing it.

"But we had a deal!" he shouted as he stood up.

Once again, Adrik shot fire from her fingers. This time, the flame landed on Kane's shirt. He screamed and dropped to the ground once more, rolling, putting out the flame.

"Does it burn?" she mocked him. "Better get used to that, boy."

Adrik turned and walked deeper into the forest while Kane lay in the dirt. He watched her as she disappeared into the Ether, right before his eyes. This time, he did as he was told and stayed put, feeling angry and dejected.

As Adrik walked through a forest in the Ether, birds, deer, and other woodland creatures fled as she made her way over rocks and through the dark trees. She reached a familiar dim, fetid glade. A fire burned in its center. Adrik slowly approached, with reverence in her gait. She knelt before the flames and bowed her head low.

"Will I be happy, my bride?" the fire spoke.

Adrik raised her head, and her face transformed in the light of the fire to that of an ancient, repulsive hag—Lilith.

Her face was so decrepit that maggots had formed deep in the folds. Her complexion was riddled with warts, and the few struggling hairs failed to cover her bald, weathered head and missing ear.

"Even if I were to fill the depths of hell with all the human souls ever born, my prince, it would bring you no happiness. Because then this war you started eons ago would be over, and you would serve no purpose."

"Regrets, my bride? Before you answer, consider this . . . Do you think He misses you?" The fire laughed mockingly, its menacing flames rising and falling.

"One cannot miss what one has never known," Lilith answered. "He has never known hatred or wickedness—the essence of what we are. So, no, He does not miss me."

"Well said. And that is why we must destroy all He holds dear . . . Which is why that child cannot be," the fire growled. "Now give me the book I have coveted to possess for eons."

Lilith held her hand to the fire, her eyes riveted to the ground. Despite touching the flames, the heat did not scorch her flesh. She unwrapped her bony fingers within the flames, revealing the blue sapphire. The flames lowered and stilled as they both examined the stone. Lilith waited in silence, her hand outstretched into the blaze. Moments of tense silence passed.

"I have taught you well," the fire spoke, its flames rising.

Lilith's eyes looked up.

"Too well," the fire snarled.

Two flaming hands shot out from the blaze and pinned Lilith to the ground, holding down her shoulders. Yet Lilith did not appear frightened. In fact, she seemed numb to the transpiring events.

"Did you think you could deceive me?" the fire shouted inches from her face. "You cannot fool me! I am the father of all lies and deception!"

The heat upon Lilith's face scorched the deep-set maggots. Their bodies popped and crackled, oozing down her gritty face.

"Are you not pleased with the book?" she asked.

"This is not the book!" the fire shouted.

Lilith's mouth became slack in shock.

"Perhaps our new recruit is more like you than we knew," Lilith said.

"This is not the first time you have been disgraced by a mere fledgling. Where has your pretty long hair gone?" the fire mocked her. "And your ear?"

Lilith's eyes turned red with malice. "I will get the book!" she snarled.

"Does the fledgling Vero have the real book?"

"I do not know. Kane said the fledgling had given him that stone to hold."

"Then Vero has played you both!" the fire screeched. "Unlike me, this Vero is smart enough to trust no one! I have given you many chances, and you have failed me each time. I will take the book myself!"

The fiery hands withdrew into the blaze, releasing Lilith. The flames shot higher than the treetops, then fell to the forest floor, scorching everything they touched before they died. Lilith stood. Without the light of the fire, her face morphed back into that of Adrik. She clutched the blue sapphire tightly in her hand and walked out of the clearing.

❖

Kane sat on the ground where Lilith had left him. Despite the fact that every instinct in his body had told him to run, he stayed, busying himself by running his index finger through the dirt.

He heard the rustling of dead leaves and looked up. A figure shrouded in shadows approached. Adrik smashed through the tree branches and, with unworldly speed and strength, jumped to Kane, clenching her hand around his neck.

"You deceived me?" she hissed.

She shook him, her long fingers meeting around his neck. With one hand, she lifted him off the ground. The blood rose into Kane's face as he gasped for air, trying to pull her hand away.

"No, no . . ." he gurgled.

With her other hand, Adrik shoved the blue sapphire in his face. "This is not the book!" she shrieked.

Kane's eyes went wide with surprise.

"It is . . ." he managed to say. "Vero gave it to me to hold. He feared he would be attacked for it . . ."

"The fledgling saw your true heart and has played us both!" Adrik hissed.

She tightened the hand around his neck, squeezing harder. Kane's eyes began to roll into the back of his head. He was losing consciousness fast. As blackness overtook him, Adrik released her grip, and Kane fell to the ground. He gulped down huge breaths of air, coughing.

"You will go back to him and get that book!" Adrik demanded. "Why did you even come to us?"

Kane looked into her black, hollow eyes.

"Why?!" Adrik screamed.

"Because they turned their backs on me!" Kane blurted.

"And are you angry?"

"Yes," Kane said sullenly.

"And do you hate them for what they did to you?"

Kane paused for a moment. Adrik moved closer to his face, waiting for a reply. Kane nodded.

"Then you will go back," Adrik said. "Use that anger and hatred, spin it into lies, deception, or aggression to get that book. Should that fledgling be allowed to take it to the garden, all will be lost."

Kane stood.

"You did not come to us because they turned their backs on you . . ."

Kane locked eyes with her.

"You came to us because you desire greatness." Adrik smiled darkly. "And only we can give you that."

She cupped his face with her long fingers.

"Bring me the book."

Kane nodded his head once in agreement.

Vero, Clover, and Tack stood on the cliff overlooking the ravine. Early rays of sun were fighting through the morning clouds.

"You sure he wasn't on the bridge?" Clover asked with concern as she looked down at the gorge below, while Tack began pulling the slack rope up.

"No, he wasn't on yet," Vero said. "The rope snapped from my weight, right after I got on."

"Bad news," Tack said as he pulled up the end of the bridge. He turned and showed it to Vero. "It didn't snap. This rope was cut."

Vero looked at the rope's end. It was frayed, but not a one hundred percent clean cut. Almost in disbelief, Vero looked across the ravine, squinting his eyes, trying to see through the mist.

"Don't get your hopes up. We're never going to see him again," Tack said. "He ran off with it."

"Maybe he's hurt. Maybe he fell when the rope broke," Clover reasoned.

"Or maybe he cut the rope!" Tack shot back.

"With what?" Clover asked. "He didn't have a knife."

Vero turned around to Tack and Clover.

"I still have to find the garden," Vero said, walking away from the cliff.

"What's the point if you don't have the book?" Tack asked, keeping pace with him.

Vero stopped. He reached into his pocket.

"Who says I don't have the book?" Vero said, showing Tack and Clover the blue sapphire in his hand.

Tack's eyes lit up with astonishment. Clover gasped.

"You had it the whole time?" Tack asked.

Vero nodded.

"So you didn't trust Kane?" Tack said. "I knew it."

"I was told to trust no one," Vero said, catching Tack and Clover's hurt expressions. "The book is too powerful. It can't get in the wrong hands. For whatever reason, I am the only one who can return it."

"But what if somebody or one of those creatures just comes after you and takes it?" Tack asked, concerned.

"That's why I need to hurry."

"Yeah, but can't you fight them off?" Tack asked. "Angels have swords."

"I can't do much on earth." Vero held back a sigh. "The garden is somewhere in the Ether. Once there, I can put up a fair fight."

"Can't we go with you?" Clover asked.

"No." When he saw his sister's distressed face, Vero smiled. "But the best way you can help me is to send prayers. Angels become more powerful when people pray."

"Okay," Clover said timidly.

"So how do we find the garden?" Tack asked.

"We've been over this. You guys don't. I do," Vero said.

"No . . ." Clover looked panicked.

"I can't put you in anymore danger," Vero said. "You need to get back on the trail and go back to Mom."

"You believe this guy?" Tack looked to Clover, who shook her head.

"Do you think that bridge just fell by coincidence?" Vero asked. "Do you? It's probably been there for years, and the moment we get on it, it snaps? Guys, there are other forces at work here!"

"You're right. It wasn't random," Clover admitted.

"Lucifer's followers did this," Vero said, grabbing the rope from Tack. "You need to go back!"

"But you said we were to help you with your mission," Clover said.

"And you have. I would have never gotten the book without you guys."

"No," Tack said.

"Please . . . if anything ever happened to you . . ." Vero said, working hard not to cry.

Once again, the rustle of the underbrush alerted them. Vero's eyes darted around the forest. It was much easier to see now that the morning sun had begun to fight through the thick vegetation, yet he saw nothing unusual.

"What's out there?" Clover whispered.

"I can't see anything, but that doesn't mean we're alone," Vero said, his eyes still searching through the dense foliage.

The crunch of the forest floor grew louder, as if something was nearing. Vero pulled Clover in close to him.

"I hear it," Tack said in a low voice.

Suddenly, something flew through the air, startling all three. It landed a few feet in front of them. As Tack stepped forward to examine it, Vero put out his arm, stopping him. Vero's head turned in all directions, eyes scanning. He still saw nothing. He stepped forward as Tack and Clover quietly followed. Vero kneeled down at what lay on the ground for a closer look. Clover gasped.

Lying on the ground was the fresh carcass of a half-eaten squirrel. Its head and torso were gone, leaving little more than a bushy tail. Clover quickly covered her mouth, as if afraid she'd gag, and Tack looked sick to his stomach. His eyes caught Vero's, who turned his head, his eyes suddenly filled with dread.

The sound of something approaching grew closer. Vero stood. He looked behind him, only to see a hulking figure on all fours in the early morning shadows. Vero put his arms out, corralling Tack and Clover so they couldn't walk any farther. He put his index finger to his lips, indicating to keep silent. Vero slowly backed them up and led them behind a massive rock. He crouched, pulling down Tack and Clover with him. The three peered over the top of the boulder.

"You see anything?" Tack whispered.

Clover elbowed him to be quiet. Vero stared straight ahead and saw a rabbit nibbling on a patch of soft grass. Within moments a figure pounced on the unsuspecting creature. It happened so quickly that Vero's mind hadn't even registered what he had just seen before the headless carcass of the rabbit was thrown high into the air and landed behind the boulder. Clover dug her nails deep into Tack's arm.

The landscape before them was nothing out of the ordinary—trees, stumps, rocks, and fallen leaves. Yet what was straight ahead made Vero very alarmed.

It was the size of a Great Dane. A mohawk of heavily matted, night-black fur ran from the top of its head down its back to the tail. The rest of its body was slimy gray skin. On its feet were sharp, long, black, dirty claws. Vero sucked in a short breath when he saw its eyes.

The eyelids were completely sewn shut. But whatever it lacked in vision, it must have overly compensated for with its nose, the snout of which was quite elongated. As it sniffed the air, searching for its next prey, Vero also noticed it lacked ears; the side of its head was all leathery gray skin.

"Are you seeing something?" Tack whispered.

Vero solemnly nodded his head.

"Should we be scared?" Tack whispered.

"Yes," Vero peeped, barely audible.

The creature turned its head in their direction. Vero instinctively ducked. Tack did not. But the beast didn't move. Vero pulled Tack's arm and yanked him down.

"You can't see it?" Vero said in a low voice.

"No."

"Me either," Clover whispered. "What is it?"

Vero considered this for a moment. Why had Tack been able to see the maltures in the elevators, but not this creature? And Clover had been able to see the maltures Duff and Blake, who had tormented Danny. Had they lost the sight because they had already fulfilled their mission in helping Vero find the book?

"Not sure," Vero whispered. "But I don't think it can see or hear. Its eyes are sewn shut and it has no ears."

"So why are we whispering?" Tack said in a low hush.

The creature breathed in the surrounding air then lowered its head as if following a scent.

"What's it doing?" Tack asked.

"Tracking us."

Vero watched as the creature's head spun in their direction.

"Run!" Vero yelled, jumping up.

Tack and Clover dashed out from behind the massive rock. The creature bounded after them. Tack hesitated, looking behind him. He was running from a pursuer he could not see. Vero grabbed his arm.

"Follow me!"

Vero ran through a grove of trees, with Tack and Clover close on his heels. Tree branches slapped their faces. Vero could feel spurs scratching his arms as they raced through the tangled underbrush.

"Vero!" she yelled.

Vero looked back and saw Clover sprawled on the forest floor. She tugged at her leg, trying to free it from the gnarled roots of a tree. Tack and Vero raced back to her. As he pulled on her leg, Vero saw the creature looming in the nearby shadows. It had momentarily lost their scent, but eagerly searched the air for them. The creature crept closer as Vero desperately tried to free Clover's ensnared foot.

The creature's malformed head whipped side to side, searching for their sent. Panic flooded Vero's eyes.

"Luckily, we must be upwind of him . . . He can't smell us yet. Hold your breath!" Vero whispered as he covered Tack's mouth and nose with his hand.

All three held their breath as the creature sniffed dangerously close to them. It breathed just a few feet from Vero's face, and Vero willed himself to ignore his burning lungs. He could smell the hot, foul stench of the creature's breath. Vero crouched uncomfortably, too terrified to move a muscle. He looked over at Clover. Her face was turning blue, and he knew she wouldn't be able to hold her breath for much longer. The creature would discover them.

Vero did not want the demonic beast to attack his sister or his best friend—have them fall victim to an attacker they couldn't even see. So as Clover's eyes started to bug out, Vero let out a huge breath right in the creature's face, and taunted the great beast by saying, "Your breath smells worse than a port-a-potty on a hot summer day!" And on that note, Vero hauled butt!

Vero left Tack and Clover on the cold jungle ground and ran through the thicket in the hopes the beast would follow him and thus leave Tack and Clover alone. His plan was working, as the beast was in quick pursuit.

"No, Vero!" Clover shouted, desperately tugging on her leg.

Breathing fast and hard, Vero was an easy target for the beast. The creature was closing in. Vero took off his backpack and threw it as far away as possible, hoping the creature would mistake the backpack's scent for him. It seemed to work. The creature bounded off in the direction of the backpack. Vero ran into a grove of trees and straightened his back up against a trunk, trying to hold his breath for a few moments in order to elude his pursuer. But then Vero saw the long snout poking through a clump of moss as it whiffed the surrounding mist.

Vero had a thought as he gazed up the long, pointed nose. If he held his breath long enough, he could give himself a heart attack and transition to the Ether. He would be free of the creature. It sounded like a perfect plan, but then Vero changed his mind. If he went to the Ether, the beast could follow him there. Even worse, if he left, it could still attack Tack and Clover.

Vero could feel the Book of Raziel in his pocket. It was as if the book was calling out to him. Without Tack and Clover to distract him, he longed to look upon its pages. Perhaps the book could tell him what this creature was and how to get rid of it? He reached into his pocket, but then the beast's snout disappeared. A few moments later, Vero tentatively stepped out from behind the tree. He looked around. There was no sign of the creature.

He walked back the way he had come, looking for Tack and Clover. It was hard to remember the path, since he had been running for his life and hadn't been paying attention to landmarks. He backtracked farther into the woods, then, to his utmost surprise, he saw Tack walking toward him, holding Kane in a headlock, with Clover grabbing onto Kane's shirt.

24

$$\diamond$$

THE MOUNTAIN'S SHADOW

You're all right?" Vero said, surprised to see Kane.

"Yeah," Kane answered. "But my neck hurts. Can you tell them to release me?"

Vero motioned to Tack and Clover. "Let him go."

"You sure?" Tack asked, tightening his arm around Kane's neck.

"Yes."

Tack slowly removed his arm, eyeing Kane the whole time. Clover let go of his shirt.

"I'm glad you guys are okay," Kane said. "My heart dropped when I saw that rope break."

"What happened?" Vero asked.

"I think you cut it!" Tack accused Kane.

"What? I was just getting on the bridge when it snapped right in front of me," Kane answered.

"How did it snap?" Vero asked.

"I don't know." Kane raised his hands. "Maybe it couldn't take the weight of all three of you. But it really hurts my feelings that you guys think I cut it. And besides, where are these magic scissors that I would cut it with?"

"Could have been maltures?" Vero's forehead creased.

"Maybe . . . Yeah, come to think of it, I do." Kane nodded. "I told you, they're coming after you."

"But we kept yelling for you. What happened? How could you not hear us?" Tack said in an accusatory tone.

"I fell," Kane said. "When the rope broke, I lost my balance and face-planted. I rolled down the stupid mountain, and lost my backpack too. But here," Kane said, removing Tack's beaten-up backpack from his shoulder, "I think this is yours . . . I found it down in the gorge. Don't worry, I didn't take any Ding Dongs."

As Kane handed Tack the backpack, Tack eyed him, and Vero could tell his friend was trying to assess if Kane was telling the truth or not.

"All I'm saying," Tack said in a low voice only Vero could hear, "is that even though his shirt is kind of beat up, he looks a little too good for someone who fell down the side of a mountain."

Vero looked at Kane. His shirt and pant legs were torn and frayed in a few places, but other than that, he really wasn't that dirty. And the holes almost looked ... scorched. Maybe Tack had a point.

"And, no. I didn't run off with the book," Kane said while under Tack's stare. "It's right here in my pocket."

"Yeah, well, it's not the right book," Tack said with a smug look. "So the joke's on you."

"What?" Kane said, looking at the gem in his hand.

"That's not the real book," Vero said. "I'm sorry, I couldn't let anyone else have it."

"Oh," Kane said, crestfallen. "Well, I can't say it doesn't sting that you don't trust me, but I get it. You were only being careful."

"If it makes you feel better, I wouldn't even give it to my own mom," Vero said, trying to lighten the foul mood.

"Noted," Kane said.

"I'm sure that demonic thing hasn't forgotten about us," Vero said. "We need to keep moving and get you two back to the path. I know you want to help, but I think your missions are done. That's probably why neither of you could see that thing."

Clover looked contemplative for a moment. "I'm not going to fight you on it anymore," she said. "I think I've had enough adventure to last a lifetime. And it seems we might be in your way now."

"Yeah, even climbing up the thousands of steps to Sri Pada's summit seems like a cakewalk compared to trekking underground rivers or hanging from rope bridges like Indiana Jones." Tack sighed.

"I have no idea how to get back to the stairs," Vero said, frustrated.

Vero saw Clover staring off into the distance as if she were in a trance. Moments later, she blinked.

"I do," Clover said. "I remember this from my dream."

❖

Clover led everyone through the woods, traversing a faint footpath. Kane quietly followed her while Tack and Vero lagged behind. Vero kept anxiously glancing over his shoulder, on the lookout for the demonic beast.

They reached a fork in the footpath and stopped.

"Which way?" Vero scratched his head.

Clover plowed ahead without any hesitation. "Left."

She led them to a narrow river with fast-moving rapids. They stood on the bank.

"How are we going to get across?" Tack asked.

"It's not very wide," Vero said. "But the currents are pretty fast."

"And it looks deep," Kane said.

Clover looked up the river, her eyes searching.

"Do we need to cross it?" Vero asked her.

"Yes. The steps should be right on the other side. But I know this river. I drew it, and there should be a fallen tree across it. Let's walk a little upstream."

Clover headed north along the banks of the river. The others followed. After a few minutes, she smiled and pointed out over the river.

"There it is!"

A massive tree trunk about three feet in diameter and about twelve feet long lay across the water, stretching from riverbank to riverbank.

"Let's go," Vero said, stepping up onto the trunk.

He turned around, held out his hand, and pulled Clover up onto the felled tree. Kane followed, and then Tack, whose feet slipped on the slick bark. He held out his arms and regained his balance.

"I might sit for this one," Tack said, his face beet red.

The others walked across the tree as if they were traversing a balance beam. Tack sat with each leg dangling on either side of the tree, like riding a horse, and made his way across. Once everyone was on the other side, the group walked a few feet up a hill, where they saw the lights on the steps to Sri Pada in the rising morning sun. But they did not rejoin the path, choosing to stay hidden in a clump of trees.

Tack breathed a sigh of relief. "We made it."

Disappointment swept across Vero's face when he glanced up the winding trail. "It looks like we're only a little more than halfway up. We're not going to make it to the top by sunrise."

"Does it matter?" Tack asked, blinking in the morning sun.

"Yes, I think the entrance must be at the summit."

"Why?" Kane asked.

"It makes the most sense. I was hoping something would just hit me when I saw the view from the summit," Vero said.

"That's lame, dude," Tack said. "You can't wait for something to just hit you. In your pocket is a book that can give you the answer, and you don't want to read it?"

"He's right." Clover looked curiously at Vero.

"It's something Raziel said . . ."

"Who is that?" Tack asked.

"He's an archangel," Kane answered.

"Raziel said when you possess that much knowledge, you feel like you know as much as God."

"But you don't," Clover said.

"Right, but Raziel said it's a dangerous feeling. Wanting that kind of knowledge is what led to Adam and Eve's fall."

"So you're afraid the book will corrupt you?"

Vero slowly nodded.

"You have to use the book to find the garden," Clover said. "You don't have much more time. We'll be with you and make sure it goes right back into your pocket."

Vero looked to Clover, considering. Kane stood, his eyes glued to Vero's pocket, awaiting his decision. After a moment, Vero nodded.

"But I'll also need you guys to be on the lookout," Vero said. "I'm afraid the second I pull it out of my pocket, maltures or whatever are going to attack."

"We've got your back," Kane said.

Vero pulled the blue sapphire from his pant pocket, nervously glancing around. The stone captured Kane's complete attention. He appeared mesmerized by its sparkling allure.

"Stand around me," Vero instructed as he crouched down on one knee in the cluster of trees. "And keep an eye out."

Clover and Tack crowded around Vero. Tack looked at Kane, who appeared to be in a trance. Tack elbowed him. Kane's head jerked up, his face startled.

"Vero needs us to keep guard," Tack sternly told Kane.

Vero stared into the stone. His index finger swiped the stone's surface several times as if he was swiping some sort of electronic screen. Before his eyes, tiny flames formed into archaic symbols. Vero was surprised that he could read the symbols, but none so far mentioned the garden. His finger swiped across the blue gem a few more times, then he stopped. Something had caught his attention. The tiny flames rose and fell. They formed a symbol that Vero read as 'garden.' Then the flames twisted into a figure—a triangle. Vero could clearly see the shape with three equal sides, and then in the center of the triangle, more flames transformed into a pair of fluttering wings.

Vero stared intently into the stone. He swiped his index finger across its surface once more, but the "pages" did not turn. The triangle image remained. What did it mean? Vero thought hard. There were the three waterfalls in the Ether that formed a perfect triangle. Was that the portal to the garden? But he was told he would have to enter from earth . . .

As Vero silently deliberated, the flames began to fade. And after a few seconds, they disappeared completely. Vero stood. Clover closed Vero's hand around the stone.

"Put it back in your pocket," she said forcefully.

Vero nodded and pushed the stone deep into his pocket.

"Well?" Kane anxiously asked. "Did it tell you?"

Vero shrugged. "It's trying to tell me something, but I don't understand."

"What?" Clover asked.

"It showed me a triangle with wings in the center."

"The waterfalls in the Ether!" Kane blurted excitedly.

"I thought that too, but no," Vero answered dejectedly. "I have to enter from earth."

"I might know," Clover said.

Vero watched curiously as Clover walked toward the edge of the mountain. He followed her.

"Where are you going?" Tack shouted after them.

Neither answered. They continued walking. Tack and Kane chased after them. Clover stood on the edge, where together she and Vero took in the vista of lofty hills, rolling green plains, meandering rivers, and, in the far distance, the sparkle of the Indian Ocean. As the morning sun illuminated the panoramic view of the landscape, Clover pointed to the sky in front of her.

"There's your portal." She smiled. "It was in my drawing the whole time."

Then Vero saw it, and an astonished smile graced his face.

In the distant sky, a shadow was cast from the mountain of Sri Pada. It was a perfect triangle! Surrounded in mist, the shadow appeared to stand upright. Awe-inspired looks came over everyone.

"How do you access it?" Kane wondered aloud.

"There were wings in the middle of the triangle," Vero said. "You fly into it."

"Then I guess Clover and I definitely can't go with you," Tack said with sadness.

"Now you really need to get back on the path," Vero said.

Clover looked to the sky, and Vero's eyes followed. As the sun climbed higher, the shadow began to retreat swiftly toward the base of the mountain.

"You better go or you'll miss it," Clover said urgently. "It looks like it might disappear quickly."

Vero looked down from the sky, and his gaze landed over Tack's shoulder. His eyes shot wide.

"The dog thing is back!" Vero shouted. "Run to the stair path!"

Clover momentarily locked eyes with Vero. Vero knew she was worried for him and didn't want to leave him.

"Pray for me," Vero said. "It's more powerful than you think."

"I promise," Clover said.

Vero gave one last look to his sister and his best friend. Through the tree branches, he saw several of the demonic dogs.

"Go!" Vero shouted.

Tack and Clover ran in the direction of the steps. Vero turned and saw a pack of the creatures running up the side of the mountain toward him. The dog beasts were coming at Kane and him from two directions, preventing Vero from reaching the edge of the mountain and the triangular shadow. Kane took off running into the forest, as did Vero, chasing the shadow. He looked up, surprised by how fast the shadow was moving across the vista. He had to hurry while the beasts pursed him at the same time.

"Vero! Help!" Kane yelled.

Vero stopped a few feet short of reaching the edge of the forest, and the shadow beyond. He looked back and saw Kane lying on the ground, holding his ankle in pain.

"I can't move!" Kane shouted.

Vero quickly ran back to Kane. He bent down and lifted Kane's arm over his shoulder and raised him to his feet.

"Lean on me!" Vero yelled, looking back at the pack of dog creatures snarling and drooling.

Kane limped along with Vero supporting him, toward the shadow. With a supernatural strength, a demon dog leapt more than twenty feet through the air and landed on Vero's leg, grasping his pants. Vero let go of Kane, who fell to the ground then scooted back away. Vero fought the dog, but it sunk its teeth into his calf. Vero screamed in agony as blood ran down his leg.

"Kane, help!" Vero screamed, looking to him. "Kane, please . . ."

Kane stood perfectly straight. Vero saw that Kane's ankle was not injured. Vero's heart sunk as his worst fears were confirmed, and he realized that Kane had never intended to help him . . . Kane had set him up. The betrayal was more painful than the bite to his leg.

The rest of the pack soon joined in the attack. They backed Vero up to the edge of the mountaintop, and then the dogs instantly grew docile and sat. Vero looked over the pack of dogs as Adrik walked toward him. Vero saw red flecks in her eyes, and he knew exactly who she truly was.

"It's over," Adrik said to Vero.

Vero shook his head. "No, Lilith!"

"Give me the book or I'll have the dogs finish you, and then I'll take it anyway."

Vero looked to Kane, his eyes pleading one last time for help. Kane lowered his gaze. Adrik held out her hand. As she stepped toward Vero, he backed up dangerously close to the edge of the cliff, his leg leaving a trail of blood on the ground.

"We're done here," Adrik said, turning to the pack. "Kill!"

The demon dogs leapt to their feet. Vero's eyes darted around, desperately searching for a way out. There was none.

Except . . .

"Please, God," Vero said. "I can't do this by myself. Don't let me be alone on the other side."

As the doglike beasts sprung off their hind legs at Vero, he stepped back, spread his arms wide, and fell into the air. Adrik's eyes narrowed in fury. Kane looked on in disbelief.

✧

At that same moment, Clover stood on the edge of the steps, looking out over the vista. She gasped when she saw Vero freefalling over the side of the mountain. But then his body caught the mountain's shadow. Wings shot out from Vero's back, stopping his fall. Clover knew Vero was an angel, but seeing him flying in midair took her breath away. Her eyes widened as his majestic wings took him higher toward the peak of the triangle shadow. Vero flew into the peak of the triangle, and disappeared.

"Go, Vero." Clover smiled.

As Clover continued to look, she saw four other young angels suddenly materialize in the triangular shadow. One was a slight boy with big ears, another a teenage girl with curly, auburn hair, the third a handsome teen boy with light brown skin, and finally a tall, athletic girl with short brown hair highlighted with blonde streaks. They flew in the same direction that Vero had, and they, too, disappeared into the peak.

A moment later, Clover's smile quickly dropped when she saw Adrik holding on to Kane, and then watched them leap off the cliff together. When they were in the shadow, their true forms were also revealed. Kane sprouted angel wings, but Adrik turned into a vile, hideous hag.

Clover gasped as she watched them also disappear into the peak of the pyramid shadow. She knew her brother and his fledgling friends were in grave danger.

In the most barren of deserts, the ground began to rumble. Red hotspots flashed just beneath the surface. The rocky, sandy soil bubbled as if tar were coming to the surface. Then the ground burst open—thousands of maltures broke through as if they had been festering in a large boil and were finally cut free. The vile creatures rocketed up to the surface, climbing over one another like a den of snakes released from their long hibernation.

As Clover kept watch over the quickly moving shadow, a tunnel of what looked like dark smoke appeared, swirling and racing toward the shadow's peak. Clover stumbled back when her eyes made out the true nature of the smoke— thousands and thousands of hideous red-eyed creatures with jagged black wings. It was a horrifying sight. The creatures disappeared into the peak when what looked like a tunnel of bright, white light spun, then grew bigger and bigger as it headed toward the peak. The lights began to take form, and Clover saw they were angels—legions of angels—flying at supernatural speeds. And when they vanished into the peak, Clover knew an epic battle had begun.

25

DEMON DOGS

Clouds and mist surrounded Vero, though he felt his feet were on solid ground. He ran his hand over his pant pocket, making sure the book was still safely there, and sighed in relief when it was. He lifted his pant leg. The bite was still there, but the blood loss had slowed a bit. As Vero looked around, he heard familiar voices in the distance and followed them. Then, through the thick, cloudy air, Vero made out a face.

"Thank you, God, for not letting me be alone," Vero said as he tapped her shoulder, startling her. Greer spun around with a surprised look.

"You little jerk!" she yelled. "Don't ever do that again! I almost had a heart attack!"

Vero grabbed Greer and pulled her into a hug. An even more surprised look came over her face.

"Ew! Get off, you loser!" she shouted, pushing him away.

"I'm just so glad you're here."

"Do that again, and I will leave," Greer said.

"That's what's so great about you. I know who you are. You're always brutally honest," Vero said wistfully, thinking of Kane.

"Is there something wrong with you?" Greer said, looking at him as if she was staring at an alien.

Before he could answer, Vero saw Ada, X, and Pax standing before him. He ran to them and pulled all three into a group hug. X looked at Greer over Vero's shoulder, his eyebrows raised.

"He's off," Greer said to X.

Vero let go of the three.

"I wish Kane would hurry up and get here," Greer said to Vero. "Then he can get his hug and we can get this lovefest over with and do whatever it is we're supposed to be doing!"

"Kane . . . won't be coming," Vero said with great sadness.

"Why? What's wrong?" Pax asked.

Vero shook his head. "Kane's no longer one of us."

"What do you mean?" X asked, panicked.

All eyes were locked on Vero; their postures were tense, their breathing quick.

"He fights for Lucifer now."

Shocked looks came over the others. Tears formed in Pax's eyes. X doubled over, as if punched in the gut.

"No," X said. "You're wrong. I know Kane. He wouldn't."

"I thought I knew him too," Vero said. "He tried to take the book from me."

Ada gasped. "You have the Book of Raziel?"

Vero nodded, touching his pocket.

"Really?" Greer asked, duly impressed.

"Yeah."

"But how were you even with Kane?" X asked, still trying to make sense of it all.

"The book was in Sri Lanka. I went there with my family . . ." Vero started.

"And Kane's from Sri Lanka," X said, putting it together.

"We ran into one another there," Vero said. "But it was no coincidence."

"Probably not," Pax said.

"And his aunt Adrik—at least she was pretending to be his aunt—was our tour guide," Vero said. "All along, she was Lilith."

X's head sunk down to his chest, as if the weight of the news was too heavy.

"Maybe she fooled him," Ada said, a look of hope on her face. "Maybe he didn't know who she was?"

"No, I begged him to help me," Vero said, anger rising. "There were these demon dogs attacking me . . . Look what they did."

Vero lifted his pant leg, revealing the gruesome bite. Ada winced.

"I went back to help him, but he set me up. He stood beside Lilith and watched them try to kill me!" Vero shouted.

"Then he's made his choice!" Greer responded, now furious. "We fight against him!"

"He was just so bitter after the Angel Trials," X explained.

"It was only a contest!" Greer yelled at X. "We all have reasons to be bitter. On earth, you can't walk. Pax bangs his head against a wall all day! I never had a family. All of us could be bitter for the fact that we have to live our lives knowing we'll never make it to adulthood!"

The fledglings exchanged looks with one another.

"But none of us ran off to make a pact with Lucifer," Greer said, a little more calmly.

"She's right," Pax said.

"So I don't want to hear anyone feeling sorry for Kane," Greer said.

Ada nervously twirled her finger through her hair. She nodded in agreement. X looked to Greer, then his eyes rested on Vero.

"We're here to help Vero," X said. "Let's do it."

"Start by wrapping that bite," Ada said, pulling her winter scarf from around her neck.

Vero lifted his pant leg. Ada bent down and tied the scarf around Vero's calf.

"That feel better?"

"Yeah, thanks," Vero said. "I hoped that it would have healed when I transitioned, but no luck."

Ada stood. "That's the best I can do."

"You really have the book?" Pax asked, with a sense of wonder.

"Yes, Rahab was right. It was a gem . . . a blue sapphire," Vero said.

"I want to see it," Pax said.

Vero reached into his pocket. X put his hand over Vero's forearm, stopping him.

"Don't," X sternly said. "We don't know who or what could be around."

"Yeah, sorry, Pax," Vero said. "He's right. It probably would just look like a blue sapphire to you. Kane tried to read it, but saw nothing."

Pax nodded, understanding.

"We need to get you into the garden of Eden, right?" X asked Vero.

"Yes, and I thought this was it," Vero said, eyes looking around in the heavy clouds. "But I don't know where this is. Do you?"

"No clue," Greer said. "I was hanging out in my bedroom doing homework when I got called back. But instead of coming to the Ether the regular way, I transitioned midflight, and passed through some shadow."

"Same for me." Pax shrugged. "It looked like a triangle."

Ada and X nodded in agreement.

"You sure you entered correctly from earth?" X asked.

"Yeah, I mean, it all made sense," Vero said. "This has got to be it. We all came the same way." Vero sighed, frustrated.

"Anybody else hear that?" Pax asked.

"Hear what?" Vero asked.

"Faint sound of running water, like a babbling brook," Pax said.

"No," X said.

"Hey, if the kid says he hears it, I believe him," Greer said. "Those giant ears gotta be good for something."

Pax gave her a look.

"If you hear it, lead us." Vero nodded to Pax.

Pax walked ahead through the mist as the others followed him. The sound of the brook grew louder the farther they walked, but mist was still thick, making it impossible to see too far ahead. Vero could feel the ground underneath his feet become softer, as if he were walking on grass. The soft cushioning gave his injured leg some comfort. The dense fog gradually began to lift.

"I see something up ahead," Pax said, squinting through his fogged-up glasses.

They walked a few more feet, and there, before their eyes, was a magnificent ornate gate made entirely from gold. Light bounced off the rails as if the rays were dancing. The gates were attached to two massive pillars and walls made of rails completely covered in ivy. Vero could see through the golden gates. On the other side was lush vegetation—green as far as Vero's eyes could see. Trees, grass, and shrubs decorated the garden. Flowers of varying vivid, pastel colors grew in beds, straight and perfect. X tugged on the gate. It would not open.

"I wonder how we get in?" X said, while peering closely at the supposed entrance.

"Are we sure this is the garden?" Vero asked.

"What else would it be?" Greer said.

"Why do you think it isn't?" Pax asked, concerned.

"I thought that it would feel different . . . If the garden's supposed to be paradise, I'm just not feeling it," Vero said.

"Maybe after Adam and Eve were expelled, the garden wasn't what it once was," Ada said.

Vero thought about that for a moment. "Makes sense."

"I say we check it out," X said, looking above to the sky. "We could fly over the gates. I don't know how else to get inside." He tugged on a rail. It would not budge even an inch. As X took a few steps back to join the others, suddenly the gates clanged and began to open. X quickly jumped out of the way as the entrance spread wide.

"Guess we don't have to fly in," X said, looking at the open gates.

"Let's go," Pax said, leading the way through the gates.

As they stepped into the garden, Vero looked around. He was standing in a large meadow. Tall grass swayed in a cool, refreshing breeze. Vero heard a nearby splash. A stream with crystal-clear water made its way over shiny rock beds. The air was filled with the songs of birds. His nose breathed in the perfumed scent of the flowers.

"It is beautiful," Ada said, her mouth agape.

"Enough sightseeing," Greer said. "We need to return the book."

"Where does it need to go?" X asked.

"Back to the tree of knowledge," Vero answered. "It should be in the middle of the garden."

Vero took a step, and then hesitated.

"What?" Greer asked.

"It's way too easy," Vero said, an unsure look on his face.

"Look." X smiled, nodding his head to the direction in front of them. "That should make you feel better."

Vero followed X's eyes. Off in the distance, he saw a herd of unicorn grazing on white snowball bushes in the meadow. The magnificent creatures seemed so peaceful and yet so powerful.

"Don't you remember about the unicorns?" X said. "Once a year they journey to the garden of Eden."

It was true. When the angels had been given the challenge of finding the unicorns, they had gone to the C.A.N.D.L.E. library to learn everything they could, and discovered the glorious creatures did journey every year to the garden. Seeing the unicorns made Vero feel more confident that they were in the right place.

"Let's find the tree," Vero confidently told the others.

As the angels walked through the meadow, Vero's sudden rush of confidence began to wane. Thoughts began to rattle around in his brain like the dried beans inside a maraca. He felt uneasy, confused. He tried to summon his Vox Dei, but it was too hard to concentrate. He couldn't think straight.

"There it is!" Pax shouted, pointing.

A splendid fruit tree stood alone in the center of the meadow. Its trunk was so smooth, Vero thought it looked like brown glass. The branches were perfectly formed, each symmetrical to the others. The leaves were waxy, with no blemishes to be found. Plump, shiny fruit of every kind, even types Vero did not recognize, hung from the branches. Each looked so delicious, so tempting to devour. Yet there was one branch that did not have any fruit hanging from it. It looked so out of place with the others. As Vero stared at it, he wondered if this was the branch from which Eve had taken the forbidden fruit. Is that why it was now so bare?

"How do you return the book?" Ada asked in a whisper, awed by the tree.

Vero studied the end of the bare branch. He approached it. As he got closer, Vero saw a hole carved into the top of the branch. He pulled the blue sapphire from his pocket. The others watched with bated breath as he held the sapphire to the hole in the branch. It looked to be a perfect fit; the sapphire would fit precisely into the carved hole.

Vero looked to X, then to the others. Everyone was uneasy. Pax shifted from one foot to another while Greer bit her nails. Vero held out his hand, grasping the sapphire. He was inches away from placing it into the branch when he closed his eyes and tried to summon his Vox Dei. Before he let the stone slip from his hands, he needed to know it was the right thing to do. His mind was spinning, but he tried to quiet it, thinking of the meditation tactics Chiko had taught him—the ability to drown out every distraction so he could only hear himself breathe.

Eventually, Vero could no longer hear Greer spit her nails to the ground. The babbling brook went silent. The songs of the birds vanished. He longed for God's truth. When he opened his eyes, he was still in a meditative state. And then as his hand grazed the top of the branch, Vero saw the truth—

Beneath the robust exterior, the tree was diseased, hollowed. It was infested with vermin. Beyond the colorful shine, the fruit was rotten to the core. Its true nature was filth and decay. Vero quickly jerked his hand away. In the split second he tried to shove the sapphire back into his pocket, a creature swooped down from the sky and attacked Vero. Razor-sharp claws dug into his sleeve, ripping his shirt. Vero screamed, while his hand instinctively formed a fist around the sapphire, protecting it.

Vero became a tangle of feathers and talons as a black raven-like creature tried to rip the sapphire from his hand. It was the size of a vulture, though it had a long tail, which wrapped around Vero's chest, forcing his arms at his side. The demonic raven hissed and its glowing red eyes narrowed in on Vero's hand. The bird's head lurched forward for the attack, until a long blade pierced clear through the creature's stomach. A look of pure rage flashed in the raven's eyes. It fell to the ground and began to spontaneously combust, and formed into a pile of ash.

Vero looked over to X, who stood, watching, his sword blade dripping with black ooze from the raven's gut. Vero put the sapphire back into his pocket.

"Thanks," Vero said to X, still in a mild state of shock.

"Dude, that was intense," Greer said to X. "And impressive."

"This isn't the garden of Eden," Vero said. "We've been tricked."

The garden's true nature began to manifest. The tall green grass turned brown and wilted. The cheerful meadow turned to dark mud. Every tree transformed into a gnarled, twisted mess of dead branches. The colorful fruit withered and dropped to the dirt, letting off a foul, putrid stench as each splattered on the ground. The air turned heavy as if fires were burning nearby. The babbling brook began to flow with a black, thick liquid resembling molten tar.

"Definitely not paradise," Greer said, with a disgusted look on her face.

"It was all an illusion," Pax said as his eyes took in the hideous landscape.

As Vero watched the unicorns grazing off in the distance, one by one their milky-white hair morphed into gray, smarmy skin. Hooves became sharp, dirty claws, and a long patch of greasy, dark fur sprouted from head to tail. Thick stitches sewed their eyes shut. The unicorns had been nothing but the demonic dogs in disguise. Vero swallowed hard.

"Swords, everyone," Vero said, backing up.

The creatures' long snouts pointed in their direction. Vero's heart sunk as he realized that they had picked up his scent. A sword sprung from the palms of each fledgling. Pax and Ada both smiled to see their swords in fact had regrown after losing them against Rahab's "severe beasts."

They held them up in a defensive position, braced for an attack.

"What are they?" Pax asked.

"Demon dogs," Vero said. "One like that bit my calf. At least this time I'm not unarmed."

The dogs dashed at an unnatural speed toward them. Vero and the others stepped back and bunched up close to one another. With their teeth barred, the beasts surrounded them, circling. Thick saliva dripped from their hungry lips as they looked ravenously upon their prey.

One broke free from the pack and leapt into the air. Its mouth was wide open, ready to clamp down on angel flesh, when Pax swung his sword, slicing clear through the beast's nose and cutting it off.

"Excellent!" X yelled.

The dog howled in agony as the same black ooze as the raven's gushed out of the spot where its nose had been only moments before.

"It's so creepy," Ada said. "Its eyes are sewed shut."

Without its nose, the demon dog stumbled along as if it were completely off balance, like a rudderless ship. It shook its head, spraying drops of the black ooze onto the fledglings. Greer winced and used her shirtsleeve to wipe the foul ooze from her face.

"Finish that thing off!" she shouted to Pax. "Or I will!"

But the injured creature fell to the ground. Its body blackened in seconds and turned to ash. Its death only angered the rest of the pack. They howled at the fledglings with intense hatred. The largest dog's mohawk bristled as it released a ferocious cry, rallying the other dogs. The hair on Vero's neck bristled too.

The whole pack attacked as the large dog pounced onto Vero, its mouth going straight for the jugular. Vero anticipated the move and rolled underneath the creature. He quickly spun, sword out, but the massive demon dog cocked its head and leapt at Vero again.

Vero's sword went clear through its chest. The dog bayed in pain. Vero pulled his sword from its chest.

"Help!" Greer yelled.

Vero looked over and saw Greer fighting off two dogs at once. As Vero swiveled to strike one of Greer's attackers, the same demon dog he had just stabbed got back to its feet. It jumped onto Vero's back, knocking him to the ground. Out of the corner of his eye, he watched as Ada struck the other dog attacking Greer. Greer then sliced the snout off the demonic canine.

The enraged dog on Vero's back reared its hulking head, readying to snap his neck in its jaws. Vero twisted his body beneath it and jabbed his sword up toward the dog's nose, cutting it off. The creature yelped as again black "blood" gushed from its snout. Vero shoved the demonic dog off him as it started to smoke. Greer quickly gave him a hand, pulling him to his feet. Greer looked down at the struggling dog.

"I thought it was dead. You killed it," she said, catching her breath.

"Apparently you gotta cut off their noses to kill 'em," Vero said.

"Oh no . . ." Greer said, looking over Vero's shoulder.

Vero followed her gaze. Pax was backed up against a gnarled tree. A dog had him cornered. Pax grabbed on to a branch with one hand, as the other held a sword toward the creature. As he climbed up the tree, the dog followed him, just beyond sword's reach. Lightning fast, the dog-beast attacked. Its teeth grabbed a mouthful of Pax's pant leg as the fledgling screamed. In a panic, he tried to kick the dog off his leg, but it wouldn't let go. Pax's wings suddenly sprung from his back. He shot up in the air with such a force that the demon dog released its grip.

"Good going, Pax!" Vero shouted as Pax stood on a branch near the top of the tree.

But then Vero's face dropped as the dog leapt from the tree branch straight up in the air—a good ten feet—and sunk its teeth into the branch, just missing Pax's ankle. Wildly flapping his wings to escape, Pax became entangled in the tree's branches. As the dog neared, Vero and Greer sprouted their wings and shot up to Pax. In a well-orchestrated move, Greer grabbed hold of the dog's neck and violently jerked its head back. With a clean cut, Vero sliced off its snout. The demon dog fell from the sky and landed on the ground with a thud. It blackened and turned to ash.

"Who knew they could fly?" Pax said, a bit dazed.

Greer untangled his wings.

"Is that all of them?" Vero asked, as his eyes scoured the ground.

"I think so," Greer said, searching below.

"Not so fast!" Pax yelled, pointing.

Vero and Greer followed his direction. A dog was sprinting after Ada, nipping at her heels as she ran. X chased after the beast, slashing at it with his sword, but falling short. Greer, Pax, and Vero landed in front of Ada. She was so terrified, she couldn't stop running and plowed into Greer, who fell back, hitting her head on the ground. The dog sprung toward Ada and Greer lying in the dirt. Then, *whack*—

Pax's sword cut through the creature's snout, and the demon dog landed on top of the girls, drenching them in black bile. Ada quickly rolled out from underneath the dog. X and Pax dragged Greer out from underneath it as the creature smoldered away.

Exhausted, the angels stood, catching their breath. Greer turned to Pax and hugged him.

"Thanks, little dude," Greer said. "I owe you one."

"We're even," Pax said as Greer released him.

"But you know I'll always have your back."

"I know." Pax nodded.

"We gotta get out of here!" Vero yelled.

The others turned their head in Vero's direction, and they, too, saw them—

Three large, red eyes peeked out from a thick mass of gnarled trees.

26

❖

THE ZIZ

Vero glanced over his shoulder as he flew at breakneck speed toward the gates. Three larger-than-normal maltures were flying after them. Vero had seen plenty of maltures over the years, but he never got used to them. Each was hideous, covered in scales and fur. They had no noses, but were armed with plenty of sharp talons and claws. Yet the most disturbing trait of all was the single eye that went clear through their heads. That and the fact these uber-maltures had wings, something Vero had never dealt with before.

Ada, Pax, X, and Greer flew on either side of Vero. The golden glint of the gates guided them like a lighthouse directing a ship to shore. The gates were open, a more-than-welcome sight as the maltures were flying close behind. X flew ahead of Vero.

"Quick! Back the way we came . . . Let's get out of here!" X yelled, pointing ahead.

The angels aimed straight for the open gates until suddenly the heavy doors slammed shut right in their faces, seemingly by themselves. Ada had been flying so fast that she slammed up against the rails. Her shoulder bore the brunt of the impact.

"You okay?" Pax asked.

"Yeah," Ada said, rubbing her sore shoulder.

"We'll have to fly over!" Vero yelled as he shot straight up.

The others followed. Just as they were about to clear the top of the gate, rails from not only the gate but the walls as well grew over their heads, trapping them underneath. The fledglings zigzagged, but the metal bars grew faster than they flew. The rails created a dome and they were trapped inside.

"What the heck!" X shouted, frustrated and angry.

"Try to fit through there!" Vero pointed to a large gap between two rails.

Vero squeezed his head through the bars, but the rest of him would not fit. His face turned red as he desperately tried to push through the rails.

"It's not gonna work," Greer shouted as the ubermaltures flew closer. "We're trapped in here, and these guys look like they mean business!"

Vero retracted his head from between the bars. He looked above—the rails had curved over, forming a ceiling that went on as far as his eyes could see. There was no escape; they were trapped, like caged animals at the zoo.

Vero heard the flapping of bat-like wings. He turned and saw three super maltures hovering over them. A truly evil smile formed on their nose-less faces and then each grew a scythe out of the palm of their claw. Vero knew they had no choice but to—

"Fight!" Vero shouted to the others.

With their jagged black wings beating furiously, the three maltures darted forward. One swiped at Ada, who barely managed to fly out of its way. The malture continued to pursue her.

"Ada! No point running from these mutants! We're in a freakin' cage!" Greer shouted. "They only have one head . . . Should be easy enough for you to separate it from their bodies!"

"You're right . . . I did decapitate that four-headed leopard," Ada said, as a fierce look came over her. She spun around in the air and faced the malture.

"Bring it," she snarled, narrowing her eyes.

The malture raised its scythe and swung it at Ada. The blade of her sword caught the blade of the scythe. The sound of metal striking metal cut through the air as Ada skillfully deflected every jab. The malture backed her up to the rails and swung its scythe at Ada's head. She ducked, and, summoning all her strength, wielded her sword, slicing the fiend in two across its midsection. Ada watched as its bottom half fell to the ground, but yet the upper half of its body remained hovering in the air, swinging at Ada. She was caught unaware as the scythe aimed for her neck. Suddenly a blade sliced the malture's hand off, and her scythe and claw dropped to the ground. Ada saw Vero hovering beside her.

"You need to cut their hands off to kill them!" Vero shouted.

Ada, a bit shell shocked, slowly nodded.

Whoosh! Vero felt the air from a scythe as it came dangerously close to his head. He pivoted in midair and saw a malture readying another swipe. To avoid it, Vero dropped out of the sky, to the ground. The malture followed him down. It stabbed at Vero, who deflected each blow. And then in a clean cut, Vero chopped the malture's attached scythe from its body. It instantly went down.

Pax and X sparred with the remaining malture on the ground. They pushed the creature back with their swords. The malture slashed his scythe at Pax, catching and ripping his shirt. Pax stumbled back and fell on his behind. The malture quickly advanced, his scythe raised, when—

X lunged forward and drove the tip of his sword straight through the creature's lone eye—all the way through the backside of it. The malture howled in agony. Instantly blinded, it stumbled forward. Pax got to his knees and swung at the malture's arm, severing it. The malture's body began to smoke. Pax got to his feet and stood next to X, watching the hideous creature burn to ash.

"Your first malture?" X asked.

"Yeah," Pax said.

"Unfortunately, I don't think it's going to be your last," X said solemnly.

The other fledglings gathered around X and Pax. Greer looked overhead.

"We're sitting ducks," Greer said, her eyes scanning the bars that surrounded them on all sides.

Vero turned to the others. "She's right. There will be more."

"There's got to be a way out!" Ada said, panicked.

"There is," spoke a low, guttural voice.

Vero jumped and turned. Behind him stood Lilith, no longer disguised as Adrik, but in her true form—the

revolting hag. Vero felt sick to his stomach, not from looking at Lilith but rather at who was standing beside her—
Kane! Ada gasped at the same sight. Crestfallen looks came
over X and Pax while Greer shot daggers at Kane. "Traitor!"
she shouted.

Kane looked impassive as he stared at Greer. She made
a move to shove him when Vero stepped in front of her,
stopping her.

"We all risked our lives to save his sorry butt in that
stupid river of acid!" she shouted. "It could have been over
for any one of us!"

Kane stood, poker-faced. Greer locked eyes with him,
then turned away and allowed Vero to walk her back to
the others. Pax turned to Vero. "Is that Lilith?" he croaked.

Vero nodded.

"Really? I didn't recognize her without all her pretty,
long hair!" Greer shouted. "Hey Lilith, do I need to yell
louder? Seems to me like you're missing an ear!" Greer
grabbed her ear in mockery.

Pax flashed Vero a puzzled look.

"Greer sliced her ear off," Vero said.

"Yeah, and today I'm getting the rest of her head!" Greer
yelled.

Lilith's black eyes instantly flamed red. But then she
quickly composed herself. She stepped toward Vero, who
defensively held out his sword.

"Give me the book, and all these bars," Lilith said,
motioning above, "will be gone."

"No deal," Greer answered for Vero.

"Quiet, fledgling!" Lilith shrieked. "Give me the stone
and all of you can live. I'm sure your Maker will reward

you. How could he not? Sacrificing your own glory to save the lives of your friends?"

Nodding, Lilith motioned Kane to step forward.

"Bring me the stone, boy," Lilith told Kane.

All eyes were on Kane, waiting to see what he would do. A moment later, Kane crossed over to Vero.

"Just give it to me for all of your sakes." Kane held out his hand. "Come on, Vero," he said, in a coaxing voice. "It's for everyone's good."

"What do you know about goodness?" Vero spat. "It's not for our good you're doing this."

As Kane stepped forward, Greer brought her sword down hard directly in front of him. Less than a split second later, Kane's sword sprung from his hand. His blade caught Greer's, and her sword flew out of her hand, landing several feet away. Ada gasped. Pax quickly scrambled and picked up Greer's weapon.

"Like I said, make this easy on yourselves," Kane said, moving his face dangerously close to an enraged Greer.

Pax handed Greer's sword to her. Vero shook his head at Kane. "You're not getting it."

"Are you so sure?" Lilith smirked.

She motioned with her hand toward the gates behind them. Once again they opened, and in flew darkness like a black plague! A great swam rushed through the gates and spread out among all of the bars. The darkness was so thick it blocked much of the light from above the fledglings. It grew eerily calm. Vero felt Ada grab his arm at the sound of the gate slamming shut again.

Shrill wails began to fill the air. Gradually, something came into view as the fledglings' eyes adjusted to the new light level . . . First thing that became visible was red glowing dots . . . and more . . . and more.

Vero stumbled back as he finally realized what he was looking at. Clinging to the bars above and on every side of him, thousands of maltures anxiously rustled. Ada closed her eyes, as if hoping what she was seeing was not real. Pax's hand began to shake. X turned to Kane with a hurt, angry expression.

"How could you?" X said, disgusted.

For a brief moment, Vero thought he saw a look of shame cross Kane's face, but then Kane straightened his shoulders and hardened his stare. The cries of the maltures split the air, and Vero felt the panic rising in his chest. They were lambs being led to the slaughter. Vero knew he had only seconds before the attack would begin. His mind was racing.

There has to be a way out!

And then it came to him. He recalled Michael's words to him: "Just like humans, we are never alone."

Vero dropped to his knees. Bowing his head, he fervently prayed, "Please, God, help us. Send your angels . . ."

The already dark sky above instantly blackened like an eclipse of the sun. Dread overcame Vero. *Are more maltures arriving outside?* And then an earsplitting screech shattered the darkness. The ground shook. Patches of light began to stream through, and Vero could finally see what was going on.

The canopy of bars was being lifted high into the air by two giant claws, easily ten times bigger than those of a megaraptor dinosaur. With no effort at all, the claws flew off with the colossal covering, freeing the fledglings. Vero watched as all the maltures released their hold on the bars and began to fly down toward them again.

"Was that the . . .?" Pax asked, looking upward.

It was so massive, Vero could only see the underside of their rescuer, but he knew.

"The Ziz," Vero said, astonished. "Thank God."

The sky began to lighten more and more as the Ziz flew farther away. And as the Ziz disappeared from sight, another one took Vero's breath away.

Uriel, Raziel, Gabriel, Raphael, and Michael stood in the sky, their swords glistening, poised for battle. They were dressed in golden breastplates. Each carried a shield, but it wasn't the kind Vero had ever seen before. Each had the definite shape of a medieval shield, but was made of light—light the archangels could hold with their hands. A feeling of awe came over Vero as he looked upon the mighty archangels, while the assured look on Lilith's face soured.

Greer turned to Lilith and Kane, flashing a cocky smile. "Now it's a fair fight."

A massive explosion of white rent the air. Heart thundering, Vero looked upward. Whirling light spun round and round, creating powerful gusts. Vero's hair blew as he firmly planted his feet in the ground. The light seemed to pierce the sky above, opening some sort of a gateway. Ada let out a gasp of joy. Vero's eyes swelled with hope.

Behind the archangels above stood legions of angels, swords poised for battle—their eyes, narrowed. Radiant, glorious beings filled the sky.

"This is all for you," Pax said in an awed hush to Vero.

In that moment, Vero felt such love and gratitude for his fellow angels. Their outpouring of support was humbling.

Greer looked to Lilith and Kane. "If I were you two, I'd run."

Disturbing wails and howls grew into a feverish frenzy. The air was electric.

Then Lilith raised her hand. Flames shots from her pale fingers and pounded down like heavy rain. The maltures attacked! Clangs of scythes striking blades broke out, both on the ground and in the air above, as the angels and maltures charged and engaged one another.

Two maltures charged Vero. His blade sliced through the scaly hand of the closer one. The creature dropped to the ground. Vero dove out of the way of the other's blade as it struck dangerously near his head. He felt something hot and sticky running down his arm. The malture's scythe had nicked his shoulder! Relentless, it swiped at Vero until a beam of light blinded the creature. Vero spun and saw Raphael holding his shield to the malture. The malture writhed in pain, hiding its face in the crux of its elbow, when Raphael sliced through its wrist as easily as a hot knife cutting through a stick of butter.

"Thanks," Vero said, impressed.

"You must leave at once!" Raphael urgently shouted. "Go to the garden!"

Vero looked to Raphael. "I'm trying!"

Vero turned and ran, dodging maltures and angels locked in violent battle. He heard loud screams and howls of pain. Ahead, he saw the source of the anguish.

Michael held his shield at four attacking maltures. Stopped, they were blinded by the light. In a flash, Michael's sword plunged straight through the chest of the first, then the second, the third, and finally the fourth.

Michael held up all four on the blade of his sword like they were shish kabob. Vero watched as the impaled maltures' bodies engulfed in flames. Yet Michael hadn't cut off their hands in order for them to die.

Michael's sword must be different from the others, Vero realized.

"Malture at nine o'clock!" Greer screamed.

Vero spun, and in a well-executed move he separated the malture from its arm. He looked around. Piles of ash littered the ground, filling him with encouragement ... then a scythe pierced the heart of an angel locked in battle. The angel stumbled back as his sword fell from his hand. Next . . . *poof!* The angel vanished, leaving a stream of mist behind. The malture turned its lone eye to Vero and smiled hungrily. A sword pierced its eye. The creature sunk to the ground. Vero stepped on its arm and cut off its wrist.

"I didn't like the way it was looking at you," Ada shouted.

Vero nodded to her. "Come with me!"

Vero and Ada darted through the battling mob. His heart dropped into his gut when he saw Kane charge X with his blade upheld.

"X!" Vero screamed.

X spun and saw Kane rushing, his sword held high. X dodged Kane's first blow. He met the second blow with the blade of his sword. As the blades pushed against one another, X's eyes met Kane's. Kane defiantly smirked and gave his old friend a cold, hard stare.

With a powerful shove, he pushed X's blade against his chest, sending X stumbling backward. Kane quickly attacked, slicing the fabric of X's shirt at his torso, barely missing the skin underneath. As Vero and Ada raced over to help X, a malture dropped out of the sky and landed right in their path, halting them with a swipe of its scythe. As Vero and Ada battled the malture, Vero caught a glimpse of the enraged look on X's face.

X's blade stabbed at Kane. Kane deflected the blow. The former best friends were evenly matched as they traded thrusts and parries with great skill and precision.

Vero raised his sword and brought it down dead center on the malture's head. The blow momentarily stunned the creature, dropping it to its knees. And in a flash, Ada cut through its forearm, severing the scythe.

"We make a good team!" Ada shouted.

As they raced toward X, yet another malture blocked their path, brandishing its wickedly sharp weapon.

X backed Kane up against a gnarled tree. The clinking of their blades rang into the air.

"I never imagined you'd raise your sword to me," X angrily spat.

"They don't care about us," Kane retorted, as his blade pressed against X's.

"And Lilith and Lucifer care about you?!" X yelled. "You're an idiot if you believe that! You can still come back to us! There's still time to make things right!"

X's words clearly sparked anger in Kane. Overcome with a surge of strength, he shoved X's sword. X staggered backward as Kane came after him again with a vengeance. X's eyes widened in shock. He quickly ducked, his head narrowly escaping Kane's blade.

X stumbled to the ground, falling to his backside. Kane charged. His blade caught flesh. Vero watched as X's outer thigh gushed blood, his heart pounding, yet he and

Ada could not free themselves as a new wave of maltures descended upon them.

"Help X! Somebody help X!" he frantically screamed to anyone who would listen while swinging madly at the scythes around him. His voice was muffled by the continuing battle still raging above them all. There were no battle lines above . . . just angels and maltures battling hand to hand.

Pax heard Vero's plea and his head whipped around. He and Greer were locked in battle with a malture.

"Go!" Greer screamed, while holding the malture at bay.

In a split second, Pax's wings carried him to X. Kane's sword was raised over X's head. Pax swung his sword solidly, striking Kane's blade. Kane turned, surprised to see Pax. Seizing the chance, X got to his feet, wincing in pain. He grabbed the open wound on his leg while holding his sword outward with his other hand. Pax sparred with Kane, who struck Pax's blade, knocking the sword out of his hand. Pax rushed off to retrieve his weapon.

X briefly locked eyes with Kane. "My legs never really did me any good anyway." He thrust his sword at Kane's chest. Kane masterfully repelled it. A surge of fury consumed X. He hit Kane's blade with such force that when Vero looked over, he saw panic in Kane's eyes. X pushed Kane, forcing him back, then relentlessly attacked him.

Vero slashed at the malture standing in his way, and seeing Pax's sword lying on the ground, kicked it over to him. Pax quickly snatched it up in his hand. They raced over to X and watched as the powerful fledgling forced Kane back. With a mighty blow, X knocked Kane's sword out of his hand. It flew up in the air and landed out of his reach. X advanced and pressed the tip of his sword on Kane's neck.

Vero watched as fear spread across Kane's face. Sweat ran down his brow. X steadied the tip against the skin of Kane's windpipe.

"X, please . . ." Kane pleaded.

X stared hard at Kane. His face was twisted in rage.

"X, don't, please . . ." Kane begged.

Vero watched, almost unable to breathe, as Greer joined him.

"Why not? You were going to kill me," X said in an icy tone.

"Please, it's still me, your friend," Kane said.

X's face went expressionless, giving no indication of what he was going to do. Kane's face was a different story—a mingle of dread and alarm. Vero thought Kane looked like he was going to cry.

"Please, X, please . . ." Kane pleaded.

Anger flashed across X's face before he decisively jerked the tip of his sword away from Kane's neck.

"You disgust me," X said harshly. "Get out of here."

Kane quickly scrambled for his sword. As he reached for it, Pax stomped down hard on his hand, pinning him.

"No," Pax said, firmly.

Kane glared at Pax. It was a tense standoff.

A shrill shriek, like a warrior's cry, filled their ears. Pax wheeled to see Lilith swoop down from the sky. She shoved him to the ground. Kane rushed for his sword, picking it up. He brandished it toward Vero, Pax, Ada, X, and Greer.

"Take it from him!" she yelled to Kane, eyeing Vero's pocket.

As Kane stepped toward Vero, Pax valiantly stepped in front, waving his sword. Kane stopped.

"You're going to let this little pathetic excuse of a fledgling stop you?" Lilith taunted.

"Don't do it, Kane," Pax said, standing stalwart. "You don't have to."

Kane momentarily paused, considering. To Vero, it looked as if Pax's words and stance had an effect on him. But then a black glint caught Vero's eyes. It streaked across Pax's ribcage. His glasses flew off his face. Vero's mind couldn't process what he was seeing. It felt as if he was watching in slow motion as blood gushed from Pax's side. A look of complete shock and fright transformed Pax's face as he staggered back. Kane's eyes bulged in dismay at the sight. A truly evil, lethal smile formed on Lilith's lips. She held up her hand—Pax's bright-red blood dripped down her scythe's blade.

27

◈

PAX

Greer caught Pax before he hit the ground. She gently lowered him down in her arms, cradling him. The others gazed on in horror; even Kane looked upset at the sight of Pax bleeding to death in Greer's arms.

Lilith cackled triumphantly. She stepped forward toward Vero, until X held out his sword, stopping her.

"Get Michael!" Greer yelled to the others. "Find an archangel! They can save him."

Ada, with tears streaming down her face, flew off to find an archangel. "Give me the stone or you're next," Lilith said in an icy tone, eyeing Vero.

Vero become enraged, and the muscles in his neck swelled. He charged Lilith, swiping wildly like a madman. X joined him as they battled Lilith who grabbed Kane and disappeared into the mob of fighting angels and maltures. X and Vero ran back to Pax.

"I was hoping he'd change his mind and come back to us." Pax weakly smiled to Greer as she held him.

"I don't care about him," Greer said, tears streaming down her cheeks.

"Do you think I'll go to the choir?" Pax said, gurgling.

"No, you're gonna be all right," Greer said, her voice breaking. Her eyes wildly darted around. "Where are the archangels?" Greer screamed.

"Hey, you have my back . . . like you promised," Pax mumbled.

"No, not like this!" Greer shook her head.

"Come on, Pax," Vero said, kneeling down to him. "Stay with us."

Pax locked eyes with Vero. "Don't let her get the book," he whispered. "You were right, Vero . . . I'm not scared." Pax's eyes rolled back into his head, and his breathing ceased. His body went completely limp. Greer let out a heart-wrenching wail as she hugged Pax's lifeless body to her own. Vero cried, placing a comforting hand on Greer's shoulder. X looked down at Pax and reverently closed his friend's eyes. A moment later, a white mist emanated from Pax's chest with the sound of a small tinkling bell. The mist grew heavy and swirled around his body, wrapping itself around him. Then the mist vanished, taking Pax's body with it.

"What a touching little scene," Lilith scoffed as she reemerged from the battle above.

All heads turned to see that Lilith had returned with Kane. Looking up at Lilith, hatred rose in Greer, igniting her. She met Lilith's eyes.

"Today is your last day to prowl this world or any other," Greer said in a steely voice.

Greer's sword shot from her palm, and she charged Lilith with an almost supernatural strength. Lilith raised her scythe, and the flat side of her blade met the tip of Greer's. Greer pulled her arm back, and in a fluid motion struck Lilith across her forehead, leaving a long gash, temple to temple. Black ooze dripped down her face, making her appear even more monstrous.

Lilith grew enraged. A scythe shot out from her other palm. She raised both toward Greer, but Greer met Lilith's gaze with a defiant stare.

Lilith swung both scythes violently at Greer, who somersaulted over Lilith's head, landing behind her. As Lilith wheeled, Greer brought her sword down, missing only because the hag stepped back.

Vero felt a puff of air as Kane's blade narrowly missed his head. X thrust his sword at Kane. As Vero and X dueled Kane, Vero could see Kane was breathing heavy as his reflexes began to slow, and his hair clung to his head with sweat.

Through his own sweat dripping down his forehead and into his eyes, Vero looked over and saw Greer skillfully and relentlessly attacking Lilith. Then his eyes went wide with fear as Greer lunged at Lilith with all her might but missed her target. Greer's own force caused her to trip and fall.

"Greer! Look out!" Vero shouted.

Both scythes came down on Greer, who rolled out of the way of the curved blades at the last second. Lilith attacked again, but Greer kicked out her foot, tripping Lilith, who fell facedown on the ground with her arms splayed. Greer jumped up, and with her right foot stomped her boot onto the back of Lilith's bald head, pushing her face farther into the dirt.

Quickly and expertly, Greer ran the sharp blade of her sword across Lilith's wrists, severing both her scythes.

Lilith hissed and howled in searing pain. A look of disbelief came over Kane, who ran into the melee of battling angels and maltures. Vero searched for Kane in the mob, but quickly lost sight of him.

"I told you today was your last day," Greer triumphantly said, removing her boot from Lilith's wretched head.

Shrieking, Lilith stumbled to her feet. She lifted her arms. They were stumps at the ends, black ooze spilling to the ground. She snarled and hissed at her attacker, lunging, almost grabbing Greer before a deafening clicking sound filled the air. It sent shivers down Vero's spine—he knew exactly what the noises meant. A mound of dirt formed, and the ground began to rumble.

"No! No!" Lilith shrieked.

Heavy black chains shot out of the mound. Vero protectively pushed X and Greer behind him, forming a tight circle. Like snakes attacking their prey, the chains slithered straight toward Lilith. They lassoed themselves around her legs, knocking her into the dirt.

"No!" Lilith screamed. "Lucifer, save me . . . your bride!"

The chains continued to wrap themselves around her body. The mound burst open, and hundreds of creatures emerged. Each had the head of a man, a locust's body, and wings paired with scorpion tails. Vero shuddered at the sight of them. The head of a man with long black hair and mouth of lion's teeth arose from the mound. His body also resembled a locust's, with iron breastplates. Greer gasped, peeking out from behind Vero's wings.

"Abaddon," Vero said in a hushed whisper.

Abaddon yanked on the chains. Kicking and screaming, Lilith thrashed against the heavy chains, but Abaddon
dragged her to the hole in the middle of the mound. She
flailed and shrieked, but then grew silent, disappearing
into the hole with Abaddon. His locust creatures followed,
and soon the hole sealed itself over with dirt, and Lilith,
Abaddon, and his locusts disappeared.

"She's gone," Greer said, stepping out from behind Vero.

As fighting continued all around them, Vero's eyes
searched. "And so is Kane."

Michael and Uriel landed with Ada in front of Vero and
the others. Michael's wings were so massive, they provided
a temporary shield from the surrounding battles.

"Where's Pax?" Ada asked, her voice full of dread.

Vero shook his head. Tears flooded Ada's eyes. She
turned to Michael. "You can do something," she pleaded.

"No, Ada," Michael said. "I'm sorry."

"Uriel, please . . ."

"Only God can give life," Uriel said, his violet eyes
downcast.

Ada cried. X wrapped her into his arms when suddenly
the air was filled with the sounds of nightmarish growling.
The hair on Vero's neck bristled. Michael turned to Vero.

"Run to the garden of Eden," Michael said, calmly yet
with urgency. "Lucifer has been watching and orchestrat-
ing all of this. He is now desperate."

The growls grew louder.

"Is he coming?" Vero asked, terrified.

"Yes, and he's bringing his demons," Michael said, looking Vero in the eyes. "We'll hold them off to give you a
running start."

"But how will I find it? I thought this was the garden," Vero said with desperation in his eyes.

Michael placed his hand on Vero's shoulder. "Have faith, and God will lead you."

Vero took in Michael's words then nodded.

"I'm coming with you," Greer said to Vero.

"Me too." X stepped forward.

Ada nodded.

"Only Vero will be granted access to the garden," Michael said to the others. "I need you to stay here and fight. It's the only thing any of us can do to give Vero a chance."

Michael raised his shield, and a beam of light shot from it, burning scores of maltures. Vero seized the opportunity and ran.

Clover and Tack stood on the steps leading to the top of Sri Pada. They were a little more than halfway up the mountain. Clover leaned on the railing, looking out over the landscape below for any sign of Vero. Tack stood next to her with an anxious look on his face.

"I don't think we're going to see him," Tack said.

"Vero's in trouble," Clover said, panicked. "I know it. But I know I have to help him!"

"Excuse me," a boy's voice said.

Clover and Tack gazed down at the step below. A small boy in monk's robes stood there.

"Did you say Vero?" the boy asked.

"Yes, he's my brother," Clover said. "Do you know him?"

"I do—we met at the start of our pilgrimages." The boy quickly introduced himself as Chiko. "Is Vero in trouble?"

"He's in very grave danger," Clover said, panicked. "He's an . . ." She stopped, catching herself.

"Angel," Chiko said.

Clover and Tack looked to him, surprised.

"Are you one too?" Tack asked.

"No, I am studying to be a monk. Is there anything I can do to help?"

Clover looked to him. "Yes. Yes there is. You can help us pray for him by sending him good thoughts. And the more of us who do, the more strength he'll get," Clover said.

"You've come to the right place for prayer and good, loving thoughts." Chiko nodded over his shoulder.

Clover followed his gaze to a small, brilliant white building on the trail that was shaped like a bell.

"What's that?" Clover asked.

"A peace pagoda."

The farther he flew away from the dead, ugly garden, the more verdant and beautiful the landscape became. But Vero had never felt more alone in all his life. He had known since the beginning only he could return the sapphire to the garden. The pressure he felt was enormous, though it was like he was on autopilot. The devil dogs, the injury to his leg, and the malture battle—they had all exhausted him, yet he kept pushing forward. And it was gnawing at him that his fellow fledglings and all the angels were involved in an epic battle, and he was flying in the other direction.

He knew on some level that he wasn't processing all the unfolding events properly. Neither Pax's demise nor the return of Abaddon seemed quite real in his mind. He felt as if his brain was compartmentalizing these things so he could move forward with his mission.

As he flew farther, the more the mist gradually gave way to rejuvenating light. Lucifer's faux garden never felt right to him. Why hadn't he listened to his gut? He vowed he would never make that mistake again.

The terrain below began to change. Ahead of him, Vero saw he was approaching massive trees. As he flew closer, they looked like redwoods, though much bigger than those on earth. He dropped down to the forest floor, as it had become difficult to fly through the dense trees. Surrounded by lush ferns as he walked, Vero looked up and saw the trees were the height of skyscrapers, blocking out much of the light. Their trunks were so wide that it would take at least a dozen people clasping hands to form a ring around the base.

Vero's eyes scanned the ancient forest. It was beautiful, and yet its deep silence made him feel uneasy. He knew it wasn't the garden of Eden, because he hadn't passed through any gates. But his Vox Dei was telling him he was on the right path.

Vero wished one of his fellow fledglings could have come with him. His feelings of loneliness and inadequacy grew as he walked quickly beneath the gargantuan trees. As he tried to hurry through the maze of trunks, he wondered what Tack and Clover were doing. He thought of his mother and hoped she wasn't worrying about him. It occurred to him that she had said she had felt pushed when she fell, and he remembered that Adrik had been with her at the time. Guilt struck him as he connected the dots, and realized he had put her in danger. But then he pushed thoughts of everyone away. He needed to quiet his mind so his Vox Dei could guide him.

Vero paused for a moment and took several deep breaths. He thought only of the garden, and moments later he knew which direction to take. He wove his way through the maze of massive redwoods. The trees were so immense, and stood so close together, that Vero was hard pressed even to walk between them.

Vero came upon a tree whose partially hollowed-out trunk was so large, he thought that twenty people could easily fit inside. Onward, Vero continued. Eventually, a light began to break through the trees, the sliver growing brighter and brighter the closer Vero came to it.

Vero squinted his eyes, trying to look into the light. Slowly, it began to take on the form of an angel. Vero looked curiously upon the angel. He was incredibly beautiful, as every part of him emitted shimmering light. He hovered a few feet off the ground.

"Hello, Vero," the angel said in the most melodious voice Vero had ever heard. "I am here to guide you to the garden, where none have entered since the beginning of time."

"Who are you?" Vero asked.

The angel replied, "I am the angel of light. Here to guide you, Vero."

It was hard for Vero to look upon the angel, as the radiance coming from him was so blinding.

"You know where the entrance is?" Vero asked, his hand shielding his eyes.

"I do, and I will lead you there," the angel said. "Follow me."

Vero hesitated for a moment, unsure of what he should do.

"Hurry, Vero," the angel said, beckoning. "Time runs short, and it's not much farther."

The angel turned and flew a few feet above the ground. A moment later, Vero followed, walking behind the angel. As they made their way through the forest, around the trees and through the ferns, Vero had the sinking feeling that he was being led away from the garden. Perhaps the angel was confused? Vero stopped.

"As my friend Tack would say . . . I'm not feeling it," Vero said. "I don't think this is the way."

The angel turned around. Vero shielded his eyes from the angel's light.

"Vero, there's no time to question. You have to move fast."

Vero had ignored his Vox Dei once before, and he wasn't about to do it again. He firmly stood.

"You never told me your name," Vero said.

"What?" the angel asked.

"Your name . . . what is it?" Vero insisted.

"As I told you . . . The angel of light."

With each passing moment, Vero felt more and more uneasy in the angel's presence.

"Your name?" Vero said in a commanding tone.

"Why do you persist?" the angel asked. "We are in a great hurry."

"Then I'll change the question," Vero said, pausing for a moment, thinking. "Do you love God?"

Vero's question caused the angel to instantly squirm and twist as if it was being tortured. As its body seized, the light shining from it extinguished. The angel became a shadowy figure.

"I command you to tell me your name!" Vero yelled, as his sword sprung from his hand.

The shadowy figure flew up to the treetops and out of sight. Its low growling voice echoed through every inch of the forest.

"Lucifer."

28

MORNING STAR

People of all different nationalities had gathered around the peace pagoda. Tack and Clover had asked every pilgrim who either walked up or down the stairs to join them. Chiko had waved many pilgrims over and had translated for those who could not speak English.

"Do we have enough people?" Tack asked Clover.

Clover's eyes scanned the area. There were about a hundred pilgrims standing in a circle around the pagoda.

"Yeah, I think we should start."

Vero raced back the way he had come. To say he was frightened was a gross understatement. He remembered that Corinthians had said Satan could disguise himself as an angel of light. In fact, Lucifer was referred to as "morning star," so he should have known right away. As scared as he was, he was furious for allowing himself to be led astray yet again.

Vero had the feeling that he was being watched. He heard rustling in the distance. His eyes shot up to the tree-tops, but he could see nothing there. Vero picked up the pace. His Vox Dei was telling him he was sprinting in the right direction. The forest blackened. A shadow cast down upon Vero. A moment later, it lifted, and once again light broke through the trees.

Suddenly, a wind whipped through the forest. Vero strained his ears and heard the faint echoes of his name as if the wind was whispering to him. He became even more spooked and goose bumps broke out up and down his arms. The sky momentarily blackened again, and then the darkness passed. Vero now felt as if he was being hunted, and paranoia began to seep into him. Yet as he nervously glanced over his shoulder, his eyes were met with only the ferns and tree trunks of the forest.

"We could be so powerful together," the wind whistled in a low voice through the leaves.

Vero's eyes darted around.

"Who said that?" he shouted.

"You know me," the wind breathed. "You have always known me."

Vero fell silent, listening.

"When the schoolchildren picked on you, I gave you the strength to hit them back. And when your mother and father accused you of wrongdoing, I put the lies in your mouth that spared you punishment."

Vero tightly shut his eyes, attempting to drive that voice from his head.

"And when you sat in church listening to the scriptures, I was the one who helped you pass the time with thoughts of amusement," the wind spoke.

Anger rose in Vero. His sword shot out of his palm. He wielded it defensively out front, ready for an attack.

"He is using you. Don't be a fool."

"No!" Vero yelled.

"Don't you think He knew where the book was all along? Don't you think He could have gotten it back Himself?" the wind asked.

Sweat began to bead on Vero's forehead.

"Yes . . . He's using you. He's putting your life in jeopardy, for what? Just to toy with you." The wind cackled. "And you think that's love?"

Doubt spread through Vero's mind like poison. Was it really true? Why did God put him through all this? Why did Pax have to die?

A shadow swirled around him. It caressed his body then wrapped itself around him. Vero felt as if a war was going on inside his body. As uncertainty seeped into every cell of his brain, convincing him that the dark shadow was correct, Vero's heart fought back. The tenderness he felt for his parents, for Clover, for Tack, the smiling faces of Greer and Ada, the warm light of the Ether, the love of the archangels—together they filled every single cell of his heart, so much that Vero felt as if his heart would burst.

The doubt that plagued his mind quickly receded as the goodness building within him shown through, revealing the truth.

"Be gone!" Vero forcefully yelled, and the shadow burst into a million little pieces then vanished somewhere beyond the treetops. Vero caught his breath as he summoned all of his strength.

He stood tall and continued on his way to the garden. As he swung his sword, he sliced through the tops of clusters of ferns, creating a path. He caught the reflection in the blade—fire. He knew that an angel with a fiery sword had been placed on the east side of the garden after Adam and Eve had been driven out. He looked hopefully over his shoulder toward the flames, and then his face went white.

Fire was raining down from the sky! His sword disappeared into his hand, and he ran. Vero sprinted as fast as he could, but the relentless, thick underbrush slowed him terribly. As he glanced behind him, a ball of fire landed just a few feet behind him, close enough to feel the intense heat from it.

Vero zigzagged as he ran. Another ball of fire landed directly in front of him, close enough that his shirtsleeve caught fire. He dropped to the ground and rolled, extinguishing it. He quickly jumped right back onto his feet and continued to run. Fireballs shot down all around him like grenade explosions, though they did not spread once they hit the ground. And no matter what direction Vero ran, the fire rained down like hail.

Vero's eyes quickly scanned the forest. He came upon the hollowed-out trunk of the massive redwood he had seen earlier, and sprinted for it. Several balls of fire fell around him, but he managed to make it to the safety of the tree trunk.

Vero sucked in huge gulps of air as he tried to catch his breath. But then several fireballs ignited the dry, ancient bark, setting it ablaze. Vero dashed out of the tree before it could trap him.

He nimbly moved through the forest, around tree trunks, glancing in all directions. This time, no fire fell down on him. Up ahead in the distance, through the thick vegetation, Vero caught sight of a glimmer of vivid colors. Could it be a rainbow? Pressing forward, he stealthily made his way to a clearing, nearing ever closer to the bright hues. He saw the source of the colors was brilliant gems—thousands and thousands of precious stones inlaid in a door that had been hung in a hollowed-out redwood trunk. Vero smiled, for his Vox Dei screamed to him that through that door lay the garden of Eden.

And then all he saw was red. The heat of a fire singed his eyebrows before he could even shield his face. He quickly backed away from the inferno. And when his eyes were again able to focus, he saw before him a massive serpent's head with devious yellow eyes, and black slits for pupils. Two razor-sharp horns protruded from either side of its head. And when it reared back, Vero glimpsed the rest of the monstrous creature. The beast's reptilian body was covered in thick gray scales. Plates ran down its back and tail like an armored suit. The four-legged creature stood upright on its hind legs and flapped gigantic, leathery bat-like wings. Vero instinctively covered his eyes as the wind buffeting from the wings kicked up a storm. When the creature stopped beating its wings, Vero lowered his arm. His eyes clearly made out the true nature of the being that stood before him: it was the dragon.

Puffs of smoke blew from its large nostrils. Vero anticipated what was coming next. He feigned right as it opened its heinous mouth, and a long, forked tongue shot blasts of fire at him. Vero instinctively dodged the jets of fire by flipping his body over midair and then quickly sprinting back onto his feet.

Almost without thinking about it, Vero's sword appeared. From several feet away, he held it defiantly toward the dragon's head. An evil smile lit the creature's face, as if Vero were holding a toothpick instead of a sword.

"Are you really going to fight me, fledgling?" the dragon cackled loudly, shaking the ground underneath Vero's feet. "Give me the book now!"

Vero looked the dragon in its yellow eyes, and definitively shook his head. The dragon grew incensed. It opened its mouth and tried to clamp down its large jaws around Vero's sword. Vero almost instantaneously shot up into the air, and thrust his sword into the creature's back.

The dragon's head reared around, its fearsome eyes seething. It snapped at Vero, who quickly flew out of its reach. The dragon unfurled its wings and lifted into the air. As Vero flew higher, the dragon followed on his heels. Its mouth opened wide, ready to devour him.

Vero flew to the left, dodging the dragon's clamping jaws yet again. He cut right then jerked hard left again, then right, trying to dizzy the creature. But no matter where Vero moved, the dragon's head followed, its eyes focused and snarling teeth bared.

Out of the corner of his eye, Vero saw the dragon's spiked tail heading for him. He quickly rose higher, but a spike caught the flesh right above his ankle, grazing him near where the demon dog had already injured him. Pain coursed through his leg. Vero shot down to the ground and hid around the base of a redwood.

He lifted his pant leg and removed Ada's scarf to check his gashes. The new cut was bleeding, but not as badly as it hurt. Luckily it hadn't reopened his previous wound, mere inches above. He fastened Ada's scarf around both wounds. As Vero looked back up, a powerful spray of fire escaped the dragon's vile mouth. Its target was not Vero but the redwood where Vero stood. The heat of the fire was so intense that it burnt straight through the trunk of the tree. Watching the tree totter, Vero ran away as fast as he could for fear of being smashed underneath it. The gargantuan tree fell with a deafening thud, taking the branches of nearby trees down with it. A mass of branches stopped Vero in his tracks. It was so large that Vero could not walk around it. Rather, he climbed his way through the tangle of tree limbs. Blasts of fire fell all around Vero, who wasn't moving as fast as he would have liked—his injured leg was holding him back. He broke through the branches and ran toward the gate, his leg dragging.

The dragon blew puffs of scorching fireballs at tree after tree, severing their trunks and causing the massive beauties to topple over. Vero ducked the colossal trees, but soon they were coming at him in all different directions. His reflexes began to slow as he fought for every breath. His leg was killing him. Vero looked up as a redwood was heading straight toward him.

He threw himself beside a fallen tree. As the redwood came crashing down, Vero pressed himself against the fallen tree trunk, tucking behind it. He covered his head with his arms and hands, bracing for the impact. The very top of the falling tree smashed down, crashing onto the tree trunk over Vero with such force that he thought for sure he'd be pounded deep within the ground. Luckily, it landed directly over Vero's hiding spot—the enormous tree trunk had saved him.

Vero quickly came to realize that he was still very much alive. He quietly began to climb out of the tangled mess of branches and leaves that now covered him. His head poked out, then the rest of him. The silence was eerie. He climbed out and stood on top of a fallen branch, surveying the forest. Fallen redwoods were everywhere. Up ahead he saw the tree with the gemstone door. It stood unscathed and seemingly so close . . . A steely resolution came over him.

The fallen trees had created a clearing. Vero sprouted his wings, and, with a huge burst of speed, he flew to the door. And then, right in his flight path, a person's face came into view. Kane! His one-time friend and former fledgling stood before the door, blocking it, sword in hand.

"Move aside, Kane!" Vero shouted.

"No," Kane said, stalwart.

"I don't want to fight you!" Vero yelled.

"Because you know I'll win!" Kane replied. "Deep down you know I'm more powerful than you! All this time, the archangels all thought you were the special one, the chosen one! Well, guess what? I've been chosen too!"

A look of disbelief registered on Vero's face.

"You think Lucifer and Lilith chose you?" Vero scoffed. "You've got it backward . . . *you chose them!*"

Vero's words seemed to give Kane pause. He looked momentarily perplexed. As Vero advanced Kane, his sword emerged. Suddenly, the dragon's tail coiled around Vero's chest, immobilizing his arms. It tightly squeezed his body, and Vero began to gasp for air. He fought against the tail that constricted him like a rodent twitching in the clutches of a hungry snake. His breathing became labored. He felt as if the top of his head would explode.

As he felt the blood rushing to his face, Vero realized the tail had turned him upside down. It violently shook him side to side. And then Vero watched; as if in a bad dream, the blue sapphire—the book—slipped out of his pocket to the ground. Kane scrambled over to the sapphire, and with lightning speed snatched it into his hand.

The dragon let out a triumphant roar, so loud that Vero thought more trees would topple over with the vibrations. The tail loosened a bit. Vero slipped through and plummeted to the ground, twisting his body in the air so he wouldn't land headfirst.

"Kane, please . . ." Vero pleaded as he got to his feet and approached him.

Kane stepped back, wielding his sword at Vero. The dragon moved toward Kane.

"On my back, Kane," the dragon said, lowering his tail so Kane could climb aboard.

"Kane, please, give it to me." Vero's eyes begged him.

"Come Kane, and reap your reward." The dragon smiled.

"What is my reward?" Kane asked. "We never discussed that."

"The glory that you deserve," the dragon answered, his forked tongue flicking out. "You will possess great power, for I will make you prince of all that I have. As it turns out, I have a new vacancy."

"All he has is hatred, envy, pride," Vero shouted. "Kane, you are none of those things. You are light!"

Vero's words upset Kane. His hand holding the sapphire began to tremble.

"Come back to the light!"

"I can't. It's too late for me," Kane said, his voice cracking. "I've done bad things . . . terrible things . . ."

"Yes, you have," the dragon snickered. "In fact, your light is disgusted with you. He hates you."

Vero watched as flames twisted in the blue sapphire, creating symbols: a horse, a horn. The dragon's eyes also focused on the symbols. Vero could tell that the dragon could also read them. Vero's mind quickly understood what the book was telling him.

"The blessing of the unicorn!" Vero blurted out. "You won the blessing of the unicorn! You won it! Not me! You have a special grace from God! I thought I had needed it. But God knew all along you would need it. He's giving you one last chance!"

"No, it's a lie!" the dragon snorted. Puffs of smoke escaped his nostrils. "You've turned from the light, Kane! You are mine!"

"He gave you this grace because . . . He loves you! He wants you with Him!" Vero shouted.

Kane's face contorted into a look of extreme agony. When he looked at Vero again, tears streamed down his cheeks.

"I raised my sword to my friends. I turned my back on God. And Pax is gone because of me!" Kane sobbed. "How can I be forgiven for that?"

Vero stepped closer to Kane, and looking him squarely in the eyes said, "Because His mercy is endless."

Kane fell to his knees as his whole body trembled with tears. Vero watched him, unsure what he would do.

"I'm sorry!" Kane shouted so loudly, his voice drowned out any other sounds of the forest. "I'm sorry!"

Enraged at the turn of events, the dragon's pupils grew larger, coloring his eyes completely black as Kane placed the blue sapphire into Vero's hand.

Vero quickly jammed the book back into his pocket, and as he did so the dragon hissed. Its head reared up, its jaws opened. Vero knew he and Kane were in great danger. He grabbed the back of Kane's shirt.

"Let's go!" he shouted, pulling Kane to his feet.

They raced for the door; they would be safe once inside it. But in a split second, the dragon's jagged black wings flapped madly. Teeth barred, claws opened, it headed straight for Vero. Vero had no choice but to turn and face the dragon. His sword was poised for battle, knowing he was no match for the dragon.

Surprisingly calm, Vero closed his eyes, and muttered a simple prayer. "Please, God, give me the strength."

At that exact moment, Clover too uttered a prayer. She held hands with Tack and Chiko, who linked hands with many other pilgrims, forming a circle around the peace pagoda. Though she had no idea why, a passage from Ephesians came to her lips:

"Put on the full armor of God, so that you can take your stand against the devil's schemes."

As the dragon closed in on Vero and Kane, Vero felt something wrap around his feet. He glanced down. Gray streaks shot from his feet, up his leg, until they covered his body, leaving only his head exposed. It was a suit of armor! A light shield like the archangels' materialized in his left hand. And in his other hand, his sword began to flame.

In that moment, Vero lost all fear. His leg no longer hurt. He stood tall as the fierce confidence of a warrior consumed him. Kane's mouth dropped at the sight of Vero suited in armor with a flaming sword. The dragon spewed fire from its mouth at Vero, who calmly held up his shield and deflected the flames. More fire spit out the dragon's mouth. Kane ducked down, behind Vero. Vero again caught the flames with his shield. He swung his fiery sword at the dragon's head, forcing it to retreat.

"You're fighting for the wrong side, fledgling," the dragon said. "I can give you everything you want."

"There's nothing I could ever want from you," Vero snarled.

"Switch to the winning side," the dragon said. "Look at your earth . . . I am succeeding. It's all my doing—the violence, the strife, the unhappiness. It's all because of me. Wars, disease, starvation . . ."

"Yes, let's look at my earth," Vero said.

The dragon looked momentarily confused.

Vero waved his sword, and an image appeared midair before the dragon. Clover and Tack stood in a circle, holding hands with the pilgrims. People of many races and religions stood together, hand in hand, praying, meditating, and sending good thoughts for Vero.

Vero waved his sword once again, and the image vanished.

"Now remind me, who exactly is winning?" Vero smirked.

The dragon grew enraged. The tip of its tail swung around, blindsiding Vero. It hit his legs, knocking him to the ground.

"Vero! Watch out!" Kane yelled as the dragon's mouth opened directly over Vero.

He couldn't get up in time. The dragon sunk his teeth into Vero's stomach. Vero screamed, but then realized its bite wasn't able to penetrate the armor. The dragon bit him again, but could not inflict harm. Frustrated, the dragon picked Vero up in its mouth and violently shook him. The shield disappeared back into his palm, and then with both hands on the hilt of his sword, with all his might, he drove the flaming sword into the dragon's left eye. Vero could see the fire instantly spread in its eye. The dragon opened its mouth, howling in pain. Vero fell to the ground and quickly scrambled to his feet, watching as black ooze gushed from the dragon's injured orb.

"Now!" Vero shouted at Kane as he raced for the door.

Kane and Vero ran to the door in the tree. Vero stretched out his hand to turn the knob, then felt himself being pulled off the ground. He looked over his shoulder. The dragon's front claws had grabbed his legs, and it was lifting him upside down high into the air once again.

The seething dragon was carrying Vero farther and farther away from the garden's door. Vero could not even wiggle his legs from within the grasp of the beast's talons. Using just his stomach muscles, Vero did a sit-up in midair. With two hands on the flaming sword, he sliced through both front legs of the dragon, just above those talons. Again, the creature howled in pain. Vero freefell with the talons still wrapped around his legs until his wings shot open, arresting his descent. With the flames of his sword, he burnt off the talons from his body.

Vero swooped down to the ground. He landed beside Kane, who stood by the door. His hand on the knob, Vero felt the hot stench of the dragon's nostrils on his neck. The dragon's forked tongue flicked out of its mouth, each tip bound for Vero's eyes. Vero spun.

With unnatural strength, in a flawless single stroke, Vero sliced the fiery blade clear through the deadly forked tongue, severing it. It thumped to the ground.

"Now I won't have to listen to any more of your lies," Vero spat.

Shock came into the dragon's remaining eye. It staggered back, flapping its wings. The dragon flew to the tops of the trees, disappearing from sight.

"Think he's coming back?" Kane nervously asked Vero.

Vero shook his head.

"But you might want to hurry," Kane nodded to the door. "In case he does."

"Maybe you could come with me . . . they might grant you access," Vero said.

"No. I'm not worthy." Kane looked down.

"If it weren't for you, I wouldn't have the book right now."

Kane looked up and a faint smile formed on his lips. "Thanks, Vero, but I need to go back and try to make things right with the others."

"Tell Greer I said not to go too hard on you," Vero replied.

Kane nodded. He turned and walked away. The moment Vero wrapped his hand around the doorknob, his suit of armor vanished from his body. He turned the knob and walked into the garden of Eden.

29

◇

PARADISE

Vero's parents had taken him to many parks and gardens in his lifetime. He had seen the beauty of the Ether with its lakes, mountains, and green fields, but nothing had prepared him for the beauty of the garden of Eden. As he walked out of the tree, he was met with the most stunning landscape imaginable.

Trees with perfectly shaped trunks and branches met his eyes in every direction. Their leaves were tremendously healthy and of a deep green hue that Vero had never seen before. Vibrant, graceful flowers perfumed the air. The beauty that surrounded him was beyond astonishing. The grass was even greener than what he had seen in the Ether. Each tree was unique in its shape and type, each with its own personality, and Vero felt he knew each one. In the distance, he saw a lion nuzzle its nose against a lamb's nose. A doe playfully chased a bear around a tree.

In this garden, there was no food chain, no survival of the fittest. All the creatures lived peacefully with one another. The grass underneath his feet was so plush, so luxurious, that it massaged his feet with each step, reminding him of his injury. He lifted his pant leg and removed the scarf once more. His wounds had been healed.

The most beautiful thing about the garden was the feeling of peace that Vero felt. Everything created a sense of harmony and unity. Nothing was in conflict.

He saw a small herd of whitetail deer grazing under the warmth of a brilliant sky. As Vero gazed upon the deer, he realized that he could understand them. They could communicate mind-to-mind.

"Hello, Vero," a huge buck said. "Welcome."

"Thank you." Vero smiled as he spoke telepathically. "I need to find the tree of knowledge. Any idea?"

"It is on the east side of the garden," the buck telepathed. "You will see the cherubim with a flaming sword guarding it." The buck nodded its antlers to its right side. "It is in that direction."

Vero smiled gratefully to the buck. He turned and walked deeper into the garden. So many sights delighted his eyes along the way. Birds resting on branches sang beautiful melodies. Rocks and boulders were shiny, glistening. The water in a babbling brook sparkled in the light like glistening diamonds. Vero bent down and stuck his hand in the water. Plump, jolly fish swam quickly over to his hand, allowing to be pet.

Vero continued in the direction indicated by the buck. He saw a grove of trees ahead. A man stood before the trees, holding a flaming sword. Vero recognized his face but he wasn't exactly sure where he had seen him. The man then turned his head and Vero saw that his face morphed into that of a lion's.

"I've been waiting a long time for you, Vero," he said as his face then changed into that of an ox.

"You're a cherubim," Vero said, eyeing the four wings coming out of the angel's back.

"Yes," the cherubim answered, his face once again transforming, this time into that of an eagle's. "You have the book?"

Vero reached into his pocket and pulled out the blue sapphire.

"Well done." The cherubim smiled.

Vero held out the gem to the cherubim. The cherubim shook his head, his face again that of a lion's.

"You deserve the honor," the cherubim said, stepping aside.

When he moved aside, Vero saw a wilted, shriveled-up tree. A perplexed feeling came over him. It was so ugly, especially in comparison to all the beauty he had already seen in the garden. Vero hesitated, not sure if he should approach the tree.

The cherubim nodded, letting Vero know that it was the correct tree. Vero stepped in front of the tree. There was a sadness to it, as rotten fruit hung from its branches.

"Any action not in harmony with God's will always has unhappy consequences," the cherubim said.

Vero looked at the tree, wondering where to return the book. As his eyes studied the branches, he saw one branch that bore no fruit. Vero realized that *this* was where Eve must have taken the forbidden fruit. As Vero held the blue sapphire to the end of the branch, the cherubim gently touched his hand, stopping him.

"Before you return the book, do you want to know what everything you've experienced was for?" the cherubim's oxen face asked Vero.

Vero nodded.

"Look," the cherubim instructed, gazing into the sapphire. "God has given you the gift of sight. Use it."

Flames danced and twisted into symbols. Vero stared intently at them. His mind totally focused.

"Daniel Konrad, Jr.?" Vero shot the cherubim a confused look.

"Read on." The cherubim motioned.

As Vero continued to study the sapphire, he voiced the things as he read them. "He is the reason the book needed to be returned," Vero said aloud, transfixed with the stone in his hand. "The child will grow to be righteous, and bring much goodness into the world." Vero paused, taking that in.

"Lucifer was desperate to know the name of this baby so he could drive the parents apart, and would have done anything to prevent his birth." He looked at the cherubim, who nodded.

Vero continued reading. "Daniel Konrad and Davina Acker are the child's parents." Vero had to pause to smile, as it all seemed to be a bigger plan unfolding before his eyes.

"Davina will give birth to the child in an alley in a big city. She won't make it to the hospital in time, but she and the child will be fine," Vero read, astonished.

"What is it?" the cherubim asked.

"I dreamt about this a few years ago. And Clover was there too!"

"As was I," the cherubim said. "Now you may return the book."

"Just . . . give me a minute. I need to see one more thing," Vero said.

"Are you sure you want to know?" the cherubim's lion face asked, having read Vero's mind.

"I need to know," Vero said, locking eyes with the cherubim. The conviction in his gaze seemingly gave the cherubim his answer.

Vero opened his hand and looked deep into the sapphire. The tiny flames began to form into shapes, then symbols. Vero stared at the symbols, reading them silently in his mind. His body trembled with tears. It was the most devastating thing he would ever read. Vero closed his eyes, trying to be strong . . . for he had just learned the date of his earthly death.

Vero held the blue sapphire to the branch where no fruit hung. Upon contact with the branch, a large fruit pit—a stone—formed around the blue sapphire, encasing it. A perfectly red and shiny skin then formed around the stone. It instantly grew into a magnificent fruit, although Vero wasn't sure what fruit it was. It was different from anything he'd seen on earth. It sort of looked like an apple crossed with a pomegranate. Before Vero's eyes, the rest of the tree transformed. It grew into a magnificent fruit tree with plump, healthy fruit clinging to its branches.

Vero had returned the book from whence it had come.

Michael hugged Kane on the steps of C.A.N.D.L.E., as Uriel stood a step below. Vero, Greer, X, and Ada sat on a ledge watching. A tear streaked Greer's face.

"Greer, you're crying?" Vero said.

"Say another word and you'll be the one crying," Greer said, throwing him a threatening glance.

Kane turned to the others. "I'm sorry, you guys. I'm so sorry." His eyes were downcast.

"Stop, it's over," Michael told Kane. "When you are forgiven, that is the end of it."

Kane nodded.

"You can't imagine how proud we are of each of you," Michael said, extending his gaze over the fledglings.

Kane looked away.

"We are most proud of you, Kane," Uriel said. "The greatest battle we fight is the one within, and in the end you emerged victorious."

Kane locked eyes with Uriel, and smiled gratefully.

"All of you were outstanding," Michael said.

"But it's not right. Pax should be here with us," Greer said. "It's not a good day."

"But it is," Michael said.

"No, he was so brave. Pax fought hard and for that he winds up in the choir?" Greer said, exasperated.

"But he is not in the choir of angels," Uriel said.

"But when we fail in our training . . ." Vero said.

"This was the real deal," Uriel said. "This was not training."

"So what happened to Pax?" Greer asked, the panic rising in her chest.

"For his bravery in the face of evil, Pax 'got his wings,' as some would say. He has become a full-fledged guardian angel," Michael said, with pride in his voice.

Vero's face lit up. "So he made it?"

Michael nodded.

"That little twerp became a guardian before me?" Greer said with an outraged look that quickly turned into a huge smile.

"All in time, Greer." Michael smiled.

"Michael . . ." Vero said, hesitant. "Um . . . we probably wouldn't have found the book without Rahab's help."

"Oh, yes, Rahab. We are grateful to him, and I'll see what I can do about having his sentence commuted."

Michael wrapped his wings around himself and vanished.

"And now it's time for all of you to go back," Uriel said.

Greer grabbed Vero and hugged him tightly. Ada smiled. She joined in and hugged Vero too. Kane looked to X, who shrugged. They joined the group hug. Vero fell over, taking everyone down with him.

"Get off of me!" Greer yelled as she fought her way out of the pile. "I'm claustrophobic, you know that!"

Everyone got back on his feet.

"You'll see each other soon enough." Uriel smiled furtively.

Vero looked to Kane. "I see you in few minutes in Sri Pada."

"If it's okay, I think when I get there, I just want to go home. Can you make some excuse to your mom?"

"Yeah, I get it."

One by one, the angels closed their eyes and vanished. Only Vero remained standing. Uriel placed his hand on his shoulder.

"Raziel would like a word with you."

There was a whirl of wind, then Raziel stood before them. Uriel nodded to Raziel and moved away, allowing them privacy.

"Sit," Raziel motioned.

"Sure." Vero nodded.

They sat on a marble ledge.

A smile formed at the corners of Raziel's lips as he looked at Vero. "Vero, I want to thank you," he said, his eyes full of emotion. "Long ago, I failed, and you made things right for me. I will always be grateful to you. You are a very fine, noble angel."

"Thank you."

"When I first saw you at C.A.N.D.L.E., I'm ashamed to say I was disappointed in you. I didn't think you were up to the task. You couldn't fly. You were scrawny, but God knew what He was doing when he chose you. And it's not only because you had the vision to read the book."

Vero looked to him, curious.

"It's because you're good. Few can resist the power that the knowledge gives them. And I know that from firsthand experience."

"You felt it too?"

"Absolutely."

"It was so tempting especially when Lucifer was messing with my mind," Vero said.

"But how much more stronger are we that we both resisted?"

"I guess we're more alike than what we knew."

"Yes." Raziel smiled.

"All these years you thought God was punishing you for losing the book. You thought having no memory of the book was your punishment . . . but maybe you've been wrong. Maybe your lack of memory was a gift."

Raziel gave Vero a curious look.

"By not remembering it, Lucifer would leave you alone."

Raziel considered for a moment then stood. He bowed his head to Vero. "I look forward to working with you."

In an instant, Raziel vanished. Uriel walked over to Vero, who stood. "We are all grateful to you," Uriel said, his eyes bursting with pride.

"Thank you," Vero said, a bit hesitant.

"What is it?" Uriel asked, concerned.

"It's, um . . ."

An understanding look came over Uriel. He had read Vero's mind. "You're time on earth is nearly over," Uriel said, gently.

Vero nodded.

"Earth is not your true home," Uriel said, cupping Vero's chin. "And it's not their true home either."

Vero looked to Uriel, taking in his words. Vero hugged Uriel tightly, for he truly loved Uriel. After a moment, they broke apart.

"All of you belong with God, and one day, all of you will be with Him . . . and everything will be as it should be."

Clover stood on the steps of the peace pagoda. The pilgrims had all left to continue their trek up the mountain.

Tack sat on a bench, drinking a bottle of water. Suddenly, a huge smile spread across Clover's face.

Vero was walking up to the peace pagoda. She screamed and ran to her brother and wrapped her arms around him. Tack's face lit up.

"Did you return it?" Clover excitedly asked.

"Yeah. We did it!"

"Woo-hoo!" Tack yelled. "Do they know that I helped? Not that I'm looking for credit or anything . . . but I could sure use some."

"Where's Kane?" Clover looked around.

"Kane and Adrik won't be joining us."

"I saw who Adrik really was." Clover shuddered. "Was Kane like her?"

"No, he's good." Vero smiled.

"Really?" Tack asked.

"Well, he went through a rough patch, but now he's okay. We'll just have to come up with some excuse to tell Mom."

"What happened? I want to know," Clover said.

"I'll tell you everything as we walk up," Vero said.

"But we don't have to now," Tack said, eyeing the many, many steps leading to the top of the mountain.

"You don't want to be a quitter, do you?" Vero asked.

"Come on, Tack," Clover said. "We've come this far, let's finish."

"You guys are killing me," Tack said, getting up.

Vero, Tack, and Clover climbed to the top of Sri Pada. Along the way, Vero told them everything that had happened, both outside the garden and inside: of the dragon, of Lilith, of Pax's bravery and Kane's conversion. They were so fascinated that Tack didn't seem to realize that after two hours of climbing, they had reached the top of the mountain.

A bell hung near the sacred footprint. As tradition, each pilgrim rang the bell for the number of times they have ascended the mountain. Clover rang the bell first, followed by Tack. When Vero got to the bell, he paused a moment, took the handle, and said, "For you, Pax, buddy. Well done." And he rang the bell once. Other pilgrims followed. As the clangs of the bell echoed into the distance, Vero knew that God had heard the sacrifice of each and every pilgrim.

30

THE ANGEL VERO

Life settled back into normalcy after the trip to Sri Lanka. Dennis got his plans approved—Sri Lanka was going to get the extra canals. Nora continued to work part time at the hospital, and Clover, Vero, and Tack went back to school. Danny and Davina were also friends again, determined not to waste a single moment before his move out West. The two vowed to stay in touch. Vero smiled, knowing that they definitely would, knowing that he would see to it.

With only a few days left in the school year, on a balmy June evening the Lelands sat down to dinner. Vero looked across the kitchen table. Dad and Mom were laughing—something funny had happened at work. Clover pushed half her peas off her plate into her napkin. It was an ordinary night around the dinner table. And Vero knew it would be his last.

"Vero, eat please," Nora said. "Since when don't you like my meatloaf?"

"My stomach hurts," Vero said.

Nora's scolding expression turned to concern. "Did you eat anything earlier? Something not agree with you?"

"Not that I can think of."

"Go lie down on the sofa."

As Vero got up from the table, he caught Clover's worried look. Vero didn't want to alarm her. He flashed her a reassuring smile. As he lay on the sofa, Vero heard the sounds of his family finishing up dinner.

This is how it will be from now on, Vero thought. *It will just be the three of them sharing a meal.* Sometimes, in moments of brutal awareness, the brain thinks of the dumbest stuff. Maybe it's a defense. But Vero wondered when he was gone, and it was pizza night, would they still order two pizzas or would it only be one? A tear escaped from his eye. He laid only a few feet away from them, yet Vero never felt so far away from his family.

He fell asleep on the sofa. Nora and Dennis watched as Vero moaned while twisting and turning in his sleep. Nora felt his forehead. It was so hot to the touch that her hand instinctively pulled away.

"He's burning up!" she turned to Dennis. "He needs the ER!"

"Vero, Vero," Dennis said, trying to rouse his son. "Come on, Vero . . ."

Dennis reached under Vero and lifted him off the sofa.

"Clover!" Mom shouted hysterically as she helped hoist Vero to his feet. "Clover!"

Clover ran into the room. She saw her Mom and Dad walking Vero to the front door. She knew. The blood instantly drained from her face.

Oh, God.

Please, not now.

I'm not ready.

"We have to get to the hospital!" Mom screamed.

"Where are the keys?!" Dad shouted, his hand fumbling under the schoolbooks left on the entrance table, while holding Vero with the other.

The table lamp crashed to the floor.

"Here they are!" Clover yelled, grabbing the keys off the table.

Dennis's car was parked in the driveway. They walked Vero to the backseat and lay him across it. Nora sat with Vero's head resting on her lap. She stroked his head and sang softly to him—lullabies that she had sung to him when he was a baby.

Clover sat beside her father up front, quietly praying. But she knew. She knew. But she still asked.

Please, God, not now.

Please, I'm not ready.

The car pulled up to the ER as an ambulance drove away without its siren blaring. Dennis jumped out of the car and ran around to the back. He and Nora gently lifted Vero from the backseat. Nora turned to Clover. "Tell them we need a gurney!"

Clover ran to the hospital's glass doors. They opened automatically, and she raced over to the nurse on duty, whom she recognized.

"Mrs. Matthews, my brother needs a gurney!" she shouted.

The middle-aged woman looked over to the double doors, and saw Nora and Dennis walking Vero inside. She sprung from her chair and ran to them.

"Nora, what's wrong with Vero?" Mrs. Matthews asked.

"I think it may be his appendix!"

"Lay him here!" Mrs. Matthews yelled as she wheeled over a gurney.

They lifted Vero onto the stretcher.

"We'll take him to room two," Mrs. Matthews said with a hint of panic in her voice.

Nora and Dennis followed the stretcher as Mrs. Matthews whisked it to the examination room. Clover did not follow. Inside the waiting room, she pulled her cell phone from her pocket and called the only person who would understand: Tack.

"Please come now," she tearfully begged. "It's happening, and I don't know if I can take it . . ."

After a CT scan, the doctor told Nora and Dennis that Vero had a highly inflamed appendix and would need emergency surgery. Otherwise it would burst, spilling infectious material into the abdominal cavity, which would most likely be fatal.

Despite the 103.6 fever, Vero was conscious. Nora, Dennis, Tack, and Clover crowded around his bed, not wanting to leave him. As the doctors and nurses stuck all sorts of needles in him, prepping him for surgery, Vero smiled to his parents.

"You still believe those cosmonauts saw angels?" Vero said in a weak voice to his dad.

"Yeah, I do, with all my heart," Dad said, then quietly wept.

"I'm glad you're the one who found me," Vero said to Nora, who kissed Vero's forehead, her tears drenching his hair.

An aid unlocked the wheels on the gurney.

"Time to go," he told the family.

Dennis leaned over, tenderly kissing Vero's cheek. As Vero was wheeled past Tack and Clover, it warmed his heart to see Clover wrapped up in his best friend's arms. He knew Tack would keep true to his word and always be there for Clover.

Eyes clouded with tears, Clover grabbed Vero's hand, but couldn't bring herself to say anything to him. But it was all right. They had already said everything that they had needed to say to one another. No stones were left unturned. Vero knew how she felt about him, and she knew how he felt about her. Before she released his hand, Vero smiled.

"Eat all your peas," he weakly said.

When the surgery lasted much longer than what the doctors had expected, Nora knew something was wrong. Standing in the very same waiting room of the hospital where she had first seen baby Vero, she knew. Something in Nora told her that Vero was not well. That she may never again hold the boy she had found lying on a chair in that hospital. That if she were to be honest with herself, since the night Vero came into her life, she had always feared that one day he would be taken away just as unexpectedly. That somehow he never really belonged to this earth, that he was a gift for only a short few years.

The doctor came out to talk to the family. He told them that Vero's appendix had erupted the moment they opened him up. For hours, the doctors cleaned him up best that they could, but Vero had slipped into a coma.

For three days, the Leland family kept a constant vigil by Vero's bedside. Clover slept in bed beside him, rarely getting up. Tack sat in a chair, reading Vero his favorite comic books. Kids from school came, bringing get-well balloons, flowers, and cards. Davina brought meals for the Lelands and a feeling of peace with each visit. The Atwoods came. Even Mr. Atwood shed a tear seeing Vero lying helpless in bed. Nurse Kunkel worked extra shifts to be near them. So many people, but one visitor in particular surprised Clover.

Danny Konrad.

The boy who had once so hated Vero. He came empty handed—no food or cards, yet he brought with him the greatest gift of all, kindness from a pure and contrite heart. And the Lelands were grateful.

On the third day of his coma, with only Clover, Tack, Dennis, and Nora keeping vigil, Clover heard Vero's voice. And it wasn't the weak one wrecked with fever, but a strong, clear voice.

"Clover, wake up," Vero said.

Clover rubbed her eyes. She thought she had heard her brother.

"Clover," Vero said with a sense of awe. "Look!"

Clover opened her eyes. The sight before her was all the more astonishing. Everywhere she looked, she saw angels. Radiant, glowing, shimmering angels!

"They've come for me," Vero said.

Clover's mouth hung open at the sight. To the others in the room, Vero still appeared to be sleeping.

Vero recognized Uriel, Raziel, Raphael, and Michael, who hovered closest to him.

"Are you ready, Vero?" Uriel asked.

Vero looked over at his mother, who was gazing upon his sleeping face with such tenderness; to his father, who had his head in his hands, silently praying; and to a sleeping Tack, who looked so different from the boy he had once been, so much like a young man now. But Clover . . . she was the hardest to leave. She looked to Vero, her eyes no longer full of tears. He saw wonder and acceptance in them. Clover gave him a faint smile.

"It's all right, Vero. You can go now. We'll be okay," she bravely told her brother. "Go fly with the angels."

Nora looked to Clover. What was she saying? The heart monitor machine began to loudly beep, waking up Tack. A panicked Dennis stood, grabbing the bed for support.

"I'm ready," Vero told Uriel.

As Clover watched, with great reverence an angel gently placed both his hands, palms down, on Vero's chest. As the angel drew his hands straight back, Vero's spirit began to gradually lift out of his body. His spirit looked very much like Vero, except it was luminous with a silvery glow. Every inch of him was shimmering. He appeared ethereal, yet his spirit also had substance. And he was smiling. Clover could feel Vero's immense joy. Nora looked upon Vero's body as his breathing became shallow. She saw a light emanating from him.

The moment Vero's spirit completely separated from the body, the heart monitor flat lined. The guardian angel Leo rushed to Dennis's side and held him so he would not collapse. And Karael hugged Nora tightly, comforting her as she wept across Vero's chest. An angel stood behind Tack, placing a steadying hand on his shoulders, and with the other, wiped his tears. It was Pax! He was Tack's guardian angel. Pax looked so different to Vero. He was not the slight little angel anymore and instead stood tall, with radiant wings.

Clover saw a beam of light shine down upon Vero. She heard heavenly singing and music. The beam formed into a staircase. Vero stood on the first step. Thousands of joyous angels lined the steps. Vero climbed a few more steps then turned back to Clover.

"I love you, Clover," Vero said.

"I love you, Vero," Clover whispered.

Vero turned, and as he continued to climb, the beam of light engulfed the entire room, then completely disappeared.

A doctor and three nurses raced into the room. As the doctor reached for the defibrillator paddles to resuscitate Vero, Clover knew they wouldn't help.

For her beloved brother was dead.

❖

As Vero walked up the stairs, he recognized them as Jacob's Ladder. He had climbed them during the Angel Trials. After walking a few more steps, Michael, Uriel, Raziel, and Raphael led Vero off the ladder. They flew with him to the trio of waterfalls. Vero stood on the shore of the crystal-blue lake as the water crashed down from above. Uriel nodded to him. Vero understood what was happening. He was being cleansed because he was on his way to meet God.

Vero stepped into the cool, refreshing water. Even though he knew there were others bathing with him, he could not see them. He scooped the water over his head and let it run down his face. After a few minutes in the cleansing water, Vero walked out to the shore. Michael, Uriel, Raziel, and Raphael flew with him, escorting him back onto the ladder.

They continued their ascent up the staircase. As they neared the top, Vero thought of his fellow fledglings. Some had made it to the top of Jacob's Ladder during the Angel Trials, but of course they were stopped at the gates of heaven. As Vero climbed on the final step, a warm, loving light surrounded him. So bright, so intense, yet it did not hurt his eyes. A deep sense of feeling loved came over Vero—unlike any he had ever felt before. A mighty voice rang out.

"Vero, my child."

And Vero knew he was in the presence of God.

Yet Vero was not afraid. Every inch of his being felt nothing but unconditional love.

"I have a few questions for you," God said.

Vero looked to Him, yet he did not see His face, only radiant light.

"Do you reject Satan?"

"I do," Vero said.

"And all his works?"

"I do."

"And all his empty promises?"

"I do."

The light grew brighter, expanding out into a glorious whiteness. Vero felt only goodness and tranquility.

"And Vero . . . do you love me?"

"I do," Vero said, his eyes full of emotion. "With all my heart."

Suddenly, the light that was God swirled around Vero. It grew even more brilliant than the sun and wrapped Vero up in it as if he were a baby being swaddled. Vero felt an utter explosion of love as the light cradled him. In that moment, Vero knew no one could have ever loved him more. He knew that he had always been a part of this light who was God, and Vero realized that he had never been far from Him. For God had always been with him. Not for one moment had he ever been alone.

Glorious stones of many stunning colors materialized in the air. They began to twinkle and solidify. Vero knew exactly what it was—his completed crown. And as promised, it was waiting for him in heaven.

ACKNOWLEDGMENTS

Chris, who started this journey through the Ether with me, and I'm proud to have your name next to mine.

Nena Madonia and Jan Miller, yeah! We did it—three books! Couldn't have done it without you by my side. Can't wait for whatever's next!

Jacque Alberta and Annette Bourland, thanks for giving Vero the chance to fly!

Guy Molinari, my third brother, thank you for all your sage wisdom.

The Lulli family, especially Daniela, your support and willingness to read each draft has been invaluable to me.

Alvaro de Vicente, thank you for your generous reads and theological insight.

The Rosen family—Vicki, Bruce, Emily and Alex . . . your showing up at Barnes and Noble meant the world to me.

Randy Gallegos, who has turned every cover into a stunning work of art.

My friend, Doug Amaturo, who constantly cheers me on with his relentless enthusiasm. And thanks, Dougie, for the title of this book.

The Ether

Vero Rising

Laurice E. Molinari

The Fiercest of Warriors?

Vero Leland always suspected he was different from others his own age, ever since his childhood attempts to fly. But he never could have predicted the truth—or how much his life was about to change. Soon after his twelfth birthday, Vero learns he is a guardian angel and is abruptly transported to the Ether, the spiritual realm that surrounds the earth. Yet before he can be counted among these fierce warriors, Vero must learn to master his growing powers, competing with other angels-in-training and battling demonic creatures known as maltures as well as mythical creatures such as the leviathan. Until his instruction is complete, Vero needs to alternate between the Ether and his regular life. If he survives training and accepts his destiny—a destiny he did not choose—he must leave everything behind, including his family and the life he loves. Meanwhile, an evil is growing—the maltures are rising, and Vero appears to be their target.

Available in stores and online!

Pillars of Fire

An Ether Novel

Laurice E. Molinari

Just because thirteen-year-old Vero Leland has discovered his true identity doesn't mean his life has gotten any easier. Middle school is humiliating at best, and his training in the Ether—the spiritual realm that surrounds the earth—has only intensified. Becoming a guardian angel, the fiercest of all warriors, is not for the faint of heart.

At any moment, Vero could be yanked from earth to the Ether, where he must face whatever trials come his way in angel school, aka C.A.N.D.L.E. (the Cathedral of Angels for Novice Development, Learning, and Edification). This year, Vero and his fellow fledglings are selected to compete in the Angel Trials, a set of three challenges that will test everything they've learned and pit them head-to-head with advanced angels from other realms.

But as Vero soon learns, there is more at stake in these trials than a crown of glory. Back on earth, his sister Clover is in trouble, and her fate may be inextricably tied to Vero's own. As the evil both on earth and in the Ether grows, Vero must choose which battles he can't afford to lose. Once again, he is tested beyond what any previous fledgling has endured, and the choices he makes will affect not only his grade in C.A.N.D.L.E., but also the fate of the world.

Softcover: 9780310735625

Available in stores and online!